# Safe
# Thus Far

## Theresa Hupp

ISBN for paperback edition: ISBN: 978-0-9853244-7-6

ISBN-10 for paperback edition: 0-9853244-7-3

Rickover Publishing

Safe Thus Far

Cover illustration adapted from Evening on the Prairie, an oil painting by Albert Bierstein, circa 1870, public domain. Original housed in the Museo Nacional Thyssen-Bornemisza, Madrid.

Back cover photograph of Fort Klamath Barracks, original found at http://www.fortwiki.com/File:Fort_Klamath.jpg

Map from A. J. Johnson's 1864 map of Washington, Oregon, and Idaho, with parts of Montana and Wyoming, published by Johnson and Ward as Plate No. 65 in *Johnson's New Illustrated Family Atlas* (1864 edition).

Title page and scene divider image from "Camping and Hunting in the Shoshone," by W.S. Rainsford, in *Big Game Shooting*, by Archibald Rogers, et al, Charles Scribner's Sons (1896)

# Dedication

This novel highlights the bonds of family and friendship. I've dedicated earlier novels to various family members, and they all remain close to my heart. I think of my family as I write, and I strive to make them proud of me.

This book is dedicated to my friends, both new and old. I have been blessed to find trusted companions and colleagues in each phase of my life. The humor and compassion of my friends shepherd me through the stresses of daily living.

In particular, I dedicate this book to Sylvia, who now has known me longer than almost everyone alive except my siblings. We see each other rarely these days, but when we do, the years fall away.

# Cast of Characters, as of March 1864

*(all ages as of opening of the novel)*

**The McDougalls:**
Caleb (Mac) McDougall, 42, attorney and businessman in Oregon City
   Jenny Calhoun McDougall, 31, Mac's wife
   Their children:
      William (Will), age 16
      Maria, age 13
      Caleb (Cal), age 12
      Nathan (Nate), age 9
      Elizabeth (Eliza), age 8
      Charlotte (Lottie), age 6
      Margaret (Maggie), age 1

**The Pershings:**
Franklin and Cordelia Pershing, both deceased
   Their children *(only those who appear in this novel)*:
      Zeke Pershing, age 36
         Hannah Bramwell, age 36, Zeke's wife
      Joel Pershing, age 34
      Esther Pershing Abercrombie, age 32
         Daniel Abercrombie, age 35, Esther's husband
      Their children:
         Cordelia, age 15
         Sammy, age 14
         Others *(rarely seen in this novel)*: Abigail, Franklin, Harriet, George, Thomas, Daniel, Esther, Abraham
      Jonah Pershing, age 16, raised from birth by Esther and Daniel

**Militia Members on the Owyhee Expedition:**

*(only those who appear in this novel are named; the names are real, but their personalities are fictionalized)*

Lieutenant Colonel Charles S. Drew

Captain William Kelly

Sergeant James Moore

Sergeant Garrett Crockett

Sergeant A. M. Beaty

Sergeant Geisy

Corporal Abner Biddle

Surgeon G. W. Greer

And 39 enlisted soldiers of Company C of the First Oregon Cavalry Militia

**Civilians hired by the militia:**

8 Quartermaster's employees, including guide, blacksmith, teamsters, 2 Indian scouts, and 23 mule packers

# Oregon in 1864. Map by Johnson & Ward

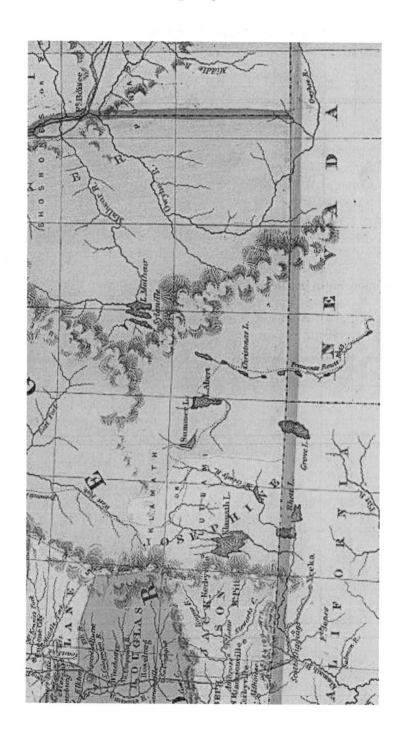

# Chapter 1: Playing Hooky

Will McDougall glanced over his shoulder, then tapped his heels against Shanty's sides to spur the gelding along the road. He should be in school, but his friend Jonah Pershing had invited him to help on his family's farm outside Oregon City. The two boys had been friends since before Will could remember, and Will was set on going. Though he hadn't told his parents he was playing hooky.

At sixteen, Will didn't see the point of attending school—he knew as much as his teachers, and he could learn what he needed from the newspapers. The Oregon City and Portland papers were full of stories about the War of Rebellion between Union and Secessionists. Violence had engulfed the nation since Fort Sumter, and it continued as of now, March 1864, almost three years later. Not only was there war in the East, but Indian attacks were frequent in Oregon. All of this was more important than classes at the academy.

As Will rode up the hillside out of Oregon City, he looked back to be sure Pa hadn't seen him leave. No one followed—he'd escaped unseen. He patted Shanty's shoulder. "Come on, boy," he said. "Let's have some fun."

He and Shanty trotted east along a dirt road, passing through fields and forests as town turned to farmland. The morning air was clear, but a stiff wind blew, and Will hunkered down in his jacket, glad he'd remembered his gloves.

Mount Hood, visible on the horizon ahead of them, was snowcapped. But the high peak was white year-round, so he couldn't tell if new snow had fallen in the mountains overnight. He shivered and urged Shanty to move a little faster.

Thirty minutes after leaving home, Will and his horse arrived at the farm where Jonah Pershing lived. Like Will, Jonah was sixteen. Jonah lived with his sister and her husband, Esther and Daniel Abercrombie. He was Esther's youngest brother, and when their mother died, Esther took on raising Jonah.

Will dismounted, tied Shanty to the paddock railing, then went to find Jonah. He poked his head in the barn and saw his friend. "I've come to help," Will said. "What are we planting today?"

"Beans, I think." Jonah called over his shoulder to Sammy, Esther's and Daniel's oldest son. "Did Daniel say we was workin' on beans today?"

"Yeah," Sammy said. "In the south field."

Daniel Abercrombie entered the barn. "Hello, Will. What are you doin' here today?"

"Jonah invited me, sir," Will said.

"Does your pa know?" Daniel asked.

Will shrugged with a glance at Jonah.

Daniel glared at Jonah. "You asked Will to leave his studies?"

Will tried to look innocent as he interceded for his friend. "I'm sure Pa won't mind. He likes me to spend time outdoors."

Daniel grunted. "When he lays into you, be sure he knows I ain't had a part in it." Then the farmer began harnessing a mule. "Grab the traces over there," he ordered Will, pointing to leather straps hanging on the barn wall. "You and Jonah harness the other mule."

"Why aren't you using the oxen?" Will asked as he handed Jonah the straps. Mules tended to bite, though Daniel had trained his team well. Still, Will would rather work with the large placid oxen.

"Jack here is pesky," Daniel said, slapping the mule's hindquarters. "Needs to get out of the barn. We'll let the oxen rest today. You ready to work, boys?"

Not sure if Daniel was talking to him or the mules, Will nodded. He untied Shanty and remounted his gelding to follow Daniel, Jonah, and Sammy to the south field.

By midafternoon, Will's muscles ached, and he could barely feel his fingers and feet. Throughout the cold spring day, he'd followed the plow mule, dropping seed, raking over the furrows, and fetching whatever Daniel asked him to fetch. Jonah and Sammy had done the same.

"Good job, lads," Daniel said, when they finished the field. "Let's head back to the barn."

Will wanted to be home in time to pretend he'd been at school. He made his excuses to Daniel and Jonah and turned Shanty toward town.

The sun hung over the hills across the Willamette River by the time Will reached the carriage house behind his family's home. He led Shanty into his stall. The two carriage horses and his little sisters' pony stood munching hay, but Pa's stallion Valiente was gone. The family dog Rufus nosed at Will's feet, no doubt sniffing at the strange smells from the country.

Will rubbed down the gelding, all the while murmuring to the horse about how much better the day had been than if he'd gone to school. As he finished grooming Shanty and was scooping out a bucket of oats for the horse, Pa entered the carriage house. Mac McDougall led Valiente into the stall next to Shanty, murmuring to his mount just like Will had talked to his gelding.

There was no hope of avoiding Pa, so Will greeted his father and offered Valiente a handful of Shanty's oats. Valiente's muzzle was turning gray, but the stallion was still a favorite in the family.

"What are you doing here, Will?" Pa asked, raising an eyebrow.

"I spent the day with Daniel and Jonah helping them plant." No sense in lying—Pa always found out.

"What about school?" Pa asked.

"Didn't have much to do today," Will said. "Thought I'd be of more use at the farm. Abercrombies were planting beans."

"I don't care what you thought," Pa said, frowning. "I'm paying your school fees. Which means you should sit in class and learn. I expect you to be there, unless I've given you leave not to be."

"But Pa—"

"Did you hear me, son?" Pa said. "Your duty is to go to school. Nothing more. Not farming. And certainly not on your friend's farm. I hire others to cultivate my claim, so there's not even a good reason for you to work on the land I own. You'll be in a town job someday, and you need an education."

"I'll rub down Valiente for you, Pa," Will offered, hoping Pa would leave the carriage house and not lecture him anymore.

"A man takes care of his own mount." Pa continued to curry Valiente. Silently, Will finished tending Shanty, measured out oats for Valiente, then headed inside their home.

When Mac finished grooming Valiente, he followed Will into the house, still with a frown on his face. The boy had no business playing hooky from school. Mac took the back stairs up to the bedroom he shared with his wife Jenny. He'd have to discuss Will's infraction with her, and she was often soft on the boy.

Jenny sat in a chair reading and glanced up. "Hard day?" she asked.

He took off his cravat and sighed. "I just saw Will in the carriage house."

"Oh?" She sounded surprised. "I didn't hear him come home from school."

Mac laughed sharply. "School? He didn't go to school today."

"Where was he?"

"He was truant. He went to Daniel's to plow a field," Mac said. "I swear, I don't know what's gotten into that boy. He used to be so easy, and now he causes problems every time we turn around."

"He's sixteen, Mac." Jenny smiled. "What were you like at sixteen?"

"This isn't about me," Mac said, unhooking his pocket watch from his waistcoat. "At sixteen, you were already his mother."

"Yes. But boys are different. They grow up more slowly." She stood and crossed the room to him. "Or so you've always told me."

Mac leaned over and kissed her. At thirty-one and after eight pregnancies, her waist had thickened, but her hair was still the light brown he'd always loved, and her smile lit up whatever room she occupied. He pulled her close. "How long until supper?"

"Not long enough," she murmured against his mouth. "So tell me again, what was William doing today?"

"You'll have to ask him. All he told me was the Abercrombies were planting beans."

"You didn't chastise him, did you?"

"What was I supposed to do, Jenny? The boy belongs in school."

"You know he's bored at the academy. Maybe a tutor would suit him better."

"There aren't any tutors in town who are any better than the academy teachers." Mac shook his head. "He needs the discipline of school."

"Don't be so hard on him," Jenny said. She patted his arm. "Wash up, then come downstairs. I'll go find him and have a word."

**10**

When Mac went down for supper, he found his whole family in the parlor. Jenny sat with little Maggie on her lap—hard to believe their baby was almost two. Eliza and Lottie leaned on their mother, pestering her with questions. Maria knitted in a chair by the fire, and Caleb and Nathan played marbles on the carpet. Will had his nose buried in yesterday's paper.

"What's the War news, son?" Mac asked as he entered the room. Eliza and Lottie left their mother and rushed to hug him. He boosted Lottie, almost seven, onto his hip.

"Secessionists beat the Union in Florida," Will said. He didn't look up from the paper. "Somewhere called Olustee. That was on February 20, almost two weeks ago."

"What else is in the paper?"

"The telegraph line from California to Portland was completed yesterday." Will sounded more animated with that news. "First telegram to arrive from California said the Union is winning in Richmond. We'll get more current war news in Oregon now."

"News from the East to San Francisco, then all the way north to Portland," Cal crowed from the floor.

"I heard," Mac said. Throughout the day, men had stopped in Mac's office in town to discuss the telegraph connection with California. It would be an enormous help to business. The speed of communications had increased considerably since Mac arrived in Oregon sixteen years ago. Then, it took months for letters to reach Oregon or California from the East. Within a few years, travel between Oregon and California became easier, but travel and communications from Eastern cities like Boston, New York, and Washington, D.C., were still slow. The telegraph would bring the nation together.

Or it would, if not for the infernal War. For the past three years, the nation had fought state against state, brother against brother. Arguments between the North and South influenced politics in Oregon as much as in the East. There might not be battles between opposing armies in the West, but neighbors abandoned friendships when arguments over the War broke out.

Mac was a Yankee through and through. But long-time acquaintances who had emigrated from Missouri, Tennessee, and Kentucky favored the Secessionists. Mac was careful before he voiced his opinions outside the house, though he tried to instill his own political sentiments in his children.

When the family moved to the dining room for supper, the boys continued to chatter about the telegraph, with thirteen-year-old Maria listening intently. She was a quiet girl, the daughter Mac adopted in California in 1850 after her mother died. Jenny had gladly taken Maria in, and the two of them were now inseparable.

After supper, the children dispersed, leaving Mac and Jenny alone at the table. Mac smoked a cigar, and Jenny sipped a cup of tea.

"What would you think if I took Will and Cal to Portland next week?" Mac asked. "I know Will played hooky today. But I have business to conduct, and I could show them the telegraph."

"There's been a telegraph office in Oregon City for months," she said.

"Yes, but I do need to go to Portland. And we could send a telegram to my agent in San Francisco—it would go along the entire line in Oregon."

Jenny smiled. "You want to watch it as much as the boys would."

Mac grinned. "Of course. It's progress." He hesitated. "Then you don't think we're being inconsistent—taking Will out of school for a day after he played hooky today?"

"It's up to you." She paused. "You wouldn't take Maria or Nate?"

"Two boys are enough. There's no telling how Will might act, whether he'll be the personable lad he can be or whether he'll fall into a churlish fit. And Cal has about all the exuberance I can manage."

"I'm sure they'll enjoy it. And they will be glad to spend time with you. Even if William will never admit it."

# Chapter 2: The Telegraph Office

The following Wednesday, Will sat at the small desk in his bedroom. Despite the burgeoning household, Will had a bedroom to himself. It was the smallest room in the house, but he relished his privacy. Cal and Nate shared a room, and the four girls slept in the largest room.

Will had to write an essay on the pros and cons of slavery for school tomorrow. He fingered the pockmarks on his cheeks as he often did when bothered. Pa was adamantly against slavery, but Mama's family owned slaves in Louisiana and Missouri. Old Samuel Abercrombie spouted off frequently in favor of the Southern Secession, and Jonah sometimes repeated his grandfather's opinions.

But Will remembered the Tanners, a free Negro family who'd lived in the small shack across the yard from his home with Mama while Pa was away mining gold. Otis Tanner had been Will's first friend. That a white person could own Otis and his parents seemed monstrously wrong. Will began to write about the Tanners.

A tap sounded on his door, and Pa came in. "I thought you might like to go to Portland with me on Friday," he said. "To see the telegraph."

Grinning, Will turned to face his father. "Really, Pa? The telegraph?"

"You seemed interested in it last week."

"Yes, sir. Just think—we can hear the news the same day it is written. And send word of happenings in Oregon to the East as well."

"We'll leave Friday morning," Pa said. "Catch the steamboat to Portland, see the telegraph office, spend the night at the Pioneer Hotel, and return on Saturday." He nodded at Will's papers strewn on the desk. "Can you manage your schoolwork around the trip?"

"Yes, sir."

After Pa left, Will returned to his essay, his words flowing quickly now.

Will woke early Friday morning, March 11, 1864. Rain splattered against his bedroom window. But wet spring weather wouldn't bother him—he'd take the steamboat with Pa no matter if it poured.

He dressed and went downstairs for breakfast. Mrs. O'Malley, the housekeeper and cook, had bacon sizzling, while Mama stirred oatmeal on the stove. "Morning, Mama," Will said, hugging her.

She smiled up at him. "Hand me bowls for the oatmeal, please. I'll need three—for your father, you, and Caleb."

"Is Cal up already?" Will asked in surprise as he reached for bowls in the cupboard. Cal liked to stay in bed in the mornings.

"Why, yes," Mama said. "The steamboat departs at nine, and he needs breakfast before you leave for the dock."

Will stopped with the bowls still in his hands. "Cal's going to Portland with Pa and me?"

"Of course. Didn't you know?"

Will shook his head. The day suddenly seemed dismal. It wouldn't be just him and Pa at the telegraph office. Twelve-year-old Cal would be there, too. The pest. He followed Will everywhere, asking questions all the time. Cal charmed folks with his ready grin, while Will felt uncomfortable talking to strangers. Will was sure everyone liked Cal better than him.

Now he'd have to spend two days with the brat, who would monopolize conversation with Pa. Will's plans to talk man-to-man with Pa evaporated.

The three McDougalls boarded the steamboat at the dock below the Willamette Falls, then the vessel churned downstream to Portland. Will had made the trip several times. He loved watching eddies in the water, trees along the riverbank, fields carved out of forests along the Willamette. Most farms showed little sign of spring growth yet. Only fields planted in winter wheat sprouted green shoots above the black earth.

Pa said the journey to Portland used to take two days by steamboat. Now, with faster boats, the trip from Oregon City to Portland took only four hours.

It was a little slower returning upriver, but only an additional hour or so.

After they disembarked, Will followed Pa. Portland was a bustling commercial town, more populous now than Oregon City, though Oregon City had once been the dominant settlement in all of Oregon.

As they walked toward the Pioneer Hotel on Front Street to check in and leave their satchels, Pa nodded at several men they passed and stopped to introduce the boys to them. Will shook their hands and murmured a bashful greeting, while Cal had a smile and a question for everyone. Pa didn't seem to mind Will's shyness, but he nodded approvingly at Cal's geniality.

The Pioneer Hotel proprietor, Mr. Arrigoni, greeted Pa by name and offered to take their bags to their room. Pa agreed, and soon he and the boys headed to the telegraph office. Will walked beside Pa, and Cal bounced ahead of them to call back questions, then lagged behind to stare in a shop window. "Cal," Pa said. "Stay with us."

Men crowded into the telegraph office, many watching the clerk behind the counter tap a key that sounded like "dit dah dah dit, dah dah dah, dit dah dit, dah." Will didn't understand Morse code, but he'd read about it. He gaped at the speed with which the operator clicked dits and dahs, tapping out messages that moved from one telegraph station to the next as fast as lightning.

Will knew there'd been a telegraph in Oregon for a couple of years, the wire going north to Portland, through Oregon City, and south to the state capital in Salem. He'd visited the telegraph office in Oregon City. But the final leg between Roseburg, Oregon, and Yreka, California, had recently been completed—the final segment connecting Portland with San Francisco, and from there to the rest of the world.

Will edged toward the counter to see the clerk better. What would it be like to be the first to get the news? Whether it be news of the War, of Indian attacks on the Plains, or of foreign catastrophes? It must be wonderful to have that knowledge and to have the duty of conveying it to all of Oregon.

Cal moved closer to Will and bumped his elbow. "Watch it, Cal," Will complained.

"Behave, boys," Pa said from behind them, clapping a hand on Will's shoulder. Pa blamed every problem on Will, merely because he was the oldest. He'd been responsible for his younger siblings ever since Pa brought Maria into their home.

Will listened while Pa talked to the telegraph operator. "I'd like to send a telegram to California. To my agent in San Francisco." Pa had business interests in San Francisco and Sacramento, in addition to his investments in Oregon. He'd made money in the gold fields—and kept most of it. Will listened to his parents' conversations at meals and to Pa's discussions with other men in town and after church. Will thought proudly that Pa was one of the leading citizens in Oregon City.

"You pay by the word, Mr. McDougall," the clerk said. "Two bits a word."

"All right," Pa said. "I'll make it brief. 'Awaiting word on warehouse completion. Please advise soon.' So that's two dollars?"

The man wrote the message on a slip of paper. "Yes, sir."

Pa handed over the coins. "May we watch you send it?" Pa asked. "The boys would like to see."

Cal pushed closer, and Will nudged his brother aside.

"Certainly." The man smiled, took the slip of paper, and began tapping. Within seconds, he'd finished.

"When will Pa get a response?" Cal asked.

Will sighed—his brother knew so little. The message would have to be transmitted from station to station, then delivered to Pa's business agent. And then the man would have to send a reply. That could take an hour, or it could take days.

"That depends on my agent," Pa said, ruffling Cal's hair. Will could have told his brother that.

They watched the telegraph operator for a few more minutes, then left. Pa had an appointment with a man in Portland, and he gave Will money to spend on candy for the children back home. Will and Cal browsed through several stores before choosing what they wanted, then returned to the hotel to meet Pa for supper.

Mac sat in the hotel dining room listening to Will and Cal spar. Will was physically larger than his brother, though Cal would catch up someday and probably would be heavier than Will's lean frame. But verbally, they were already a good match. Will had more years of schooling, knew more, and had a broader vocabulary. But Cal was quicker with repartee. Mac knew Will detested having his younger brother snap at his heels like an errant puppy, and so Will frequently ragged Cal, causing the younger boy to insult him in return.

Mac was the youngest of three brothers, so he sympathized with Cal's desire to keep up with his older brother. Plus, with his sullen attitude these days, Will deserved the indignities Cal heaped on him.

Nursing the whiskey he'd ordered, Mac let the boys' sniping fade into the background. He focused instead on his business problems in California—the reason for his telegram earlier in the day.

Torrential floods in Sacramento in early 1862 had knocked several warehouses he owned off their foundations. The structures and their contents were a total loss. Mac had rebuilt the warehouses, but the economic downturn after the floods reduced demand for goods, and orders were only now picking up. Mac wanted to increase his purchases of goods from the East, but he needed an update from his agent before filling the new warehouses.

Flooding had occurred in Oregon as well. The Willamette's tributaries sent water cascading downstream, and the river valley had suffered the same fate as Sacramento. Many farms along the rivers and streams flooded, and Mac lost money he'd lent to local farmers. Only now was prosperity returning to the West. Meanwhile, the War back East prevented the regular flow of merchandise to Oregon and California.

The completed telegraph line would make an enormous difference. Between what the local papers published and what Mac could learn directly via telegrams to his agent, he would know within hours or days what took him weeks to learn in the past.

After leaving the telegraph office, he'd visited William Ladd, a prominent businessman in Portland. Ladd was a major investor in most commercial projects in Oregon—a bank, steamships, roads, and rail development. For that matter, Ladd was president of the Oregon Telegraph Company that developed the communication line Mac had just viewed.

Now that Portland had overtaken Oregon City as the center of Oregon commerce, Mac needed to build relationships with men like Ladd. He'd asked Jenny whether the family should move to Portland, but she enjoyed the company of long-time friends in Oregon City. For now, then, the McDougalls would stay put.

Will said something, causing Cal to shout in dismay.

"Pipe down, boys," Mac said, returning his attention to the dinner table. "We're in public, so act like young gentlemen."

Saturday morning, Will and his father and brother boarded the steamboat to return to Oregon City. Other than Cal's presence, it had been a stirring visit. Will enjoyed the telegraph, the sights and sounds of Portland, and the fine supper at the hotel. Mama and Mrs. O'Malley made good meals, but they didn't offer rich sauces for meats and vegetables like the hotel chef provided. Hollandaise sauce—that was new to Will. He'd have to ask Mrs. O'Malley whether she knew how to make it.

The boat chugged upriver slowly. The spring current was strong, and men constantly fed wood into the firebox. Steam from the boiler turned the paddlewheel, and occasionally excess steam spouted from the pipe high above the boat.

Will watched the boilermen. What would it be like to spend one's days throwing wood into the boiler and cleaning out the coals? Will liked physical labor well enough, but these men were sweating in their shirtsleeves despite the cold spring day. Pa told Will repeatedly he should go to college so he could later hold a professional job, but Will wasn't sure that's what he wanted to do with his life.

He was supposed to finish this school term, but he didn't want to. He hoped he wouldn't have to return to the academy in the autumn. Pa wanted him to go East to Harvard. But only because that's what Pa had done. Will wasn't sure he wanted to follow in Pa's footsteps, but he didn't know what else to do.

Will moved to the boat's railing and leaned over the side to stare at the water. Where would he be in the fall? In Oregon or far away in Boston? Or somewhere unexpected?

Mac sat on the boat deck reading the newspaper. Every few minutes he looked over the pages to be sure neither son had fallen overboard. Cal flitted from place to place, and Mac envisioned him tripping over a coil of line or a misplaced gaff. Will leaned out over the railing and could lose his balance if the boat hit a log or snag.

It had been a good trip. Both boys had been enthusiastic observers at the telegraph office. Mac was glad he'd given them the experience.

Soon, he and Jenny would have to make some decisions about Will's future. The boy had grown beyond the Oregon City academy where they sent him. Mac had read the essay Will wrote about slavery. He'd started with his memories of the Tanners and made a compelling case against holding people like his Negro friends—indeed, any people—as slaves. Mac agreed, though he wondered if he could have made as convincing a case as Will had. The boy had talent.

Jenny didn't want her oldest son leaving home yet. But Will needed more education. He could be a fine lawyer or judge someday. Or a writer. With his intelligence and flair with words, Will could be anything. It was Mac's responsibility to be sure he was prepared.

It was time for Will to leave, Mac thought. Nearly time.

# Chapter 3: Sunday Services

Sunday morning, the day after Mac and the boys returned from Portland, Jenny sat at the breakfast table with Will. The family had eaten, but she lingered to talk with him.

It was a struggle to get the entire family ready for Sunday services on time. She should braid Eliza's and Lottie's hair, but Maria could probably manage the younger girls without her. Jenny needed to be sure Nate washed his face, or it would remain sticky with pancake syrup. And little Maggie would need help with everything—at almost two, she threw tantrums if anyone other than Jenny tried to dress her.

But Will was eager to converse with her, and she needed to listen. He rambled on and on about the telegraph office. "Pa sent a telegram while we watched, Mama. All the way to California. Right while we watched."

"Did your father's agent respond?" she asked.

"Not while we waited. But his response came to the hotel before supper. You should have seen the meal we had." Will raved on for another minute. "Do you know how to make Hollandaise sauce?"

She nodded, holding back a smile. "Did you like it?"

"It made the vegetables so tasty."

Cal entered the room. "Mama, Nate ain't washed up yet."

"Hasn't, dear. Nate hasn't washed yet."

"Well," Cal said with a sigh. "You'd better help him. He won't listen to me."

Will's face soured at Cal's arrival. She didn't know why, but there seemed to be a problem between her two oldest sons. At least on Will's side. He'd been such a cheery baby and toddler, back when the two of them were alone while Mac was in California. But over the past year, Will had turned surly. He hid his intelligence behind a wall of moods, and she didn't seem able to break through. She was sorry she couldn't sit and talk with him longer, but she needed to get her brood ready for church.

The only part of the church service Will enjoyed was the singing. He tried to match his tenor harmony to Mama's clear soprano. Pa sang a baritone beneath them all. Today, they sang all the verses of "Amazing Grace."

As soon as the congregation finished the final hymn, Will slunk outside behind the rest of his family, then sought out Jonah. He hadn't seen his friend since the day on the farm.

"Did you get in trouble for playing hooky?" Jonah asked.

"Pa mustn't have cared too much," Will said. "He took me to Portland on Friday. We sent a telegram to California." He didn't mention Cal's participation in the trip.

"Gosh." Jonah looked impressed. "I ain't never been on a steamboat. And telegrams are like magic—messages written on a wire."

Will grinned. He didn't want to explain Morse code to his friend—Jonah's spelling was atrocious, and his penmanship worse.

But Jonah didn't let him boast any further. "Look across the churchyard. See Iris Hayes with her family." Jonah gestured with his head. When Will started to turn, Jonah hissed, "No, don't stare."

"What about them?" Will asked, facing his friend again.

"Not all of them. Just Iris. Ain't she purty?"

Will took a quick glance. "I suppose."

Jonah sighed. "She's the purtiest thing I ever did see. I'm gonna marry her."

Will chortled. "She'll never have you."

Jonah pulled himself to his full height, still shorter than Will. "I don't see why not."

"Have you kissed her?" Will asked. Not that he'd kissed a girl, but he was fairly certain Jonah hadn't either.

"No. But I will."

Will grinned. "Bet you can't kiss her before April Fool's Day."

"That's only two weeks off," Jonah protested. "How'm I gonna do that?"

"Then don't take the bet." Will saw Pa gesticulating as he talked with other men across the yard. Their conversation might be more interesting than teasing Jonah. "Let's go see what our fathers are talking about."

After the service, Mac stood in the churchyard discussing his trip to Portland with other men. The weather had warmed, though it looked as if another spate of clouds and cold would reach town by the end of the day. Daniel Abercrombie and his father Samuel were in the group chatting with Mac. The Abercrombies had traveled from Missouri to Oregon in the same wagon train as Mac and Jenny, back in 1847.

"What news of the War?" Samuel asked. "Any advances by the Confederacy?" Abercrombie came from Tennessee, and his sympathies lay with the South. Daniel kept a closed mouth when his father spouted off, but Mac thought Daniel was on the fence—wanting peace between the states, yet not passionate about ending slavery.

"Not since the Battle of Olustee in Florida late last month," Mac said. "Though with General Grant in charge now, the Union Army should do better against Richmond."

"The Confederates pushed back the Union invasion in Florida, that's for sure," Samuel crowed. "We'll send the Yankee bastards hightailing it north all the way to Maine, even against Grant."

Mac didn't respond—it would only encourage the old buzzard. Samuel Abercrombie had been a thorn in Mac's side since they'd met, and Mac had learned to ignore the curmudgeon's tirades whenever he could.

"Any news of Indian raids in Southern Oregon? Those'll hurt us more'n battles in the East," Daniel said. Daniel might not express strong opinions about slavery, but Mac knew the farmer feared Indian attacks.

"Relations between the Klamath tribes and miners in the Rogue Valley are terrible," Mac said. "Every few weeks there's talk of an attack. And with the Homestead Act bringing more settlers and miners, the Indians feel even more threatened."

Samuel spat a stream of tobacco juice. "Threats come more from the tribes, not the settlers. White men just want to farm, build a home."

"The tribes might say they've had homes here for centuries," Mac said mildly.

"Savages can't even count centuries." Samuel followed his words with another spit. "Nor build proper homes. They move from place to place with the seasons, following their food rather than growing it. 'Tain't a proper way to live."

At that point, Will and Jonah joined the men. Mac wanted to impress on Will what he believed about the rights of Indians, so he said, "As long as both sides follow the treaties, we should be able to live in peace with the tribes. When we break the treaties—or when the tribes do—that's what brings violence. But the settlers can't keep pushing the Indians into smaller and smaller territories where they can't survive."

"They don't do nothin' with the lands they got," Samuel objected. And he continued his tirade against the tribes.

Mac pulled Will aside. "Let's head home." After they walked away, Mac continued, "There's no reasoning with that man. And no point in listening to him any further." He hoped Will agreed.

That afternoon, after a huge Sunday dinner, Will lounged in the parlor reading a book, the family dog Rufus asleep at his feet. Mama didn't insist on the Bible on Sundays, but she did like the family to engage in quiet activities. He thought about moving to the porch to finish whittling a little horse he was carving, but he was too sated with roast beef to budge.

While he read, Maria entered the parlor with her sewing basket in hand. "Oh," she said, "I didn't realize anyone was in here."

"Just me," Will said, sitting up straight on the sofa. "I don't mind your company. As long as you don't have any of the little ones trailing behind you." Maria was almost fourteen, the next sibling after Will. He liked his adopted sister better than his natural-born siblings. He remembered when Mac brought her home—she'd been only a baby, and Will had been three. He'd thought she was a pretty baby then, and he still thought she was pretty. More so than any of the other girls he knew. A lot prettier than Iris Hayes.

"Tell me about your trip to Portland," she said, as she sat and began working on her sampler. Rufus moved to curl up beside her sewing basket.

Will grunted. "You must have heard it all from Cal already."

She smiled at him. "Yes, but I haven't heard what you thought."

That was all the encouragement Will needed. He started with the steamboat trip and recounted the journey step by step, telling Maria everything he could remember about the telegraph office and the hotel. "Maybe someday I'll be a telegraph operator," he said. "I'd like knowing the news before anyone else. Though think of the trouble if I got the message wrong. I could start an economic catastrophe, or maybe even a war."

She laughed, a musical trill. "You used to want to be a Pony Express rider. Remember?"

He grinned back. "But that didn't last any longer than the Pony Express. And the telegraph is much faster. Only minutes to transmit information across the nation, instead of days."

Maria's face turned solemn. "What do you really want to do, Will?"

"I don't know." And that was God's truth. Will had no idea what he wanted to do with his life. Just that it didn't involve any more schooling at the Oregon City academy. He was ready to leave that place behind.

# Chapter 4: Preparing for a Party

A week after Mac's trip to Portland with the boys, Jenny woke up with a queasy stomach. A familiar feeling—she was likely with child again. And today, March 18, her youngest child Maggie turned two. Another baby was not a surprise, but Jenny wondered when she would be done with birthing.

She remembered her friend Esther's mother, Cordelia Pershing. Jenny was carrying William—her first—while they traveled the Oregon Trail, and Cordelia was pregnant with Jonah. Cordelia had died with Jonah's birth. Jenny shivered at the memory. She may not be scrabbling in the wilderness as Cordelia had been, but women died of childbirth everywhere. As did their babies.

Jenny's morbid thoughts turned to the two children she had lost. A miscarriage in 1853 between Caleb and Nathan. And poor little Abram, born in February 1859—that mite had died mere weeks after his birth. She mourned him every day.

Jenny sighed and sat up in bed. Mac had left already. He worked too hard these days, trying to make up for losses from the floods two years earlier. The family had plenty to be comfortable, but Mac treated business like a battle, a battle he intended to win.

She rose, dressed, and went to wake Maggie. Jenny and Mrs. O'Malley had a long day of cooking and baking ahead. Tomorrow they were hosting a party for Maggie and Maria, both of whom had birthdays this month.

Jenny tiptoed into the girls' bedroom, only to be greeted with shouts of glee. "Good morning, Mama," Eliza and Lottie crowed. "It's Maggie's birthday," one of them added with excitement.

"Yes, it is." Jenny smiled.

"Two," Maggie said from her crib. She held up all her fingers, causing Eliza and Lottie to giggle.

Maria stood dressing in the corner. "I tried to keep them quiet, Mama," she said. "Did they wake you?"

Jenny shook her head. "It's time to be up." She hefted Maggie out of the crib and onto her hip. "Happy birthday, little one."

"Two," Maggie said, resting her head on Jenny's shoulder and sticking her thumb in her mouth.

Jenny nuzzled the toddler's blond curls, taking in the morning baby smell. Maybe another one wouldn't be so bad. "Shall we go get ready for a party?"

Esther Abercrombie and Hannah Pershing arrived in midmorning to help Jenny and Mrs. O'Malley with the cooking. Esther's waist had thickened with yet another pregnancy—this would be her eleventh child, due in late June. She'd miscarried one, but birthed two sets of twins.

Hannah had only two children—twelve-year-old Hope and four-year-old Isaiah. She'd had trouble with other pregnancies and lost several before birth. Privately, Jenny wondered if Hannah's injured leg—she walked with a pronounced limp—contributed to her difficult pregnancies. But Hannah and her husband Zeke had raised several of Zeke's orphaned younger siblings, and two of his brothers—grown men now—still lived with them. Hannah seemed happy with her life as a farmer's wife, though it offered her little opportunity to use the education she'd had in the East.

As usual, Esther chattered non-stop. She complained about her feet hurting. "And I have three more months of my belly growin' afore I'll get any relief. Not that birthin' brings any relief from standin' and fetchin'."

Jenny murmured sympathetically. She wasn't ready to mention her suspicion that she was also pregnant—she hadn't even told Mac yet.

"I used to pooh-pooh Ma," Esther continued. "Remember how she always needed to sit and rest as we walked the trail?"

Jenny nodded.

"Well, I understand her a lot better now," Esther said, stirring the cake batter. "She weren't much older'n I am now. And I've borne more young'uns than she did." Her expression turned sad. "Oh, how I miss her still."

Jenny patted Esther's shoulder on her way to get a ham out of the larder.

"You're both fortunate to have so many children," Hannah said. "They're such a help on the farm."

Jenny smiled. Trust Hannah to be the practical one. "Maybe, but here in town, they just fill up bedrooms and eat everything in sight."

"They do that in the country as well," Hannah said. "But the boys in particular are good workers. Isaiah isn't old enough yet, but we have Zeke's brothers."

"I'm glad they all stayed near Oregon City," said Esther, who was Zeke's sister. "All us Pershings stayed close, except Joel."

"What does Maggie think of her birthday?" Hannah asked.

"Oh, she doesn't understand birthdays yet," Jenny said. "Though the older children try to explain."

Esther chuckled and gave the batter a final stir. "She'll understand cake once she gets a slice."

Jenny laughed. "Cake she understands already."

"And Maria?" Hannah asked. "Does she feel slighted to play second fiddle to her little sister this weekend? After all, this party is for her also."

Shaking her head, Jenny said, "Maria never acts slighted about anything. She's such a docile girl. Grateful for everything. Sometimes I think she doesn't trust that we are truly her family."

"But she's lived with you since she was a baby," Esther said. "How can she think you aren't her family?"

"Mac has always made it clear she's adopted," Jenny said.

"That's just to squelch the rumors he's her father," Esther said. "You've never thought he was, have you?"

"Of course not." Jenny shook her head. "He told me he wasn't, and that's enough for me."

Mac rubbed his forehead after spending the morning in his town office catching up on correspondence. His investments finally seemed to be on a path to growth. He'd written bank drafts to cover the building expenses in Sacramento. But those costs were offset by income from his mining interests in California and from Oregon farmers repaying the loans he'd made them.

He glanced at his pocket watch. Time to head home for the noon meal. As he left his office, he remembered today was Maggie's birthday. How had he forgotten? The household had been in an uproar all week with preparations for the party tomorrow afternoon.

And Maria's birthday came later in the month. He smiled, remembering Maria as an infant. Her mother Consuela, part Spanish and part Indian, had been Mac's friend in California. She'd been a stubborn and independent woman who returned to whoring soon after Maria's birth, only to have a customer kill her. On her death bed, Consuela pleaded with Mac to take the baby. So Mac brought Maria home to Jenny to raise. Jenny loved the baby as soon as she saw her, and they'd become a family.

Mac locked up his office and stopped at Myers Mercantile on his way home. He found a cloth doll with a china head for Maggie. While he browsed the store for a gift for Maria, he overheard a small group of men talking as they sat around the stove near the counter.

"Confederate deserters been flocking to Oregon," one man said.

"They ain't all Confederates," another said. "Union men, too."

"Some ain't even soldiers, just men looking for a quick fortune in the mines, or easy labor," said a third.

The first man chortled. "Ain't nothin' easy 'bout any labor. Least ways, not any I ever found."

Mac picked up a roll of lace. A piece of this might do for Maria. "Are the deserters dangerous?" he asked the men.

"No more so than other men with nothin' to do," came the reply.

"But most of 'em absconded with their Army weapons," another said. "So they's armed. I'd keep an eagle-eye on my farmland and barns if I was you."

"I live in town," Mac said. "But I'll pass on the news to my farming friends." Many of his guests tomorrow would be farmers, and he'd make sure they were aware of potential intruders.

# Chapter 5: A Party for Two Sisters

The party for Maria and Maggie had barely begun, and already Will wanted to leave. There were too many people for him to enjoy the occasion. But his parents had pressed him into greeting guests and taking their wraps. "Why can't Maria and Cal help?" he asked Mama.

She reached up to pat his shoulder. "It's Maria's party, she shouldn't have to work. Cal can carry the coats upstairs. I need you to man the door."

Cal was nowhere to be found. After carrying one load of cloaks to the girls' bedroom, the brat disappeared. So Will grabbed Nate by the collar as he passed through the hall from dining room to parlor. "Stay here," he ordered. "Help with the coats."

The younger boy pulled away. "Can't. I'm taking this plate to old Mrs. Abercrombie."

Jonah's grandmother Harriet was a nice old lady but didn't stray far from her husband Samuel Abercrombie. Samuel was a right old bastard—as Will heard Pa say often enough.

The Abercrombies weren't really Jonah's grandparents, but Harriet treated him like a grandson. Samuel mostly ignored Jonah.

At least Jonah had the semblance of grandparents in Oregon. None of Will's grandparents had come West. Pa's family all resided in Boston, and Will had never met any of them. He also didn't know Mama's family. Mama's father died when she was only a girl. Will was named after him— William Calhoun. Mama's mother remarried and lived with her husband and their son in Missouri. Mama didn't speak of them often, though she and her mother exchanged letters from time to time.

It might be nice to have family around. Particularly a grandfather, if he were nicer than Samuel Abercrombie.

Nate raced back toward the dining room. Will collared him again. "Sorry," Nate said. "Now Mr. Abercrombie wants some ham."

Family? Will grumbled to himself. They were more trouble than help. The door knocker sounded, and he greeted the next guests.

After all the company had arrived, Will and his friend Jonah found chairs in the dining room near the laden table. They could keep their plates full of food and hear the conversations flowing around them. "You been goin' to school?" Jonah asked Will.

Will nodded. "Mama and Pa make me." His face brightened. "But they say this is my last year at the academy. Don't know what I'll do when the term is over."

"I ain't goin' to school no more," Jonah said. "Daniel wants me workin' with him on the farm."

"Does Esther agree?"

"She says if I don't want no more schoolin' and Daniel'll keep me busy, that's fine by her."

"Are you going to file your own land claim once you're old enough?" Will asked. Some of the Pershing men had filed claims, others worked as hired hands. The original Pershing claims were six hundred and forty acres, before the Homestead Act reduced the maximum size of a claim to three hundred twenty acres. Six-forty was enough land to support several families.

Jonah shrugged. "I ain't decided. I still have several years afore I can. Maybe I'll prospect for a while first. Like Joel."

Joel was one of Jonah's older brothers. Joel had left to prospect for gold in California not long after the Pershings arrived in Oregon. He returned to Oregon City for short visits occasionally, and Will had met him. "Does Joel want you?" he asked Jonah.

"I dunno." Jonah bit into a slice of bread slathered with butter. "Maybe I won't ask him. Just go."

"Esther and Daniel will never let you do that." Will couldn't imagine taking off for southern Oregon by himself. His parents would be frantic with worry—and Esther and Daniel would be equally concerned if Jonah left without telling them.

Old Samuel Abercrombie lumbered into the dining room to refill his plate. "That younger brother of yourn didn't bring me no ham. I still got a hankering for it," he said to Will.

"May I help you, sir?" Will said. It was his parents' party, so he needed to be polite.

"I'll get it myself." Samuel joined other men beside the now mostly bare ham bone. "What do you hear about Indians near the Rogue?" he asked the sheriff, close enough for Will to hear.

"None of my affair," Sheriff Thomas responded. "I'm only responsible for Clackamas County. Only news I get is what I read in the paper. Last I read, Rogue River Valley is teeming with tribes returning to spring camps."

"Those savages need a firm hand," Samuel said. "No Indian's a good Indian."

The men around Samuel and the sheriff talked on and on about the tribes in the south. They all seemed to believe the Indians should be removed from the lucrative farmland and mines in Oregon.

"What do you think about the tribes?" Will asked Jonah as the men moved on.

"Makes sense to me, what they say," Jonah said. "Whites make better use of the land than Indians, whether it's farmin' or minin.' They hunt for their food—they can do that anywhere."

"Not all land can support hunting," Will said.

Jonah shrugged. "There's always game, if you know where to find it."

As he chewed his food, Will wondered whether Indians were as savage as Mr. Abercrombie said. They didn't dress the same as whites, they didn't live in houses, they did little farming. But Pa didn't think Indians were all bad.

Plus, Maria was part Indian, and she certainly wasn't a savage. She was as genteel as Mama, sometimes more so, because Mama could get mad, and Maria never did.

Mac noticed Will and Jonah tucked away in the dining room. Spying the frown on Will's face, Mac walked toward the boys. As he entered the room, he heard Abercrombie ranting about savages. That was only one of many differences Mac had with Abercrombie. In Mac's opinion, many of the problems between the races resulted from how the whites squeezed the tribes off their land, precluding them from living as they had for generations.

He joined the group of men, if only to rankle Abercrombie. "If we let the tribes have portions of their native lands, they'd be happier and leave the white farmers alone," Mac said.

As Mac anticipated, his comments set Abercrombie to pontificating. Samuel might be in his sixties now, but he was as cantankerous as ever. Age hadn't made the old fool worse because he'd always been a difficult man.

But Samuel was a good man to have at one's side in a fight, Mac thought. Mac had been on hunts and posses with Abercrombie, and the codger could shoot with the best of them.

To change the subject, Mac mentioned the rumors he'd heard in the general store the day before. "Men in Myers Mercantile told me there are Secessionist deserters in the area."

"Be damn proud to have 'em in our state," Abercrombie said. "I'd help out any Tennessee boys what come to Oregon."

"If they're deserters," Samuel's son Daniel said, "they're probably not good for much. They're running away from the War."

"If they's Tennessee Rebels, they's good men," Samuel said with a sniff. "Army ain't for everyone."

"Be forewarned," Mac said. "Have a care, particularly out in the country. They'll hide in your barns and steal your food. Maybe kill some chickens. And scare your women."

Zeke Pershing chimed in. He didn't usually mingle with Samuel Abercrombie. There was bad blood between the two men. "I've dealt with marauders afore. Men on the run can be dangerous. They have nothin' to lose. Thanks for the warning, Mac."

Jenny signaled to Mac that it was time to slice the cakes. He left the men and moved toward his wife, nodding at Will as he left the dining room.

That evening, when the guests had left, Will helped carry plates and platters to the kitchen. Once the house was returned to order, Will headed toward the stairs to his bedroom. Pa called him into his small home study. It was a windowless room, lit only by an oil lamp Pa kept on his desk. No wonder Pa spent most of his time at his office in town.

"Thanks for your help today, son," Pa said, barely looking up from the document in front of him. A glass of whiskey sat at Pa's elbow.

"You're welcome." Will stuck his hands in his pockets, wondering if that was all Pa meant to tell him.

After a moment, Pa turned his full gaze on Will. "Did you hear Samuel Abercrombie spout off about the tribesmen this afternoon?"

Will nodded.

"What did you think of what he said?"

"You've always told me Indians act the way they do because of how they're treated."

Mac picked up a cigar and motioned Will to have a seat. He lit the cigar and puffed on it to get it going. "Yes, that's what I've told you. But what do *you* think?"

Will frowned. What did Pa want from him? "I suppose same as you. The Indians aren't like us, but the white landowners don't treat them well."

Pa raised an eyebrow. "You wrote a fine essay on slavery a few weeks back. I was proud of you. Just like Negroes, the tribesmen can do whatever they're allowed to do, whatever they're educated to do. Our laws don't let them own land, not full bloods anyway, and if we cut off their livelihoods, they'll turn to slovenliness. And from there to violence."

Will considered Pa's comments—they made sense. But why did men like Samuel Abercrombie believe so differently? He supposed that's why the Secessionists had rebelled. And why there were frequent skirmishes with Indian tribes in Southern Oregon.

Pa sat smoking, and Will thought some more. Then he said, "Pa, what did you think about what Mr. Abercrombie said about the deserters?"

Pa glanced at Will. "You mean about the deserters being fine men?"

Will nodded.

"Some might be, and some are probably villains. It's not safe for families to take them in until they get to know the men as individuals."

"And the Army?" Will asked. "What do you think about soldiering?"

"I haven't had much experience, myself," Pa said. "A short stint with the militia back in forty-seven, when we pursued the Cayuse who killed the Whitmans. And some posses from time to time, both in California and Oregon." He puffed on his cigar. "Some soldiers are fine men, like Robert O'Neil, and others are as mean as Samuel Abercrombie."

Will rubbed the pockmarks on his cheek. Mr. O'Neil had left the Army and come to work for Mama while Pa was away mining gold. Mr. O'Neil cared for Will when he had smallpox, back when Will was very young. He'd been as kind and gentle with Will as Mama. "Mr. O'Neil is a good man," he said.

"That he is," said Pa. "Talk to him about the Army someday. He'll tell you the good and the bad of it. As for me, I didn't take well to following orders I thought were foolish. I don't think you would either."

# Chapter 6: Is She My Sister?

Maria's birthday, Jenny thought as she woke up on March 30. They'd celebrated the occasion with the party two weeks earlier, and last Sunday they'd celebrated Easter with another large meal. But Jenny still wanted to make today special for her oldest daughter. She hadn't borne Maria, but family was who we loved, Jenny reflected, not who was ours by blood. Maria had become her treasured child and companion.

Jenny increasingly felt nauseated in the mornings—a sure sign another baby was coming. She still hadn't said anything to Mac, but she must do so soon.

After dressing, Jenny went downstairs to the kitchen where Maria assisted Mrs. O'Malley with breakfast. Jenny's stomach turned at the smell of frying bacon, but she managed to smile and hug Maria. "Happy birthday, daughter," she whispered into Maria's hair. "Go sit down, I'll help Mrs. O'Malley."

Maria hugged her in return. "Thank you, Mama. I don't mind helping."

"Sit," Jenny said, more firmly. "I won't have you working on your birthday."

"I told her I'd make chicken pot pies for supper," Mrs. O'Malley said. "Her favorite."

"With vanilla custard for dessert," Jenny said, smiling. "And you get the first portion. Make your brothers wait their turn."

"Thank you, Mama," Maria whispered.

Jenny wondered whether she should have taken Maria out of the girls' school in Oregon City when she turned twelve. The other girls had not been kind to Maria because of her Spanish and Indian ancestry. But keeping Maria at home had not increased her daughter's self-confidence—she remained timid and self-effacing.

Mac came downstairs to a breakfast table laden with bacon and pancakes. Maria sat in her place, cutting up a pancake for Maggie beside her. "Good morning, girls," Mac said. "Where's your mother?"

"In the kitchen helping Mrs. O'Malley," Maria said.

Then Mac remembered—it was Maria's birthday. He bent and kissed her cheek. "Happy birthday," he said. "Fourteen. You're a young lady now." Then he turned to kiss Maggie's sticky face.

Maria's face brightened at his kiss. Maria was an easy child to love, he thought. Serene and even-tempered. She had her mother Consuela's dark beauty, though Mac hadn't noticed her mother's stubborn streak in Maria. No way of knowing who'd fathered her, of course. Though he felt like Maria's father—he'd known her since birth and had been the first person able to calm her as an infant.

Some things happened for reasons known only to God, Mac mused. If Consuela had lived, Maria would probably be with her mother in a brothel in California. Instead, Mac had made her part of a large, loving family.

And someday Mac would give her away in marriage. He felt a pang of sadness. Someday far in the future, he hoped.

Will, Cal, and Nate clomped down the stairs and into the dining room. Mac's quiet moment with his oldest and youngest daughters had ended.

Will trudged home from the academy, a crumpled piece of paper in his hand. His teacher had written all over his essay about the Tanners and why slavery was wrong. The teacher had given Will a failing grade because the essay was based on personal experiences, not facts. Wasn't an essay supposed to be personal? An opinion? An attempt to express that opinion? Mama had told him "*essai*" meant "attempt" in French. And Will had attempted his best to explain how he felt about the Tanners.

Pa had liked the essay, and Pa was the smartest man Will knew. He kicked at a stone as he entered the yard, wondering what Pa would say about the bad marks he'd received on the essay.

"Hello, Will." Maria sat outside the back door peeling potatoes. "Why do you look so mad?"

Will's mood lifted. He'd hoped to find Maria alone today, so he could give her the birthday gift he'd made. He carried it in his pocket all day—a small wooden horse he'd whittled with the Bowie knife Pa had given him a year ago. He'd tried to make the carving look like Shanty. He'd finished it just the day before, and it was his best carving ever.

"Happy birthday, Maria," he said, smiling. "I thought Mama said you didn't have to do any chores today."

"Mrs. O'Malley said if I wanted potatoes in the pot pies, I needed to peel them."

"Give me the knife," Will said. "I'll do a few. As a birthday gift."

She laughed and gave him the paring knife. "I suppose you won't cut yourself," she said. "You're always whittling at something."

"That reminds me." Will set the knife down and pulled the little horse out of his pocket. His hand trembled as he held it out. "This is for you."

"Oh," she exclaimed. "How beautiful. It's Shanty, isn't it?"

Will grinned, relief surging through his chest. "You recognized him?"

"Of course," she said, tracing the blaze on the tiny horse's nose and the spots on his rump. "Here are his markings."

"Do you want to go riding with me?" Will asked. "Maybe on Saturday? We can take Shanty out to the Abercrombie farm. See Jonah and the rest of the Abercrombies."

"Perhaps," Maria said. "If Mama doesn't need me."

"I'll ask her," Will said. "I'm sure she'll say yes."

Maria smiled. "Mama doesn't refuse you much, does she?"

"That's because I'm so reasonable." Will didn't think Mama favored him over the others. If anything, Mama expected more of him as the oldest. Just as she expected more of Maria than the other girls because she was older. Though Maria was more responsible and nicer than any of his other siblings.

After supper, Maria showed the family the wood carving Will gave her. Will beamed with pride—Maria seemed more taken with his whittling than with any other gift she'd received. Eliza and Lottie wanted to touch the little horse. Nate pretended to trot it around the parlor floor until Mama told him to stop. Cal fidgeted as if he wanted to get his hands on the wooden figure.

Will sat in a corner across the room while the younger children crowded around Maria. She was fourteen now, almost grown for a girl. Mama had barely been fifteen when Will was born, and he knew several girls who'd married at fourteen. Would Maria marry soon? The idea made him angry, and he wondered why.

Must be because she's my sister, he mused. No boy wants to think of a man touching his sister.

But she wasn't really his sister, only an adopted sister.

As he'd grown older, Will realized from comments his parents made that Maria's mother had been a prostitute. Once he'd learned what a prostitute did, he'd wondered if Pa wasn't Maria's father after all, despite what Pa and Mama said. So perhaps Maria was his sister—his half-sister anyway.

He still thought she was the prettiest girl he'd ever known. Her black hair turned almost blue in sunlight. Her dark eyes were deeper than the starry sky. She flashed a smile brighter than the sun. Will wished she'd smile at him more often.

Will would fight any man who wanted Maria for a wife. Only if she loved the man would Will let her wed. And then, only if the man were good enough for her.

# Chapter 7: An Uncertain Future

On Friday afternoon, April 1, Will came home from the academy in bad humor, as he had earlier in the week after seeing the poor grade on his essay. Last night, he'd forgotten an algebra assignment, and the teacher ridiculed him in class today. It was just a mistake—he didn't forget assignments often. The teacher made him stay after school and do the problems before he left. And he still hadn't told Mama and Pa about the essay.

When he got home, he found Maria in tears. "What's wrong?" he asked.

"I can't find the horse you gave me. I lost it."

His school problems seemed less important as he put an arm around her shoulders. "I can make you another." Though the next horse probably wouldn't be as good. He discovered the animals as he carved the wood, and every piece of wood was different. But he could whittle her something new.

"Thank you," she said, stifling a sob. "But the first one was so nice."

The evening meal was glum. The whole family debated where Maria's horse might be.

"It's only a silly carving," Cal said.

"Maybe to you," Maria retorted. "But Will gave it to me. I loved it."

Later that evening, after the younger children were in bed, Will, Maria, and Cal sat with their parents in the parlor. Maria took her usual chair near the fireplace. "Ouch," she exclaimed after she sat. She stood and picked up the seat cushion. "It's Shanty," she said, holding up the missing wooden horse.

"April Fool's," Cal crowed. "I hid it."

"The tail broke off." Maria picked up the tail from under the cushion and cradled the two pieces of Will's carving in her hands.

39

Distraught at seeing his hard work damaged, Will examined the figurine. The tail had snapped off cleanly. "Maybe I can glue it back," he said to Maria.

"I'm sorry," Cal said. "I didn't mean for it to break." His exuberance shifted to a remorseful tone.

Will's temper flared at Cal's heedlessness. "Saying sorry isn't enough," he hissed. "I worked hard on that horse. I made it for Maria." His fist shot out and cracked against Cal's cheekbone.

The younger boy fell to the floor.

"Will," Pa shouted. "Go to your room."

Will hesitated, already repenting his action.

"Now," Pa said.

As Will turned to go, Mama knelt beside Cal. "It's not even cut," she said. "But it'll bruise. Let's go put some meat on it." And she led Cal toward the kitchen.

Once in his room, Will threw himself on the bed. He'd seen Maria's reproachful stare after he hit Cal. He hadn't intended to hit his brother. But Cal's foolish act damaged Will's gift to Maria, a gift she treasured.

How could he and Cal be brothers? Will wondered, as he often had over the years. Cal ambled blissfully through his days, not caring what happened. Will cared about everything.

He remembered when Cal was born. Until then, he'd been the only boy. Maria had been there, but she was a girl. And she was adopted. Will was Mama's firstborn, her real child, and that made him feel special.

Then Cal came. After Cal was born, Will watched his parents smile at each other and down at Cal as if the baby were the only child in the world. Will felt left out of their triad, distant from his parents and their newborn. Maybe that's when he decided it would be him and Maria against the world. Cal was the interloper, the one who stole Will's parents.

Mac followed Jenny and Cal into the kitchen. "Let me see, son," he said, tipping Cal's chin to inspect the injured cheek. It was already swelling—the boy would have a shiner for sure. "It's a whopper," he said. "But it'll heal."

Jenny put a piece of steak on Cal's cheek. Cal whimpered when the meat touched the bruise. Jenny looked at Mac. "We need to talk to Will," she said.

"I'll do it," Mac said.

"You gonna whup him?" Cal asked, his expression brightening.

"We don't whip children in this family," Mac replied. "But we also don't hit each other, and Will should not have hit you."

Mac climbed the stairs slowly, wondering how to talk to Will. He would have to get the older boy to apologize to Cal. But there was a bigger issue. What were he and Jenny to do with Will? The boy's anger against Cal was out of place, but there was something more going on in Will's head, and Mac needed to find out what.

He knocked once, then entered Will's room. Will lay on his back on his bed, staring at the sloped ceiling above his head. He sat upright when Mac came in.

Mac sat at Will's desk chair. "Tell me why you hit Cal."

Will blew out a long, slow breath. "I don't know." He paused. "I didn't mean to hit him." Will's jaw jutted out, reminding Mac of Jenny when she turned stubborn. "But he ruined Maria's horse. The horse I gave her."

"He shouldn't have hidden it," Mac agreed. "It was a silly prank. But he did apologize."

"So he gets off scot-free?" Will looked defiant.

"You didn't give your mother and me a chance to punish him. Your fist did the punishing," Mac said. "What more do you think he should have to do?"

Will stared at the floor. "I don't know."

They sat silently for a moment.

"What's wrong, son?" Mac asked. "You haven't been happy all year. I know school isn't suiting you, but you need an education."

Will shrugged. Then he reached under his bed, pulled out a wrinkled paper, and handed it to Mac. "I failed on the essay."

"Failed?" Mac was shocked—the boy had written a fine essay. He read the teacher's comments, then looked at Will. "This man doesn't know what he's talking about. A personal story about your experience is a fine theme for an essay."

"Doesn't matter to him." Will sighed. "I want to quit school."

"Seems you've done as much as you can at the academy. After seeing what this man said about your essay, I'd support your wish to leave the school. Though I should talk to your mother before we decide."

"Thanks, Pa." Will's face relaxed.

"Are you ready for Harvard, do you think?" Mac asked.

Will stared at him. "Harvard?"

"We've talked before—you know I'd like to send you to Harvard. The college was the making of me, a time to be exposed to great teachers, good fellows as companions. A time for growing up."

"When do you want me to go?"

"Sometime this summer, perhaps," Mac said. "The autumn term begins in September. I could take you to Boston, see you settled, and visit my parents and brothers."

"Just you and me? Not Mama or Cal?"

"We'll see." Mac paused, wondering why the boy cared who accompanied him East. "Do you want to go?"

"I don't know," Will said. "Could I go into business with you?"

Mac nodded. "You could. Or you could farm—I have plenty of land. But those endeavors could wait until after you further your education. You'd learn a lot at Harvard, maybe find a calling of your own, rather than following me. The law—you'd be good at that, better than the bit of scrivening I've done." Mac had obtained a law degree at Harvard, and he wrote some contracts and other legal documents for friends in Oregon. But practicing law had never appealed to him.

Will was silent.

"Think on it, son," Mac said. "And I expect you to apologize to Cal before you go to bed tonight. To your mother and Maria as well."

After Pa left, Will sat on his bed, head in his hands, elbows on his knees. Pa let him off too easy. He should be punished more for hitting Cal. Even if Cal deserved it.

Instead, Pa had given him leave to quit the academy, which is what Will wanted. Though Pa said he should go to college.

Did he want to go to Harvard? He'd been truthful when he told Pa he didn't know. Boston was so far away. Did Mama and Pa want to get rid of him? He'd been at loose ends this past winter, though he didn't know why. Nothing suited him. He didn't understand his own restlessness, so how could anyone else understand? He yearned for something he couldn't identify,

42

something impossible to find.

The only time he felt happy was with his friend Jonah. Sometimes with Maria—like when she'd smiled at him when he gave her the horse.

He'd have to fix the horse for her. Or make her another one. He could do it, and she'd love the new one.

But it wouldn't be the same, thanks to Cal.

Will sighed and stood. Time to go apologize to Cal. Even if the little dunderhead didn't deserve it.

# Chapter 8: A Letter from Missouri

The morning after he hit Cal, Will rode Shanty to Jonah's house. This time he'd asked for permission, and Pa had given it. Pa frowned awhile before agreeing, but Will stood waiting for the answer, ready to do what Pa wanted. It was his way of telling Pa he regretted hitting Cal.

The morning weather was bright, promising warmth later in the day. Will took Maria with him. Sitting behind him on Shanty, Maria chattered as they rode, eager to see her friends Cordelia and Abigail Abercrombie.

When they arrived at the Abercrombie farm, Will checked for Jonah in the barn while Maria ran to the house. Not finding Jonah, Will followed her. Esther shooed him back outside, saying Daniel had the boys tilling the fields already. Will took a hoe from the barn and found them in a cornfield nearby. He started hoeing in the row next to Jonah so they could talk as they worked.

"Pa says I don't have to go to the academy anymore," he told Jonah. "But he wants me to go to Harvard."

"Where's that?"

"A college in Boston."

Jonah stopped hoeing and stared at Will. "Boston? In Massachusetts?" Will nodded.

"That's awful far." Jonah started tilling again. "Are you goin'?"

"I don't know."

"I'm stayin' right here," Jonah said. "Daniel's got plenty of work for me. He'll pay me a wage, too, he says. Though not a man's wage, not as long as I live at home. Still, I can save up to wed Iris."

"Don't you want your own land?" Will asked, deciding not to comment on Jonah's plans to marry.

"Sure, but I can't file a claim till I turn twenty-one. I don't want to wait that long to marry."

"Wish I knew what I wanted like you do," Will said.

Jonah snorted. "Farming is all I can do. Or prospect, but that ain't certain to earn me nothin.' Or the Army, but then I might get shot."

"You're lucky to have Daniel to help you get started."

"Hah," Jonah spat. "You're the lucky one. Fine house in town. Your pa sendin' you to college. You'll see the world. And you got a family. I'm an orphan."

Will rarely thought of Jonah as an orphan. Jonah's parents were dead, but Daniel and Esther had raised him along with their brood since birth. He fit in with their family better than Will fit with his. Or so it seemed.

"Are you mad at Daniel?" he asked Jonah.

"I suppose not," Jonah said. "Though he acts like my pa when he ain't."

"He treats you like he does his own children," Will said, voicing his earlier thought.

"But I ain't a child no longer. I'm a man, ready for a man's pay. Ready to start my own family."

If Jonah was a man, what was Will? He was only a few months younger than Jonah, but he didn't feel ready to be on his own. Perhaps that's why he didn't feel eager to leave for Harvard.

After eating the noon meal with Jonah's family, Will rode Shanty alongside Esther Abercrombie's wagon. She had errands in town, so Jonah drove her and some of her younger children. Maria sat in the wagon with Esther until they reached town, where she joined Will on Shanty's back.

"I'll visit your ma after I do my shoppin'," Esther called as Will and Maria turned to ride up the hill to their home. "We'll see you in a bit."

When Jenny heard Esther would be there soon, she mixed a batch of muffins. An hour later, Esther and her children arrived. Jenny ushered Esther into the parlor, while Maria took the younger Abercrombies upstairs to play with Maggie. Will and Jonah stayed in the parlor with the women—probably because she offered them warm corn muffins, Jenny thought with a smile as she passed around a tray.

"I stopped at the post office," Esther said. "Nothin' for us, but when I asked after your mail, the clerk gave me this." She took a letter out of her pocket and handed it to Jenny.

Jenny recognized the handwriting. "From my mother," she said. "She writes so seldom. I wonder what her news is."

"Do you want to read it now?" Esther asked.

Jenny set the letter on a table and shook her head. "Let's talk. I can read it later."

Esther plopped on the divan after taking a muffin. "I don't know how I'll bear two more months of this," she said, with a sigh and a wave at her belly. "Each time I'm carryin' seems harder."

"It must be because we're busier," Jenny said. "More children, more household to care for."

"And, of course, we're gettin' older." Esther grinned, then stared at Jenny sharply and whispered, "Are you carryin', too?"

Jenny glanced across the room at Will and Jonah. Could they hear the women's conversation? She still hadn't talked to Mac. She nodded and murmured, "But I haven't told anyone yet. It's too soon."

Esther beamed. "More of our young'uns to be friends." She tilted her head, gesturing toward the boys. "Like those two." As usual, Esther lumped Jonah, her youngest brother, in with her children.

"Yes," Jenny said. "Will and Jonah have been the best of friends."

Tired after tilling the fields all morning, Will was glad for the chance to sit in the parlor with Jonah and eat muffins with none of the younger children there to pester them. Mama and Esther Abercrombie talked and nodded across the room, but he couldn't hear their conversation. He was only half-listening to Jonah, until Jonah asked, "Who are you sweet on?"

"Huh?" Will said. He wasn't sweet on anyone.

"I'm gonna ask Iris Hayes to the next dance. Who you gonna ask?" Jonah took another muffin from the plate between them.

"Hadn't thought about it."

"I danced with Iris at the last harvest ball. I aim to ask her to be my wife by year-end." Jonah bit into the muffin.

"Did you ever kiss her?" Will asked, remembering his dare.

"Not yet. But if I want to be a farmer, I'll need a wife."

"You think you're ready to be a husband?" Will choked out. "I ain't."

Mama didn't like him saying 'ain't,' but she wasn't paying him any mind now.

"It won't be long. When I have a cabin ready, I'm set on Iris. What about Cordelia?"

"What?" It took Will a moment to follow Jonah's shift from Iris to matchmaking for Will. "Your sister?" He'd never thought of marrying the oldest Abercrombie girl, though she was close to him in age.

"Then you and I'd be brothers almost." Jonah seemed to have both their lives all figured out.

"Cordelia's n-n-nice enough, but—" Will stammered.

"Or Meg Bingham, if you don't want Cordelia," Jonah said, taking another muffin. "Meg's been sweet on you since you was young'uns. Because you both have pockmarks."

Will's fingers went automatically to his cheek. Meg hung after him anytime their families met. Her pockmarks were much worse than Will's. He had three on his face, and a few others on his stomach. Meg's face was covered—she'd suffered in the same smallpox epidemic as Will and nearly died. But that didn't mean he should wed her. "I don't want to marry her either."

"Then who?" Jonah demanded.

Maria's face flashed into Will's mind—her smile when he'd given her the carving of Shanty, another smile as she'd run toward the Abercrombies' house that morning. But he couldn't marry her either. She might be his sister, no matter what Pa claimed. He wasn't ready to marry anyone. "No need to decide now," he told Jonah.

It was late afternoon before Jenny had time to open the letter from her mother. She broke the seal and read:

> *January 30, 1864*
> *Ma chère Geneviève,*
> *    I appreciated your Christmas wishes and should have responded to thank you sooner. But the winter weather and the War have had me in vapors. The news is not good from*

*Louisiana. The Yankees have ejected my brother from his home there and dispersed his slaves.*

*Here in Missouri, the news is little better. The Yankees hold the state, though our neighbors are mostly of a common sentiment with us.*

*The Confederacy will rally, I am sure. I pray daily for the South to rise and smite the enemy from our land.*

*I do hope the vile War ends soon. Otherwise, I fear my son Jacques will be off to soldier. Thankfully, my dear Mr. Peterson is too old and suffers dreadfully from the gout, so he will not be called into service.*

*And what of the news in Oregon? It troubles me you are so far away, depriving me of the comfort of my daughter's companionship during these evil days.*

*Mr. Peterson and your brother send their greetings. Write me again when you can spare a moment,*

*Ta chère mère,*
*Hortense Peterson*

Jenny shuddered as she set the letter on the table next to her. The mention of her stepfather never failed to rouse terrible memories. She would like to meet her half-brother Jacques, born just months after she fled Missouri with Mac. But if it meant also seeing her mother's second husband, then she would stay in Oregon.

Several years ago, Mac had offered to take her back to Missouri to see her mother. "You haven't returned to Boston to see your family," she replied. "Why should I visit my mother?"

"I'm willing," he said, kissing her cheek. "It's whatever you want, my love." He ignored her suggestion that he visit Boston.

Jenny wondered whether the children missed knowing their grandparents and other relatives. Though her mother and Mac's parents were not the loving elders of fairy tales. Neither she nor Mac had grown up with parents given to affection.

Except for Papa, she remembered. She'd loved her father without reserve, but he had succumbed to fever in Missouri when she was thirteen. She smiled, thinking of how much Will reminded her of her father. The same light hair and slender frame, the same love of books and pensive demeanor.

As Mama read the letter from her mother to the family over supper, Will wondered about his half-uncle in Missouri. That boy wasn't much older than he was, just like Jonah wasn't much older than his niece Cordelia. And Jonah had a younger half-brother, the son of his father and stepmother, who'd left Oregon with his mother when he was a toddler and hadn't been seen since.

Families were strange things, Will thought. Relationships braided together until no one could pick them apart. Maria was part of their family. Jonah was part of Esther's. Each person somehow became part of the whole. But how many braids could a family take before it got tied up in knots?

Will shook his head. This notion of braids and knots—no one else in the family seemed to have strange ideas like his. Why did he?

Then he thought about his grandmother's fear that the Army would conscript her son. Was the Army so desperate they needed sixteen-year-olds? How would Will feel if he were called up? The thought of men shooting at him made his insides churn.

What was worth fighting for? Was there anything he believed in firmly enough to die for? If there was, he couldn't name it.

"Will." Pa's voice broke into Will's reverie.

"Yes, Pa?"

"I've been talking to you. Did you clean out the horse stalls today, like I asked?"

Guilt descended on Will. He'd meant to do the chore in the late afternoon, but Jonah had come to visit, and he'd forgotten. "No, Pa."

"Well, do it now. It's dark, so take a lantern." Pa sounded irritated. "And don't burn down the carriage house."

"Yes, Pa." Now that the spring sun had set, the carriage house would be cold. He'd have to don a coat and gloves. But the horses needed his attention.

"Why can't you keep your mind on your responsibilities?" Pa called after him as Will left the room. "Like Cal does."

That wasn't fair, Will thought. Cal shirked his chores often enough. Though his younger brother was glib enough to finagle his way out of trouble. It simply wasn't fair.

Not for the first time, Will wondered why his parents had named Cal after Pa. Will was the oldest son—why wasn't he named after Pa?

Will had asked Mama one time why they'd named him William. She'd hugged him. "You're named after my father—William Calhoun. I loved my father, and I wanted to name my first son after him."

"And Pa agreed?" he asked.

A far-away look came over her face as she answered, "Yes, he did." Then she'd focused on Will again. "And so you became William Calhoun McDougall."

But she named her next son—Cal—after Pa.

# Chapter 9: Another Birthday

Mac was up early on Tuesday, April 5—his birthday. He dressed silently and crept downstairs so as not to wake Jenny or the children. There, he found Mrs. O'Malley preparing breakfast. He took a slice of ham on a biscuit from her, nodded his thanks, and strode down the hill to his office in town.

He had a meeting scheduled with Daniel Abercrombie this morning to discuss a loan. Daniel said he needed money to tide him over until harvest. Many of the stores in town offered farmers credit on their accounts, but for some reason Daniel wanted a cash loan. Mac was one of the few men in Oregon City willing and able to loan money to farmers.

Mac invested in real estate and kept abreast of which landowners farmed their fields productively and which men were too shiftless to get paying crops to market in the fall. Daniel was a good risk, as well as being a friend. Mac would gladly help Daniel if the man's plans were viable.

Mac's business had not completely recovered from the floods of 1862. It was expensive to purchase goods during wartime, though his California warehouses should be built and filled soon. Plus, Oregon farmers were now paying Mac back for earlier loans. He could afford to take a chance with Daniel.

Daniel arrived not long after Mac settled in. He rose to shake Daniel's hand. "What's on your mind, Daniel?" he asked.

"I want to build another house on my land," Daniel said, sitting across from Mac and fidgeting with his hat. "Not large, but big enough for Jonah to start. I'm thinking of deeding him forty acres with the house."

"Jonah?" Mac was surprised. The boy was only sixteen—same age as Will, and Will was nowhere near ready to live on his own.

"He's done with schoolin'," Daniel said. "Truth be told, he ain't gone to class much for the last two years. He prefers farmin.' He's as tall as me and almost as heavy. He can plow and reap as well as any man in these parts. And he's started talkin' about a wife."

Mac chuckled. "Does he have a girl in mind?"

Daniel grinned back at Mac. "Question is, does any girl have *him* in mind? If he has a girl, he ain't told me. But he's a growin' lad, and he'll sow some wild oats soon enough. I'd rather he did so in his own house, rather than under my roof with all my young'uns."

"What land do you want to deed to him?" Mac asked.

Daniel described a wooded parcel of his land claim with a small creek running through a corner. "Water don't flow there all year round, but a well wouldn't need to be too deep."

Mac recognized the description. "That's a nice piece. Is Jonah aware of your plan?"

Daniel shook his head. "His birthday is in July. I want the deed ready by then. I'm startin' with you. I need funds to have the lumber milled, buy nails and glass, and the like. I won't start the house until after Jonah's birthday, but I want the house built between his birthday and harvest time."

They talked and came to terms. Mac shaved a bit off the interest rate for an old friend like Daniel. "I'll draft the loan document and a deed from you to Jonah dated in July," Mac said. "Mind if I ride out to view the parcel before we sign the loan?"

"Of course not," Daniel said. He sat back in his chair, then turned the conversation to small talk. "I hear tell more deserters been seen in these parts."

"Are they causing any trouble?" Mac leaned back and put his feet on his desk, ready to chat.

"Nothin' much. Men camped in fields where they shouldn't be. One man scared a settler's wife when he come into their yard while she hung out her wash."

"You've told Esther to be careful, haven't you?" Mac asked.

"Of course. And told her to keep the young'uns close to home." Daniel tapped his hat on Mac's desk. "You best tell young Will to watch himself when he rides out to visit us. Particularly if he's bringin' Jenny or Maria. Y'all should be safe enough in town, but the country roads is another story. Some of them deserters are dangerous—whether they be Yankee or

Confederates. If they couldn't make it in the Army, they ain't worth much."

Later that morning, Mac rode Valiente toward Daniel's claim. He inspected the parcel Daniel wanted to deed to Jonah. It was a handsome gift—a sign Daniel truly treated Jonah as his son. Mac hoped he could ease Will's path in life as Daniel was planning to do for Jonah. Will hadn't seemed keen on a Harvard education. Maybe Mac should help him invest in a business.

As Mac turned to leave the property, he spied Daniel's father Samuel trotting toward him on his old nag. Mac didn't relish an encounter with the blowhard, but he didn't want to be churlish, so he greeted the older Abercrombie.

"What're you doin' on Abercrombie land?" the old man demanded.

"I talked to Daniel about a loan this morning, so I came to inspect the collateral."

"Why's my boy need a loan? He ain't said nothin' to me 'bout no loan."

"You should ask him then," Mac said. It wasn't his place to get between Daniel and his father. He probably shouldn't even have mentioned the loan. But if he didn't give Samuel a valid reason to be on the land, the man might haul Mac into the sheriff's office at gunpoint. A rifle hung in a scabbard on Abercrombie's saddle.

"I got another beef with that friend of yourn, Zeke Pershing," Samuel announced. "Might have to sue him again."

"What's your quarrel this time?" Mac asked. Samuel would only give him half the story. He'd have to talk to Zeke to get the rest of it.

"Creek between our claims changed course," Samuel said. "Now it runs through Pershing's land. By rights, I should get the water what used to flow on my land."

"How is your deed written?" Mac asked.

"Don't matter what the damn deed say," Samuel replied, spitting a stream of tobacco juice. "I got rights to the water."

"Why don't I talk to Zeke?" Mac hoped he could mediate this dispute before Samuel filed a lawsuit. But once Abercrombie got his dander up, it was hard to calm him down. "How's your family?" Mac asked. Samuel lived with his wife Harriet and daughter-in-law Louisa. Samuel's older son Douglass had been killed in a gunfight many years earlier. Douglass's widow Louisa relied on Samuel for support.

"Doin' well enough," Samuel said. "Annabelle's expectin'."

Annabelle was Douglass's and Louisa's oldest daughter. She'd married Zeke's brother Jonathan a year ago. Despite the animosity between Pershings and Abercrombies, their families were becoming interconnected through the generations. Mac smiled. "Congratulations. This will be your first great-grandchild, won't it?"

"Darn straight." Samuel's face beamed. "I'm hopin' for a boy." The man had a soft spot for his family, and Mac couldn't begrudge him that.

Jenny drove her buggy to Hannah Pershing's farmhouse. Hannah had invited her to tea to meet a woman who ran a boarding school in Lafayette, a town across the Willamette River from Oregon City. Both Jenny and Hannah had taught country schools in the past. When Jenny arrived, she was surprised to see Esther Abercrombie there as well. Esther had never taught school and had less education than Jenny and Hannah.

After making introductions, Hannah limped about her kitchen as she served her guests tea and cake. Jenny rose to help her, then they sat at the table with Esther and Mrs. Duniway.

"Abigail and I became acquainted at a Women's Temperance Society meeting a few months ago," Hannah explained. "She asked me about my days as a teacher in the country before Zeke and I were married. I told her I took over the school from Jenny, and she requested to meet you. She runs a boarding school for girls."

Jenny smiled. "My teaching was a matter of necessity," she said. "I was alone while my husband was in California, and the children needed schooling."

Mrs. Duniway nodded. "I understand. Due to an unfortunate accident, my husband is an invalid. I must support our family. I taught before we were married, though I have only a year of formal education myself. Still, I have read widely, and I kept the accounts for my husband's business."

Jenny wondered how a woman with little education could manage a roomful of children, and she asked Mrs. Duniway about her school.

"I teach only girls," Mrs. Duniway explained. "I have set aside two rooms in our home to house them, and another room for lessons."

"What do you teach?" Jenny asked.

Mrs. Duniway listed her classes, and Jenny's eyebrows rose in appreciation. The woman had developed her lesson plans in some detail. Mrs. Duniway instructed the girls not only in the basics of reading, penmanship, and arithmetic, but also in history and household management.

"Do you have books and other materials?" Jenny asked. "Slates, paper, and the like? Those were in short supply on the frontier when I taught, though that was more than a decade ago. Now there are regular ships from the East."

"The situation had already improved by the time I took over Jenny's school in fifty-one," Hannah said. "My problem was that many of my students were not interested in learning."

Jenny laughed as she and Hannah shared a glance. "Of course, we taught both boys and girls. And half of the children were Pershings." As she spoke, she felt Esther bristle beside her—the Pershing students had been Esther's younger siblings.

"My brothers wanted to farm, not spend their time on book learning," Esther said. "Our mother had died on the trail, and our father died here in Oregon—"

"Oh, I'm so sorry, Mrs. Abercrombie," Mrs. Duniway exclaimed. "My mother died on our journey west also."

"Mine died after birthing my youngest brother," Esther said, her expression softening as she smiled at Mrs. Duniway.

"And mine of cholera," said Mrs. Duniway. Jenny remembered Mac's near-death from that dreadful disease, but she let Esther and Abigail tell their stories of grief along the trail.

From there, the conversation flitted from tales of their pioneer journeys to the need for school sessions that accommodated farm schedules to the weather in Oregon. Jenny concluded Abigail Duniway would do a fine job as a teacher.

"But it would be helpful," Jenny told Mrs. Duniway, "if you had an assistant. I had Esther's sister helping me. Rachel took the younger pupils while I worked with the older."

Hannah nodded. "And my niece Faith often performed the same role for me. She later became a teacher herself."

Mrs. Duniway shrugged. "I can see the value of an assistant, but it would be a squeeze in my household. Plus, I do not know any young women I would trust. Can you suggest anyone?"

Jenny eyed Esther and almost mentioned Esther's oldest daughter Cordelia. But with a new baby coming, Esther would need her daughter at home. She smiled at Mrs. Duniway. "We shall think on it and let you know. In the meantime, you might find a girl in Lafayette who suits you."

After his conversation with Samuel, Mac decided to stop by Zeke Pershing's claim before returning home. He might as well hear Zeke's side of the water dispute. He found Zeke sowing corn in a field near his home with his younger brothers.

"It's as Samuel said," Zeke told Mac. "The creek changed course during this spring's run-off. Now it flows through my land, instead of formin' the border between our claims. I'm willin' for him to take some of the water, but that's still my land on both sides of the creek, same as always. It's twenty acres of prime pasture."

"Then you'd work with him to divert water from the creek to his land?"

"Don't see why not," Zeke said. "Unless he decides to make a mountain out of a molehill. But you know Samuel—that might be his preference."

Mac shook his head with a grin. Then he remembered his conversation with Daniel. "Did Daniel tell you there are deserters in these parts? He said folks should be careful. And after what happened with Hannah years ago, I wouldn't want any of your family attacked." Zeke's wife Hannah had fended off an intruder on their homestead who was later convicted of killing a man.

Zeke nodded. "I heard. I've told Hannah to keep a rifle handy. And not to let Hope or Isaiah out of sight."

Mac arrived home in late afternoon and went upstairs to wash for supper. Jenny followed him. "Happy birthday, husband," she said.

He turned to kiss her. "Thank you, wife."

"What kept you away all day?"

"Business. First with Daniel Abercrombie—I needed to inspect a parcel of his land. Then I ran into his father."

"Samuel?" She sighed. "And I suppose he chucked a problem in your direction."

"Unfortunately, yes." Mac poured water into the bowl on the washstand, then splashed some on his face and lathered his cheeks with soap. "He has another land dispute with Zeke Pershing."

"Poor Zeke." Jenny shook her head. "Will you get dragged into their argument?"

Mac shrugged. "I talked to Zeke—that was my last stop before returning to town. Zeke seems reasonable, so I hope Abercrombie will accept his proposal."

Jenny settled herself in a chair while Mac took out his razor strop and sharpened his blade. "I visited Hannah today as well," she said. "I'm surprised we didn't run into each other on the road."

"Were you alone?" Mac asked, grimacing at himself in the mirror. More and more gray at his temples each week. He supposed that was to be expected—he was forty-three today.

"It was a women's meeting," Jenny said. "No need for Maria or the little ones to be there."

"There are deserters around." Maybe he shouldn't worry, but he did.

"I can take care of myself, Mac." Jenny sounded offended by his concern.

He changed the subject so as not rile her further. "How are the children behaving?"

Jenny sighed. "The boys were unruly again. Mostly Caleb and Nathan, but Cal dragged William into it."

"Will is old enough to know better," Mac said.

"Cal knows exactly how to needle his older brother." Jenny sounded tired. He glanced at her in the mirror—she'd leaned her head back on the chair and closed her eyes.

"I've told Will he should go to Harvard this autumn. I've a mind to take him to Boston myself."

"Oh."

Surprised at Jenny's short response, Mac turned to face her. "What is it? You've always said I should visit my parents. They're not getting any younger."

"I'm with child again."

Mac's razor dropped into the bowl. "Are you feeling all right?"

"The usual queasiness. I'll be fine."

In two steps Mac crossed the room and dropped to his knees beside her, gently cupping her face in his hand. "You look pale. Are you eating well?"

She smiled and touched the hand on her cheek. "I'm fine, Mac. Just like always. We'll be welcoming this child in October. Around my birthday, I think."

"A little more than six months still." Mac thought for a moment, frowning. "I could take Will to Boston in mid-summer. Leave him with my parents and be back before the baby comes. If the ships sail as they ought."

She frowned. "Do you think that's wise? Leaving William with your parents? Given everything—"

"He'd be fine," Mac said. "He'd soon move into rooms at the college. I'll look into sailing schedules later this week."

Jenny stayed seated after Mac headed downstairs for a whiskey before supper. The children shouted in the hallway as they raced after their father, but she wasn't ready to face the clamor yet. Mac had given her a new worry—what would happen when his parents met William? What questions would they have about the boy?

William had been born while Jenny and Mac traveled to Oregon. Would Mac's parents question when and how he'd met Jenny? When they'd married?

Mac and Jenny had mostly buried the truth. Only a few friends in Oregon knew what had happened, and they'd never explained the full story to their families back home. Would it all come out now?

And what would the impact be on William?

Jenny sighed, put a smile on her face, and went to celebrate her husband's birthday with their family.

# Chapter 10: Another Letter

Will stayed close to home for the rest of the week after his father's birthday. Now that he'd stopped attending the academy, he'd hoped to spend more time with Jonah. But Pa told the family to stay in town unless he accompanied them to the country. "Deserters are flocking to Oregon," he'd said. "Most of them probably only want work and shelter. But some are up to no good. So, keep away from strangers."

The younger children's eyes grew round—Eliza and Lottie bursting into tears. "Don't scare them, Mac," Mama said. Then she looked around the table. "But, children, obey your father. Stay close to home or school."

Will had complied all week. Still, working with Jonah would be a better use of his time than sitting around the house. Will was a good shot, and Shanty had a lot of speed in him. They could out-run or out-shoot any ex-soldier riding an Army nag.

He might have disobeyed Pa, but he didn't want to worry Mama. He dutifully ran errands for her. Friday afternoon, she sent him to the Post Office. He collected their newspapers, but the only other mail was a letter for Pa from California.

On a whim, Will asked for mail addressed to Daniel or Esther Abercrombie. Maybe there would be an excuse to ride out to Jonah's.

To his surprise, the clerk handed him a letter addressed to Esther. "You goin' that way, boy?"

"Yes, sir," Will said, taking the letter. "I'll deliver it."

Will stopped by Pa's office and gave him the letter from California. "Esther Abercrombie has a letter. The Post Office clerk asked if I would deliver it to her. I said I would."

Pa frowned at him. "That's not your responsibility, son."

"No, sir. But I don't mind."

"Talk to your mother. She might like a visit with Esther. I don't want either of you traveling alone."

"Yes, sir." Will was elated to have his father's permission. Though waiting for Mama would slow him down. He wouldn't be able to spend much time with Jonah.

Jenny sat in the parlor mending Nate's trousers when Will asked if she wanted to go with him to deliver a letter to Esther. "She'll likely be in town for church on Sunday," Jenny told him. "It can wait until then."

"The clerk at the Post Office seemed to think it should get to her right away," Will said. "And Pa said I could."

"Who is the letter from?" Jenny asked.

Will shrugged. "I don't know."

Jenny held her hand out, and Will gave her the letter. "Probably her brother Joel," Jenny said after inspecting it. "All right, I'm sure she'll want his news as soon as possible." She packed the mending in her sewing basket and gathered her cloak and bonnet. A light mist fell, and she sighed at the damp. She thought about taking Maggie with them, but Will seemed antsy to be on his way, and getting the little girl into her hat and coat might take another half hour. He'd already harnessed one of the carriage mares to the buggy by the time Jenny was ready.

Will helped her into the buggy, tapped the traces on the mare's hindquarters, and they headed out of town. The evergreens lining the route were heavy with rain from earlier in the day, and the road itself was muddy. But they trotted along at a good clip. Like Shanty, the mare was bred out of Jenny's old Indian mare Poulette and sired by Mac's Andalusian stallion Valiente. Mac bought Poulette for her at Fort Laramie as they traveled to Oregon—she'd loved that Indian pony, which had died five years ago.

"Have you thought about your father's plan to send you to Harvard?" she asked.

Will shook his head.

"It's a fine opportunity. Mac has always spoken fondly of his years in college."

"Boston is so far away," Will said.

"Yes," she said. "It is. I hate for you to be so distant from us. But your education is important. You could be a great man here in Oregon." She swallowed. "Or wherever you decided to settle." There was always the possibility he'd stay in the East.

He glanced at her. "Are you afraid I wouldn't come back?"

"I would hate it if you didn't," she said sadly, patting his arm. "A mother always worries about losing her child."

"Nothing bad'll happen to me," Will said.

"I'd be devastated if it did," Jenny murmured.

They arrived at Esther's house. Jenny knocked on the door while Will tethered the mare to a fencepost. "We won't stay long," Jenny told him. "No need to unharness her."

Esther opened the door and ushered them in with a smile and offer of coffee. Jenny handed Esther the letter.

"From Joel," Esther exclaimed. "I recognize his handwritin'.' Do you mind if I read it?"

Jenny shook her head. "I figured you'd want to read it right away. I'll pour the coffee." She knew Esther's house as well as her own. She took mugs out of the cupboard and poured steaming drinks for Esther, Will, and herself.

"Where's Jonah?" Will asked. "Maybe I can go talk to him."

"He's with Daniel and Zeke. Cuttin' timber. I ain't sure exactly where. You best not traipse after 'em if you and your ma ain't staying long," Esther said as she perused the letter. "This is news—Joel is in the Rogue River Valley. Last he wrote, he'd been minin' near Ruby City. Now he plans to stay 'round Jacksonville for a while."

"That's in Southern Oregon, isn't it?" Jenny asked. She'd never been that far south in the state—in fact, she'd never been south of where the steamboat stopped in Eugene.

"Mmm-hmm," Esther mumbled distractedly. "He says to send letters to him in Jacksonville. Though he'll be prospectin' in the mountains 'round those parts." She looked up. "I'll have to write him and beg him to visit us."

"For your sake, I hope he will," Jenny said. Joel had prospected with Mac in California, but he only rarely traveled north to see his siblings. He seemed to prefer mining to life on Esther's or Zeke's farms. "Have you seen any sign of deserters nearby?" she asked after Esther finished reading the letter.

Esther shook her head. "Not a one. Daniel warned me and the young'uns to stay close. I don't go to town without a rifle and at least two young'uns to watch from the back of the wagon."

"Well, be careful," Jenny said. "You remember what happened to Hannah."

"That was more'n a decade ago. And the man who attacked her was a murderer, not just a deserter," Esther said. "Have you seen any strangers in town?"

"I've stayed close to home, so no," Jenny said. She smiled at Will. "William has been good enough to run errands for me. I won't let Maria out alone, but Will is sharp enough to spot trouble."

Will was pleased to hear Mama's compliment, but he soon grew bored with the women's talk. They whispered about babies and such, and he overheard Mama say she was expecting again. He glanced at her—he hadn't noticed her puking in the chamber pots like she usually did before she started showing a big belly. But then, he hadn't paid her much attention. He'd been caught up in his worries about whether to go to Harvard.

Will wandered into the other downstairs room where Esther's younger children squabbled. Cordelia, the oldest Abercrombie daughter who was almost Will's age, smiled at him. "Hey, Will. Would you play marbles with George and Tom? I've got my hands full with Dan, Essie, and Abe."

Will shrugged. He hadn't come visiting to shoot marbles with little boys, but it was better than listening to Mama and Esther. So he played until the younger boys calmed down. Meanwhile, Cordelia got twins Dan and Essie to play quietly with blocks, then took toddler Abe upstairs for a nap.

Once the children were soothed and Cordelia left with Abe, Will could overhear pieces of the women's conversation from the other room. Mostly he ignored their talk, until he heard his name mentioned.

"Does Will know yet?" Esther asked.

Mama murmured some response that Will didn't hear.

"But Mac isn't his father," he thought Esther said. Will shook his head. He must have misunderstood. Of course, Pa was his father.

# Chapter 11: A Stranger in Town

On Saturday, the day after he visited the Abercrombies, Will went to Myers Mercantile, the general store their family patronized, to buy thread for Mama. "All I need is black," she told him. "I'm sure you can get that right." He wouldn't have wanted to sort through the blues or greens, but he agreed—black thread he could handle. "And here's an extra nickel," she said. "Bring home some penny candy for the children."

He walked to the store, glad to be on his own for an hour or so. He picked out the thread under the eagle eye of the proprietor's wife. Then he stood beside the candy jars on the counter, trying to choose. A group of men sat by the stove smoking and talking.

"Got a little extra spending money, boy?" one man asked with a grin. He wore a Confederate kerchief, but otherwise had no military paraphernalia.

"Yes, sir," Will said, continuing to inspect the candy—peppermint or molasses?

"Take your time, Will," the man behind the counter told him.

"You lived in these parts long?" another man near the stove asked. He had a beaten-down Confederate cap on his head. Was this a group of deserters? Will wondered.

"All my life," Will said. "I was born while my parents were emigrating."

"Where'd they come from?" the first man asked idly, striking a match to light a cigarette.

"Mama lived in Missouri and Pa in Boston." Then Will told the proprietor, "Two cents' worth of peppermints, please. Two of molasses, and a penny of licorice."

The store owner wrapped the candy in parchment paper.

"Boston, eh?" the man in the kerchief said. "What's your name, boy?"

"William McDougall," Will said, handing over his nickel and taking the candy.

"McDougall." The man glowered at Will. "My name's Johnson. Jacob Johnson." He seemed to want a response from Will.

Will nodded as he turned to leave the store. "Pleased to meet you, Mr. Johnson."

Mac rode Valiente out to Zeke Pershing's claim again Saturday afternoon. He'd researched the descriptions of both Zeke's and Samuel Abercrombie's deeds filed in the land office. Both deeds predated the survey of Oregon completed in 1855, but the descriptions were clear enough—the land was described in terms of distance from the road into Oregon City, which had existed when the men staked out their claims in 1847. Neither deed referenced the creek that formed the boundary between their land before this spring's change of course. Where the creek flowed was irrelevant to the men's ownership rights, and Zeke had a strong claim to the land.

Mac told Zeke the results of his research, and said, "I'd like to talk to Abercrombie about the deeds. You want to come with me?"

"You think I should?" Zeke asked. "Might be, he'd take it better if you talk to him alone."

Mac grinned. "He doesn't like me much better than he likes you."

"All right, then." Zeke nodded, then grabbed his hat and coat and saddled his gelding.

As they rode to Abercrombie's claim, Mac asked, "Seen any strangers around?"

Zeke shook his head. "Our hen house was broken into a few nights back, and Hannah said someone stole most of the eggs laid that day. Wish old Blackie was still here. New hound ain't near the guard dog Blackie was. We didn't hear nor see nobody."

"I've seen some scurrilous men in town," Mac said. "No problems yet, but they don't look like they're up to any good. They sit around the saloon or the stores, watching people and gabbing."

When they arrived at Abercrombie's house, Samuel came outside before they could knock. "What'd'ya want?" the old man asked as they dismounted.

"I'm following up on our conversation earlier in the week," Mac said. "I looked into your deed, to see what it said about the creek."

"I ain't asked you to," Abercrombie said. "This is twixt me'n Pershing."

"Just thought I might help," Mac said, trying to keep his tone calm. "Turns out, neither deed says anything about the creek forming your boundary. Your property lines are measured in metes and bounds from the road. The hilltop at the corner is also referenced."

"That don't mean nothin'," Abercrombie said.

Mac ignored his comment. "The description makes sense—we filed our claims late in the year, when the creek was probably dry or nearly so."

"That's right," Zeke said. "I was surprised the next spring to see so much flowin' water."

"I need the water," Abercrombie stated.

"I don't mind you having a portion of it," Zeke said. "If you'd asked, I would've told you so. I'd be glad to help you dig a ditch or a well, as long as at least half the runoff still goes through my land."

Abercrombie eyed Zeke. Mac could see the old man trying to find a reason to object to Zeke's offer. "Lemme think on it," Abercrombie said.

"If you two want me to draw up an agreement, I'll do it," Mac offered. "No charge. But for now, I have other business in town."

He remounted Valiente and turned to leave. Zeke followed him.

"What'd'ya think he'll do?" Zeke asked.

"Only heaven knows," Mac replied.

Back in town, Mac stopped at Myers Mercantile to ask about strangers in town. The clerk told him, "I seen a lot of new men in these parts. Can't say if they're just passin' through or if they mean to stay. Your boy Will was talkin' to a group of 'em earlier today."

"Will was here?" Mac asked.

The man chuckled. "Seems his ma sent him to buy thread. And bribed him with a nickel's worth of candy." Then he turned serious. "But one of the men, name of Jacob Johnson, was askin' about you afterward. You know him?"

Mac felt his blood leave his head and congeal in his stomach. "Not in Oregon. I met a Jacob Johnson once in Missouri. No way of knowing if it's the same man."

"Was he a friend?"

"No," Mac said, remembering his only encounter with Johnson. "No, he wasn't a friend."

Mac stopped by the Post Office to get his mail—he had a letter from Portland and one from Eugene. He took them to his office, lit a cigar, and leaned back in his chair to read them.

Before he could concentrate, however, he had to shake off his fear at hearing of a Jacob Johnson in town—surely, it wasn't the man he'd confronted in Missouri. Still, he would have to warn Jenny, and she would be upset.

Taking a deep breath, he turned to his mail. The letter from Portland dealt with a bank proposal he was considering. The National Banking Act had passed a year earlier, and men like Mac who had loaned money to their neighbors were considering whether to incorporate as a bank under the new law. William Ladd in Portland was the farthest along in his planning, and Mac should return to Portland to meet with Ladd again.

Ladd was also involved with men in Eugene who proposed to incorporate a company to build a road through central Oregon. He'd referred one of the road surveyors, Byron Pengra, to Mac. Pengra wanted Mac to invest in the road enterprise, and Mac should travel to Eugene to investigate that possibility.

The banking plans sounded more developed—Portland should be his first trip. The sooner the better. And he could talk to Ladd about the road project at the same time.

After Mac dashed off a letter to Ladd proposing they meet on the following Tuesday morning, he returned home.

"I have a trip to Portland planned. I'll leave Monday and be back the next evening," he told Jenny. "Will you and the children be all right without me?" He hated to leave her, particularly after what he'd heard in the store.

She smiled, seeming unconcerned. "Will's been a tremendous help this week. I'm sure we'll be fine."

"Be careful," Mac warned. "There's a man in town named Jacob Johnson, who's been asking about us."

She gasped. "No."

"I don't know if it's the man you knew in Missouri," Mac said. "But watch out for him. And I'll make sure Will stays nearby."

Sunday evening, as Will sat reading in his room, Pa knocked on his door. "I need to go to Portland tomorrow," Pa said.

Will sat up and grinned, thinking Pa wanted him to go along.

But Pa continued, "I need you to stay close to home and watch out for your mother."

Will's face fell—Pa only wanted Will to keep toting and fetching for Mama. "I can't come with you?" he asked sullenly. He wasn't allowed to visit Jonah these days, at least not alone. And he'd been humiliated on Saturday, buying thread for Mama. Those ex-soldiers watched him, and the storekeeper and his wife smirked at him. Jonah got paid a wage to farm, while Will ran errands in town like a schoolboy, even though he was done with school.

Pa shook his head. "Not this time. I need someone to watch things here. I heard a man in town was asking about us—a Jacob Johnson. You talked to him?"

Will shrugged. "Just for a minute. I didn't recognize him."

"I knew a Jacob Johnson in Missouri," Pa said. "I can't say it's the same man. But if it is, we don't want him anywhere near our house or family. If you see him nearby—or any other stranger, for that matter—you get the sheriff. Do you understand?"

"Yes, Pa."

# Chapter 12: While Mac Is Away

Jenny felt Mac's absence when he left for Portland on Monday. She'd spent plenty of time without him—first while he was in California for two years, and even after he returned when he had business elsewhere in Oregon and California. She'd even been alone during earlier pregnancies.

But somehow this felt different. Maybe because William seemed so unsettled. Maybe because of the possibility that Jacob Johnson was nearby.

She shuddered, remembering the last time she'd seen Johnson. That was the day she met Mac. She should focus on the happy events that flowed from that day, not the terror.

Monday evening, Jenny sat in the parlor with Will, Maria, and Cal. She'd let Cal stay up later than usual but sent the younger children to bed. When Cal yawned, she told him, "Off with you, Caleb. To bed."

"Aww, Mama," he protested.

"Now," she said more firmly.

"I'll go up with you," Maria said. "I'm tired, too."

Jenny was glad for a chance to speak with Will. "Have you thought more about your father's plans for you?" she asked.

He looked up. "You mean Harvard?" He shrugged. "I suppose I'll go. There isn't much else to do." He didn't sound very excited.

"If you could do anything you wanted, William, what would you do?"

"I don't know. Maybe go to California."

"California?" That surprised her. "Why?"

"Pa made a fortune there. Maybe I could, too."

"We could help you get a start," she said. "But wouldn't you rather have

**68**

an education first?" She remembered the days she'd spent with her father in his study. "Your namesake—my father—loved reading his philosophical treatises. He liked nothing better than to think and dream. You're a lot like him." She smiled at William, so like his grandfather.

"I enjoy studying," Will said. "When I'm interested. But too much of school is doing what the teacher wants, not what I want."

Jenny raised her eyebrows. "Much of life is doing what others want, not what you want." She sighed. She hadn't wanted to go West and dreaded the journey when it started. She only went because Mac insisted. "You'll find that out as you grow. But knowing what you want, that's important. Because otherwise, there's no hope of getting it." She almost waited too late to determine what she wanted—she let Mac go to California, not realizing *he* was what she wanted. She was grateful every day that he returned, and they had found their happiness.

Tuesday morning, Will and Maria sat in the parlor after the younger children went to school. "Mama says you don't want to go to Harvard," Maria said.

"It's not that I don't want to go," Will said. "I'm just not sure."

"I'd miss you," Maria said. "But you'll probably leave us someday."

"How do you know?" Will said. "Maybe I'll stay right here and pester you all my life." He kept his tone light, but he was serious. Maybe he would stay in Oregon City, despite his comment to Mama last night about California. Did he really want the work and responsibility of earning a fortune? If he asked, Pa would probably find something for him to do.

Maria shook her head. "You're destined for better things, bigger things, than Oregon City, William McDougall. I believe you can do whatever you set your mind to."

"So you're pushing me out, too?" he asked.

"No, silly." She frowned. "But you'll figure it out. You'll find your way."

"What of you, Maria?" He'd never wondered about her plans before. "What do you want from life?"

"Like Mama," she said. "A family. A home. That's all a girl can want."

He harrumphed, sounding to himself like an old man. "You could teach. Like Hannah Pershing did. And Hannah also clerked in a store. Or Ruth Pershing—she's still teaching. Or Faith Bramwell before she married. Or you could nurse soldiers, like Clara Barton. Girls can do lots of things."

"But it's harder for girls." Maria sighed. "Particularly girls like me."

"What do you mean?"

"With Indian blood. You forget about it, but I remember my mother was part Indian every time I walk into a store and see people staring at me."

"That doesn't matter," Will scoffed. "You've always been part of our family."

"But it does matter, Will. It does."

Later that morning, Will was in his room reading. But he couldn't concentrate on his book. He kept thinking about what Mama and Maria had said—they both had great plans for him. Mama thought he could be a great scholar, like her father. Maria thought he was destined for something grand. Should he go to college? Was Harvard right for him? Should he stay and work with Pa? Should he strike out on his own?

Why did life have to be so hard?

Shouts sounded from the parlor. Then a scream.

Will raced downstairs.

Jenny stitched a pinafore for Maggie in the parlor, grateful for the silence in the house. Mrs. O'Malley had taken the toddler to the market with her, and Will and Maria were occupied on their own tasks.

A knock sounded on the front door. Jenny went to the foyer, opening the door with a smile. "Yes?"

A man burst inside, grabbing her arms and pushing her against the wall. "Jenny Calhoun?" he snarled, peering into her face. "It's you, ain't it?"

He was tall, burly, with bearded face and uncombed hair. His right hand grasped her tightly enough to bruise, but his left arm seemed weaker. "Who are you?" she quavered.

"You don't remember me?" he growled into her ear. "I remember you. Every inch of you. I'm Jacob Johnson."

"No," she whispered in dread, searching his face in an effort to recognize the boy she'd known in Missouri. It *was* him. Her stomach clenched, and she grabbed her belly to protect the babe inside.

"Now you remember." His left hand grabbed her chin and turned her face toward him. "Look at me good. Be sure you remember everything."

"G-go away," she said. "Or I'll scream." Visions of her last encounter with Johnson flashed through her memory.

He guffawed, the sound low and mean. "Like you screamed last time? McDougall ain't here to save you now."

"He-he'll be back soon."

"Scuttlebutt in town says he's in Portland."

"The sheriff knows to watch for you." She would say anything, anything to make him leave.

"There ain't no sheriff here now, is there?" Johnson pushed her into the parlor. "So we'll close this door and have ourselves a nice chat."

Jenny prayed Will and Maria stayed upstairs. She didn't want them to find her with Johnson. He'd hurt them. She knew what he could do to young girls—she didn't want Maria to suffer as she had.

Keeping a hold on her, Johnson looked around the room. "You got yourself a fine home. Musta done all right over the years, you and McDougall."

"Do you want money? I don't have any here, but I could get some in town," she babbled. Anything to make him leave.

"Well, now, that might be nice. But first I want you to say you're sorry for killin' my pa."

"I didn't kill him—"

"McDougall did," Johnson said, his fetid breath stifling her. "And he ain't here. I'll just take your apology instead."

"I-I'm sorry. I never meant for anyone to get hurt."

"Is that why you shot me?" he demanded, shaking her with his right arm. "See this?" He flapped his left arm. "This arm ain't never been much good since you put a bullet in it."

"I'm sorry." Jenny meant it. "Truly sorry. But you were going to—" She couldn't even say what he'd been going to do to her then.

"I was gonna what? Have a little fun?" Johnson leered. "That weren't worth maiming a man, was it?"

"N-no." What would it take to make him go away?

"Let's start up now where we left it back in Missouri. Shall we?" He pushed her onto the divan and threw himself on top of her.

She screamed.

Will rushed into the parlor. A man sprawled on top of Mama. Will pulled at the man's shirt. "Get off her. Get off!"

The man turned from Mama and grabbed Will's neck, slamming him into a wall. "You little bastard."

It was that Johnson fellow from town. Pa told Will to keep him away, and now Johnson was in the house. Will had failed his father. He flailed, trying to land a punch. Johnson crowded close to Will to avoid the blows and squeezed Will's neck with one arm.

Only one arm, and still the man could choke him. Will saw stars. Though his hearing dimmed, Will heard Mama yelling and beating on Johnson's back.

"Leave him alone—don't hurt him," Mama cried.

Will struggled. He had to protect Mama.

Maria screamed from the doorway.

"Don't hurt him," Mama shouted. "Don't! He could be your son."

Johnson's grip slackened, and Will slumped to the floor.

"My son?" Johnson kicked Will. Will gasped for air through his bruised throat and stared at Johnson, who stared back.

Then Johnson chortled wickedly. "Or my brother?" He grabbed Mama's chin and forced her face close to his. "Or *your* brother?" he said, grinning.

Will didn't understand. His father? Or his brother? Or Mama's brother? How could this man be any part of them?

"Yes," Mama whispered. She seemed to shrink.

Johnson cackled uproariously. "You little bitch." He pushed Mama, and she staggered. "You took my kin away with you."

"He's mine," Mama said, regaining her feet and thrusting her chin forward. "Not yours. You can't have him."

Johnson snickered. "We'll see about that."

"You better leave, mister. Or I'll shoot." Maria's voice dripped icy calm. From his position on the floor, Will saw she had Pa's rifle trained on Johnson. Briefly, he wondered if it was even loaded. He'd never seen Maria shoot anything. Could she do it now? But watching her face, he thought she might.

Johnson raised his hands. "Well, now," he said to Mama, "like mother, like daughter." He sidled toward Maria, "Don't worry, little miss," he said,

"I'm leavin'."

Maria backed away from the door to let him pass, but didn't lower the rifle. Johnson passed inches from the barrel, and Will feared Johnson would attack her. But Maria didn't flinch.

"I'm leavin'," Johnson repeated, and he slunk through the door. Maria slammed it behind him and turned the key.

With the terror over, Will blurted, "What did he mean, Mama?" He still couldn't understand what Johnson had said. Then it dawned on him—Mama had had intimate relations with that man. And others. That's the only way the man's words made sense.

"Mama," he said in horror, "were you a whore?"

From the hallway, Maria gasped.

Mama's face paled as if he'd hit her. "Will, let me explain—"

But Will couldn't take any more. He stood shakily, staggered past Maria, and raced out the back door. He halted in the yard and retched. After emptying his stomach, he ran to the carriage house.

When Will reached Shanty, he buried his face in the gelding's mane and keened. All he could think of was escape. He saddled the horse and rode away blindly.

# Chapter 13: Aftermath of Evil

Will urged Shanty into a canter. He didn't know where he was headed, and he didn't care. He only wanted to get away from the house. Away from Mama, from whatever sins she'd committed. Away from Maria, who'd witnessed Will's annihilation.

That's how he felt—annihilated, destroyed. He wasn't who he thought he was. If he was Johnson's son—or the son of some other man, then Pa wasn't his father. He'd tried all his life to be like Pa, to make Pa proud of him. If Pa wasn't his father, he didn't know who he was.

Shanty took them on the road toward Jonah's house. When Will realized where they were, he slowed Shanty to a walk. He couldn't visit Jonah—he couldn't face anybody, not even his best friend. He didn't understand what Mama and Johnson had said. But he understood enough to realize it was a secret. A huge secret. A secret Mama never wanted him to find out.

As they approached the fork in the road leading to Pa's claim—could Will even call him Pa anymore?—Will turned Shanty in that direction. That claim was the earliest home Will remembered, a snug little cabin where he and Mama lived while Pa—Mac?—was in California. Later, after Mac—Pa?—returned, they moved to town, to the big house where they now lived.

A tenant named Eben Coates lived in the cabin on the claim now—an old codger Mac hired to farm the land. Across the yard from the cabin stood the barn. Beside the barn was a disheveled shack, the shack the Tanner family lived in when they helped Mama. Some of Will's earliest memories were of playing on the dirt floor of that shack with Otis Tanner, son of Clarence and Hattie Tanner. Hattie had smelled of molasses and cornbread, and Clarence of the smoke from his forge.

Will tied Shanty to a tree just off the road and crept toward the old Tanner shack. The door creaked open when he pushed on it. No one from the larger cabin came out to inspect, so Coates must be working the fields. Will peered inside. The shack was filthy, but large enough for him and Shanty to spend the night.

Will retrieved Shanty and led him toward the shack. The gelding balked when Will tried to pull him inside, but finally followed. Then Will went to the barn and took a bucket of oats back to the shack. Shanty at least would eat tonight. Will would go hungry unless he scrounged a few eggs in the henhouse. He foraged around until he had three eggs.

After eating the raw eggs, Will laid on a burlap bag in the shack and closed his eyes. He puzzled through what he'd heard again. According to Mama, he might be Johnson's son. Then Johnson said Will might be Johnson's brother, meaning he and Johnson might have the same father. Or Will might be Mama's brother, which would mean her father—no! Will's mind couldn't accept that Mama had been intimate with her father. But that's who she always said Will looked like.

His stomach rebelled. He rushed to the bushes behind the shack and vomited the eggs.

Jenny's whole body shook as she left the parlor, this new assault resurrecting memories she thought she'd buried. Memories of terror. Now, she feared not only for herself, but for Will. Her worst fear for him had come to pass—he'd learned the truth. Or part of it.

But now she needed to calm Maria, who lay sobbing on the floor after bravely chasing off Jacob Johnson. "Maria," she said gently, dropping to her knees beside the girl, though she still trembled from the shock of the encounter with Jacob. When Maria flung herself into Jenny's arms, the two of them wept together.

"Who was that man?" Maria asked a bit later, wiping a hand across her eyes.

"Someone I knew long ago," Jenny murmured. "He's not important." But he was, and she'd have to face the truth.

"You said he was Will's father." Maria's stricken expression mirrored Jenny's own anguish.

"He might be," Jenny said. "But it doesn't matter." But it did. It mattered horribly.

"Is what Will said true?" Maria whispered. "Were you a whore?"

"No," Jenny said, appalled at the girl's conclusion. "Oh, no. Is that what you thought?"

"My mama was."

"That's different." Jenny didn't know how to respond without disparaging the woman who had borne Maria. "Mac rescued me."

"Pa was my mama's friend as well."

Jenny settled herself beside Maria, both of them seated on the hall floor. She took a deep breath and braced herself for the truth. "I was raped," she said bluntly. "When I was fourteen—your age. By three men. One of them was Jacob Johnson. That's why he might be Will's father."

Maria's face blanched. "Oh, Mama." She threw her arms around Jenny. "Poor Mama." She leaned back against the wall. "Poor Will."

"Yes," Jenny said. "I never wanted him—any of you children—to find out. You mustn't say anything to anyone."

Will spent the night shivering in the shack. Coates returned at dusk, and Will feared the tenant would hear Shanty's soft snuffles, but apparently he only wanted to feed his mules and himself. Soon, Coates shut the door to the cabin, and Will neither heard nor saw anything further from him.

It started to make sense to him, why he hadn't felt a part of his family for so long. Why Mac seemed to favor Cal. Why Cal was the one named after Mac, not Will—Cal was Mac's true son, not Will.

Will was that odious Jacob Johnson's son. Or his brother. Or Mama's brother—and Will's mind stopped working again. What had Mama done?

He thought he'd never sleep, but finally, when the narrow sliver of moon shone through cracks in the roof, he dozed.

Mac arrived home from Portland around supper time that evening, drained after his discussions with Ladd about establishing a bank. Mac wanted to open a banking office in Oregon City, but Ladd insisted Portland was the better location. Since Ladd possessed greater funds to invest than

Mac, Ladd's opinion prevailed. He would continue his work to incorporate the bank, but he still wanted Mac as an investor.

Mac brought connections with banks in the East to their enterprise, and he agreed to write his brother Owen to establish a link between his family's Boston bank and the new operation in Oregon. With an established partnership in Oregon and New England, they could better attract shipping clients. The law required the banks to remain separate corporations, but good relationships between the two banks could get around the lack of a formal legal relationship.

Mac let himself into the house. Jenny came into the foyer, and their children—all but Will—rushed past her to greet him.

Jenny hung back, her face pale. He worried about her and the baby, and after brief hugs, he sent the children into the parlor. "What's wrong?" he asked his wife.

"It's happened," she whispered. "The worst."

"What?" He frowned, immediately concerned. Had she lost the baby?

"Come. We need to talk." She turned and started up the stairs.

Mac called to Maria to watch the younger children, then followed Jenny to their bedroom.

She sat on the bed and pulled him down beside her. "Jacob Johnson—it was him. He was here this morning. Will and Maria saw him."

Mac's stomach clenched, but he kept his fingers gentle as he brushed an errant strand of hair from her face. "Did he hurt you again? Or the children?"

"He grabbed me. And choked Will."

Mac made a guttural sound and cupped her cheek in his hand. "Jenny."

"I'm all right," she said, though Mac didn't believe her. "It's Will."

"Is he hurt?" Mac asked. The boy was not used to physical violence.

"He ran away." Jenny stood and paced the rug. "He heard me say Johnson might be his father. Or one of the other two."

She didn't have to say anything more—Mac had been there. Not the day Jenny was raped, but the day the three men had come after her again. Jacob Johnson and his father Isaac. And Bart Peterson, Jenny's stepfather. Mac killed Isaac that day, and Jenny shot Jacob. The craven Peterson stood there, doing nothing. Then Mac fled, taking Jenny with him.

"Where's the boy now?" he asked.

"I don't know," she whispered. "He left. He didn't let me explain. I'm so afraid for him."

"And Maria? You said she was there?"

"She had your rifle. She chased Jacob away." Even now, Mac noticed, Jenny called the villain "Jacob." They'd known each other as children in Missouri. But he'd proved to be an enemy, not a friend. "You should have seen her," Jenny continued.

Mac smiled. Consuela had been fearless. He wasn't surprised her daughter took after her.

"But she's been crying all afternoon. You need to talk to her," Jenny said. "And you have to go after Will. Find him."

"What about you?" Mac asked. "And the baby?"

Jenny hugged her stomach. "I almost forgot the baby. This is about William. We must tell him the truth. He can't live knowing only part of it. You need to find him."

Mac sighed, his head pounding—he had no idea where Will might have gone. "Let's give it until morning. Maybe he'll come home."

# Chapter 14: Finding Will

Jenny couldn't sleep that night. Visions of Johnson, then and now, raced through her mind. She laid awake, listening for Will to return, but only heard Mac snoring softly beside her.

At dawn, she nudged him. "Mac," she whispered, "William still isn't home. You have to go after him."

Mac grunted and slowly awoke. "Where do you think he went?"

"I don't know." Her stomach tightened.

"Then where do you suggest I search?" He sounded testy, but he sat up and swung his legs to the floor. "Did you talk to the sheriff about Johnson yesterday?"

"No. Do you think we should?"

Mac swore. "The man attacked you, Jenny. You and Will both. And scared the living daylights out of Maria. He's a violent criminal." He began to dress. "I'll go see Sheriff Thomas right after breakfast."

"What will you tell him? You can't let rumors spread around town about us."

Mac turned to her. "You did nothing wrong. Not then, and not now."

"But Mac, we never wanted Will to find out—"

"I won't tell the sheriff any more than necessary to convince him to go after Johnson."

And Jenny had to accept Mac's assurances.

As soon as Mac ate, he headed to the sheriff's office. "A man attacked my wife and son yesterday," he told Sheriff Thomas. "Jacob Johnson is his name. My wife and I knew him back in Missouri."

"What happened, McDougall?" the sheriff asked. His deputy, a man named Albee, looked up from cleaning his rifle.

Mac and Sheriff Calvin Thomas had known each other for years. Mac had joined several posses at the lawman's request. Still, he weighed how much to tell the sheriff about their past with Johnson. "He and his father Isaac assaulted Jenny in Missouri, shortly before we headed to Oregon in forty-seven. I defended Jenny, and Isaac Johnson died in the fight. It seems Jacob has not forgiven us. I don't know why he's in Oregon City now, but he came to our house yesterday. That's when he hurt Jenny and our son."

"Why didn't you report it immediately?" the sheriff said.

"I wasn't home. My wife was afraid of leaving the house."

"And your son?" Albee asked. "Which one was it?"

"Will." This was the part Mac had difficulty explaining. "He ran away afterward. We haven't seen him all night."

Sheriff Thomas was a smart man. "Why'd he run off?"

Mac shrugged. "Maybe he was frightened. Maybe he went after Johnson. I'd left Will in charge of the household while I was gone—maybe he thought he'd done something wrong."

"Seems odd," the sheriff said.

"Teenage boys don't always use good judgment." Mac leaned forward over the lawman's desk. "What are you going to do about Johnson?"

"We'll look for him. But he could be anywhere now. I'll let you know if we find him."

"And Will?"

The sheriff shook his head. "We ain't got time to search for a runaway. If me or my men see him, I'll bring him home. But he could be anywhere, too."

Will shivered in the early morning, wishing he had more than a burlap bag between him and the ground, and more than a shirt to stay warm. He'd eaten nothing but the raw eggs he'd puked up. Shanty, however, seemed calm, though his piles and urine stank up the small space. Will listened for Mr. Coates, the tenant, to leave. Then Will would muck out the shack and move on.

But where would he go? He could go to Jonah's, but how would he explain why he'd left home? He couldn't stay there, though Esther would probably give him a good meal. Could he spend days working with Jonah and Daniel and nights in this shack? Sooner or later, someone would find him.

Will felt terrible about what he'd said to Mama—calling her a whore. It couldn't be true. Could it? How else could she explain why three different men might have fathered him?

Who was he now? If Mac wasn't his father, was he even a McDougall? Had Mac adopted Will like he'd adopted Maria?

The questions spun in Will's head, and he couldn't answer any of them.

The notion that a man like Jacob Johnson might be his father made Will want to retch again. But he had nothing in his gut to puke.

Coates started banging around in the barn, then the man's wagon creaked as his mules pulled it into the yard and onto the road. Soon silence surrounded Will again. He laid on his pallet and dozed, wondering whether to sneak into the cabin for food.

After visiting the sheriff, Mac rode Valiente to Daniel Abercrombie's claim. Will often ran off to spend time with Jonah. Perhaps that's where the boy had spent the night. Mac wanted to search the obvious haunts before returning to Jenny. He wanted to have something to report to her.

Daniel and his older sons had already left for the fields by the time Mac arrived. Mac talked to Esther. "Have you seen Will?"

"Will? No. Why—is he missing?" she asked.

She knew the full story, so Mac described who Jacob Johnson was and the man's attack on Jenny and Will. "Will found out Johnson might be his father."

Esther gasped. "Oh, no. Come inside and sit. Have some coffee."

"I don't have much time," Mac said, doffing his hat and entering the house. "Do you have any idea where Will might be? Any places he and Jonah would go off to?"

Esther shooed her younger children outside, all except the littlest toddler. Then she poured Mac a mug of coffee. "No. They ramble through the woods huntin' sometimes. Fish in the creek. I can ask Jonah when he returns."

"Where are Daniel and the boys working today?" Mac asked. "I'll go talk to Jonah myself."

"The fields toward your old claim," she said. "Least ways, that's what Daniel said this mornin'."

Mac thanked Esther for the coffee and rode Valiente down the road in search of Daniel and Jonah. He found them planting corn in a field near the creek between their property and Mac's claim. Mac remembered clearing that field with Daniel and other men the winter after they'd arrived in Oregon. It was one of the first fields planted on Daniel's farm.

Mac greeted them, then asked Jonah, "Have you seen Will since yesterday?"

"No, sir," Jonah said, shaking his head. "Ain't seen him since Sunday services."

"Do you know where he might be?" Mac demanded.

Jonah seemed puzzled at Mac's vehemence. "No, sir. What's wrong?"

"Will ran off, and I need to find him."

"Somethin' wrong?" Daniel asked.

"I explained to Esther," Mac said, certain Esther would tell Daniel the story later. "I need to find Will. Jenny's worried about him." He turned to Jonah again. "Is there someplace you boys hide? A secret place? I used to have a tree fort I'd go to as a lad."

"Not really, sir," Jonah said. "We hang around our barn, or the barn over at your claim. Where Mr. Coates lives now. But we only go there when it's cold or wet. Otherwise, we stay in the woods when we ain't helpin' on the farm."

"All right," Mac said. "I'll ride by my claim before I head back to town." He nodded at the others. "If you see Will, please send him home."

Mac trotted Valiente toward his claim, wondering why Will would seek refuge there. They hadn't lived on that land since the boy was three years old. Mac had built a cabin for Jenny, a home for her and her baby. But Mac never intended to live on the land with her, and he'd left as soon as the worst of the winter was behind them in early 1848.

He was sorry soon enough that he left her. He'd intended to travel back to Boston, but when he learned of the gold strike in California, he stayed there. After two years in California, when he realized the riches he'd found hadn't made him happy, he returned to Jenny and married her. They'd been together ever since. Should he have stayed with her in forty-eight? They might not have been as wealthy without his gold diggings, but they would have had two more years together.

Would it have made a difference to Will if Mac had stayed? Mac often sensed a distance in his relationship with the boy, an uneasiness he didn't feel with Cal or Nate. He tried to treat Will the same as his other children, but maybe the awkwardness was Mac's fault, not Will's. Maybe Will remembered when Mac was away. Maybe Will sensed Mac withholding his affections, though Mac tried to treat him the same as the other children. And maybe, in fact, Mac hadn't loved the boy enough.

When he pulled into the yard at his claim, it was quiet. Mac shouted for the tenant, then for Will. No answer.

Valiente whinnied and tossed his head. An answering whinny came from the old Tanner shack near the barn.

Mac dismounted, looped Valiente's reins around a fencepost, and strode toward the shack. He pushed open the door and saw Shanty.

Will lay on the ground beside the gelding.

When the door to the shack opened, Will sat up with a gasp.

"Are you all right, son?" Mac asked.

Will frowned—he wasn't Mac's son. "How'd you find me?"

"Your mother sent me to look for you."

Will sat silently. He'd known people would search for him, and someone was bound to find him eventually.

Mac sat beside him. "Your mother said you protected her yesterday. I'm proud of you."

Will rubbed his pockmarks. Mac must not know how ineffectual Will had been, how Mama had beaten Johnson while the man choked him, how Maria had scared the intruder off with the gun. Will had done nothing.

Except find his world destroyed.

Mac sighed. "You learned some things we hoped you'd never find out."

"You mean things you wanted to hide from me," Will blurted.

"Has it done you any good to know I'm not your father?" Mac asked.

"So who is?" Maybe Mac would explain what Mama had said.

Mac heaved a deep breath. "This won't be easy to tell you." He turned to Will. "Nor for you to hear."

Will waited. When Mac said nothing, Will croaked out, "I can take it."

Mac nodded. "All right. Man to man. Here's what happened. Your mother was raped by three men. Before I met her. One of them fathered you."

Rape—why hadn't that occurred to Will? He knew of such evil, but he'd never heard of it happening to any woman he knew. "And Jacob Johnson was one of them?" He felt better about Mama, even as the horror of his own paternity began to sink in. He'd been fathered by a rapist.

"Yes."

"Who were the others?"

"Jacob's father Isaac. And a man named Bart Peterson."

That name Will knew. "Mama's stepfather."

"Yes. I told you it's not a pretty story."

"What happened to them?"

"The men?" Mac blew out a long breath. "A couple of months after their first attack, I stopped in Arrow Rock where your mother lived. That day, I found the three of them assaulting her again. I shot and killed Isaac Johnson. Jenny shot Jacob in the arm."

"Is that why his arm doesn't work right?" Will asked, remembering Johnson's weak left arm.

"I didn't know that," Mac said. "Could be."

"And Peterson?" Will asked. "He's still in Arrow Rock, isn't he?"

"Yes. He told us to leave town, and I took your mother to Independence. She told me the story along the way. I couldn't leave her alone, so I took her to Oregon with me."

"Did she want to go?"

Mac smiled wryly and stared toward the cracks in the roof. "I've never been sure. But she didn't have much choice."

Will looked at Mac, wondering how the love between Mama and Mac had developed. That they loved each other had always been obvious to him. "But she married you?"

Mac shook his head. "Not then. And not before I left the two of you on this claim. But we married when I returned."

"Then I'm a bastard," Will said, trying the word on for size.

"You're my son," Mac said, putting an arm around Will's shoulders. "As much as Cal or Nate. I love you as I love them."

Will shrugged off Mac's arm. "But you're not my father, and you don't even know who is."

"Come on home, son," Mac said, standing and holding his hand out to

Will.

Will stood without Mac's help. "Don't call me that. Don't say it ever again. I'm not your son."

"Well, come home," Mac said. "Your mother is worried."

Will turned to Shanty and led him out of the shack, tethering him beside Valiente. Without a word, he found a shovel in the barn, cleaned out the shack, mounted the gelding, and followed Mac toward town.

# Chapter 15: Back Home

Will and Mac arrived home and stabled their horses in the carriage house. As Will trudged into the house, Mac clapped him on the shoulder. "Go see your mother," he said. Will went upstairs and found Mama reading in her bedroom.

"William." She rose and hugged him tightly.

"Mama." At first he stood rigidly, then he awkwardly patted her back. She seemed so little. He thought of the violence she endured with Johnson and the other men. "I'm sorry, Mama. I'm sorry I ran away. Sorry for everything." He hoped she understood what he meant.

She reached up and touched his cheek. "I never wanted you to know."

Will shrugged. He still couldn't make sense of it. He felt alien in his own skin—which scoundrel's skin had he inherited?

"You look so much like my own papa," she murmured.

"Which man do you think was my father?" he asked.

She closed her eyes and shook her head. "I don't think about it. I can't. You're mine—all mine." She opened her eyes, met his gaze, and shook him by the shoulders gently. "Mac is your father. He has raised you as his own. And he loves you as much as I do."

Will didn't answer. He no longer felt any kinship with Mac. But he grieved the loss.

Jenny watched Will for the next few days. He didn't speak much to Mac or her but seemed to act the same as always around the other children. "What can we do to help him?" she asked Mac one evening when they were alone in their room.

"Let it slide, Jenny," Mac said. "Will's a bright boy. He'll sort it out."

"He seems so lonely. Aloof." She sighed. "I wish he were still a baby. He was so happy then. Remember?" She smiled, recalling baby William's winsome smiles and coos. Her first child. A part of her. As soon as she'd held him, his paternity ceased to matter. She'd worked to put his violent conception out of her mind. "He's keeping himself so distant from me now."

"Boys do that." Mac took off his cravat and threw it on a chair. "They can't stay tethered to their mothers forever."

"We can't let the other children know. It's terrible enough that Will and Maria do."

"Have you talked to Maria?" Mac asked.

She shook her head. "I did that day. But not again." She sighed. "What do I say?"

"Just answer her questions," Mac said, taking Jenny into his arms. "And tell her to keep her thoughts to herself. Or talk to us. You're right—the other children shouldn't know. They're too young."

The next afternoon, Jenny and Maria polished silver in the dining room. The younger children were at school, Maggie napped, and Will was nowhere around. Mac had gone to his office in town. "I'm sorry you were there when Jacob Johnson came," Jenny said, broaching the subject with Maria. "And I'm proud of you for scaring him off."

"I was so frightened, Mama," Maria whispered. "And now I'm so afraid for Will."

"Why for Will?" Jenny asked.

"He's brooding. Like he doesn't know who he is or how to act around us."

The girl's perceptiveness startled Jenny. That's exactly how Will behaved—like he had to probe a wound, to test his relationship with each one of them. "Maybe he doesn't know how to act," she said. "We must show him we love him still." She hesitated. "You know, I've never loved you less because you aren't my daughter. I mean, you *are* my daughter," Jenny amended. "As much as if I'd given birth to you. And Mac feels the same way. About both you and Will. We're your parents."

Maria smiled, tears shining in her eyes. "I know, Mama. Folks in town might call me a half-breed, but I've always known you loved me."

Jenny stared in surprise. "They don't call you a half-breed around me."

Maria shrugged. "They know you'd give them a piece of your mind."

"No matter your heritage, you are our daughter."

Maria's face remained impassive.

"Can you keep your knowledge about Will to yourself?" Jenny asked. "If you have questions, come talk to me. Or Mac. But don't let the little children know. Will would be embarrassed, and so would I."

Maria touched Jenny's hand. "You shouldn't be. Those men were the villains, it wasn't anything you did."

"Good did come from their heinous acts," Jenny said, with a rueful shake of her head. "Because they brought me Will. And then Mac. And you." She waved her hand to encompass the house. "And all our family. I am more blessed now than I ever was before they assaulted me."

"If anyone should be embarrassed, it's me," Maria said. "My mother was the whore."

Jenny took the girl's shoulders and forced Maria to look at her. "You mustn't ever say that. You are not responsible for your mother's actions. No more than Will is responsible for his father's. We are each what we do in this life, not what others have done to us."

Several days passed with no sign of Jacob Johnson anywhere in Oregon City. Mac decided it was safe to make his long overdue trip to Eugene. He took the steamboat upstream to Eugene. When he disembarked, he went to the newspaper office of Byron Pengra, the man planning to build a road from Eugene east across Oregon to Fort Boise. Pengra had arranged for Mac to meet other investors in the road project.

Once the men were gathered, Pengra said, "We have good transportation between Oregon and California. At least by sea. We still need better roads south to Sacramento and San Francisco. But equally important are connections from Oregon to the East. Boise is the first stop."

"The folks back East are too busy with the War to worry about Oregon," another investor said. "But the War will end. The South can't stand much longer. Then people will pour into our state."

Mac wasn't as optimistic as these men that the War would be over soon.

But eventually it would end, and settlers would flock west again. Indian tribes and emigrants would continue to fight over the land, and someone would need to police them both. "A military road?" he asked. "Is that the idea?"

Pengra nodded. "That would be its primary use. At least at first. And that's what we're surveying this year."

Another man chimed in. "But over time, our road should become the rail bed between here and Boise, and from there all the way to St. Louis. There will be a transcontinental railroad within the decade. I'd bet money on it. In fact, by building this road we *are* betting money on it."

"But the transcontinental railroad is starting in San Francisco and Sacramento, not Oregon," Mac said.

"We want another railroad east from Oregon," the railroad proponent replied.

"That's not likely," Mac said. "California is far larger than Oregon now. The first route is already determined."

"Then we'll have to demand a rail connection soon after," another investor said. "That's how we'll make our money—from federal land grants along the track lines."

"And how do we recoup our monies if the railroad never comes?" Mac asked. "If the road never develops into a rail bed?"

"Tolls, perhaps," Pengra said. "But we truly believe the railroad will arrive at some point. Are you with us?" he asked Mac.

Mac nodded. "I'll invest. But in phases. I'll help with the surveying costs this year. But that's all I can commit to now."

"That's all we're planning at the moment," Pengra said, smiling. But Mac knew the man hoped for more.

# Chapter 16: Quiet Before the Storm

Will tried to keep to himself in the days after Mac brought him home. He had to interact with his younger siblings—he supposed they were his siblings, or at least his half-siblings. Cal still pestered Will daily, and Nate followed Cal's lead. Lottie and Eliza and little Maggie clung to him, wanting piggyback rides and stories. It all felt normal, and yet he felt like a stranger.

Will escaped the bustling household by visiting Jonah whenever he could. It was mid-April, and the air had finally warmed. Farm work kept Daniel, Jonah, and Sammy busy all day, and they welcomed Will's help.

The first time Will joined them after he'd run away, Jonah questioned him about why he'd left home. "Leave Will be," Daniel ordered. Will wondered what Daniel knew about his past, but he didn't ask. He didn't want Jonah to know any of it—Jonah would look differently at Will, and his friend might also think poorly of Mama.

Whatever happened, Will needed to protect Mama. She'd been through too much already for his sake. She must not have wanted him to be born, at least not at first, though he didn't doubt she loved him now. He tried not to think about how he'd come to exist. He tried to work and work, to exhaust himself each day, so he could sleep at night.

One evening, Will found himself alone with Maria in the kitchen. She washed dishes after supper, and he volunteered to dry for her. If he stayed in the kitchen, the other children wouldn't badger him—they'd already hightailed it upstairs to avoid doing any chores.

"Are you all right, Will?" Maria asked as she handed him a wet plate.

"What do you mean?" He swirled a towel over the plate, then set it on the table.

"I heard everything that man said." She handed him another plate. "And I talked to Mama afterward."

"Did she tell you?" he whispered. "About the three men."

Maria nodded.

"Any of them could have been my father," Will murmured. "Any of them. They were all wicked, and one of them is my father."

"It doesn't matter, Will. You're still the same boy—"

"But I'm not," he exclaimed. "I don't feel the same. I don't feel like me."

"It doesn't matter about those men," she insisted. "Pa raised you and me both. Neither of us is his, and I'm not your mama's either. But they're our parents."

"Don't you ever feel like a stranger?"

She waved a soapy hand around the room. "This is all I know. This is what made me."

Will grunted in response. How could she believe it didn't matter who her parents were? Her mother had been a prostitute and part Indian. Neither Mama nor Mac were her parents—though Will sometimes wondered whether Mac was in fact her father.

Then it dawned on him. Even if Mac was Maria's father, he wasn't Will's. He and Maria had no common blood—both their mothers and their fathers were different. She was no more his sister than Cordelia Abercrombie or Meg Bingham.

He would have to think about what that meant to him.

The next morning after breakfast, Jenny carried a load of clean dishes from the kitchen into the dining room to put away. As she set them down on the table to open the cupboard door, a sharp pain sliced through her belly.

The baby! She immediately worried about another miscarriage. But the pain only came once. After that, she merely felt a slight tenderness across her lower abdomen.

It must not be serious. She'd borne most of her babies with no problems. In the course of eight pregnancies, she'd experienced every symptom possible, she told herself, and she'd only had one miscarriage. This pregnancy would go fine, she was sure.

But she took her time lifting the plates into the hutch, no more than two at a time.

Mac sat in his office reading his mail. A letter from Ladd in Portland, wondering when he would receive Mac's funds to invest in the banking operation. A letter from Pengra in Eugene, asking for confirmation of Mac's support for the Central Oregon road survey.

And now correspondence from the People's Transportation Company, a steamship company operating on the Willamette. Mac had invested with the P.T. Company in 1862 when it formed. Asa and David McCully, the company's founders, were long-time friends. When they wanted funds to compete with the larger Oregon Steam Navigation Company, Mac agreed. Competition was a good thing, and unless the P.T. Company grew, the larger O.S.N. Company would monopolize steam travel on the Columbia River. William Ladd was one of the principal investors in the O.S.N. Company, but Mac still thought the upstart P.T. Company was a good bet.

Now, however, the stakes were higher. The P.T. Company had added a boat on the Columbia River, operating between the Cascades and Celilo Falls, and the McCullys also contracted with other steamboat operators to transfer passengers and cargo farther up the Columbia beyond Celilo. But the O.S.N. Company had started a fare war that spiraled the P.T. Company into debt. The McCullys needed more funding, and they wanted Mac to increase his stake in their corporation.

He most definitely would invest, Mac thought, reaching for quill and paper to respond to the McCullys. But he wondered—would he be able to support all these new ventures or was he overextending himself? He had a large family to support, and that family was still growing.

Mac had been lucky in California—he'd arrived early at the gold fields and made a fortune when mining was profitable. Later arrivals faced slim pickings. And Mac left mining at the right time as well—he moved into storekeeping and transporting gold, more lucrative operations than physically digging ore from the ground.

He increased his fortune over the years in both California and Oregon. Until the floods. Never had he anticipated water would inundate both states in the same year.

Was Mac ready to expand after rebuilding his investments? Only time would tell whether taking on all these risks was wise. He set his pen to paper and drafted his agreement to the P.T. Company's request.

As he sanded the paper to dry the ink, Mac remembered Samuel Abercrombie's threats against Zeke Pershing. What would come of that? Would the old bully take Zeke to court again, as he had many years earlier? Once again, water caused difficulties—if that creek hadn't changed course, Abercrombie would have no basis for his claim against Zeke.

Will worked all day with Jonah. They were lumbering today, and they had the help of old Mr. Abercrombie, along with Zeke Pershing and his three brothers.

At the noon break, Will and Jonah sat a short distance away from the others while they ate. Jonah grumbled about how hard Daniel made him work. "He ain't nearly as hard on the other men as he is on me," Jonah complained. "And they's all bigger'n me."

"You're always saying you're full grown now," Will said. "Not like me—Mama says I'm lean as a sapling. I don't have any muscles yet."

Jonah sighed. "Daniel says if'n I want to farm, I need to do the work of a man. I try. But it's hard."

"Don't you want to be a farmer?" Will asked.

"He treats me like I'm his slave," Jonah continued. "I ain't even his son."

"He's raised you." It dawned on Will that both he and Jonah were being raised by men who weren't their fathers. He opened his mouth to tell Jonah that, then decided against it. What would Jonah think if he found out Will was a bastard? If he knew a rapist had fathered Will?

Jonah whined on about how easy Will's life was. "Your pa's going to send you to some fancy school in the East. You'll come back to Oregon with fine airs, won't you?" He threw a pinecone at Will. "You won't want to get your hands dirty no more."

Will threw the pinecone back. "Or maybe I won't come back at all."

What would he do? Where did he belong in the world?

# Chapter 17: Responsibilities

Jenny continued to feel occasional cramping over the next few days. One evening, when she gasped and grabbed her middle, Mac asked, "What's wrong?"

"Just a little pain," she said, sorry she'd let him see her wince.

"Is it the baby?" He crossed the room to her and led her to a chair.

Shrugging as she sat, she said, "I'm fine." He couldn't do anything to help, even if it were the baby—no need to alarm him.

"Have you seen the doctor?"

She laughed. "For a baby? This early? I'll let you get him when the real pains start."

"I'll stop at his office tomorrow morning and send him to the house to see you." Mac rubbed the back of his neck. "I wish Doc Tuller were still alive. I trusted him. I'm not as sure about the new doctor."

Jenny smiled at the memory of Doc Tuller. Their Abram was born shortly after Doc Tuller died, and they named the baby after him. But tiny Abram followed Doc to the grave a few months later. Her only comfort had been the thought of the gruff old doctor watching out for his wee namesake.

"Let Will and Maria do more of the chores," Mac ordered. "I'll talk to them. They're old enough to help—Will's older than you were when he was born, and Maria's already taller than you."

"That's not saying much," Jenny said. She was short for a woman, and Maria had passed her up two years ago.

94

The next evening, after the doctor checked on Jenny and prescribed frequent rests, Mac took Will and Maria into his home study. "Your mother is having trouble with this baby," he told them. "You're old enough to understand what that means. I want you both to help her."

"Yes, Pa," Maria said, nodding. "I'll do everything I can. I won't let her lift anything."

Mac turned to Will, who stood silently. "And you?" He almost called the boy "son," though Will now cringed whenever Mac did so. Mac's conversations with Will had been awkward since he'd brought the boy home after Johnson's attack. Would they ever find their way to a comfortable relationship?

"Yes, sir." Will said.

"Stay close to home," Mac told Will. "No more gallivanting off to see Jonah. I need to be able to rely on you."

"Yes, sir."

He wasn't likely to get any more out of the boy, Mac thought. But Will must still love Jenny and would care for her—surely he didn't blame his mother for what had happened.

The next day was bitterly cold, despite the late April date on the calendar. Will stayed indoors after breakfast, but he was fidgety. Mama didn't need him to run any errands, and he'd read everything in the house.

Will wandered downstairs, hoping to find a new book or magazine in Mac's office. He found nothing and drifted into the parlor to stare out the window. He wondered what Jonah was doing. Despite the frigid temperatures, Daniel would have some task to keep them busy. They'd probably be working outside, which would be better than sitting cooped up in the house with nothing to do.

Will put on his coat and dashed out to the carriage house to check on Shanty and Valiente. Rufus followed, yapping at his heels until distracted by a squirrel. Even the horses ignored him when he didn't offer them a carrot or apple.

When he returned to the house, Will climbed the stairs toward his room, but on a whim continued up the next flight to the dusty attic. Maybe he could find something to do there. He rummaged through old toys and books, but nothing interested him. Foraging into the darkest corner of the attic, Will spotted an old trunk, which he didn't remember seeing before.

He opened the dusty trunk and found a pair of worn-out saddlebags. Something was inside one bag—a notebook, which he pulled out. Flipping it open, he recognized Mac's handwriting—a journal. The first entry began, "I killed a man today." He read on. It was Mac's account of how he met Mama, starting in March 1847.

Will set the journal aside and reached into the trunk again. Wrapped in calico was another notebook. Mama's journal, beginning, "In six days I start for Oregon. Will I survive?" Her record of the wagon journey.

He took the saddlebags and notebooks to his room and read all morning.

Will finished the journals before the noon meal. After they ate, he was restless again, prowling the parlor, thinking about what he'd read. Mama had been so young. Mac seemed so uncertain, yet he'd taken over the wagon train as if he'd been born to lead.

Will felt more like Mama than Mac—he should have realized long ago Mac wasn't his father. They were nothing alike. Will didn't belong here.

Maria entered the parlor. "What are you doing?" she asked.

"Nothing," Will said, sorry and yet not sorry to have his reverie interrupted. "Where's Mama?"

"Resting. I think she's asleep. So is Maggie."

"It's so quiet." Will paced the room, peering out each window in turn.

"Sit down, won't you?" Maria said. She'd settled in her favorite chair and pulled out her sewing.

"You always have something to do. How do you stay so busy?"

She lifted a shoulder. "There's always mending. Cal and Nate go through clothes so quickly. And Lottie and Eliza aren't much better."

He continued to pace.

"Can't you be still?" Maria said, sounding annoyed.

"No."

"Why don't you take Shanty for a ride? I can manage here. Just be back by dusk."

Will's heart leapt. "Are you sure?"

She nodded.

That was all the encouragement Will needed. He grabbed his coat, hat, and gloves, then ran to the carriage house. Ten minutes later, he and Shanty were on the road to Jonah's.

Will spent two hours at Jonah's house. The boys peeled potatoes for Esther and mucked out the barn. Jonah was still upset with Daniel and complained the whole time they were together. "I'm grown enough to set my own chores," was Jonah's complaint today. "I don't need him tellin' me every last thing."

Will listened, wanting to tell Jonah about his own woes, which were far more serious than Jonah's. But once again, Will demurred from telling Jonah what he'd learned about Mac.

Will left well before dusk, wanting to be home before Maria's deadline. She'd been kind to him, and he didn't want to abuse her offer. After he curried Shanty and mucked out the horse stalls, he snuck in the back door and found Maria in the kitchen helping Mrs. O'Malley. Maria's face was flushed pink from standing over the stove. She looked very pretty.

"You're back," Maria said. "Mama's in the parlor now. She doesn't even know you left."

Mrs. O'Malley raised an eyebrow at Will, but said nothing. Will thought he ought to stay on Mrs. O'Malley's good side. "Can I help here?" he asked.

She gave him a bowl of potatoes to peel and slice. Will shook his head at the irony of peeling potatoes for two families in one day, but quietly set to work.

After supper, Will offered to help Maria wash dishes. He dried while she washed. "Thank you," he said. "For covering for me this afternoon."

"What'd you do with Jonah?"

He chuckled. "Peeled potatoes. And cleaned the barn."

She giggled. "You could have stayed here and done that."

"I did—I cleaned our horse stalls and peeled potatoes for Mrs. O'Malley, too."

She laughed again. "Serves you right for leaving."

"You said you didn't mind." Will hoped he hadn't hurt Maria's feelings.

"I didn't," she said. "I'm teasing you."

They bantered back and forth until Maria dried her hands. "That's the last dish," she said. She moved to pick up the washtub.

Will put down the plate he'd dried. "Let me get that," he said. "It's heavy." He moved next to her and put his hands beside hers on the tub's handles to take its weight. She looked up at him, smiling.

He leaned over and kissed her. Her lips tasted sweet. Then he grabbed the tub and took it outside.

Out in the cold, he dumped the wash water. Then stood stark still. He'd kissed Maria.

He went inside with the empty tub. She'd fled the kitchen.

# Chapter 18: Repercussions

The next morning, Jenny roused and dressed Maggie and took the toddler downstairs. Maria sliced bread while Mrs. O'Malley fried bacon. "Good morning," Jenny said, putting Maggie down to hug Maria.

"Morning, Mama," Maria murmured.

Jenny turned to pick up a platter of pancakes to take to the dining room where the boys sat waiting.

"I'll get that, Ma—Ouch," Maria cried. "I cut my thumb."

Jenny put down the platter and examined her daughter's bleeding thumb. "We'll need a towel, Mrs. O'Malley," she said. When the housekeeper offered her one, Jenny wrapped it around Maria's hand. "Come with me," she said to Maria. "That needs a plaster."

They went upstairs, and Jenny treated Maria's thumb. Her daughter trembled uncontrollably. "It's not that bad, child," Jenny said.

Maria sobbed.

"What's wrong?" Jenny asked. The towel had stanched the bleeding, and the injury didn't warrant the girl's tears.

"Will kissed me," Maria mumbled.

"Pardon?" Jenny didn't think she'd understood correctly.

"Last night. While we washed dishes. In the kitchen."

"He kissed you?" The children had always been affectionate, and Jenny had seen Will buss his sisters on the cheek many times. "What's the fuss?"

"On the lips, Mama," Maria whispered. "Like Pa kisses you."

Stunned, Jenny spent a moment to attach the plaster. Then she asked in as nonchalant a tone as she could muster, "How did you feel about it?"

"I don't know," Maria wailed. "I think I liked it. Does that make me bad?"

"No, no." Jenny put an arm around her daughter. "It's not bad to like a boy kissing you." The possibility of William and Maria forming an attachment beyond brother and sister had never occurred to Jenny. In her mind, they *were* brother and sister. How should she handle this situation?

Jenny took a deep breath. "You mustn't be forward with a boy. Any boy. Even William. And you're way too young for any romantic notions with any young man."

"But you were my age when you—"

"I didn't have a choice, dear," Jenny said. "In any event, I was too young for a romantic attachment. I was still too young the next year when Mac left for California. I grew up a lot before he came back. I was eighteen then."

"I wasn't forward, Mama, I swear."

Jenny ran her hand over Maria's dark hair. "I'm sure you weren't, dear. I'll have a word with William."

"I don't want to get Will in trouble."

"He's not in trouble." Jenny sighed. "But I will talk to him nonetheless."

Jenny fretted all day about how to approach William. How did a mother talk to her son about whether it was appropriate to kiss a girl? A girl who was his sister . . . but wasn't. There was nothing wrong with the two young people becoming sweet on each other, though it could cause great awkwardness in the family.

When Mac arrived home from his office, Jenny followed him to their room. "We need to talk," she said.

He turned to her. "Are you all right? Any more cramping?"

She shook her head. "That's not it." She swallowed hard, then said, "William kissed Maria last night."

"He did what?" Mac bellowed. "Damn that boy." Apparently, Mac understood immediately what William had done, unlike Jenny's confusion that morning.

"Mac," Jenny admonished.

"How did you find out?" Mac threw his cravat on the bed and his cuff links followed.

"Maria told me."

"Did he hurt her?"

"Mac, it was a kiss," Jenny said. "No more. She's confused, but she's fine."

"Damn him," Mac grumbled again.

"I don't know what to say to him," Jenny said.

"I'll talk to him," Mac stated, his mouth set in a thin line. "And to Maria."

Mac stormed down the hall to Will's room and threw open the door. Will lay on his bed with a book in hand. The boy dropped the book and shot to his feet. "Sir?"

Mac slammed the door behind him. This conversation needed to stay between the two of them. He didn't want the entire house in an uproar.

"Jenny says you kissed Maria."

Will blushed a deep red and stared at the floor.

"Why in the hell did you do such a thing?" Mac wanted to hit something. Not the boy, but something.

"She looked pretty," Will muttered. "She'd done me a favor. I don't know. I just wanted to." By the end of his little speech, Will glared at Mac with his chin thrust out, like Jenny did when she was mad.

"She's your sister," Mac hissed.

"No, she's not," Will shot back. "She's not your daughter, I'm not your son, and she's not my sister."

Mac stood dumbfounded. He couldn't deny the boy's statements. He managed to choke out, "In this household, she is your sister. In this household, you are my son. In this household, you will not behave so rashly again. Do you understand me, Will?"

Will's jaw clenched. He looked mutinous. But finally, he nodded.

Will plodded downstairs for supper but barely picked at his food. Every time he glanced at Mac, his stomach churned. And looking at Mama wasn't much better. They hated him. All because he'd kissed a pretty girl.

Maria wasn't his sister. Why shouldn't he kiss her? Other girls wanted him to kiss them. Cordelia Abercrombie had caught him under the mistletoe last Christmas and pecked him on the lips. Meg Bingham stared at him whenever they were together. He'd danced with her once, and she'd blushed the whole time.

Maria was nicer than either Cordelia or Meg. Why shouldn't he kiss her?

Will looked over at Maria. Her cheeks turned pink when he caught her eye, then she smiled softly. He'd like to kiss her again, he realized. And take more time at it. Would he ever get to try again? Not if Mac had a say in it.

Will hid in his room after supper. How was he going to live in this house until he left for Harvard in the fall? If that's what he did.

# Chapter 19: Growing Pains

Before dawn, while everyone in the house was still asleep, Will crept out to the carriage house. He'd barely dozed all night. After reading Mama's and Mac's journals, after the argument with Pa over Maria, he couldn't relax. He needed to get away. Despite his promise to stay with Mama, he was too restless to sit at home. Let Mac stay with Mama for a day. Why should Will be responsible?

Shanty and Valiente and the carriage horses all whinnied at the interruption, but he quieted them with oats while he saddled Shanty. He'd ride out to Jonah's house. If he left now, he'd get there about the time the Abercrombie family began their day.

The cold air nipped at his ears, but the rising sun promised better weather as the day wore on. Will hunched low over Shanty's neck and urged the gelding faster. Shanty tossed his head, but obeyed Will's nudges.

As Will expected, Daniel and Jonah were doing morning chores in the barn when he arrived.

"You're here early," Daniel said. "Come to spend the full day with us?"

"I hope to," Will said. "What do you have planned?"

"Tilling the last of the cornfields," Daniel said. "Ground's warm enough to pull a plow through now."

"Morning, Jonah," Will said to his friend, who grunted in response. Jonah in a churlish mood would make for an unpleasant day. Maybe Will would leave at noon.

But he was so glad to be away from his own home that he tried to be friendly to the other Abercrombies. He cheerfully offered to help Esther, flipping pancakes for her brood while she fried bacon. After they all ate,

Daniel ushered Will, Jonah, and Sammy out to the fields.

The sun came out by midmorning, and the wind gentled. Will was still glad for his coat and gloves, but he was comfortable laboring under the bright sky. He willingly agreed to guide the plow behind the mules while Jonah took the easier place by their heads. Across the field, Daniel and Sammy worked with the other mule team.

Daniel's daughters Cordelia and Abby brought food to them at noon. The men and girls all sat on a flat piece of ground in the sunshine.

"Where's Esther?" Jonah asked, as he dug into the plate of stew Cordelia handed him.

"Abe is fractious," Cordelia replied. "Ma didn't want to leave him. But me'n Abby was glad to get out of the house."

Will grinned. "I don't blame you."

Cordelia smiled back at him coyly, batting her eyes.

Will groaned inside. He hadn't intended to encourage Cordelia's flirting.

While Will talked to Cordelia, Jonah and Daniel got into an argument. Will didn't hear what started it, but he heard Jonah yell, "You treat me like Abe. Like one of your young'uns. Don't you trust me to do a man's work?"

"Not when you throw tantrums like Abe—" Daniel began.

"Damn it, Daniel," Jonah shouted, "I—"

"Don't you cuss at me, boy," Daniel said. "I can still tan your hide."

"I'd like to see you try." Jonah stood and loomed over Daniel. "Try it now."

"Back off, son," Daniel said.

"I ain't your son," Jonah said through his teeth. "You ain't my pa. You'll never be my pa." Jonah ran off into the woods.

Will squirmed while watching the exchange. Jonah's shout at Daniel was exactly what Will had said to Mac. The difference was everyone knew about Daniel and Jonah. And everyone knew who Jonah's father was.

But no one knew Mac wasn't Will's father. And no one—not even Mama—could identify who his father was. He shivered despite the sun, once again feeling alone in the world.

After Jonah stormed off, Will continued plowing with Daniel and Sammy. Sammy took Jonah's place with the mules, and Daniel managed the other team alone. At dusk, Will returned home.

As he rode Shanty into the backyard and dismounted, Cal entered the yard from the kitchen. Rufus rushed out behind Cal and sniffed Will's feet. "Where you been all day?" Cal asked.

"Jonah's." Will took Shanty into his stall and started currying him.

Cal followed. "Pa asked where you were."

Will shrugged and continued caring for his horse.

"You'll get in trouble." Cal brought a handful of oats over to Shanty. The gelding pulled away from Will to nibble the treat from Cal's hand.

"Leave Shanty be," Will said. "I need to rub him down."

"He likes the oats."

"Maybe he does, but I need to finish here before supper, and clean myself up as well."

Cal held his hand up to Shanty's nose again.

"Quit being such a little pest," Will shouted.

"I hate you," Cal shouted back. "You take Shanty off all day to see your friend, while I'm stuck parsing sentences in school. It's not fair."

"I had to parse sentences, too, when I was your age."

"I don't care," Cal said. "I still hate you."

"Well, I hate you, too," Will said, violating Mama's rule not to speak ill of their siblings. But then, Cal broke the rule first. "I worked hard all day, and I want my supper on time."

"You're not too old for Pa to whup you," Cal said. "You left home again without telling anyone."

Will cringed at the reminder Mac was Cal's father, not his. "You should be the first he whups," he said. "After stealing Maria's horse the way you did."

"You already whupped me," Cal said. "And you got in trouble for it."

"I'd whup you again," Will said. He wouldn't really, but Cal didn't need to know that. "You broke my best carving, and I don't want to live in the same house as you. You wreck everything."

Cal's face fell, and he turned away. As the younger boy left, Will murmured to himself, "Ever since you were born, I've had no place here. No place in my own home."

When Mac walked through the hallway before supper, he saw Maria alone in the parlor. He still hadn't said anything to her after he'd learned about Will kissing her. He went into the room and sat across from her. "What are you doing, daughter?"

"Sewing on buttons." The movements of her hands were as quick and sure as Jenny's—Maria had been trained well.

"About Will—" he began.

The blush on her tan cheeks rose immediately. "Pa—"

"I told your mother I'd talk to you."

She shook her head. "You don't have to. I talked to Mama."

"I've spoken to Will."

Maria looked up, her face now paling. "Don't blame Will—"

"Well, then, who do I blame?" His anger at the boy rose as quickly as her blush had.

"No one, Pa. There's no need to blame anyone."

Despite Cal's prediction that Will would get in trouble, nothing was said at supper about his absence that day. Mac glared at him, but that was it.

That evening Will kept his oil lamp on late and re-read Mama's and Mac's journals. Their words filled him with awe, even on a second reading. They'd left their homes to travel to Oregon, a place they knew little or nothing about. Mama took off into the wilderness with a man she didn't know, and she'd been carrying a baby. Mac started the journey on a lark but ended as captain of the wagon company.

Will wondered if he was as brave as his mother. He fretted about going to Harvard, an established college in a settled city. It would be different from Oregon, but how bad could college be? He had nowhere else to go. If Mama had left her home for Oregon, maybe he needed to leave home, too. Maybe leaving home would lead him to his place in the world.

Will turned out the lamp, then lay awake past midnight. He heard a hoot from the yard below his window. It came again—the signal he and Jonah used.

He opened his window and peered out. Jonah stood in shadow under the stars. "Will," Jonah whispered. "Come out."

Will dressed quickly and crept downstairs. Rufus slept by the kitchen stove, but only gave one soft woof as Will eased out the kitchen door. Jonah beckoned him toward the mounting block by the carriage house.

"Where'd you go this afternoon?" Will asked.

"I had to get away," Jonah said. "Had to do me some thinkin'." He grabbed Will's arm. "I'm leavin.' I'm gonna find Joel."

"All the way to Jacksonville?" Will asked, surprised.

"I'm gonna prospect with him. It's gotta be better'n workin' for Daniel. He treats me like a slave. You wanna come with me?"

Jonah was overreacting—Will thought Daniel treated Jonah fine. And going to find Joel in Jacksonville was a harebrained notion.

But why not? Will had just been thinking he had nowhere to go except Harvard. He shrugged, then said, "When are you leaving?"

"First thing in the mornin'," Jonah said. "I'm goin' home to pack now."

Will nodded. "I'll meet you at dawn. At the turnoff from your house to our old claim."

# Chapter 20: Runaways

Will packed some clothes and a blanket in the old saddlebags he'd found in the attic. He tied his stash of coins into a sock and thrust it into his pocket. He only had a few dollars—not much for a journey to Jacksonville. Seeing Mama's and Mac's journals on his desk, he grabbed a blank notebook and pencil and crammed them in with his gear. Maybe he would keep his own journal on this adventure. Maybe he'd have a story to tell, a story that would shape him as much as Mama's and Mac's journey shaped their lives.

An hour before dawn, he crept downstairs with the saddlebags. In the kitchen, he rummaged for some biscuits and bacon. He packed as much food as he could find easily, filled a canteen with water, and snuck to the carriage house to saddle Shanty. The horses must be used to his early morning intrusions, because they didn't even nicker when he entered.

After tying the saddlebags to the back of the saddle, Will walked Shanty outside. He glanced once at the house—when would he see it again? Then he mounted and turned Shanty toward the country road.

This morning was warmer than the day before. Will hoped he and Jonah would have good weather on their journey south. That's about all he knew of Jacksonville—it was south of Oregon City. South of Salem and Eugene, almost to California. Will had never been farther than Eugene—he'd ridden the steamboat there once with Mac.

Jonah waited for Will when he arrived at their meeting place. "Ready?" Jonah asked.

Will nodded, and the boys turned their horses south.

"Anyone see you leave?" Jonah asked.

"I don't think so," Will said. "The house was quiet. You?"

"Nah," Jonah said. "Sammy grumbled when I left the bed, but he was sleepin' again afore I was dressed."

They rode in silence. After a while, Will asked, "What made you decide to leave?"

"I'm tired of workin' for Daniel," Jonah said. "Esther says Joel has the wanderlust. Like our pa. Guess I take after them more'n I do Esther and the others. They're all happy stayin' put. Zeke and Daniel, they like farmin.' Me, I want to be my own boss."

Will didn't comment, but he didn't think Jonah was ready to be his own boss. "What about Iris?" he asked.

Even in the early dawn light, Jonah's expression turned dreamy. "I'll come back for her someday."

Then what did Jonah hope to gain by leaving now? Will shook his head. Jonah was too impetuous. But if Jonah was impetuous, why was Will so ready to follow him? Will shrugged. No matter. He was committed now.

The boys rode south on the post road toward Molalla, sometimes in silence, sometimes pointing out what they saw, sometimes arguing about how long the trip to Jacksonville would take. "At least a week," Jonah said.

"More like two," Will responded.

Jenny rose and woke the girls, readying them for the day ahead. Maggie wanted to snuggle while Jenny dressed her. Eliza and Lottie groggily took care of their own morning routines. Only Maria seemed to have any vitality today.

"Maria," Jenny said, "go wake the boys."

Jenny heard Cal and Nate grumbling, then Maria came back to the girls' room. "Will isn't here," Maria said.

"Maybe he's up early," Jenny said. "Eating already."

Maria's feet tapped down the stairs, then the sound of her return. "Will's not there," she told Jenny. "Mrs. O'Malley hasn't seen him."

Jenny found Mac shaving in their room. "William isn't home."

Mac swore. "Did you check the horse stalls? Is Shanty there? Yesterday the boy rode to Jonah's without permission."

"Maria?" Jenny called. "Go look in the carriage house."

A few minutes later, Maria raced upstairs. "He's not there. And Shanty's gone."

Jenny clutched Mac's arm. "You need to go after him."

"Why?" Mac said. "The lad came home yesterday in his own good time. He'll do so again. But he'll get a talking to, that's for sure."

Jenny heaved a deep sigh. "Something doesn't feel right." She went into Will's room. She picked up clothes he'd strewn on the floor—that wasn't like him. Then she noticed two familiar books on his desk. "He found our journals," she murmured. "I wonder what that means."

At Jenny's insistence, Mac rode toward the Abercrombies' farm. "I don't know whether William is with Jonah, but it's worth asking," she'd said. So he saddled Valiente and headed there straight after breakfast.

"What in the devil is wrong with that boy?" he asked Valiente. The stallion snorted and tossed his head.

Were Will's frequent departures Mac's fault? Mac had little guidance in being a strong paternal figure—his own father had been distant, except when disciplining Mac. As Will had grown, and particularly in recent months, Mac's relationship with the boy had been strained. And Will's discovery about his paternity had only made the situation worse.

He should have done a better job talking to Will, Mac thought. He'd tried to present the facts clearly, but there wasn't any way to sugar-coat the violence that led to Will's existence.

Mac ached to take vengeance on the two villains who'd survived his last encounter with Jacob Johnson. Mac no longer regretted killing Isaac Johnson, as he had in the immediate aftermath. He'd been glad at the time that Jenny didn't have a death on her hands, that her bullet had merely wounded Jacob. Now he wished Jacob had died as well—now that the past had returned to haunt them.

At least Bart Peterson remained far behind in Missouri.

Will's discovery of the truth about his parentage was a tragedy. Mac hoped the boy would learn to cope with the misfortune of his beginnings and find his way back to them. If Will had left them for good, Jenny would never be the same—losing Will might destroy her.

When he arrived at the Abercrombie claim, he found Daniel and Esther in a tizzy. "Jonah's gone," Esther told Mac. "Sammy said Jonah left before dawn."

"Do you have a horse missing?" Mac asked.

Daniel nodded. "The mare Jonah usually rides. She's gone, and so are my saddlebags."

Mac frowned. The boys were probably together, but he and Jenny hadn't noticed any missing saddlebags. He told Daniel that. "Perhaps they don't intend to be gone long," he said. "Any idea where they might be headed?"

Daniel shook his head. Behind him, Esther did the same. "He didn't tell Sammy," she said.

Mac remounted Valiente. He couldn't search for the boys with no idea where to look. "You'll send word if you see either of them?" he asked.

Daniel nodded. "Of course. And you'll do the same for us."

Jenny peered out the kitchen window in late morning, hoping Mac would return soon with William. Of course, he and Daniel might have gone elsewhere to search for the boys, so it might be hours before Mac got home.

But shortly before the noon meal, Mac rode Valiente into the yard. She rushed out to meet him.

He dismounted and shook his head. "Jonah's gone also, but there's no sign of where they went. I rode by our claim in addition to checking with Daniel and Esther. Nothing."

"Then the boys are together?" she asked.

Mac shrugged. "Can't tell for certain. But it stands to reason. I doubt they'd both disappear at the same time unless they left together."

"Where could they be?" Jenny asked, fear creeping into her voice. William was her oldest, the child who'd been with her through the dark days after Mac left her. She thought she and Will were close, but he'd left home without a word to her.

Mac grimaced. "I don't know." He led Valiente into the carriage house.

Jenny whispered, "Oh, William. What have you done?"

# Chapter 21: Starting for Jacksonville

After a few hours of riding, Will and Jonah reached the Molalla River. "There's the ferry," Jonah said, when the river came into sight. "You got money, or should we ford it?"

"How much?" Will asked. He fingered the coins in his pocket. He had enough for the ferry, but they might incur many more expenses before they found Joel Pershing.

Jonah shrugged. "The rate for a horse and rider across the Willamette is fifty cents. I expect it's about the same here."

"Let's look at the current." It was a warm day, and Will would rather not spend his money.

They rode to the Molalla's northern bank. The current was fast. "We best take the ferry," Jonah said, and Will nodded. They urged their horses up the bank. Jonah grabbed a cow horn hung on a fence post to hail the ferryman.

"Where you boys headed?" the ferry operator said after they paid their coins and walked their horses on board the wooden vessel.

"Jacksonville," Jonah said. "My brother's a prospector in them parts."

The man raised an eyebrow as he pulled them across the river. "Jacksonville's a fur piece from here."

"Yes, sir," Jonah said, at the same time Will asked, "How far?"

The ferryman's eyebrow rose higher. "Some three hundred miles, give or take." He frowned. "You know where you're goin'?"

"Yes, sir. Mostly, we do," Jonah said.

The man spat into the water as he squinted at them. "Keep heading south to Roseburg, then you'll hit the old Applegate Trail. Follow that to Grant's Pass. Then to Jacksonville."

"So there's a road all the way?" Will asked as they hit the far bank.

"It ain't more'n a trail in parts," the ferryman said. "To get a wagon through, you might have to clear out brush. But ridin' good mounts—" He nodded at their horses. "You'll be all right."

They thanked the man and continued south.

That night, Will and Jonah camped in a copse of woods near a farm. They could see lights in the farmhouse windows, but didn't dare approach it, and they built only a small fire. Will got out his biscuits and bacon, Jonah his ham and bread.

"How much food did you bring?" Jonah asked, chewing a piece of ham.

"Enough for a couple of days," Will said. "Not for two weeks."

"Same here," Jonah said. "I guess we'll need to hunt. I brung my rifle and some bullets. A shotgun, too."

Will hadn't thought to bring a gun or ammunition. The only weapon he had was the Bowie knife he used for whittling.

The lights in the farmhouse flickered out, and the night was darker than Will thought possible. He'd camped on occasion with Mac and Cal, but they'd been near their claim. Once Jonah had gone with them. It had seemed like an adventure, but he'd felt safe with Mac in the bedroll next to him.

Now he and Jonah were alone. No one knew where they were.

"Do you think they're looking for us?" he whispered.

"Most likely," Jonah said. "But they won't find us."

Jonah quickly fell asleep. In the dim light of the ebbing fire, Will took his blank notebook and pencil out of his saddlebag. He felt self-conscious— what should he write? Most of Mac's journal entries had been brief notes about distances traveled and where they camped. But Mama sometimes wrote more.

Will hesitated, then wrote:

*April 29, 1864. Left for Jacksonville this morning. Took the Molalla Ferry. Made about 20 miles.*

The sky lightened after a long night. Will hadn't slept much—worried, then scared. He hated frightening Mama by leaving, but he'd been miserable at home. He had no idea what lay ahead.

"Let's pack up," Jonah said, sooner than Will wanted to leave his bedroll. "We don't want that farmer finding us on his land."

After relieving himself against a tree, Will scrabbled his belongings back into his saddlebags and reached for a biscuit.

"We'll eat as we ride," Jonah said.

"Who put you in charge?" Will demanded. "I'm hungry now."

"Come on," Jonah urged. "We need to go."

Will stuck the biscuit in his pocket and mounted Shanty. "I'm ready."

They crossed a couple of streams flowing west. "Should we follow a creek?" Will asked. "They all reach the Willamette sooner or later. Doesn't the Applegate Trail follow the Willamette as well?"

"Ferryman said to head for Roseburg," Jonah replied.

"Roseburg is on the Willamette," Will argued.

"But we'd have to pass through river towns to get there. We best stay on back roads," Jonah countered. "You don't want to go through Salem and Albany, do you? Them places is too big."

"I've been as far south as Eugene by boat," Will said. "I'd recognize the way along the river. How far have you gone?"

Jonah shrugged. "I ain't never been south. I only been to Portland once. Daniel keeps us on the farm." And he began ranting about Daniel's unfairness again.

They came to another creek with a scattering of buildings on both sides of the stream. A sign on one building read "Silverton Mill."

"This is Silverton," Will said. "Road west from here goes to Salem. I'm heading that way."

Jonah complained but followed Will.

They rode west and in midafternoon came to a high hill that looked out over the Willamette Valley. Will pointed at the silver line of the river in the distance. "There's the Willamette. Salem's on the far side."

"Well, we're stayin' on this side," Jonah said.

Will let Jonah have his way, and they turned south, trying to stay on paths that kept the Willamette in sight. Though so long as the creeks continued to flow west, Will wasn't too worried they'd lose their way. He liked knowing where the river was—a landmark that could take him back home if he wanted.

They camped in the open again on their second night out, risking a bigger fire because they couldn't see any human habitation nearby. Their supper was meager, and in the morning, Will ate the last of the food he'd brought. "What do you have left?" he asked Jonah.

"Only enough for our noon meal," Jonah said. "I best hunt for a rabbit or bird to shoot now. Game's more apt to be out in the early mornin.' You stay with the horses."

Jonah crept away from their fire, leaving Will alone. Tall evergreens loomed overhead, with the rising sun barely shimmering through the pine boughs. His stomach growled, wanting more than the one biscuit and slice of bacon he'd eaten for breakfast. He hoped Jonah would return soon.

While Jonah was gone, Will wrote:

*May 1, 1864. Made another 20 miles or so yesterday. Now past Salem. Weather is warm. Jonah hunting.*

A shot rang out through the woods. Soon Jonah came crashing back. "Got a duck," he said. "She was on a nest, and I got her eggs, too. Six of 'em."

"Where's your pan?" Will asked, ready to cook the eggs.

"Pan?" Jonah said, sounding chagrined. "I ain't got one. I ain't thought of that."

Will shrugged. He'd seen eggs cooked in their shells, and he'd try that in the coals. He went about the task while Jonah dressed the bird.

When he tapped the shells off the eggs, they were solid—too solid with half-formed embryos inside. He didn't relish eating the embryos, but he swallowed down his portion anyway.

"Duck for dinner," Jonah crowed, holding up the plucked and gutted carcass of the bird. "We'll feast tonight."

They rode south all day, again keeping the Willamette visible on their right. The forests grew denser, and the trail moved closer to the river. As they approached the water, however, the land grew marshy and difficult for the horses to walk.

"Ain't there a road in these parts?" Jonah complained.

"There should be," Will said. "We passed Albany earlier. I saw it off to the west. But I haven't seen any sign of Corvallis yet."

They rode on until Will spotted buildings on the far side of the Willamette. "There it is—there's Corvallis."

"How'd you know it's Corvallis?" Jonah asked.

"I've been there," Will said.

"Your pa brung you this far south?" Jonah seemed skeptical.

"I told you—we took the steamboat to Eugene." Will pointed. "See beyond the town? There's another river joining the Willamette. That's Mary's River. That's how I know it's Corvallis." He sighed. "Next big town is Eugene. Beyond that, I won't know any more than you do."

"How far to Eugene?" Jonah asked.

Will shrugged. "On the boat it only took a few hours from here. I don't know how long it'll take on horseback."

Jonah sighed. "Wish we had money for the boat. It'd be so much easier."

They camped on a rise along the east bank of the Willamette not far south of Corvallis. And, as Jonah had promised, they feasted on duck. "Tastes mighty good, don't it?" he said, patting his belly.

"It does," Will said. "But what will we eat tomorrow?"

*May 1, 1864, evening. Got past Corvallis. Ate duck tonight.*

The boys saved the duck legs for breakfast, but then they were out of food. "Shall I hunt again?" Jonah asked.

Will shook his head. "Maybe this evening. Or if we come across a town, I can buy flour and we'll make biscuits."

Jonah guffawed. "How we gonna make biscuits without a pan?" he asked.

Will chuckled, too. "I guess we need more practice in running away."

By afternoon, their predicament didn't seem so amusing. Will was famished—hungrier than he'd ever been, despite the duck leg he ate that morning. "We should be about halfway to Jacksonville," Jonah said, sighing. "Joel told me it was a ten-day ride from Esther's house."

"That can't be right," Will argued. "We aren't even to Eugene yet."

The boys bickered, but neither of them had a basis for resolving the dispute.

That night, after they found a campsite, Jonah set out to hunt. Again, Will noted their progress in his journal:

*May 2, 1864. We haven't reached Eugene, and we're out of food. Hope Jonah can shoot another duck.*

Will heard a gunshot, but Jonah came back empty-handed except for two eggs. "I snuck into a barn and got shot at when I come out," Jonah reported. "But the farmwife missed these two eggs in the chicken coop."

Will coddled his egg in the shell over the fire and ate it. At least it didn't contain an embryo. Then he rolled up in his blanket and tried to sleep.

The next morning, Will's ribs seemed to touch his backbone. Shanty was happy enough on the grass near their campsite—Will was glad his horse wasn't suffering as he was.

The boys rode grumpily until around noon, when Will spotted Eugene across the river. "There's the town," he said. "We need to cross the Willamette and buy provisions."

"You got enough money?" Jonah asked.

"I got some. Let's hope I can buy enough to get us to Jacksonville," Will said. "I'll get flour and potatoes. Maybe cornmeal. And a pan. That and your hunting should keep us from starving."

The road led to a shallow crossing of the Willamette upstream from the steamboat landing. Boats couldn't travel any farther south due to the shallowness of the river. The boys backtracked into town and dismounted outside a general store near the dock. Once inside the store, Will recognized the proprietor from when he and Mac had patronized this establishment the year before. He hoped the man didn't recognize him.

Will asked for two pounds of flour and two of cornmeal, plus a spider pan. Then he added two strips of jerky so he and Jonah could eat immediately. That took most of his coins. Jonah added birdshot to their purchases, and that took the last of Will's money. They'd have to live off the provisions he'd bought and whatever Jonah could shoot.

As they headed out of town, Shanty started limping. "We ought to stop at the blacksmith's," Will said. "I want to check his shoes."

"How long'll that take?" Jonah complained.

"Don't matter," Will said. "I won't ride him while he's limping."

Jonah grumbled, but Will dismounted and led Shanty into the smithy. The blacksmith took a look and said, "Got a nail loose in his left hind shoe. Won't take long to fix."

"How much will it be?" Will asked, remembering that he'd spent all his money. "I'm out of coins."

The smith frowned. "What you got to trade?"

Will fingered the Bowie knife in his pocket, reluctant to offer it. The knife had been a gift from Mac. "How about some birdshot?" he asked.

"We might need that," Jonah objected.

"I bought it, and I'm giving it up in trade," Will said. "I won't ride Shanty with a loose shoe."

The blacksmith took the birdshot Will had just purchased, then nailed Shanty's shoe on snugly. When the task was done, he asked, "You boys headed far?"

"Jacksonville," Jonah said, repeating what he'd told the ferryman back in Molalla. "My brother's a prospector. We're joining him."

"How far you come?" the man asked.

"From up north," Will interjected, elbowing Jonah. There was no sense in telling anyone more than they needed to. Not if they wanted to avoid discovery.

"You got a long ride ahead," the smith said. "Jacksonville's about a week's ride from here."

Will's heart sank. Jonah had been optimistic on the length of the trek.

"Roseburg's about two days," the man continued. "Follow the road south out of Eugene. Ain't but one good road to get there."

After thanking the blacksmith, Will and Jonah left the store and headed toward Roseburg, chomping on the jerky they'd bought as they rode.

*May 3, 1864. Bought provisions in Eugene. Out of money, but we ate tonight. It'll be at least a week until we reach Jacksonville.*

# Chapter 22: Worries Back Home

Jenny's cramping continued in the days following the doctor's visit. One morning, she noticed spotting when using the chamber pot, and she took to bed on her own initiative, asking Mac to call the doctor back.

The doctor was firm when he came. "Mrs. McDougall, you must rest," he said. "Stay in bed. Have your meals brought upstairs. Your only chance to save the baby is to be still."

How could she stay in bed? Jenny wondered. She had a family and household to care for.

"It's Will's fault," Mac said, pacing the room after the doctor left. "If the boy hadn't run off, you wouldn't be in such distress."

"I am fearful about Will," Jenny admitted. "But I worry about all the children. Nate's birthday is on Saturday. I need to get ready for that."

"It won't hurt if Nate misses a party this year," Mac said.

"But he's ten," Jenny protested. "That's a big milestone."

"Maria," Mac bellowed.

"Yes, Pa?" Maria said, rushing into the room.

"Can you plan Nate's party?"

Maria looked from one parent to the other. "I think so," she said hesitantly.

"It's too much for her, Mac," Jenny protested. She turned to her daughter. "Talk to Esther and Hannah. They'll help."

Mac sighed. "I'll speak with them, Maria. In the meantime, your mother is not to leave this room." He turned to Jenny. "Agreed?"

Jenny murmured, "All right, Mac." She turned her face toward the wall and wept. Where was William? Would her coming child live? Finally, worn out from anxiety and tears, she slept.

The next morning, Esther Abercrombie and Hannah Pershing visited. Esther was only weeks from delivering her own child and seemed to take up half of Jenny's bedroom. "I'll be glad when this one's out," she declared, clasping her swollen belly. Then in a hushed voice, she said, "I'm sure you'll be fine, Jenny. You and your baby."

"You haven't heard anything from Jonah, have you?" Jenny asked.

Esther shook her head. "Not a word. Daniel has asked everyone. No one saw the boys leave. No one's seen 'em since."

"They'll turn up," Hannah said, plumping Jenny's pillows and helping her to sit up. "This too shall pass."

"Hannah and I have sorted everything out," Esther said. "Maria?" she called the girl, and Maria joined them.

"Now, Maria," Esther continued, "this is what we'll do. Hannah will bake Nate's cake, and we'll all celebrate at my house on Saturday afternoon. Just our three families, but we're large enough to throw a good party for the boy." Esther prattled on about her children's excitement over hosting the celebration. "We'll take care of everything. Maria, all you need to do is get your family ready. I assume Mac can drive you all to my house."

"Yes, Mrs. Abercrombie." Maria's head bobbed.

"And your ma will stay home quietly and rest." Esther turned to Jenny. "Won't you, dear?"

"Yes, Esther," Jenny whispered. When Esther was in her bossy mode, it was best to accommodate her. But oh, how Jenny would hate missing Nate's birthday.

Mac's business interests in Eugene weighed on him, but he didn't want to leave town. He only left the house to pick up mail and check his office for deliveries or notices. Otherwise, he worked out of his small home study.

Byron Pengra had written to inform Mac the Eugene investors wanted to meet to outline their plans for the road survey. But with Will missing and Jenny confined to bed, Mac didn't see any way he could leave Oregon City.

Will and Jonah had been gone a week now with no news. The other children alternated between their usual exuberance and tears over their missing brother. Maria seemed particularly depressed. When Mac asked her what was wrong one evening, she wailed, "What if he's dead? What if we never see Will again?"

Mac wasn't used to dealing with female hysterics—Jenny usually handled the girls' upsets. But he didn't want to bother Jenny with Maria's fears, so he tried to calm his daughter. "I'm sure he's fine," he told her. "Will and Jonah are capable fellows."

Mac chafed at his inability to manage both family and business. He needed to stay home during Jenny's illness, but he also needed to travel to handle his investments. Their child wasn't due until October. Would Jenny be restricted to bed for the next five months? How would the family cope without her?

Then there was Jacob Johnson—another reason Mac dared not leave town. The man hadn't been seen since the attack on Jenny and Will, or so Sheriff Thomas reported. Where could Johnson have gone? Mac didn't believe he'd left Oregon quietly.

Sighing, Mac re-read Pengra's letter, then drafted a response:

*May 5, 1864*

*Dear Mr. Pengra:*

*Unfortunately, pressing personal matters keep me in Oregon City for the foreseeable future. I trust in your judgment regarding the road survey and schedule.*

*I firmly support the need for a new road from Oregon to Boise. Any improved connections between our State and places east of us will improve our economy. While we cannot predict future rail development, I am convinced road travel will be essential in any event.*

*Please continue to keep me informed as to your progress. And rest assured that you will have my funds when needed for this enterprise.*

*Respectfully,*

Mac signed the letter and sealed it. After the noon meal, he would post it.

That evening Mac spent an hour with Jenny in their room before supper. "So Esther and Hannah visited," he said. "Did they plan the party?"

Jenny laughed. "Oh yes. If the Union Army had them for generals, the War would be long over."

"What orders did they leave for me?" Mac asked.

"Only to drive the family to Esther's house on Saturday afternoon."

"I think I can manage that," he said, chuckling.

"Don't be so sure," Jenny said with a smile. "The children will be excited. Especially Nate. You'll need to be sure they all have clean clothes and faces."

"They'll get dirty again out on the farm," Mac said, leaning over to kiss Jenny's cheek.

"But they need to present a good image at the start," she replied. "Oh, Mac," she said, turning serious, "what are we going to do about Will?"

"If I had any idea where to search," Mac said, "I would go after him. But it's pointless without a place to start."

"Esther didn't have any notion where Jonah might have headed either," Jenny said. "She wondered about Portland and a ship, but Jonah has never expressed any desire to sail. She thought about Illinois, where their half-brother Franklin lives, but Frankie left when Jonah was still young, and the boys weren't close. She mentioned Joel, prospecting in the Rogue River Valley, but she doesn't know why Jonah would head there."

"Joel seems the most likely possibility," Mac mused. "But why would Will go with him? Will's never shown any interest in mining."

"He was so upset, Mac," Jenny said. "About Jacob Johnson. About me. About how we reacted after he kissed Maria."

Mac shook his head—he'd done many things during his teenage years without good rationale. And as Jenny noted, Will did have reasons to run away. "When I see Esther on Saturday," he said, "I'll ask her to write Joel. It can't hurt to tell him to watch out for the boys."

Jenny grew bored lying in bed all day. She hadn't noticed any additional spotting, but she still felt occasional cramps. This pregnancy was unlike any of her others. Most of them had been uneventful after the early months of nausea. Even her miscarriage had started as a normal pregnancy until one violent spell of bleeding.

She felt fine most of the time. Only the cramping caused her continued anxiety. And each spate of pain made her anticipate the next, dreading when it might come again.

Over everything lay her fears for William. She'd heard Maria ask Mac, "What if he's dead?" and she had wept alone in her room. She brooded about them all—Maria, Mac, the other children. And William most of all.

She'd been so afraid when she learned she was pregnant that first time— alone, traumatized, not knowing what to expect in childbirth. On the trail, Cordelia Pershing, Esther's mother, and Elizabeth Tuller, the doctor's wife, had befriended her. But neither of them had known the root of her fears— they'd both thought Mac was the baby's father. Doc and Mrs. Tuller later guessed he was not, and Jenny poured out her heart to the older woman. The Tullers urged Jenny and Mac to marry. Perhaps they should have, but Jenny had been too afraid to consider marriage, the brutal attack by the Johnsons and her stepfather still on her mind.

She could talk now about her family's past with Esther and Hannah, both of whom knew her story. But she didn't want to burden them—they had their own families to handle.

Jenny thought of her mother. They'd never been close—Jenny had been more attached to her father than to her mother. She'd received her mother's letter in early April, and with all the worry about Will and the coming child, Jenny hadn't yet responded. She decided to write her mother now, and called Maria to bring her paper, quill, and ink.

Then she sat at the little desk in her room. But what should she write? Mama didn't know her husband Bart Peterson and the two Johnsons had raped Jenny. She couldn't tell her mother about their latest encounter with Jacob Johnson, nor about the reason Will ran away, even though those were the thoughts that haunted her day and night.

And so she wrote:

> *May 6, 1864*
> *Chère Maman,*
> *Thank you for your letter, which I received a*
> *month ago. I am with child again, though I*

*am currently confined to bed and having a difficult time. My oldest boy William has run away from home, and I do not know where he is. The rest of the family is distraught, as am I.*

*. . .*

Jenny stopped. By the time her mother received this letter, William would most likely have returned. Maybe her baby would be healthy, and Jenny could resume her activities.

Or maybe there would be more tragedy to report.

She crumpled up the paper and tossed it toward the fireplace.

# Chapter 23: Along the Applegate Trail

The land was all new to Will as he and Jonah continued their journey south of Eugene. The road deteriorated into not much more than a trail, but contrary to what they'd been told, it was wide enough for a wagon in most places, and Will and Jonah rode side by side when they could.

Mac had told Will about the Applegate Trail. In the late 1840s, the Applegates sought a southern approach into the Willamette Valley after two boys in their family drowned while rafting down the treacherous Columbia River. Mac said learning of the Applegates' experience on the Columbia led him to take their wagon train on Barlow Road around Mount Hood. But Barlow Road had proven almost as dangerous as the Columbia.

Mama also told Will how terrible Barlow Road had been. "I carried you up that mountain just days after your birth," she said, shuddering. "I don't ever want to be so tired again."

Mama had done so much for him, Will thought with a pang. He missed her. He missed Maria and the other girls. He even missed Cal and Nate.

And Mac. There was a hole in Will's heart and mind where Mac had been. And he didn't know how to fill it.

Will had always been proud of being Mac McDougall's son. Mac was a leader in Oregon City, a wealthy man, a kind and good husband and father. Will often wondered if he could live up to Mac's image and expectations. Now he knew that was impossible—Mac wasn't his father.

Will's father was a violent criminal, a vicious rapist. How could he overcome such evil? Could he ever be as easy in his skin as Cal was, knowing what he did about himself?

The store owner in Eugene had predicted it would take the boys two days to reach Roseburg. But by the evening of the second day past Eugene, they still hadn't reached the town. They camped on the banks of a river larger than most of those they'd encountered. "Must be the Umpqua," Jonah said. "That ain't far north of Roseburg."

"How do you know?" Will asked.

"Joel told me. He prospected on the Umpqua for a while. But he says the Rogue River is better diggin's." Jonah sounded authoritative, but Will still questioned whether Jonah's estimate of their location was accurate.

They would find out soon enough.

After they made camp that night, Jonah continued spouting what Joel had told him. "Umpqua's panning ain't great," he said. "But do you think we should try?"

"All we have is the spider pan," Will said.

Jonah shrugged. "Joel says any pan'll do."

"You try," Will said. "But I'd rather you tried fishing." His stomach was full of corn pone, and he just wanted to sit, to leave the activity to Jonah. The horses grazed in their hobbles not far away, and the evening was peaceful. They were higher in the hills now, but still well below the snow line. Will wondered if the trail would take them into snow before they reached Jacksonville.

The Umpqua—if that's what it was—burbled along with a swift current. They weren't far upstream from its confluence with the Willamette, but far enough that the tributary ran clear. Will tried to remember what he'd heard about the Umpqua. Mac told him once about a shipwreck at its mouth, but Will couldn't recall any particulars.

He took out his notebook:

*May 5, 1864. Camped on the Umpqua, we think.*

After a while, as Will dozed, Jonah shouted. "Got one?"

Will sat up. "A nugget?" It couldn't be that easy.

"Nah," Jonah said. "A trout." He splashed up the bank to Will. "I caught it, you clean it."

Will shrugged. "Fair enough. Shall we eat it now or save it for morning?"

Jonah's teeth were chattering. "I got wet enough I wanna keep the fire goin.' Let's eat now."

Will gutted the fish, rolled it in a bit of cornmeal, and fried it. Without any oil or grease, it stuck to the pan, but the boys ate the pieces nonetheless.

Afterward, Will's full belly let him sleep soundly.

The next day, the boys crossed the river and continued south. They arrived at Roseburg in late morning.

"See, I told you it was the Umpqua," Jonah said. They had no money to spend, so there was no point in stopping in town. They skirted the edge of the village and kept riding under the hot sun.

"Sure would like a glass of lemonade," Jonah said.

"Can't without money," Will said. "So no use thinking about it. Cold river water's the best you'll get."

"Think about ices," Jonah said. "A little fruit juice on ice. Wouldn't that taste good?"

"Of course, it would," Will said. "But I'll make do with a full canteen."

Jonah rambled on about fruit and ices until Will wanted to kick Shanty into a trot and leave his friend behind.

"Maybe we should stop early today," Jonah said. "Go for a swim."

That suggestion appealed to Will. "Maybe. Let's see what the next creek looks like."

The trail mostly followed a branch of the Umpqua. In midafternoon, they came to a little creek to the east of the larger river. It wasn't deep, and a gravel bar split the creek in two. "How 'bout stopping here?" Jonah said. "Sun's still high enough to keep us warm. I'm ready for a bath."

"We didn't bring any soap," Will said.

"No need for soap," Jonah said. "Current'll wash us clean enough."

Will agreed. They tethered their horses to bushes on the creek bank and undressed. Jonah plowed into the ice-cold water and cursed, sounding like old Samuel Abercrombie. As Will followed Jonah into the frigid water, he let a few "damns" and "hells" pass his lips as well. What Mama didn't know wouldn't hurt her. He felt his private parts shriveling as he floated in the water, hanging onto a branch to keep from rolling downstream. After he got used to it, the cold creek felt mighty good.

"Bet I can catch a fish with my hands," Jonah said. He nodded at a deep hole by the bank. "Probably a big one over yonder."

"Bet you can't," Will said. "But I don't mind watching you try."

Jonah waded softly toward the hole until he yelled and disappeared. He surfaced once. "Help," he cried, then went under again.

Will splashed after him and grabbed Jonah's arm.

Jonah rose out of the water, sputtering. "Sink hole," he said. "I ain't expected that."

"Can't you swim?" Will asked.

"Not much," Jonah said.

"Then be careful." Will moved away from the sink hole and sat on the gravel bar in the middle of the creek. He kept an eye on Jonah, ready to rescue him again.

Jonah cupped his hands under the water and peered into the waist-deep hole near the bank. The boys remained motionless for a quarter hour or so, and Will started dozing in the sun.

"No good," Jonah called. "I can't see nothin.' Guess we're stuck with corn pone again tonight."

"If you lend me your gun," Will said. "I'll try shooting a rabbit."

Jonah nodded, and the boys found their clothes and dressed. Will took Jonah's rifle and a few shells and found a clearing near the creek bank. He sat and waited for something to appear. Maybe he should have brought the shotgun and the little birdshot they had—he might find quail more readily than rabbit.

But after a bit, as the sun lowered behind the hills, he saw movement. Will aimed, pulled the trigger, then heard a cry. He ran over to the critter—a rabbit.

*May 6, 1864. Passed Roseburg. I shot a rabbit. Best rabbit I ever ate.*

The next day, their ninth after leaving home, the Applegate Trail wound from one creek bed to the next, staying mostly in the lowlands, but sometimes climbing a hill and dropping on the other side. The horses had no trouble with the terrain, but Will wondered how oxen or mules could pull a wagon through the underbrush and up and down the slopes. Maybe the trail had been in better shape in its early days.

And to think this route was supposed to be easier than Barlow Road or rafting the Columbia. His respect rose for Mama and Mac, for Daniel and Esther, and for all the Pershings and Abercrombies who made the journey. Mama and Esther had been younger than Will and Jonah were now, yet they'd cooked and washed clothes like grown women. Mac and Daniel and other men had scouted the unmarked route and led their wagons across rivers and mountains.

Today was Saturday, Nate's tenth birthday, Will realized when they made camp that night. He wondered what festivities Mama planned for Nate. She made each child's birthday a special occasion. Mac sometimes teased her, and Will sometimes did also—though he secretly enjoyed the attention when the celebration focused on him.

Last September, when he turned sixteen, Mama turned their parlor into a dance hall. She invited other youngsters his age, and the party was just for them. Maria was allowed to attend, but none of the younger children. The boys and girls danced together shyly, the boys mumbling their requests and the girls their acceptances. But then, at the harvest dance a month later, Will felt experienced. And again at Christmas parties.

Mama knew what she was doing, showing him with his birthday party he was now grown, a man. He'd had confidence in himself, based on hers in him.

Where would he be for his birthday this year? Who would bake him a cake?

The boys had finished the rabbit Will shot at their noon meal, so in the evening Jonah hunted for another. But no luck. Their dinner consisted of corn pone and water. He could take a day or two of that, but Will looked forward to finding Joel soon and getting a proper meal. Maybe even a proper bed.

*May 7, 1864. No meat tonight. We should reach Jacksonville soon.*

# Chapter 24: Nate's Birthday

Jenny's week passed slowly. She heard the commotion of the household but didn't leave her room. In late afternoons, Maria brought the younger children to see her, and she hugged and spoke with each of them briefly. But Maria took them away when they grew boisterous. Jenny missed their chatter and even their arguments.

Mac came and went. He stayed home through breakfast, she knew, because he brought up her breakfast tray after he ate. He stayed with her while she picked at her food, then took her dishes back to the kitchen. He was usually home for the noon meal, and he repeated his visit while she ate. And again at supper.

From time to time, his deep voice rumbled as he talked with one or more of the children. Sometimes he stuck his head in to check on her while she rested. And at night he crawled into bed beside her and gathered her into his arms.

"How are you feeling?" he asked Friday evening when he came to bed.

"Fine," she said. Then with a sigh, "I can't stay in this room forever. When can I get up?"

"The doctor comes again on Monday," he said, pulling her closer. "We'll see what he says."

"I'll miss Nate's party," she murmured.

"No matter. He'll have others."

"Any word of William?" Her eldest was seldom far from her mind.

"No." Mac heaved a breath against her cheek. "I rode out to Daniel's today. He and Esther haven't heard anything either. And Sheriff Thomas has seen no sign of the boys or Jacob Johnson."

"Did Esther write Joel?" Jenny asked.

She felt Mac nod. "Said she posted the letter yesterday."

"Then there's nothing more we can do," she said.

"No," Mac replied drowsily. After a minute, he relaxed into sleep, his arms growing heavy around her.

Saturday morning Mac was awakened at dawn by shouts from the hallway. "It's my birthday," Nate cried. Sticking his head out into the hall, Mac told the boy to hush, but the rest of the household was already roused.

"Dress and go down for breakfast," Mac ordered, and for once the children rushed to obey.

Twenty minutes later, Mac entered the dining room to find them eating sausage and eggs. Maria aided little Maggie, who held out her sticky hands to Mac for a hug. He kissed the toddler's cheek, then Eliza and Lottie demanded their turn. This felt like the first happy morning since Will had left, now some eight days ago.

How much longer would it be before they found Will?

After they ate, Mac told the children to amuse themselves quietly—they wouldn't leave for Esther's and Daniel's house until almost noon.

When he took Jenny's breakfast tray up to her, she laughed when he told her about the children's antics. "I wish I could go with you." She sighed wistfully.

"I know," he said. "But you need the quiet time to rest. I'm sorry Nate woke you so early."

"No matter," she said. "I wasn't sleeping. I nap so much during the day I can't sleep at night. I lie here and worry about Will."

"I've asked Sheriff Thomas to have Deputy Albee ride by the house while we're out," Mac told her. "But the deputy won't bother you. He'll just check to be sure all is quiet. And Mrs. O'Malley will stay until we return. And I'll put Rufus in the kitchen."

"I don't need—"

"Maybe not," Mac said. "But I'll feel better knowing someone is checking on you. No one knows where Johnson is."

Mac thought Esther outdid herself, despite her advanced pregnancy. The children shrieked and shouted happily and ate more than their fill. When Nate found himself the center of attention of children and adults alike, his head swelled to twice its normal size. Mac had to tell the boy to settle down.

While the children played in the barn and the women gossiped inside, the men sat on chairs and barrels in the yard. The early May afternoon was warm and sunny, and the plum tree Esther had planted years ago was in full bloom.

Samuel Abercrombie accosted Zeke Pershing about his land dispute. Apparently, the creek still maintained its new course, even as the runoff slowed.

"I told you, Abercrombie," Zeke said. "I'll help you dig that ditch as soon as all my crops are planted. But it's goin' more slowly than I'd like."

"Mine, too," Daniel said. "Without Jonah's help, I'm down a worker."

"Don't know why you couldn't keep track of him," Samuel growled to Daniel. "Young Jonah is as unreliable as his pa Franklin Pershing. You shoulda put a firmer strap to the boy when he was a young'un."

Mac's jaw clenched at Samuel's words. Daniel treated Jonah well—as well as Mac treated Will. Mac had never hit any of his children. "Is that how you raised your sons?" he demanded of old Abercrombie. "With a strap?"

"Darn tootin'," Samuel said. "Only way to raise a boy. Both of 'em turned out fine."

"If you raised Daniel so well, he probably handled Jonah just fine." Though he shouldn't bother arguing, Mac thought—Samuel would say whatever he wanted.

The party continued until late afternoon. The children enjoyed themselves, but Mac grew weary of the men's bickering. Samuel Abercrombie had a bone to pick with every man there—after arguing about water rights with Zeke and about Daniel's child-rearing, he started in on Mac's investments.

"Don't know why you put money into steamships and railroads," he told Mac. "What we need is farm roads to town, so's we can move our grain."

"I'm looking into road opportunities as well. A road from Eugene to Boise. Would you like to invest?" Mac asked.

"And loans to farmers." Abercrombie shook a finger at Mac. "You could do a world of good if you charged less interest than them damn storekeepers in town."

"Come see me," Mac said. "I'm happy to finance your needs, assuming we agree on suitable collateral and terms." As he suspected, Abercrombie had no interest in obtaining a loan—he merely wanted to complain.

Later, as Mac harnessed his horses for the ride home, Zeke took him aside. "Heard any more about Jacob Johnson?" he asked.

Mac shook his head. "I asked the deputy to ride by our house today. I didn't like leaving Jenny alone. Not with Johnson on the loose."

"I've asked folks in these parts," Zeke said. "No one's seen any strangers about. Maybe he's gone."

"I hope so," Mac said. "But somehow I doubt it. A man doesn't like to be chased off by a fourteen-year-old girl." He gave a wry grin. "And our women beat him off twice—both Jenny and Maria have pulled guns on him."

As Mac drove the wagon home, the younger children all fell asleep, curled together like a litter of kittens. Nate, the birthday boy, was the first to nod off. Maria sat on the bench beside Mac, and Cal sat right behind him, talking into his father's ear. "Where do you think Will is, Pa?" Cal asked. "Why'd he leave?"

"I don't know, son."

"Do you think he'll come home soon?" Cal asked.

"Maybe, son. Depends on what he's looking for." Mac hoped Will would tire of the adventure soon, but there was no telling.

"Do you think he left because of me?" Cal demanded. "Because I took Maria's horse?"

Mac and Maria both stared at him. "Of course not," Mac said. "I'm sure he had his reasons. Or just wanted an adventure."

Cal moved on to another subject. "When can we go to Portland again? Can I see the telegraph again?"

"I'm not planning any trips while your mother is ill."

"Can I come see your office in town? Can I help you there?" Cal's questions fired one after the other.

Finally, Mac snapped, "Hold your tongue, Cal. I can't hear myself think." And then he felt guilty—he'd reacted just as his father might have reacted when he was young.

Cal sat back with a huff, leaving Mac free to brood about his troubles.

His irritation with Cal. His broken relationship with his father. His business troubles. Abercrombie's continued threats to Zeke. Will's absence. Jenny's difficult pregnancy. Jacob Johnson. Each problem loomed larger than the last.

He pulled the wagon into the carriage house, and Mac asked Cal to unharness the wagon. "I'll be back to care for the horses in a moment." Mac carried Maggie up to bed, then returned to help Cal. The boy's exuberance had returned, and he talked the whole time they curried and fed the horses.

# Chapter 25: Searching for Joel

The trail left the Umpqua and headed due south, moving from creek to creek. The surrounding forest grew denser, with few farms in the area. Will and Jonah shot more small game and caught enough fish to stretch their cornmeal and flour until Sunday. Occasionally, they came across prospectors panning in the streams. Jonah asked them if they knew his brother Joel. The men shook their heads with barely a glance at the boys.

By Sunday afternoon, Will and Jonah reached a much larger river. "It's the Rogue," Jonah said. "It's gotta be the Rogue."

A few houses, a store, and a mill sat near the river. "We should ask how far we are from Jacksonville," Will said. "We're almost out of food again. Maybe we can work in exchange for provisions."

They tied their horses outside the store and walked inside. It was a small establishment, nowhere near as large as the stores in Oregon City, or even the store they'd visited in Eugene.

When they asked for directions, the storekeeper told them, "Two ways to Jacksonville. Trail heads southeast to Applegate, then northwest into Jacksonville. That route is purty well clear of brush, though might still be snow on parts. But the shortest route is to follow the Rogue. It's rough, and snowmelt has the river running wild. Still, if your horses are surefooted, you can make it easy enough."

"How long until we get there?" Will asked.

The man shrugged. "'Bout two days. Three if the trail is snow-covered."

"Let's follow the river," Jonah said. "We might run across Joel if he's prospectin.' We don't know exactly where he is."

"Who's that, young man?" the proprietor asked.

**135**

"My brother, Joel Pershing. Do you know him?" Jonah asked.

The man nodded. "I seen him in here. Late last fall. Said he'd hole up in Jacksonville for the winter. But no tellin' where he is now."

"Any place we can earn some money?" Will asked.

The man frowned at them. "You boys low on supplies?"

"Yes, sir," Will said. "We'd work in your store for flour and pemmican." He nodded at the barrels and bins along the store walls.

"Tell you what," the man said. "You stock shelves and sweep out this room and the barn back yonder, and I'll give you enough food to get to Jacksonville. And you can sleep in my barn tonight."

Will and Jonah worked for the storekeeper until dusk. When the man closed the shop to return to his rooms above the store, he gave them flour and pemmican and more birdshot for Jonah's shotgun as well. "No fires in the barn," he admonished. "But you should be warm enough in the straw."

"Thank you, sir," Will said, and the boys took their bounty to the barn.

*May 8, 1864. Storekeeper let us sleep in his barn. Let us work for food, too.*

Early the next morning, Jonah rousted Will from his bedroll. "Come on," Jonah said. "We're almost there." Will chewed a strip of pemmican as he saddled Shanty, and the boys headed up the Rogue toward Jacksonville.

As the storekeeper said, the Rogue River raged alongside them. Often, the path along the bank was submerged, and they had to pick their way to hills above the river. In some places, cliffs spotted with pines rose steeply from the river's edges. Elsewhere, the watershed widened into a reedy marsh where creeks flowed into the larger Rogue. The current raced through chutes and boulder-lined banks, its sound loud enough to make talking difficult. It was rough country, and Will wondered whether they should have stayed on the Applegate Trail.

But when he shouted the thought to Jonah, his friend started talking about finding gold. "It's in the hills. All around us," he said, waving an arm excitedly. "Joel told me. I hope he's prospectin' this spring. I'd like to find my fortune. I could marry Iris right quick then."

Will thought the miners they'd passed between the Umpqua and the Rogue looked half-crazed, as if they didn't trust anyone and only had eyes for the dirt in their pans. Come to think of it, Joel often had that same expression when he'd visited his family, always spouting off about finding gold.

Maybe running after Joel hadn't been a good idea.

But it was too late for second thoughts, Will decided. They were almost to Jacksonville.

*May 9, 1864. Traveling along the wild waters of the Rogue. Hope to make Jacksonville tomorrow.*

Late in the afternoon of the second day after they left the Applegate Trail, Will and Jonah reached Jacksonville. It was the largest town they'd seen since leaving Eugene. "How we gonna find Joel?" Jonah asked Will.

Will shrugged. "Ask for him in the stores, I suppose."

There were several shops and saloons in town. They dismounted in front of the nearest saloon. Will held the horses, while Jonah ducked inside to ask about his brother. Within seconds, Jonah was outside again.

"Did they know Joel?" Will asked.

"Wouldn't tell me nothin'."

"Let's try a store," Will said, and the boys walked down the street leading their horses.

Jonah went in each establishment to ask about his brother. On his fourth attempt, he came out beaming. "Man inside knows him," he said. "Saw Joel last week, but he don't know where he is now."

"What do we do now?" Will asked.

"Accordin' to this fella, Joel'll be here soon. He said Joel's runnin' mules to Fort Klamath."

"Where's that?" Will hadn't heard of Fort Klamath.

Jonah shook his head. "A few days east of here. Near a big lake."

"We just wait?" Will asked, his stomach sinking.

"What else can we do? We gotta find Joel."

"But we don't know when he'll be here." Will shrugged. "*If* he'll be here. And we're almost out of food."

"We got enough for tonight, ain't we?" Jonah asked. "Let's camp outside town. See what tomorrow brings."

*May 10, 1864. Reached Jacksonville. No sign of Joel, but he was in town recently. I hope we find him soon.*

Tomorrow brought more of the same. They asked about Joel in the last few stores, then also at the livery and forge. The man at the livery said Joel would probably return to Jacksonville the next day. "He's got a string of pack mules," the man told them. "Likely haulin' supplies between Klamath and here."

"How'd he get into that business?" Jonah asked.

The man shrugged. "If it makes him money, Pershing'll give it a go. He ain't fussy. I think the militia hired him."

"What're we going to do today?" Will asked.

"I could hunt," Jonah said. "Or fish. That river looks mighty good for salmon."

"I could use a hand cleanin' out the stables," the livery owner said. "You boys look like you got strong backs."

"We'd work for enough to buy dinner at the hotel," Will said.

The man nodded. Jonah groused about working in the stuffy stables on the fine warm day, but Will insisted they'd be better off eating a real meal for a change, instead of roughing it.

At the end of the day, the liveryman paid them. "Here's an extra ten cents," he said. "It'll buy you some grub for tomorrow as well."

"Will you let us know if Mr. Pershing gets here?" Will asked. "We'll be camped by the river tonight after we eat."

The man smiled. "I'll tell him. And you boys come back tomorrow. I'll keep you busy until he gets here."

*May 11, 1864. Ate fried chicken in the hotel tonight. We might see Joel tomorrow.*

# Chapter 26: Which Child Needs Me More?

Mac hovered in the bedroom Monday morning while the doctor examined Jenny. "You've had no more trouble, Mrs. McDougall?" the doctor asked.

"No," she replied. "And I'm tired of being confined to bed."

"I'll allow you to get up," the doctor said. "But you must stay in the house. No lifting. And a lie-down every afternoon." He smiled. "Same as your toddler. If you have any more pains, I want you back in bed. Otherwise, I'll visit you again next week."

By the time Mac ushered the doctor out and returned to their room, Jenny was dressed and ready to go downstairs. "You should take it easy today," he protested. "Your first day up."

"I'll spend the morning mending," she said. "That's restful enough. You go on to your office. Maria and Mrs. O'Malley will be here."

Mac carried her sewing basket to the parlor, then walked to town. He sorted through his mail, drafted a response to William Ladd in Portland about the status of the bank incorporation, and then wrote Byron Pengra in Eugene to request an update on the road survey.

He was about to return home for the noon meal when Sheriff Thomas stopped by. "You got a minute, McDougall?" the sheriff asked.

"Certainly." Mac leaned back in his chair, trying to seem relaxed, though he couldn't think of any positive reasons for the sheriff to stop by.

"Sounds like Johnson's back in the county," the sheriff said. "Deputy Albee heard tell of a man asking about your family on Saturday."

Mac sat up straight. "And you're only now telling me?"

"Yesterday was the Sabbath," the sheriff said virtuously.

"Is Johnson still in town?" Mac asked.

"No telling. All Albee knows is a man asked about you, your wife, your son—though whoever it was didn't seem to be aware the boy is missing." Sheriff Thomas frowned at Mac. "Is there something I should know?"

Mac shook his head. He still didn't want to reveal the full story to the lawman. "I told you before, my wife and I were acquainted with Johnson back in Missouri. My wife grew up in those parts and was acquainted with Johnson as a child. I had a falling-out with him shortly before we left there."

"What kind of falling-out?"

Mac swallowed, then said, "I told you—he assaulted my wife, as he did here. His father assaulted her as well. I killed the older Johnson in self-defense. Jenny shot Jacob."

Sheriff Thomas cursed. "No wonder Johnson has it in for your family."

"He was in the wrong, Sheriff. He and his father both. They had it coming."

"No matter. He's had years to nurse his grudge. And it seems that's what he's been doing."

"Seems so," Mac acknowledged. He asked again, "Is Johnson still around? How do we keep Jenny safe?"

The sheriff raised an eyebrow. "I don't know where he is now—he ain't been seen since Saturday. You best stay close to home. And Albee and I'll keep our ears to the ground."

After the sheriff left, Mac returned home. As he strode up the hill, he debated how much to tell Jenny. She needed to know Johnson was in the area, but he didn't want to worry her, not while her health was fragile. But any warning he gave would make her anxious.

She would worry not only about their safety, but about Will. A part of Mac had wondered if Johnson had followed Will and Jonah wherever they'd gone—if the ruffian had confronted the boys, maybe hurt them. But it sounded as if Johnson didn't know any more about Will's whereabouts than Mac did.

Jenny beamed as the family ate dinner, seeming happy to be downstairs with the children. She presided over their noon meal with a pleasant chatter Mac hadn't realized he missed until she was back at the table.

After they ate, he asked her to join him in his study. "Sheriff Thomas came to see me this morning," he said, after he sat her in a chair across from his desk. "Jacob Johnson was spotted on Saturday. He asked about our family. But the sheriff doesn't know where he is now."

"Why is Jacob bothering us?" She twisted a handkerchief in her lap.

Mac shook his head. "I don't know, and neither does Sheriff Thomas."

"And William?" Jenny asked, twisting the handkerchief tighter. "Does the sheriff know where William is?"

"No," Mac said. "There's no sign of Will."

"Oh, Mac," Jenny said. "It's been almost two weeks now. Can't you find him?"

Mac rubbed his forehead. "Where do you suggest I look, Jenny? No one has seen any sign of the boys. They could be anywhere by now." He wished he could do more for her, but he didn't know how to begin.

Jenny rested in the afternoon, as the doctor ordered. She'd argued with Mac, more about Will than about Johnson. She was frantic with concern over her son—he'd never been away from her this long in his life. But every time she thought of Johnson, she remembered the rape again. And she could not sleep. She'd tried to put it all behind her, but now that ugly day was in her mind again. This time, the villain menaced not only her, but her son.

When Mac returned home that evening, she begged him again to search for Will. "I don't know where he is, Jenny," he said. "And I'm not leaving you while you're still ailing, let alone while we think Johnson is still around."

What if Johnson found Will before they did? Jenny worried. Would the man kill Will? If not for Maria, Will might already be dead.

Late the next morning, Esther visited Jenny. "Esther—it's so good to see you." Jenny exclaimed in delight as she let her friend in the front door.

"I been shopping," Esther announced. "Got the nesting instinct, with this baby comin' any day." Truly, Esther seemed to get bigger with every pregnancy. She was as heavy as her mother had been on the wagon trek to Oregon. "I'm glad to see you up and about. I thought you might take to your bed for the duration."

Jenny shook her head. "The doctor says I can be up if I stay home. And

141

no lifting. Maggie doesn't quite understand why I don't pick her up."

"Must be nice," Esther said, sighing as she sat in the parlor. "Not to have to tote and fetch. I'm mighty glad to have Cordelia and Abby to help, but I'm still on my feet from morning till night."

"Have a rest here," Jenny said. "And won't you stay for the noon meal?"

"Can't," Esther said, shaking her head. "Got to get home. Cordelia was cookin.' She can manage the kitchen, but if I ain't there, one of my brood'll kill another one."

"You left Cordelia in charge of all of them?" Jenny asked. "Usually you bring one or two with you."

Esther tsked. "Do you realize that girl is older'n we were on the trail?" she said. "And we grew up pretty quick. You were carryin' Will already, and I was carryin' Cordelia soon as Daniel and I married."

"Yes," Jenny smiled, remembering.

"You hear anything about Jonah and Will?" Esther asked. "I can't believe those boys ain't back yet."

"Not a word," Jenny said. "Jacob Johnson was seen, but we've heard nothing about William."

"Why in tarnation would Will drag Jonah with him when he left?" Esther demanded.

"We don't know it was Will's doing," Jenny said, irritated at Esther's assumption. "It could have been Jonah's idea."

"Why would Jonah want to leave?" Esther asked. "Daniel was about to deed over a parcel of land to him, soon as the boy turns seventeen this summer." She sniffed. "Will's the one found out his pa weren't who he thought. He's the one with a reason to run."

"I just hope we find them," Jenny murmured, wondering if Esther was right about Will.

That afternoon Jenny rested again. When the children returned home from school, their stomps and teasing sounded through the walls. She considered getting up to calm them, but Maria shushed the younger girls and sent the boys outside. The family could manage without her, Jenny thought as she sighed and put her hand on her belly—at least this child needed her.

She felt a faint fluttering. So far, the child lived.

And what of William? Jenny wondered. Was he still alive?

She dozed until supper time.

Mac frowned when he saw Jenny come downstairs for the evening meal. "I would have brought you a tray," he said.

"But I want to spend time with you and our children," she protested. "I'm fine. The doctor said."

"You were sound asleep when I got home," Mac said. "I checked on you. You need the rest."

She smiled and moved toward her place at the end of the table without further comment.

Mac didn't want to press her further in front of the children. "Cal," he ordered, "seat your mother."

Cal bounded to her side and pulled out her chair. After she sat, Jenny pasted a kiss on Cal's cheek. The lad winced.

After supper, Mac led Jenny upstairs. "We can sit here as well as in the parlor," he said. "And it will be quieter."

She sat in her rocking chair by the fireplace. Mac started a fire, though the warm evening did not require it. He didn't want Jenny to get chilled.

"I felt the baby move today," Jenny said. "So far, it's healthy."

Grinning, Mac leaned over and placed a hand on her belly. "That's good." He sighed in relief. He still needed to get to Eugene sometime and wondered if he could leave her soon. But with Johnson in the area, it would be best to wait.

"How are your business interests?" Jenny asked him, as if reading his mind. "You haven't mentioned anything recently."

"I didn't want to worry you," he said. Then he explained about Ladd's banking developments and the Eugene group's road surveying project. "I might need to travel to Eugene soon. But it can wait a few weeks." Just until they found Jacob Johnson or learned he had left the area.

# Chapter 27: Joining Up

Will and Jonah worked at the livery Thursday morning, then the proprietor fed them a hearty meal at noon. Will thanked him as he shoveled food in his mouth. "This is pay enough, sir," he said, and the man laughed.

After they ate, Will and Jonah lounged outside the livery. A man rode into town pulling a string of mules behind him. Will nudged Jonah's arm and pointed. "Is that your brother?" He'd only seen Joel Pershing a few times, but the man reminded him of Jonah's oldest brother Zeke.

"Yes," Jonah shouted, and ran to greet his brother.

Joel stopped in the street as Jonah approached. The two brothers gesticulated, but they were too far away for Will to hear their conversation. Joel didn't act happy. After a few minutes, Joel led the mules toward the livery, while Jonah ran alongside Joel's horse.

"Well, Will," Joel said when he dismounted. "Never expected to see you here."

"No, sir," Will said.

"Jonah tells me you're both after prospectin'," Joel said, his face expressionless.

At that point, Will realized Joel didn't want them there. "I'm sorry, sir." He rubbed at his pockmarks.

"Sorry for what?" Joel asked. "For runnin' away? For wantin' to prospect? For searchin' me out? Which is it?"

"Yes, sir," Will said.

"We'll be fine, Joel," Jonah said, with a skip beside Joel's horse. "We can help, you'll see. You can teach us, and we'll help you find gold, and we'll all be rich."

144

"But I ain't prospectin'," Joel said. "I've signed up to run pack mules for the Army."

"The Army," Jonah said, his eyes growing wide. "Are you a soldier?"

"Nah," Joel said. "I'm a contract packer for the Oregon militia. There's an expedition headin' out from Fort Klamath to reconnoiter the Owyhee Basin. The Army wants a better route from Klamath to Boise. And they need pack mules to carry their provisions. I've signed on to lead a string."

"Then there's nothing here for us?" Will asked. Should he and Jonah turn around and head back home? Though he had nothing to do there either.

"I know mules," Jonah said. "So does Will. We been plowin' with Daniel and Zeke for years. We can lead mule teams."

Joel frowned at Will. "I thought your folks lived in town."

"We do, sir," Will said. "But I've spent a lot of time on the farms. I know how to work with mules."

"The militia might not need more packers," Joel said. "And I ain't sure I want to be nanny to you two young'uns for the summer."

"C'mon, Joel," Jonah begged. "We don't wanna go home."

"Why'd you leave?" Joel squinted at his younger brother.

"Daniel treated me like a baby," Jonah said. "Told me what to do right and left, mornin' till night."

"Maybe you needed tellin'. Act like a man, you'll be treated like a man."

"I'm almost seventeen." Jonah stood up straight. "You left home when you was 'bout my age."

Joel sniffed, then turned to Will. "What's your excuse?"

Will shrugged. "Jonah asked me to join him. I had nothing better to do."

Joel frowned. "Your folks know where you are?"

"No, sir." Will shook his head.

"When you aim to tell 'em?" Joel demanded.

"We need to decide what we're doing first, don't we?" Will responded.

"Let us stay," Jonah pleaded. "At least for a while."

Joel stared at the boys until his horse nosed him in the back. He turned to his mount. "I gotta deal with these beasts," he said. "Then we'll see what the officer in charge says."

After tending to his mount and mule string, Joel led Will and Jonah to the Army office in Jacksonville—a set of rooms on the ground floor of a small two-story building near the east end of town. Inside the front room, a uniformed militia officer sat with his feet up on a desk. "What is it, Pershing?" he asked Joel when the three entered.

"Afternoon, Captain Kelly," Joel said, taking off his hat. "You still hirin' mule packers?"

"If I can find qualified men," the captain said.

"My brother and his friend come to town," Joel said. "They want to sign on."

Captain Kelly eyed the boys. "Seem kind of young."

"They're old enough," Joel said. "Jonah farms with mules, and Will says he helps. They're both good with horses. I'd trust 'em with my team."

As Captain Kelly squinted at them, Will stood straighter. He wasn't sure he wanted to run a mule team, but he didn't want to be thought incompetent either.

"Why are you boys in Jacksonville?" the captain asked.

Jonah stuttered about coming to visit his brother, maybe do some prospecting.

The captain cocked an eyebrow at Joel. "You weren't expecting them, were you?"

"No, Cap'n. They surprised me," Joel said.

The officer turned to Will. "You run away?"

Will was silent.

"What about your schooling?"

"I finished the Oregon City Academy, sir."

Captain Kelly sniffed. "Packers have little need for education. You think you can run mules?"

"Yes, sir." Will said, while Jonah nodded.

The officer inquired about their experience. After a few questions to Jonah, he seemed satisfied that Jonah was a farm boy well used to handling mule teams. He interrogated Will further, asking about Will's riding experience. He seemed impressed when Will pointed at Shanty outside the building. "My mount's part Andalusian and part Indian pony," Will said. "He's a good horse. I've ridden him since I was not much more than a toddler."

"You ever trained mules?" the officer asked.

"Not mules, sir," Will said. "But I've helped train plenty of horses. Both for riding and for pulling. I can drive teams behind a wagon or a carriage, and I can manage plow mules. And I know dogs and ponies, and—"

"All right," the captain said. "I'll give you boys a try. We have some time before the expedition begins." He frowned at Joel. "You're responsible for these boys, Pershing. Get them mustered in. Lowest pay grade for both of them."

"Yes, sir," Joel said. "What's the word on when Colonel Drew will get here?"

Captain Kelly shrugged. "I'd like to know that myself." He frowned at Will and Jonah as if he had another thought. "If you boys don't measure up, I'll boot you out. Plenty of men in these parts ready for work. At least you two don't look like you drink much." He peered at the boys. "You don't get lickered up, do you?"

"No, sir," Will responded, glad of a simple question to answer.

"You gotta say you're eighteen to join up," Joel told them as they walked to the quartermaster's office. "So don't balk at the roster when you're told to sign."

"Who's Colonel Drew?" Will asked, hoping he wouldn't have to lie about his age out loud.

"Lieutenant Colonel Charles S. Drew, I'm told," Joel said. "We ain't seen him yet. We're all waitin' on him. Captain Kelly's in charge till Drew gets here. Kelly's a good man."

After the boys signed the pay roster for the militia's contractors, Joel took them back to the livery. "You must do exactly as I say," he said. "We'll be traveling through rough country, rougher'n what you been through to get here. No trails through a good part of it. Only Indian trails in other parts."

"Yes, sir," Will said.

"I still don't understand why you boys are here," Joel said. "What made you leave home?"

"I told you," Jonah said. "Daniel's too rough on me."

Joel snorted. "That ain't likely. Esther wouldn't let him treat you poorly."

"It's true," Jonah protested.

"And you?" Joel asked Will. "Your folks treat you bad?" He sounded skeptical.

"I-I just wanted something different," Will said. He couldn't imagine telling Joel and Jonah that Mac wasn't his father.

"Different." Joel chortled. "You'll get different all right."

He showed them how to cinch the packs on the mules and make sure the straps were tight. "You gotta balance the loads each day afore we head out," he told them. "Or somethin'll come off on the mountain hillsides, go crashin' down to the bottom of the gullies. We're packin' our own provisions as well as the militia's. If you lose somethin', you don't eat."

"Yes, sir," Will said.

Joel cuffed Will on the side of the head, though not hard enough to hurt. "I'm no 'sir,'" he said. "Call me Joel."

*May 12, 1864. Found Joel and joined the militia as a mule packer. What would Mama and Mac think of me now? No word on when we leave Jacksonville.*

The mule packers spent a boring week in Jacksonville waiting to hear when Drew would arrive. Jonah pestered Joel to take them into the hills outside of town to pan for gold. Will thought looking for gold was as good a way to spend the time as any, but he let Jonah argue with his brother.

"Ain't much easy pickin's left around here," Joel said in response to Jonah's cajoling. Joel lazed on his bedroll in the middle of the day.

"C'mon, Joel," Jonah said. "Ain't nothin' else to do."

"You'll wish you could rest once we get underway," Joel said, striking a match to light a cigarette. "Might as well take it easy now."

But the next morning, Joel rousted the boys and told them he would take them prospecting.

Despite the warm spring weather, Will shivered when they stood in the shallow creek that fed into the Rogue River. Plunging the pans Joel gave them into the icy water and sloshing the sediment until it settled was hard work. By the end of the day, Will's back hurt from stooping.

"Ain't as much fun as you thought, huh?" Joel asked his brother.

"Guess you was right," Jonah said. "Not much gold left in these parts. Didn't find more'n a couple flakes."

"Not even worth keeping," Joel said.

When they returned to camp that afternoon, Will wrote,

*May 18, 1864. Panned for gold. Slim pickings and hard*

*labor. Still waiting for word from Lt. Col. Drew.*

"What do you know about this Colonel Drew?" Will asked Joel as they got into their bedrolls that night.

Joel shrugged. "Some soldiers say he's a ditherer—not much of an officer. There's been talk of need for a road from Jacksonville and Klamath to the east for years, but Drew ain't done nothin' about it. Now, finally, he's been ordered to. But he can't seem to shake himself loose from the politics in California. Men been callin' him a Copperhead."

"Then he's a Southern sympathizer?" Will asked.

"Seems so," Joel said. "Lots of other men in these parts are, too. They want the Union to negotiate peace with the Confederates. They think the Army ought to focus on fightin' Indians, not whites."

Will nodded. There were plenty of Rebel sympathizers around Oregon City.

"Drew had charge of building Fort Klamath," Joel said. "Gave a lot of the contracts to his Copperhead friends." He spat. "Jacksonville's become a backwater, no trade comin' south because there's no good road. All the trade to Idaho Territory goes north along the Columbia and into Portland." He kicked at the campfire ashes to find live embers, then lit a cigarette from a glowing twig. "We'll have to see what kind of soldier he is once he gets here."

# Chapter 28: Heading to Fort Klamath

Monday, May 23, began with heavy rain. After tending their horses and mules and eating breakfast, the packers hunkered down in their tents. Every step outside added another layer of mud to their boots.

After the noon meal, Captain Kelly called a muster. The men milled around near the officers' tents, waiting for Kelly to speak. By that time, the rain had lessened to a light mist, but the dank air chilled Will to his bones.

"I received a message from Colonel Drew," Kelly began. "He is still delayed in California. But he has ordered me to lead the militia and our civilian support to Fort Klamath. The reconnaissance expedition will depart from there after the colonel arrives."

"When do we leave Jacksonville?" one of the cavalry sergeants asked.

"At dawn on Thursday," Kelly replied. "Be ready for inspection Wednesday at noon." He turned to the teamsters and packers. "Men, if you have any questions, see Sergeants Crockett, Beaty, or Geisy. Sergeant Crockett will act as quartermaster on this expedition, with the other two reporting to him. Sergeant Beaty will oversee provisions, and Sergeant Geisy will have charge of wagons, packers, and mules."

The next two days were a blur of activity. Will did whatever Joel told him to do. He often fumbled, but he tried his best. The packers turned their horses and mules out to pasture to graze their fill. They cleaned and checked their weapons, examined mule harnesses and panniers, and repaired even the slightest damage to any equipment. They counted and double-counted the provisions. And they washed their clothes.

"Why do I have to wash my clothes?" Jonah complained.

"Might be your last chance for weeks," Joel replied. "May only be in

Klamath for a day or two afore we set out into the mountains."

The men lined up for inspection shortly before noon on Wednesday, as Captain Kelly had ordered. The cavalry lined up on one side of the road out of Jacksonville, with the teamsters and packers on the other side.

Captain Kelly walked the militia line first, commenting on one man's uniform, another man's mount. Then he turned to the civilians. He signaled Sergeants Crockett and Geisy to walk with him. As they passed by Will, the captain nodded, and Will stifled a grin of pride.

Another packer wasn't so fortunate—Captain Kelly looked at how the panniers sat on that man's mules and said to Sergeant Geisy, "Beast is unbalanced. He'll wear blisters before we camp the first night."

The sergeant pointed at Joel. "Show him how it's done." Will stood even straighter, glad to be associated with Joel, whom Sergeant Geisy used as an example.

After finishing the inspection, Kelly shouted at the entire company, "Be ready to leave at dawn."

That evening, Will couldn't help but feel both excitement and trepidation as he wrote in his journal.

*May 25, 1864. We leave for Fort Klamath tomorrow. What will this expedition bring? Can I keep up with the older men? Can I fit in with the militia?*

Will slept poorly and was not ready when Joel rousted them while it was still dark. "Time to leave. Git your gear together."

Jonah moaned, but Will dressed silently. The three of them buckled their saddlebags to their saddles and loaded the mules—two mules each for Will and Jonah, and four for Joel.

When the boys struggled to heft the packs onto the mules, Joel laughed. "This ain't much. Only a hundred pounds or so total. On the expedition, each mule'll carry four packs, and each pack'll weigh at least a hundred pounds." Will swallowed hard, wondering how he would manage to lift so much.

After Joel inspected the ropes securing the packs to the mules' backs,

Will took the leads of his two mules and mounted Shanty. And to think Joel had managed eight mules on the trip from Fort Klamath to Jacksonville.

At Sergeant Geisy's command, they fell into line with the other mule packers. Most of the packers were men about Joel's age, though a few were grey-haired. The other packers led either four mules like Joel, or six. Will and Jonah were the only two packers who had only two mules. They plodded along in single file out of Jacksonville, each leading their mules.

It was a four-day trek from Jacksonville to Fort Klamath with the lightly loaded mules. For two days they climbed into the Cascades east of Jacksonville until they reached the path through the divide. On a rest break right past the summit, Will stared at the land ahead of them. Tall pines still covered much of the land, but the ground became noticeably more arid, and sage spotted the open areas. He'd never been east of the Cascades before— already he was in unfamiliar territory.

Then for two more days they descended the hills toward Fort Klamath. Long before the fort came into view, Will saw a large lake surrounded by green marsh. "Lake Klamath," Joel told him. "Fort is on the eastern side, a few miles to the north."

The four-day trip to Fort Klamath exhausted Will. He thought he and Jonah had ridden hard on their journey to Jacksonville, but the cavalry mule train was far more demanding. They were fed well, but they had to care not only for their horses but also for the mules. Each evening, the packers unloaded the packs from the mules so the beasts could rest. And each morning they loaded the mules again.

*May 29, 1864. Fourth day out from Jacksonville. I can heft the mule packs by myself now. Though Joel says heavier loads will come. Should reach Klamath tomorrow. I hope we get a rest before Lt. Col. Drew arrives.*

The expeditionary force arrived at Fort Klamath late in the afternoon of May 30 after a long, hot day descending the eastern foothills of the Cascades. Once out of the mountains, the men and their beasts crossed an open plain leading to the fort. Tall grass covered much of the plain, grass that would likely be cut for hay.

Fort Klamath had only been constructed the year before, Joel told them.

"Captain Kelly built it. He and Company C of the First Oregon Cavalry Militia. Just opened last year."

"I thought you said Drew built the fort."

Joel snorted. "Drew was the commander, but Kelly led the actual work. I like Kelly. Drew—we'll have to see."

As they approached the fort, Will could identify the stables and two large barracks. But smaller structures dotted the grounds as well. "What are all those buildings?" he asked Joel, waving his arm at the fort.

"Well, you see the barracks. And the stables."

"Yes, but what are all the other buildings?" Will pressed.

"Officer quarters." Joel pointed at some small houses. "The guardhouse, of course. And the offices, arsenal, hospital, and some storehouses."

"Why ain't there a stockade around the fort?" Jonah asked.

"Guess it ain't been built yet," Joel said. "Don't know what Kelly intends next."

"Why was the fort placed here?" Will asked.

"Protection from Indians," Joel replied. "A lot of people movin' to these parts. Some come for gold. Some for land. Some just want to escape the War. But the tribes threaten 'em all."

"Escape the War?" Will asked. "Are there deserters?" He wondered if Jacob Johnson would head south. He never wanted to face the man again.

Joel nodded. "I seen some."

They entered the grounds of the fort, unpacked their mules near the storehouses, and turned their horses and mules out to pasture. At least the pastures were fenced, so the fort needed only a minimal guard for the animals.

"We'll get worked into the guard roster soon enough," Joel said. "So let's eat and pick out a campsite."

Only the cavalry could bunk in the barracks. The civilian teamsters and packers camped in an open field near the fort, setting up their tents and cooking utensils.

Will was thankful not to have guard duty the first night. He clambered into his bedroll with his journal and wrote:

> *May 30, 1864. Fort Klamath is a rough outpost. Not much to recommend it. I wonder if this is like the forts Mama and Mac encountered on their journey to Oregon.*

# Chapter 29: A Possible Lead

As the days wore on and Jenny's health improved, Mac decided he should no longer delay his trip to Eugene to meet with Byron Pengra and the road construction group. He could invest his funds without this meeting, but he wanted a better understanding of the consortium's plans. Was this the best place to put his money? His finances were still precarious.

On May 31, Mac took the steamboat upstream to Eugene. The trip took most of the day, but he arrived in time for supper at a hotel near the dock. After he ate, Mac sat at his table sipping a cognac. The last time he'd left home was his trip to Portland the day Jacob Johnson attacked his family— how long ago that seemed now, though it was less than two months ago. Their family would never be the same again.

The next morning, Mac met with Pengra and his partners. "We have incorporated our operation as the Oregon Central Military Road Company," Pengra said, puffing on a cigar. "At this point our investments are minimal, but we will expand soon."

"Why the delay?" Mac asked.

"We're pursuing grants from Congress," Pengra said. "We hope the federal government will deed public lands along the road to our company in compensation for the public good our road will achieve. Then we can sell the land to finance the road construction and compensate our investors."

"You think the government will award you land?" Mac queried. "Isn't that premature?"

"Railroads receive grants of this nature. Our road is the first step toward rail development in this portion of Oregon." Pengra folded his arms across his belly. "If we can obtain alternate sections of public lands along the road's right of way, same as the railroads are granted, then we will be able to profit from our enterprise." He leaned toward Mac. "Are you with us?"

Mac considered the matter. Oregon could not grow without better roads. Ultimately, a railroad would be necessary to tie the state to the East. But as Pengra said, a road would have to come before the railroad. He nodded. "I am. What do you need from me?"

"At this point, we want a pledge for one thousand dollars," Pengra said, as the other men smiled at Mac. "Whether we will need more funds depends on how soon we complete the survey and whether Congress acts expeditiously. Of course, we cannot promise any profit from this enterprise, though we believe future land sales will justify our investments."

"In other words," Mac said, raising an eyebrow, "you can't predict what will happen."

Pengra shrugged. "We have no control over Congress, though there are several representatives who favor our cause. But there will be no profits until after the road is built and we sell the lands Congress grants us."

"I'll invest at this point because I agree Oregon needs better roads," Mac said. "But I cannot commit to anything more than the thousand dollars you are asking for now. Not until your plans for this enterprise are more certain."

Pengra nodded. "I understand."

After the meeting, Mac had a little time before the steamship departed on its downstream trip to Oregon City. The day was warm, and it was a pleasure to wander outside in the commercial area near the dock.

He saw a store he'd patronized before, a general store near the river. He strolled inside to buy candy for the children. He gathered licorice strips and peppermints, as well as the hard lemon candies Jenny liked, and took them to the counter. As he counted out the coins, he told the proprietor the candy was for his family back in Oregon City.

"Saw your son in here a few weeks back, Mr. McDougall," the proprietor said. "He and another boy."

"My son?" Mac asked in surprise.

The man nodded. "I recollect you and him comin' in my store last summer. He didn't give his name, but his companion called him Will. That's your boy's name, ain't it?"

"Will was here? When?" To his own ears, Mac's tone sounded strident.

The storekeeper's eyebrows shot up. "I don't rightly remember the date," he said. "Sometime early in May, I suppose. I ain't as good with dates as with names and faces." He frowned. "Is there a problem?"

"Will ran away," Mac said. "We haven't seen him since late April. This is the first news I've had of his whereabouts. Did they say where they were headed?"

"I don't think they did," the man said, stroking his beard.

"Did he mention Jacksonville?" Mac asked, thinking of Joel Pershing. Will didn't know anyone else to the south. "Or a Joel Pershing?"

The proprietor shook his head. "I think I woulda remembered if he'd said a name, but I don't."

The blast of the steamboat sounded, signaling its imminent departure. Mac debated whether to stay in Eugene another day and ask others in town whether they'd seen Will. But Jenny expected him tonight. "Let me leave you my address in Oregon City," he told the storeowner. "Please send word if you remember anything else."

As he rode the steamboat north, Mac wondered how Jenny would take the meager news. All the storekeeper knew for certain was that a boy had been in his store, a boy whose companion called him Will. The man hadn't heard Jonah's name. He hadn't heard Joel's name. He hadn't heard any reference to Jacksonville. It was the flimsiest of information.

Jenny sat in their room lengthening Nate's trousers as she waited for Mac to get home. She expected him shortly before supper, soon after the steamboat was scheduled to dock.

He arrived when she'd predicted. "How was your business?" she asked when he came upstairs.

"Fine," he said. "Pengra and his partners have thought through their plans. I think their road is worth my investment, though their goals may be overly optimistic." He described the meeting.

She listened with half an ear. "So your trip was worthwhile?" she asked when he finished, turning back to her mending.

"For more reasons than that." Mac hesitated, then blurted, "A storekeeper in Eugene thinks he saw Will a few weeks ago."

"William!" Feeling her heart jump, Jenny dropped the half-hemmed trousers to the floor. "In Eugene? Why would he go there?"

Mac held up his hands. "All the man said was that two boys came into his store, one called the other Will, and he thought one boy looked like our Will.

I'd taken Will into the store last year."

"When did this happen?" she asked, wanting every bit of information Mac could give her.

"He wasn't sure. Sometime in early May."

She stood and grabbed Mac's lapels. "You have to go back to search for him."

"Jenny, I questioned the man as best I could. He didn't know where Will was headed. If it was Will. He wasn't sure. And I'm not either. As you said, why would Will go to Eugene?"

"But it's our only clue," Jenny protested. "We need to tell Esther and Daniel. Maybe Daniel can go after them." She paced the room. "Esther's confinement is so soon. Daniel can't go." Her skirts whirled as she turned back to Mac. "You have to return to Eugene."

"Let me talk to Daniel. I'll go see him tomorrow," Mac said.

The next morning, June 2, Mac left for Daniel's farm shortly after breakfast. He spoke to Esther at their house. "There's been a possible sighting of the boys in Eugene," he told her, and he described his encounter with the storekeeper.

"Was it Jonah and Will?" she asked, pressing her hands to her chest above her swollen belly. "Have we found them?"

"Not yet," Mac cautioned. "Possibly they were in Eugene a month or so ago. We aren't sure. And we don't know where they went from there."

"They must have gone to see Joel," Esther said. "I wrote him, but I ain't heard back yet. He's a poor correspondent. He might not write, even if they show up on his doorstep."

Mac cleared his throat. "Where's Daniel today? I want to speak with him about our next steps."

"He's cuttin' timber with his pa and our Sammy," Esther said. "In the woods between our claims."

He tipped his hat to Esther and left. It was too bad Daniel was with his father—the elder Abercrombie would surely interfere.

Mac found the men where Esther said they'd be and called out as he approached. Daniel walked over. Old Samuel leaned on a bandsaw and spit a stream of tobacco juice, and Sammy waited with his grandfather. Mac dismounted to speak with Daniel.

"What is it?" Daniel asked, and Mac described his meeting with the Eugene storekeeper again.

Initially, Daniel thought they should investigate further. "But I can't leave home till after Esther has the baby. Our Cordelia can handle the household, but I don't want her responsible for the birthin.' If the Tullers were still alive, I'd get Mrs. Tuller, but—" He shrugged.

"What about Hannah Pershing?" Mac wasn't eager to embark on a wild goose chase, but if Jenny insisted he go, he wanted Daniel with him.

"I don't know," Daniel said. "We have so many young'uns now, it's hard for anyone to look after 'em all. And you're not sure it's worth the trek to Eugene."

"No, I'm not," Mac said, glad Daniel agreed with him. He'd wondered why Jenny and Esther were so sure the sighting in Eugene was true. He hoped he cared about Will as much as Jenny did, but maybe he didn't. Maybe that's why this lead on the boys' whereabouts didn't seem substantial enough to pursue.

Daniel continued to plan out loud. "But after Esther's confinement, I can go. Pa can deal with the timbering and Zeke with my crops. They can manage while I'm gone. How long do you think a trip would take?"

Mac threw out his hands. "I have no idea. We don't know anything except the boys might have traveled through Eugene. In the meantime, we'll wait to see if Joel responds to Esther's letter."

# Chapter 30: Supply Train

Lieutenant Colonel Drew was not at Fort Klamath when the cavalry and mule trains got there. For two days, the reconnaissance unit milled about the fort with little to do. The sergeants kept the soldiers doing drills, but the civilian packers received little supervision. Only Sergeant Geisy paid the packers any mind, and he harangued them daily over caring for their horses and mules. He also put them on alternating day and night guard duty. But when they weren't occupied with these tasks, the packers' time was free.

Jonah went fishing in a creek near the fort, and Joel hung around the campsite with the older packers.

Will took out his Bowie knife and scrounged a small piece of a fallen oak limb to start whittling. Before long, the rough shape of a mule emerged from the wood. By evening, Will was bored, and pulled out his journal.

> *June 1, 1864. Heavy rain today. First rain in many days. I'm carving a mule. So far, Army life doesn't have much to recommend it—it's mostly waiting, with occasional hard work thrown in. And no sleep when I have night guard duty.*

About noon on their third day at Klamath, a soldier rode into camp and delivered a message to the fort adjutant's office. An hour later, Sergeant Geisy called the packers together. "Cap'n Kelly wants to talk to you," he told them. "Look sharp when you fall in."

Some of the men were away from the fort, but Will, Joel, and Jonah were among those who gathered. "Colonel Drew is further detained," Kelly announced. He seemed perturbed but did not elaborate on the reasons for

Drew's delay. "We will not leave for the Owyhee Basin for several weeks."

Some packers grumbled, but Joel murmured to the boys, "As long as we get paid, I don't mind. I'll take the easy life."

"To earn your keep," Captain Kelly continued, as if he'd heard Joel, "you packers will haul supplies between Fort Klamath and the public storehouse in Jacksonville."

At that, the grumbling increased, and now Joel joined in.

"You will be paid per pound of freight hauled, instead of per diem," Kelly said. "The more you haul, the more you'll make. There's an opportunity here for those of you who work hard."

"We'll have to hustle," one man muttered. "Pound rate ain't likely to be much."

"How long will we run supplies?" another packer shouted.

"I don't know," Kelly said. "Until the colonel arrives. You start on Saturday."

*June 3, 1864. We leave on a supply run tomorrow. Back across the Cascades to Jacksonville with laden mules. Loading my mules will be hard. Joel is upset about the pay.*

The next morning, the packers rose before dawn. Will washed down ham and biscuits with coffee. "Won't eat this well on the trail," Jonah grumbled.

"That's up to you," Joel said. "We'll be cookin' for ourselves. No quartermaster on the supply runs." The packers were to carry their own provisions on their mules. Sergeant Geisy and a small cavalry squad accompanied the packers, but they had no other military support.

The mules were heavily laden for the supply trip, each mule carrying four panniers weighing about one hundred pounds each. The packers loaded the panniers each morning and unloaded them at night. The only diminution in weight was what the packers ate each day.

Will struggled to load his two mules, which left his muscles quivering by the time he pulled himself into Shanty's saddle to ride.

The journey itself was wearying. Some of the snow melted in the pass, but at the summit it was still deep underfoot, requiring careful footwork by the horses and mules. As with the trek from Jacksonville to Klamath, it took four days for the return trip to Jacksonville.

Will slept well but awakened each morning with aching muscles. Shanty seemed content enough, as long as he could graze. But Shanty didn't have to load and unload the mules.

Will sat by the campfire on the last night before they arrived in Jacksonville. He wondered if he could find a way to leave the expeditionary force.

*June 6, 1864. We will arrive in Jacksonville tomorrow. I signed the militia contract, so I suppose I must continue. But I can't see how running mules on a supply train will improve my future.*

When they arrived back at Jacksonville on June 7, the mining town felt familiar to Will. After the packers unloaded their supplies at the public storehouse, Sergeant Geisy told them, "You're free tonight. Post a guard for the animals, but anyone not on duty can do as he pleases. Tomorrow we'll rest, then head back for Klamath on Thursday."

Will and Jonah were assigned to guard duty the first night. "You boys ain't drinking anyway," Joel told them. "You'll get your night in town tomorrow." And Joel left for the saloons with the other packers.

The next day, Will and Jonah wandered through the shops in town. They greeted the livery owner who had befriended them before they found Joel. The man offered them a hot meal in exchange for mucking out his stables. The boys agreed, not wanting to cook.

In the afternoon, they packed the panniers with goods to take back to Klamath. Afterward, Jonah wheedled Joel to take him to the saloons in the evening.

"Ain't no way I'm takin' you with me," Joel said. "Esther'd have my hide if I let you drink at age sixteen."

"Bet you had your first drink afore you was sixteen," Jonah said.

"Bet I did." Joel frowned at his younger brother. "You boys show yourself capable on the return trip to Klamath, and I won't keep you outta the saloons when we come back to Jacksonville the next time."

Jonah had to accept that as his answer. Will didn't mind. He'd tasted whiskey and didn't much care for it. He wondered at what age a man took a liking to alcohol.

Joel staggered into their camp near dawn. In the morning, Will was the first packer out of his bedroll, but despite his drinking Joel was ready about the same time Will was. The pack train left Jacksonville as soon as they loaded their mules.

As they climbed into the Cascades, the sun beat down brightly. Sweat trickled down Will's cheeks from his hat brim, and his shirt stuck to his back. Even his gloves were damp with sweat. But he didn't dare ride without gloves—he'd have blisters on his palms and every finger if he did.

On the second day of the return trip, they went through the pass, again picking their way through slushy snowfields. By the time they descended into the heat again, Will welcomed the warmth.

"Why are we doing this?" Jonah asked Joel, midmorning on their third day back toward Klamath. "Takin' these supplies twist Klamath and Jacksonville? This ain't like any soldiering I ever heard of."

"We're earnin' our keep, boy," Joel responded. "So take it like a man. Army pays us to do what they ask. If Cap'n Kelly tells me to haul goods, that's what I do. Though I'd prefer to hole up one place or the other till Drew arrives."

The supply trips between Fort Klamath and Jacksonville became tedious. The route remained a challenge, moving from the desert heat of Klamath to the mountains and through the snowy pass, then downhill to Jacksonville. The mules were steady on their feet, despite the heavy packs. But the beasts could be cantankerous.

One morning on their second trip from Klamath to Jacksonville, Will hefted a hundred-pound pannier onto one jack mule. The animal stepped away causing the pack to fall to the ground. The momentum took Will with it. He cursed while Jonah laughed at him. "All your book learnin' ain't made you as smart as that ol' mule, has it?" Jonah said, chuckling.

"Damn mule," Will muttered as he picked the pack up again. The mule shifted again, but this time Will was ready and kept his balance. "Hold the damn beast steady, won't you?" he asked Jonah.

Jonah did so, braying as loudly as the mule, until Will finally got the beast loaded.

As they rode through the pine-scented forest that morning, Will wondered whether he'd rather be back in Oregon City. However miserable he'd been at home, life there was a lot more comfortable than leading ornery mules along a snow-packed trail.

That night he wrote:

*June 15, 1864. If it weren't for the accursed mules, riding through this country might be pleasant. Though I miss my bed and Mrs. O'Malley's cooking.*

The next morning, Will was slow to load his mules, not wanting to repeat the experience of the day before. He tied his two mules to each other, then worried that if one shied, they both would. They might even run off, which would cost him time to retrieve them.

"Hurry up," Joel shouted. "We ain't got all day. We'll be eatin' the others' dust as it is." His four mules were loaded, as were Jonah's two. "Go help him, Jonah."

"Now you got us in trouble," Jonah said, as he did what Joel ordered. "Tomorrow, you owe me some help."

As Joel predicted, the three of them brought up the rear of the pack train that day. At least the snow in the mountains was well packed by the animals ahead of them. But Will smelled the other equines' fresh dung all day, and flies pestered man and beast alike.

Hauling supplies was not a job Will relished. Nor did he like the military regimentation, doing everything by another man's schedule, following the group. He remembered Mac telling him he'd chafed at following foolish orders. "Why do we have to stick together?" he asked Joel on the noon break. "Can't we split up and go at our own pace?"

"Indians," Joel said simply. "It's safer to stay in groups. We only got one cavalry squad to protect us." He turned and caught each boy's eye. "You listen to me on this. Don't go off on your own, you hear?"

Will and Jonah nodded.

They arrived at Jacksonville again on Friday, June 17. After they unloaded their supplies, Sergeant Geisy announced an extra day in town. "Rather than leave on the Sabbath," he told the packers, "we'll wait until Monday. Supplies don't need to move so fast you can't have a restful

Saturday night." He flashed a wicked grin.

"Joel," Jonah said, "will you take us to the saloon? You promised."

Joel nodded. "You've earned it. But if the barkeep throws you out, I ain't leavin' with you."

"They won't throw us out if we're with the cavalry and packers," Jonah scoffed. "We ain't that young."

Jonah was right. No one looked twice at Will and Jonah when they entered the bar and ordered their whiskey. Will sipped his slowly, shuddering as it burned his gut. Jonah started slowly as well, but soon ordered a second.

When Jonah finished his second drink, Joel cuffed him on the side of the head. "You two young'uns better head to camp," he told his younger brother and Will. "You've had enough."

"What about you?" Jonah challenged.

"I'm used to drinkin.' I'll be back soon enough." But Will saw Joel wink at a scantily clad woman across the room.

"You gonna spend time with that whore?" Jonah asked.

"Esther'd have my hide for sure if I taught you more bad habits," Joel replied.

Will swallowed hard as he stared. The woman's breasts were almost fully bared. He wondered if Maria's mother had dressed similarly. Then he and Jonah ambled out the door and back to their campsite. He didn't hear Joel return, but the older Pershing spent most of Sunday sleeping and lollygagging around camp.

And so the days passed. The supply train hauled cargo back and forth from Jacksonville to Klamath. Will learned to predict most of his mules' wiles and counter them. He grew easier in the rough mountain terrain. He even enjoyed the days outside as the weather warmed and the snow melted—though snow remained on the mountaintops of the Cascades the entire time.

Pay from hauling freight on two mules wouldn't make him wealthy, but it was enough to feel he was earning a man's wage, an honest living. Jonah spouted about how he'd never go back to farming, but Will had already decided the life of a packer was not for him—he had to fulfill his obligation on the expedition, but then he would leave.

But what then? Would he work outside or mostly in an office like Mac?

Even Mac enjoyed spending time outside. A man in the West needed to be comfortable in the fresh air, and Will was a man of the West.

*June 21, 1864. Heading to Klamath. I wonder if the reconnaissance expedition will be harder than these back-and-forth treks to Jacksonville. How will I adapt when we move into uncharted wilderness? Surely, if Mama and Mac could handle the Oregon Trail, I can manage in the militia.*

# Chapter 31: Abercrombie Interferes

On Sunday, June 19, Mac took his family to church. After the service, Daniel approached Mac. "Esther had a baby girl Thursday. Esther'n the baby are doin' well, but we ain't settled on a name yet. I can go to Eugene soon, if you still wanna go."

"What if we leave Tuesday?" Mac suggested. "On the steamboat. We might need to stay a few days if we learn where the boys went after Eugene. But if not, we could return on Wednesday."

Daniel agreed.

But Monday morning as Mac dealt with his pending correspondence in his office, Milton Elliott, an attorney with an office down the street, walked in. "Morning, McDougall," Elliott said. "Do you still represent Ezekiel Pershing? You've handled legal matters for him in the past."

Mac stood and shook the lawyer's hand. "Does Zeke need representing?" he asked.

"He will," Elliott said. "I'm filing a lawsuit this morning on behalf of Samuel Abercrombie. I've brought you a copy."

Mac swore as he took the proffered papers. "What does Abercrombie allege?"

"That Mr. Pershing has reduced Mr. Abercrombie's water rights." Elliott gestured at the papers. "Apparently, the two men have a dispute over a creek channel."

"Did you try talking to Pershing?" Mac asked as he skimmed the document. It dealt with the shift in the waterway from its former location. "I've spoken to them both. I thought they'd resolved their differences."

"Not to Mr. Abercrombie's satisfaction," the attorney said. "Good day."

He tipped his hat and left.

Mac put aside his correspondence and went home to saddle Valiente. He would have to talk to Zeke. He wondered whether he and Daniel could leave town tomorrow if he had to deal with this lawsuit—assuming Zeke wanted Mac to represent him. Still, Mac thought he was the best person to try to settle the dispute between Abercrombie and Zeke—he'd known them both for more than fifteen years.

He rode first to Zeke's claim and found him tilling corn fields. "Damn weeds," Zeke said, wiping his brow against the heat of the day. "Can't stay ahead of 'em."

"Here's something else to get ahead of," Mac said, handing Zeke the legal papers. "Abercrombie is suing you."

"Again?" Abercrombie had sued Zeke years ago over another land dispute. That had been resolved in Zeke's favor, and Abercrombie still bore a grudge. "We whupped him last time."

"I don't see how he wins this case either," Mac said. "But we need to respond in court. Unless we can get him to drop the matter."

Zeke snorted. "Abercrombie drop a lawsuit? That'll be the day."

"I'm going to visit him next. Find out what he says."

"Ain't you leavin' town tomorrow? You'n Daniel?" Zeke asked.

"I'd planned to. But maybe we should delay. I don't like leaving you to deal with Samuel while I'm traveling with his son. It's been so long since the boys left that a week's delay probably won't make any difference."

"I hate to see you lose a chance to find Jonah and Will," Zeke said. "That old bastard Samuel probably filed the case now just to spite us."

"If so, he's succeeding," Mac said.

He then rode to Daniel's claim and found Daniel and his father both working there. By now, the hottest hour of the afternoon bore down on them all. Mac was increasingly irritated at Samuel's fractiousness. "Fancy finding you both," he began. "What's the purpose of your lawsuit against Zeke?" he asked the elder Abercrombie.

"Ask my lawyer," Samuel responded, leaning on his hoe. "He said it's the only way to settle the matter once and for all."

"What matter?" Daniel asked, looking bewildered.

"Your father sued Zeke," Mac snapped. "Because the creek channel

**167**

shifted."

Daniel frowned. "But Zeke said you could have the water, Pa."

"Zeke's word don't make it so," Samuel said. "I want it written down."

"Will you drop the lawsuit if he gives you a written easement for the water rights?" Mac asked. Maybe this matter could be resolved. But not by tomorrow.

"I need to talk to my lawyer," Samuel said. "See what he says."

Mac shook his head. Samuel had no problem giving his own opinion on most matters, but when it served him to rely on someone else for delay or chicanery, he did so. "Do I have your permission to negotiate a settlement with your attorney?" Mac asked.

Samuel shrugged. "Do as you please. I ain't sayin' what I'll agree to yet."

Mac turned to Daniel. "We should delay our trip to Eugene. I hate it, but I don't feel right leaving Zeke alone to deal with your father and his lawyer."

"Pa—" Daniel began.

"You ain't likely to find them two rapscallions anyway," Samuel said. "They's probably sailed for China by now. Jonah's just like his pa—Franklin Pershing was a foolhardy drunk."

Daniel glared at his father. "Jonah is my son in all but name, and I'll thank you to—"

"He ain't your son, not in name and not in blood. He's Franklin Pershing's, and he's no better'n his father."

The feud between the Pershings and Abercrombies had gone on since they'd met. Marriages between the families hadn't helped. Sharing farm duties on their claims hadn't helped. And it wouldn't help for Mac to respond to Samuel's harsh words now.

Despite Mac's allying himself with the Pershings, Abercrombie usually treated Mac with grudging respect. That could end if Abercrombie learned of Mac's and Jenny's past. Abercrombie didn't know Mac wasn't Will's father, and Mac didn't want him ever to know. If Samuel found out, he'd likely use the information against Mac and his family. No point in riling the bitter old man now.

Jenny was furious when Mac told her he and Daniel would postpone their trip to Eugene because of Samuel Abercrombie—another delay in finding her son. "I've a mind to talk to Samuel Abercrombie myself," she fumed as she paced the parlor.

"I don't think that's wise, Jenny," Mac said in a soothing tone that irritated her further.

"How can you let him do this?" she demanded. "Don't you care William is traveling farther and farther from us every day? He's been gone for weeks now." Her throat caught on the last few words.

"We don't know he's still on the move," Mac said. "We don't even know whether he and Jonah were in Eugene."

"But it's the only clue we have," she wailed. She crossed her arms over her stomach. Will seemed lost to her, and the life of the child she carried felt equally precarious. She prayed for God to protect them both. She wanted her family back together, all safe. She wanted the normal bedlam of family life they'd enjoyed before Jacob Johnson intruded. Now, Will and Maria knew of her darkest moment, a day she'd tried so hard to bury for so many years. Will hadn't been able to handle the knowledge, and her loving family was gone.

"I'll still go to Eugene," Mac said, taking her into his arms. "It won't be long."

Jenny sagged against him, but his embrace didn't comfort her. "When?" she asked, her voice muffled in his shirt. She wanted to run after Will herself, but she couldn't, not while pregnant. "When will this all end?"

"Abercrombie says he'll consider a settlement. I need to work that out with his lawyer. It'll only take a few days," Mac said, his hand moving gently up and down her back. "We'll find Will."

But would they? Jenny wondered. Would she ever have William home again?

By the end of the week, Mac and Abercrombie's lawyer had worked out the terms of a written lease permitting Samuel to have a ditch dug, just as Zeke had promised him weeks earlier. The agreement specified how much water Samuel could take from the creek, what would happen in low water seasons, and even how much Zeke would contribute to the building of the ditch and pond to capture the water.

"We can leave next Tuesday," Mac told Daniel. "I'll trust your father and Zeke to dig the ditch and pond while we're gone. Abercrombie's attorney has agreed to supervise the construction. He's a good man." With a bad client, Mac thought, though he didn't say so—he tried to keep his feelings about Samuel out of his dealings with Daniel.

"I'll be ready." Daniel said. "I'm glad of the extra week at home. Esther's now fully up and about after Martha's birth. Bustlin' about like she always does."

"You named the baby Martha?" Mac asked with a smile. "How did you decide on that?"

Daniel shrugged. "We're runnin' out of names. We have a George already. Martha seemed to fit."

On Tuesday, June 28, Mac and Daniel boarded the steamship south to Eugene. They brought their horses and extra clothing, and Mac had cash to buy provisions, in case they needed to travel beyond Eugene. "Depends on what we find," Mac told Jenny as he packed. "We might get to Eugene, learn nothing, and come straight home."

She took his arm, gripping it. "If you hear anything that indicates where William has gone, you must follow that lead. Find our boy. Please."

He kissed her. "I'll do my very best." He hoped he could give Jenny what she wanted most—Will home safely.

After watching Mac ride Valiente toward the ferry dock, Jenny took her knitting to the parlor. She tried to work on a baby blanket for Esther. She hadn't seen Esther's new baby yet, and she hoped to take the gift to Esther soon.

Jenny had promised Mac she would stay in the house while he was gone. But she couldn't focus on her knitting. She had no idea how long Mac would be gone, no idea where Will was, no idea whether her next child would be born healthy. She dropped a stitch, then stuffed the half-done blanket in her sewing basket in frustration. She couldn't sit at home waiting.

Esther would be waiting as well. Jenny decided to take her knitting to Esther's house.

She called to Maria, "We're going to visit Esther."

"But Pa said to stay home," Maria protested.

"I can't simply sit here, Maria," Jenny said. "You can come with me, or

I'll go alone."

Maria sighed as if she were mothering Jenny. "I'll harness the horses."

Jenny asked Mrs. O'Malley to watch the children, little Maggie and the others who were out of school for the summer. When Maria drove the horses and buggy into the yard, Jenny took her knitting bag outside. Once Jenny was settled in the buggy, Maria headed the horses toward the road.

When they got to Esther's house, Maria clambered out and knocked. "Are you ready for visitors?" she called inside.

Esther came to the doorway holding her newborn. "You shouldn't be here," she said as Jenny climbed out of the buggy. "I thought you were confined to home."

"I'm too tense," Jenny said. "Aren't you anxious, too?"

Esther laughed, gesturing to the baby in her arms and then to the turmoil in her house. "I don't have time to worry." She ushered Jenny and Maria inside. Maria went with Esther's older girls to check the chicken coop for eggs, leaving Jenny and Esther alone with newborn Martha.

"May I hold her?" Jenny asked, stretching her arms out for the baby.

"I gladly give her to anyone who'll take her," Esther said, sighing and handing over the infant. "Every time, I forget how much work a new young'un is." She frowned at Jenny as she moved about the kitchen. "How are you doin'?"

"I'm fine," Jenny said, trying to convince herself as much as Esther. "William is my biggest worry at the moment."

Esther nodded. "I wonder which I'll do first when I see Jonah—hug him or wring his neck. Maybe both at the same time." She poured coffee, then put a plate of day-old bread and a jar of jam on the table.

"I hope I have the chance to choose with Will," Jenny murmured.

# Chapter 32: The Expedition Sets Out

Crossing the Cascade pass in late June brought the mule train weather of every kind. They had rain, hail, snow, and wind as they wended their way along the mountain trail, careful not to slip on the wet scree.

"I'll be damn glad when we reach Klamath," Joel muttered to the boys as they shivered in camp on the morning of June 22. "I wouldn't have signed up if I'd known we'd be stuck in the mountains. I was told we'd be explorin' the desert country east of here."

When they rode into Fort Klamath the next afternoon, a corporal greeted them at the stables. "You've made your last run to Jacksonville," he said. "Cap'n Kelly heard from Drew."

"That right?" Sergeant Geisy said with a grin. "We'll be doin' real militia work now?"

Will and the other packers crowded around the corporal to see what he knew. But all he said was, "Ain't sure when we're headin' out. Kelly says he'll call muster tomorrow mornin.' Seven o'clock sharp."

"What do you think?" Will asked Joel while they unpacked the mules and rubbed down their mounts. "Will we leave soon?"

"We'll have to wait till morning," Joel replied. "As long as I'm gettin' paid, I'd rather rest in camp awhile."

> *June 23, 1864. We may be done running the supply train. I hope we leave on the expedition soon. I'm curious about Lt. Col. Drew.*

Will thought he would sleep well, given the relative comfort of their camp at the fort compared to the mountain cold. But he tossed and turned well after midnight, wondering where the militia would send him next.

"Joel?" Will whispered when Joel staggered into bed after drinking with other packers and soldiers.

"Huh?"

"How long will we be on reconnaissance with Colonel Drew?"

"How should I know? Go to sleep."

But Will couldn't relax. Joining the expedition was the most exciting thing he'd ever done, and the real journey was about to start.

"Colonel Drew has been detained in California," Captain Kelly began after the cavalry and packers assembled the next morning. The captain looked peeved at the groans that followed—he seemed as eager as the rest of the men to get underway.

"But he is on his way," Kelly continued. "We are to leave Fort Klamath on June 28, next Tuesday. He will catch up to us as we travel toward the Sprague River."

Cheers arose from some of the cavalry. Joel remained stoic. "Not much time in camp," he muttered. "Won't have a minute's rest whilst we're packin' provisions for the trek."

But Will grinned. He'd be seeing unfamiliar territory soon. Even the thought of pulling mules for weeks on end didn't daunt his spirits.

Still, as Joel predicted, the men worked from dawn to dusk for the next few days. They checked and rechecked their horses' and mules' hooves. They rubbed down the animals, making sure the beasts were healthy. They packed and repacked the mules' panniers, cramming as much as they could into the leather bags and tying on odd-shaped tools and harness pieces that wouldn't fit anywhere else.

Will and Jonah were given four mules each for the expedition. Joel took eight, as did a few of the other experienced packers, with most of the men taking six beasts. Only one wizened old packer, a man named Felix Bagley, led just four mules like the boys.

"That's twice as much weight to lift as we had on the supply runs," Jonah complained.

"So it is," Joel said. "But it ain't much harder to lead four mules than two. You'll get the hang of it."

That week, all men were furnished with rifles, even the packers. The cavalry also had Colt revolvers and sabers, but Captain Kelly refused to issue the packers those military weapons.

Sergeant Crockett, the quartermaster, supervised the packing. He argued with the packers over whether the mules could carry more. "We got the quartermaster's wagon," he told them. "An ambulance wagon and a third wagon. But the rest of our provisions must go by mule. Load 'em up. Leastwise, this time we'll be eatin' from their loads—they'll get lighter each day. So start as heavy as we can."

*June 27, 1864. Rained today, our last day at Klamath. Tomorrow we leave! Sgt. Crockett is a tough taskmaster. Drew can't be any tougher.*

On June 28, the expeditionary force finally left Fort Klamath and headed southeast. The force consisted of forty-seven men from Company C of the First Oregon Cavalry Militia under the command of Captain Kelly. The cavalry unit also had a surgeon and several civilian employees, including a guide, a blacksmith, three teamsters, and two Indian scouts.

Two teams of Army mules pulled two wagons and a hired team pulled a third wagon. In addition, fourteen civilian packers, including Joel, Jonah, and Will, handled eighty-six pack mules. Sergeant Geisy and his cavalry squad guarded the packers, as they had on the supply runs.

June 28 was the first time the entire company traveled together. Despite several days of preparation, Will was appalled at the lack of organization. He'd thought the military always moved in aligned ranks, but Captain Kelly let the men spread out along the trail, most of the cavalry in front and packers next. The wagons brought up the rear, except for a small cavalry guard behind them.

The mules all carried between four hundred and four hundred twenty-five pounds. In addition, the three wagons were filled to the brim. The supplies needed for so many men headed into rough country amazed Will. "Why do we need all this stuff?" he asked Joel, gesturing at the long line of mules and wagons. "And how will we get it through the mountains?"

"Some of it's your food," Joel said. "Wagons also carry blacksmith tools, ammunition, medical supplies, whatever Sergeant Crockett thinks we might need. Just do your job like a man. And keep your mouth shut."

Captain Kelly led the company almost due south toward a marsh at the north end of Upper Klamath Lake, then they traveled east up a ridge on the far rim of the Klamath basin and north to a ford on the Williamson River. Tall pine forests blanketed much of the land, with occasional clusters of fir trees and cedars. The ground beneath the trees was rocky once they passed the marsh.

They only traveled nine miles that day, which annoyed Will. "How are we going to reconnoiter anything if we only go nine miles a day?" he asked Joel. "Even Jonah and I traveled twice that far most days coming south."

Joel grimaced. "What'd I tell you? Hold your tongue. It takes a while for a group to get a rhythm." He chuckled. "Our first day on the trail in forty-seven, Pa was fit to be tied. One family had to stop and repack everything an hour out of Independence, or their wagon would've capsized."

"And we almost made a circle today," Jonah complained. "South, then east, then north again."

"You know better," Joel chastised his younger brother. "Wagons can't move well in the marsh. Nor over big rocks. We had to detour where the scouts took us. That's the way it's gonna be, so get used to it."

Will unloaded his mules and made camp with Joel and Jonah. He was crawling into his bedroll when Joel tapped his leg with the toe of his boot. "You got first watch. You can't rest till midnight."

Will sighed and moved off.

"Don't forget your rifle," Joel reminded him.

They made better distance the next day, traveling seventeen miles from the Williamson River to the Sprague. Peaks of the Cascades rose on all sides as they rode through low gravelly hills patchworked with grassy glades. Joel pointed out Mount Shasta to the south in California, as well as smaller Mount McLaughlin to their west.

Once they reached the Sprague River, they traveled along its north bank through undulating hills. A spur of the Cascades reached down from the north, and the river wound through the foothills. Again, they meandered through rises and gullies, as the scouts tried to find an easy path for the wagons. Will and the other packers simply followed behind the soldiers, pulling their mule strings.

They camped their second night out along the bubbling Sprague, a lively stream lined with cottonwood and aspen. They set up camp about six miles from where the Sprague flowed into the Williamson.

*June 29, 1864. Two days out from Klamath. Camping on the Sprague River. Country is pretty. I have the last watch tonight. I hope I sleep well until then.*

As Will finished his journal entry, a rider trotted into their camp and dismounted. Will wandered over to see who the newcomer was.

"Have I found a cavalry unit?" the stranger asked breathlessly. "Who's in charge?"

"I am." Captain Kelly came out of his tent. "Captain William Kelly. And who are you?"

"Richardson," the man said. "I'm leading a wagon train from California north to The Dalles. Indians attacked us a few days ago. We didn't have enough men or rifles to fend them off. And another wagon train joined us, led by a man named Allen."

Captain Kelly took Richardson into his tent, and Will didn't hear any more of their exchange. Before the men went to bed, however, Captain Kelly passed the word. "Extra guards tonight. We'll stay here until Colonel Drew reaches us."

Will had the early morning watch that night. After tossing restlessly, wondering if tribes were about to attack, he got up bleary-eyed and took his rifle to his post. The packer he relieved was Felix Bagley, the old man who only pulled four mules like Will and Jonah. "Damn savages," the crotchety packer said, spitting tobacco juice. "Cain't leave decent Christians alone."

Mac had often told Will white men violated many of the treaties they made with the Indians, pushing the tribes farther into remote and desolate lands. "We deserve a lot of the injury the Indians heap on us," Mac said. "That doesn't mean you shouldn't watch out for them. Their ways are not ours. But if we leave them alone, most of the tribesmen won't bother us."

Will spent his watch pondering whether Mac or the old packer was right about Indians—when he wasn't looking over his shoulder every time a twig cracked.

As Will came off watch and headed toward the quartermaster's wagon for breakfast, Captain Kelly called the men together. Will grabbed a plate of eggs and ham and stood at the back of the gathering to listen while he ate.

"We learned last night of an attack on eight wagons near Silver Lake," Captain Kelly informed the group. "Mr. Richardson, who arrived here last night, has sought our militia's protection. The attack happened several days ago. A war party of Klamath or Modoc Indians—they don't know which—wounded two white men, stole cattle, and destroyed most of their provisions. Their wagons and those of another train from Jacksonville with nine wagons are now camped at the John Day's ford on the Sprague River."

Murmurs rose from the men, and one soldier shouted, "Are we gonna kill them red bastards?"

"I am awaiting instructions from Colonel Drew," Kelly replied. "As good cavalrymen, I know you want to avenge the wrongs done to innocent settlers. But we have our own reconnaissance mission, and I cannot abandon that without approval from my superiors. We will wait here for Colonel Drew."

The rumblings among the soldiers continued. Will finished his breakfast and returned to his tent. Joel and Jonah were there, and Will asked the older Pershing, "What's this mean for us?"

Joel finished rolling a cigarette and licked the paper closed. Then he said, "Means we might find ourselves in a real war. Not just a surveying trek."

"An Indian fight?" Jonah said with a grin.

Joel lit the cigarette and took a draw. "Nothin's gonna happen today. Today we take it easy."

Since Will didn't have to load his mules, he lay on his bedroll. Although Mac said Indians wouldn't bother whites, it sounded as if tribesmen had assaulted this wagon train without provocation. Surely, the Richardson party wasn't to blame for the violence against them.

He wondered how long it would be before Lt. Col. Drew caught up with them. For the time being, however, Captain Kelly seemed content to wait. At least they were in a pleasant camp.

Jonah got out his fishing pole, and Will joined him on the banks of the Sprague. They ate fresh trout that night instead of Army rations.

*June 30, 1864. Richardson train attacked by Indians. Waiting for Col. Drew. I wonder what he'll have us do. Will we end up fighting?*

# Chapter 33: Colonel Drew Arrives

The expeditionary force waited in camp for two days. Every man stood a four-hour watch each day, but otherwise they lolled around their tents with little to do. Finally, on Friday, July 1, an officer rode into camp, accompanied by three enlisted men. The officer went into Captain Kelly's tent, while the enlisted men took their horses out to graze.

"Must be Colonel Drew," Will said to Joel, nodding toward Kelly's tent. "You recognize him?"

Joel shook his head. "I've only dealt with Kelly. Kelly don't malign his senior officers, but the sergeants say the good Colonel Drew spends his time lickin' the boots of generals in California. As I told you afore, Drew's a Copperhead."

"Grandfather Samuel is a Copperhead," Jonah said. "He's always spoutin' off about how great the Confederacy is."

Joel spat. "Samuel Abercrombie ain't your grandfather. He's just Esther's father-in-law. Our father must be spinnin' in his grave hearin' you call old Abercrombie 'Grandfather Samuel.'"

Will had never understood the animosity between the Abercrombies and Pershings. "Why don't you like Mr. Abercrombie?" he asked Joel. "I know he's a mean son-of-a gun, but—"

"Mean don't say it all," Joel replied. "He spent the whole first few months of our time on the trail trying to kick my pa out as wagon train leader. Finally did it, too. Though Samuel didn't get the job. Your pa got it instead."

Will knew Mac had become the wagon train leader part-way through the journey to Oregon. But he hadn't known Samuel Abercrombie wanted the role. And he'd never heard the circumstances.

"Why didn't Mr. Abercrombie like your father?" he asked Joel.

Joel sniffed. "Pa was careful, wouldn't move as fast as Abercrombie wanted. Then Pa didn't do himself any favors—he got drunk one too many times after Ma died. Abercrombie took advantage of Pa's weakness."

As Will and the Pershing brothers talked, the newly arrived officer and Captain Kelly exited the tent. "Fall in, men," the captain shouted.

The cavalry unit moved into a loose formation, with the civilians standing slightly apart.

"Colonel Drew," Captain Kelly said. "I present Company C of the First Oregon Cavalry Militia."

Colonel Drew frowned and walked along the line of men. The cavalry soldiers straightened as he passed. Seeing them, Will also stood in his best posture. Mac and Mama had trained him well, and he thought he spruced up better than most of the other packers—certainly better than Joel or Jonah. Or old Bagley. Joel didn't bother to change his stance as the officers walked by, and Will wondered if Joel knew more about the colonel than what he'd said.

While the colonel made his inspection, Will studied him. Drew was a short man, but he wore his uniform smartly. Although his hairline receded, his mustache was full and neatly trimmed with a shaved chin beneath. His official rank was Lieutenant Colonel, but Captain Kelly called him "Colonel."

Drew didn't say anything to the teamsters and packers, and he made only an occasional comment to a few of the sergeants and corporals he seemed to recognize. Then he gave a little speech, pacing back and forth between the cavalry and the civilian lines as he talked. "General Drum has ordered me to proceed on our reconnaissance mission across the Owhyee River basin. Our departure was delayed by the need to find adequate mules and men, but Captain Kelly assures me we have a full complement now. Recently, I have been delayed by pressing business in California."

Standing next to Will, Joel snorted softly.

"And now," Drew continued, "the Richardson and Allen wagon trains need our escort. I must assess the situation before we continue. And so our reconnaissance force will rendezvous with the stricken settlers."

The colonel paced a moment, then said to the line of soldiers. "The tribes north of here remain difficult. I anticipate skirmishes with the natives as we proceed. You must stay on your guard at all times."

"And you," he said, turning to the teamsters and mule packers. "Captain

179

Kelly has confidence that you men are fit for duty after your supply runs to Jacksonville. There will be no malingering along the trail. We must keep together for the safety of all."

Then he said to the group at large, "We leave this camp at dawn on Sunday, two days hence, for the rendezvous. After we reach the wagons, I will determine our best course of action and how to fulfill my reconnaissance orders."

"Two more days here?" Joel muttered. "I wonder why he's waiting."

The men scurried around camp through the afternoon, picking up their belongings and washing clothes. Now they had a date certain for proceeding with the expedition, though their immediate mission seemed to have shifted from reconnaissance to protecting wagons. Still, it sounded as if they would be away from Klamath for months.

That night, Will and Jonah lay in their bedrolls beside the campfire. "You think we'll ever go home again?" Will asked wistfully.

"Not for a long while," Jonah replied. "Ain't you havin' fun?"

Will's muscles ached from hefting saddles and panniers all afternoon. "Packing mules is hard work."

"We're out under the stars. We spend our days with horses and mules. It's work," Jonah acknowledged, "but no worse'n farmin.' And Joel's easier on me than Daniel ever was. Easier'n your pa, too."

"So you're glad we left?" Will asked.

"Sure as heck am," Jonah avowed. "And when Colonel Drew heads us toward the Owyhee, I'll be even gladder. All day in the wilderness. We'll have our mules to contend with, but nothin' else."

"I thought you wanted to marry Iris."

Jonah sighed. "Well, at some point we'll go home. Once I've earned enough to marry her."

*July 1, 1864. We leave the Sprague on Sunday. Then the true adventure begins. I'm excited to go, but sometimes I wish I hadn't left home.*

Saturday the expeditionary force continued to prepare for the trail. Jonah and Will managed to get away from camp for an hour of fishing in the Sprague River, though the skies were overcast and threatened rain.

"Hope it don't rain tomorrow," Jonah said. "It's bad luck to start out in a storm."

"Who told you that?" Will scoffed. "One of the old codgers?"

"Just stands to reason," Jonah said. "All our clothes are clean, everything's packed away. We'll be miserable if we get wet on our first day."

Unfortunately, Sunday, July 3, dawned gray and misty. By the time the militia left camp, the rain fell steadily.

# Chapter 34: Searching in Eugene

Late on the afternoon of June 28, Mac and Daniel disembarked from the steamboat in Eugene and found a hotel. "No use approaching the storekeeper tonight," Mac said as he paid for their room.

The next morning, Mac took Daniel to meet the storekeeper who thought he'd seen Will. "Do you remember any more about my son's visit here?" Mac asked. "Or about the other boy with him?"

The man shook his head. "'Fraid not. Recognized your boy, but that's it."

No matter how much Mac and Daniel pressed, the proprietor had nothing more to offer. They spent most of the day visiting other stores in the area and talking to dockworkers near the steamship and the nearby livery. None of the men they spoke to remembered two boys on horseback passing through the area in early May.

"We left it too long, I'm afraid," Mac told Daniel that afternoon. "I hate going home to Jenny with no new information."

"Same here," Daniel said. "Esther's pesterin' me somethin' fierce. And she's worse since the baby come."

Mac left Daniel on his own for supper and ate with Byron Pengra to discuss the road project.

"We are successfully promoting the Oregon Central Military Road," Pengra told him. "We have sufficient investors to proceed with a survey."

Mac looked up from his plate. "Is that what you're calling it—the Oregon Central Military Road?"

Pengra nodded. "Associating the road with a military purpose helps during wartime." He leaned forward. "And I've decided to argue immediately for a railroad along the right of way. No sense waiting until after the road is built. I want to increase our chances of getting land grants along the path."

Mac shook his head. "You don't even have the route surveyed yet. How do you know the land can support a rail bed?"

"The survey will start soon," Pengra argued. "We need to lay a foundation for expanding the road to a rail bed now. As we survey, we must be sure the passage is wide enough to carry a train safely. That'll take more than a wagon route. Don't you agree?"

"I'm not against the proposal," Mac said. "But I think you should proceed slowly. We still don't know when the transcontinental railway to San Francisco will be complete. How will your plan integrate with the California route?"

"We need to be ready to link into the transcontinental train as soon as it's finished. So our route must be laid out before then." Pengra took a sip of wine. "Will you increase your investment to fund the railway?"

Mac sighed and sipped his own wine to delay his answer. How could he tactfully decline? A road was one thing. And Oregon would need a rail connection to the East someday. But was Pengra's design the best the state could do? Why not a railway from Portland—the largest town in Oregon? Or farther south than Eugene—closer to San Francisco? "Let me think about it," he said. "I can't commit tonight."

Pengra glared across the table as he chewed his steak. Mac hadn't improved his alliance with the man this evening.

The next morning, June 30, Mac and Daniel rode a short way south of Eugene, talking to storekeepers and landowners they met. They learned nothing and headed back to town to catch the steamship back to Oregon City. Mac stood at the rail and stared at the water as the boat chugged along, stewing both over his failure to find Will and over the dispute with Pengra.

Jenny waited for Mac all afternoon, though she knew the steamboat wouldn't arrive until evening. As she stitched a pillowcase in the parlor, Cal wandered into the room. "Can I talk to you, Mama?" he asked.

"Of course, Caleb." She looked up from her needlework with a smile, then frowned when she examined his demeanor. Cal was an easy-going child, but now his face contorted in a grimace. "What's wrong, dear?"

"Is Pa going to bring Will home?" he asked.

"I hope so, though probably not on this trip." Jenny beckoned to Cal, and he sat beside her. "Don't you want to see your brother?" She put an arm around his shoulders.

Cal nodded, his expression still sober. "Is it my fault he's gone?"

Jenny leaned away from him to peer into his face. "Why would it be your fault?"

"We fought after I took Maria's horse. Will don't like me much."

Jenny smoothed Cal's hair. "Doesn't, son. And you're wrong—William likes you. All brothers squabble sometimes." Mac had assured her that was true.

Cal shook his head. "It's more'n that. He's jealous of me, but I don't understand why. He's oldest. He gets to do more'n me. I don't know why he don't—doesn't—like me, but he doesn't."

Jenny stroked his hair again. "It isn't your fault William left, Caleb. Sometimes boys have growing pains and need to get away." She hugged him. "But when they leave, it hurts their parents terribly." She tipped his chin toward her. "Can you promise me you'll never run away? Come talk to your father or me if something bothers you?"

Cal nodded. But would a twelve-year-old remember his promise? He hadn't faced any challenges beyond arithmetic yet. Jenny wondered what future heartaches her children would bring her. William was only the first of her offspring to test his wings.

After supper, Jenny paced in the parlor, waiting for Mac. Finally, Maria told her to rest. Jenny tried to calm down, but she couldn't concentrate on her needlework.

Sunset came late in Oregon in June, but it was after dark before Mac let himself in the house. Jenny ran to him. "William?" she asked. "Is there any news? Did you find him?"

Mac shook his head.

"What did you learn?" she asked, grabbing his arms.

"Nothing." Mac sighed. "It was a waste of time."

"Nothing?" Jenny's heart fell.

He led her into the parlor, and they sat. Maria was the only child still awake, and she followed them. "We talked to the storekeeper I'd seen before," Mac said. "He didn't remember anything more. We talked to other men in the area—none of them remembered the boys or their horses."

Pain radiated throughout Jenny's body, from her womb where the baby kicked to her heavy heart. She groaned low in her throat and sagged against Mac.

"You shouldn't be up," he said, lifting her into his arms.

She sobbed. "William. Where's my boy?" As Mac carried her up to bed, Jenny heard Maria crying as well.

The next morning Jenny rose and started her usual routine, but her feet dragged. "You need to rest," Mac said, urging her to return to bed.

"I can't," Jenny said. "Our family needs me." She forced herself downstairs, helped Mrs. O'Malley with breakfast, then set the younger children to their tasks and chores.

All the while, she thought about William. It had been two months now since she'd seen him. Two months of not knowing where he was or how he managed. She touched her belly as she did frequently these days. This little one might never meet its oldest brother.

Maria convinced Jenny to sit in the parlor after the noon meal. "What do you think has happened to Will?" Maria asked, as they sewed.

When Jenny saw the pain in her daughter's eyes, she did her best to smile. "I'm sure he's fine," she said, with a quick hug for the girl. "William is very resourceful. And so is Jonah Pershing. Those boys will cope with whatever they find."

She tried to persuade herself that what she told Maria was true.

# Chapter 35: Rendezvous with the Wagons

The reconnaissance force left camp on the Sprague River at first light on Sunday and traveled through the river valley. It rained off and on through the day, and the group only made eleven miles. They crossed the Sprague at another gravel bar, a crossing very like the ford on the Williamson River, and continued through the broad valley.

The Sprague was a pretty stream, wide and shallow, with a gentle babbling current. "How wide you think the river is?" Will asked Joel.

Joel squinted. "I'm guessin' thirty yards."

Jonah pointed. "A fish jumped over yonder. Might try my luck with my pole again tonight. Fresh trout beats jerky any day."

Joel laughed. "Sergeant Crockett'll thank you for savin' his provisions. But the mules don't wanna carry their loads any longer'n they have to. They'd prefer we eat what's stowed on their backs quick as we can."

They camped on the Sprague again Sunday night. Cottonwoods and willows fringed the riverbanks. Spongy marshes and grasslands covered the lowlands, and a pine forest spread over the valley and up the mountainsides. Lava outcroppings poked through where winds or mudslides had eroded the hillsides.

Drew's presence seemed to subdue the cavalry. The soldiers sat upright on their horses all day, despite the dripping skies. And their tents in camp evenly spaced in rows along the riverbank.

The packers didn't change their ways, Will noted, their ramshackle camp set slightly apart from the soldiers. "We can drink easier by ourselves," Joel commented. "The officers won't let the soldiers imbibe. Not if we're underway again tomorrow. But they hold less sway over us."

"Even Sergeant Geisy?" Will asked.

"Geisy can shout, but he needs us packers," Joel said. "Not much he can do."

*July 3, 1864. Traveled eleven miles under rainy skies. Our first day with Drew. Camped on the Sprague. Jonah caught trout for dinner.*

The next day was July 4, and Will was awakened by cavalrymen shooting off pistols. Will had hoped the expedition would celebrate Independence Day, but Drew quickly stopped the gunfire. "Don't waste your bullets," Will heard him shout. "Might need them for Indians or bears."

As he spoke, the cavalry's howitzer shot off one round, and Captain Kelly chastised the soldiers severely.

After hearing the captain's tirade, Will and Jonah kept their rifles in their scabbards and didn't emulate the soldiers. Instead, they feasted on the trout Jonah caught the evening before. "That's all the Independence Day we'll get," Jonah muttered. "Old Drew don't seem inclined to honor the Fourth."

"We gotta meet those wagons," Joel said. "He's delayed in gettin' us there long enough, and now he's fixin' to make up time."

But Drew still seemed in no hurry. That day they only traveled eight miles through the Sprague River Valley. Their camp that night was on a smaller creek, not on the Sprague itself. They had neared the rendezvous point, and the creek was a decent camp where they could wait.

*July 4, 1864. Independence Day. Camped on a creek. Only made eight miles.*

The next morning, Drew and Mr. Richardson rode out of camp, along with the expedition's Indian scouts and a small squad of mounted soldiers. "Where are they going?" Will asked Joel.

Joel shrugged. "No idea. Lemme see what Sergeant Crockett says." And he sauntered off.

An hour later, Joel returned. "Quartermaster says Drew went with his scouts to see if he can find the Indian bastards what attacked the trains."

"By themselves?" Will asked, surprised. "They only took a small cavalry guard with them."

"Seems Drew wants to question an Indian he knows in these parts. He ain't gonna attack nobody."

"So are we just waiting here?" Jonah asked.

"That's what Crockett says."

And for the next few days, they remained in camp on the little creek, waiting for Drew and Richardson to return or for the wagons to arrive. There was little for the packers to do. Joel took the boys hunting one day, and they shot a deer, which made them heroes with the rest of the packers who feasted with them on venison. Another day the boys lazed fishing in the creek, which teemed with salmon and trout. That night, too, they skipped the quartermaster's rations.

*July 6, 1864. Still on the creek. Caught more trout. Army life is a lot of waiting. At least we aren't loading our mules.*

On July 7, Drew and his scouts returned to camp. Following the colonel's return, Sergeant Geisy ordered the packers to be ready to move the next morning. "Cap'n Kelly says we'll rendezvous with the wagon trains on the south fork of the Sprague," he told them.

The next day, Will and the others loaded their mules and followed the cavalry through the Sprague Valley. When they found the Richardson wagons, the expedition's officers talked with the wagon company's leaders, leaving the rest of the men to entertain themselves.

Joel told the boys to stay close to their mules. "We won't unload 'em till we're told to," he said. "Ain't no tellin' what we're doin' next."

That made sense to Will, who didn't want to lift the heavy packs any more often than he needed to.

"Make camp here," Geisy finally ordered them.

Will saw Captain Kelly leaving camp and riding back along the route they'd traveled earlier in the day. "Where's Kelly going?" he asked.

Joel shrugged.

They later learned Captain Kelly had returned to Fort Klamath to report on the status of the Richardson wagons and the details of the Indian attack. Meanwhile, Drew and the rest of the expedition would escort the wagons to

Fort Boise.

Will was sorry to see Captain Kelly leave the expedition. That night he wrote:

*July 8, 1864. Rode twelve miles to meet the wagons. Camped on South Fork of Sprague. Captain Kelly returned to Ft. Klamath. Should I have asked to go with him? Mule-packing is not how I want to spend my life. But what would I do back home?*

The cavalry spent Saturday helping the emigrants repair their wagons. Will and Jonah aided the settlers as well, but Joel declined. "I got guard duty," he said. "Then I aim to take a nap."

Will helped the emigrants sew patches on wagon covers, repair wheels and axles, and make new handles for axes and hammers. As he worked with the travelers, he learned about the Indian assault on the wagon train.

"We was near Silver Lake," one man said. "Headed toward John Day from Yreka when the savages attacked. We thought they was Klamaths or Modocs, but couldn't be sure. Two of our men got shot. Indians stole some cattle and threw all our flour in the dirt. We couldn't salvage none of it."

He spat on the ground, then continued. "We come across another train, Allen's group, headin' from Jacksonville. We decided to stay together for safety, and we all backtracked to the John Day ford on the Sprague. That's when Richardson set out to get help and found your militia unit."

"What's Colonel Drew doin' now?" Jonah asked the man. He nodded toward Drew and Richardson talking outside the colonel's tent.

The settler shrugged. "Your colonel believes our attackers were Klamaths. But Richardson don't think so. And Drew's scout Moshenkosket don't think so neither. Moshenkosket is Shoshoni. His band rides with a mix of Shoshoni and Klamaths, and they'd know if Klamaths went after us. So that's where Drew and the scouts went—to inspect the Klamath camp."

"What'd they find?" Will asked.

"Richardson didn't recognize any of the Indians in the camp as those what attacked us. Moshenkosket said it 'tweren't them. So now they think we was attacked by a band of Paiutes. The Paiutes are wicked. We was lucky only two died if it was Paiutes."

Will pounded a new axe handle onto a sharpened blade. "What's going to happen now?"

The settler shook his head. "Now we'll head to Fort Boise. Travel through the Owyhee Basin with your unit. Your colonel says your force'll stay with our wagons."

When Will repeated this information to Joel, the older man swore. "That'll slow us down, travelin' at wagon speed. Drew don't seem very interested in finishin' his reconnaissance mission anytime soon."

The next day, Sunday, July 10, Will began to understand Joel's comments as they began their trek to Fort Boise. Slowed by the wagons, they only traveled ten miles through easy terrain along the river. Again, they found a camp on the banks of the Sprague. And they stayed at this camp site for three days, while their Indian scouts went ahead to mark a path the wagons could follow through the Goose Lake Mountains.

"What in tarnation is Colonel Drew doin'?" Jonah griped as they sat by their campfire on the evening of July 12. "We coulda reached Boise by now, I bet."

"It's a lot farther than you think," Joel said. "And a lot of desert twixt here'n there. But we ain't makin' good time, that's for sure. We're two weeks out of Fort Klamath, and we've traveled less'n seventy miles."

*July 12, 1864. Still in camp on the Sprague. Scouts are back. Word is, we leave tomorrow. Sure isn't much happening on this expedition yet. Are we exposing ourselves to Indian attack?*

On July 13, they followed the route the scouts had selected. But they made only six miles to the foothills. Colonel Drew had them stop near a grove of pine trees on the riverbank.

The sun beat down on them all day, and Will was glad of the shade in camp. "Reckon we can start the climb tomorrow when we're fresh," Joel told the boys. "Maybe that's why Drew stopped so early."

The next morning, they wended their way through the foothills. The scouts had done their job well because the grade was easy, and Will's mules didn't object to the climb. They traveled eight miles around the northern edge of a lake to a valley in the mountains.

As Will unloaded his mules that night, he overheard a conversation between Joel and Felix Bagley. "Hear what Drew's done now?" the old packer asked.

When Joel shook his head, the grizzled Bagley said, "He done named this valley after hisself. Callin' it Drew's Valley."

"Well," Joel asked, "did it have another name?"

"Who the hell knows?" The old man spat past his beard. "But that's what the Army'll call it now."

It must be nice, Will thought, to have as much power as the colonel had—naming the terrain he passed through. Would there ever be a McDougall Valley? Then he remembered—he wasn't really a McDougall.

They continued in Drew's Valley through July 15, then moved into Goose Lake Valley. The weather was sunny, even hot during the days, but with fresh mountain air that smelled of pines. The evenings were pleasant, cool once the sun went down, and the moon rose more brightly each night as it moved toward its full face.

Although his surroundings were beautiful and pristine, Will's mood was surly. What place could he find in the world when he didn't even know who he was?

# Chapter 36: Worries in Oregon City

A few days after Mac and Daniel returned from Eugene, Jenny went to visit Esther again, taking Maria and Maggie with her. Jenny also took a cake, so Esther wouldn't feel obligated to feed guests. After they arrived, the older girls took the toddlers off to play with the barn cats, leaving Jenny and Esther in the house with the baby.

"I hate that Daniel and Mac couldn't find any trace of the boys." Esther sat in her rocking chair and nursed Martha. "I'm betting Jonah and Will passed through Eugene on their way to find Joel. But Joel hasn't answered my letter, darn the fool."

"He's never been a good correspondent," Jenny said. "You've waited months for him to respond in the past."

"Yes," Esther sighed. "But this time I begged him to answer right away. Surely he must realize how anxious I am about Jonah." She moved Martha from breast to shoulder to burp the baby. "Jonah's birthday is later in July."

"The twenty-first, isn't it?" Jenny asked. "I remember your mama each year as the time approaches. Seventeen years since she died—how time has flown."

"Poor Ma," Esther said, her voice choking. "I still miss her. Every day."

"I do as well," Jenny murmured. "She taught me so much in the few months I knew her."

As the women talked, Hannah Pershing arrived to visit Esther as well. As soon as Hannah was seated, Esther launched into her worries about Jonah all over again. Jenny listened, feeling the same pain as Esther, though she let Esther talk and didn't voice her fears for William.

Until Esther said, "I'm sure it was Will's idea to leave home. Jonah would never have caused me such anguish without someone eggin' him on."

"And you think William would deliberately cause me heartache?" Jenny asked quietly.

"Well, he's the one fathered by a criminal," Esther said.

Jenny gasped and rose. Esther knew what had happened to her. Esther knew Will's parentage wasn't Jenny's fault. Not Will's. Yet now Esther maligned Will. Jenny couldn't stay any longer.

"Now, Esther," Hannah said, standing to put an arm around Jenny and urged her back to her seat. "Jenny isn't to blame. And she loves Will same as we all love our children. Who fathered him doesn't matter."

"Blood do tell," Esther murmured. "But I know you care for Will," she acknowledged. "I'm sorry. I'm so anxious about Jonah my mind is addled."

Jonah was Esther's brother, not her son. Though Jenny spared her friend that thought, she felt certain she had a greater right to grieve the boys' departure than Esther did. She wondered whether their friendship could survive this trial.

Jenny spoke little for the remainder of the visit. Hannah and Esther discussed their farms and families. While they talked, Jenny grieved for herself and for Will, and for the loss of innocence they had both suffered at the hands of Jacob Johnson, his father, and her stepfather. Why had the vile felon appeared in Oregon to haunt her? Why couldn't he have stayed in Missouri?

That evening, Mac listened to Jenny describe her conversation with Esther and Hannah. "Why would Esther accuse William? Why would she say such terrible things about me and about him?" Jenny cried. She sounded as emotional as she had in the days right after Will's departure.

"She's hurting also, Jenny," he said, trying to soothe his wife.

"Yes," Jenny said. "But to say it's William's fault—we don't know that. Sometimes, I wish Esther would hold her tongue."

"She's always been forthright," Mac said. "More so than she ought to be." Privately, he thought Esther's theory was quite possible. Will was distraught after learning of his paternity. And angry after Mac chastised him for kissing Maria. The boy had acted irrationally all year—he might well have initiated the boys' disappearance.

"You must be careful," Mac warned Jenny. "We still haven't located

Jacob Johnson. I suspect he's in the area, maybe even in town."

"Why can't he leave us alone?" Jenny moaned. "He's destroyed my life for the second time. And this time he's destroyed William and our family as well."

The next morning, Jenny heard Rufus barking in the entry, then Mrs. O'Malley answered a knock on the front door. Fearing it was Jacob Johnson, Jenny reached for her sewing scissors. When she heard Hannah Pershing's voice, Jenny gave a sigh of relief and escorted Hannah into the parlor. Then she asked Mrs. O'Malley to bring tea and muffins.

"I'm sorry about Esther's comments yesterday," Hannah said after Mrs. O'Malley left the room.

Jenny shrugged. "I was upset, but Mac calmed me down. Our greater worry is Jacob Johnson, not Esther's inability to curb her tongue."

Hannah smiled. "I love my sister-in-law dearly, and I know you do as well. But we both know what assault feels like. Unlike Esther, who can be quite outspoken."

"She worries about Jonah, as I do about William." Jenny said as Mrs. O'Malley walked in with the tea tray.

Jenny poured a cup for Hannah and handed it to her friend. "How are your children?" Hannah spoke about her daughter Hope and little boy Isaiah. Hope relished her school lessons, and Isaiah caused trouble, just like his Pershing uncles had as boys. "So Hope might be another teacher, as you and your niece Faith were?" Jenny asked.

"That is my dream for her," Hannah said. "I do not want her to rush into marriage. And what about Maria? Are you still teaching her at home?"

"I haven't had much time for Maria," Jenny confessed. "And without William here, she mopes about the house—she misses him as much as I do. She is a great help to me, of course. But sometimes I wish I had not let her quit school."

"Why did you?" Hannah asked, then sipped her tea.

"She was not treated well by the other girls." Jenny sighed, remembering Maria's frequent tears.

"How so?"

"Because of her parentage."

Hannah looked at Jenny quizzically.

"Her mother was Spanish. And Indian."

"Ah," Hannah said with a nod.

"And no one knows who her father was," Jenny continued. "Though he was probably white. At least, that's what Mac says."

Hannah took another sip, then said, "You know the rumors about Mac being her father."

"He says he isn't," Jenny said. "I trust him."

Hannah sighed. "That's all you can do." After a pause, she asked, "What about sending Maria to board with Abigail Duniway? Lafayette might be far enough to give her a new start. I had a letter from Abigail yesterday. She is still looking for a girl to help her."

Jenny couldn't let another child leave her. Swallowing hard, Jenny said, "Oh, Hannah, I rely on Maria so much. Her presence at home is a comfort, particularly with Will gone."

"But what is best for Maria?" Hannah asked.

"I don't know," Jenny whispered. "I'll have to think on it."

Jenny tried to occupy her days with her children. They were all growing so fast. There was Maria's schooling to worry about. It seemed Cal and Nate needed new trousers and shirts every time she turned around. And she and Maria had let down Lottie's and Eliza's skirts twice already this year. Maggie learned new words daily and used them to ask question after question. Jenny was hard-pressed to keep up with the toddler.

But at nights, she often lay awake long after Mac slept. Her scare with the coming child seemed behind her. The baby now kicked and rolled as soon as she laid down for the night, and she couldn't relax. While Mac snored softly beside her, Jenny's mind flashed back to her assault in Missouri. And she fretted over William. Where was he? Was he safe? Healthy? She had no way of knowing.

Still, she had a family at home, and they needed her attention. Mac was distressed about something—a business matter, she assumed—but he didn't talk to her about it.

Mac put on a cheerful face around Jenny and kept his concerns to himself.

Jenny didn't need to know how worried he was about his new investments.

He'd received a letter from Byron Pengra after their discussion in Eugene:

*July 8, 1864*
*Dear Mr. McDougall,*

*My competitors are moving ahead with other road projects. I need your answer on increasing your investment in the Oregon Central Military Road within two weeks, as I hope to begin the survey shortly thereafter. I must know how much funding is available before I start the construction....*

Mac sighed as he read Pengra's urgent request. He didn't agree with the Eugene surveyor, but the man had the backing of state leaders and financiers such as William Ladd. Maybe Mac was too cautious. But he didn't like investing his money when he couldn't see a path to a profitable return. Could Pengra convince Congress that a railroad into Eugene made more sense than one into Portland or into the Rogue River Valley nearer San Francisco? Mac had his doubts.

And then there were the problems facing the People's Transportation Company. Mac had recently met with the McCullys, the owners of that steamship enterprise. Asa McCully told him of the cutthroat competition the P.T. Company encountered from the Oregon Steam Navigation Company. "O.S.N. is more established, and can undercut our prices," McCully said. "If we are to compete, we need funds to outlast their fare war."

The McCullys wanted to buy another boat to run on the upper Columbia River. If they could expand on the Columbia, competition with O.S.N. would lower shipping costs between the ocean ports of Portland and Astoria and the Willamette River towns. That would benefit both businesses and residents in Oregon City. But should Mac invest more money in the P.T. Company?

He didn't have the cash to invest in all the opportunities before him, Mac told himself bluntly. He had to finish stocking his warehouses in San Francisco, and until they produced a profit again, he wouldn't have more cash. He had to choose between competing projects—Pengra's road and possible railway, Ladd's bank in Portland, and helping the McCullys' steamship company.

Frankly, the bank appealed to him most. Lowering the costs of river traffic would be of immediate benefit, more roads were necessary in the near term, and trains were the way of the future. But the bank would allow him to increase his correspondence with his brother in Boston.

He was long overdue to repair his relationships with his family back East. It had not seemed important for most of the years he and Jenny had resided in Oregon. But since Will's departure, Mac thought more about his own fractured ties with his father.

Mac sighed and picked up another piece of correspondence—a letter from Samuel Abercrombie's attorney. Samuel still argued over the building of a channel from the creek now on Zeke's land to his claim.

Mac swore. He'd have to make another trip to the country to mediate between Abercrombie and Zeke.

# Chapter 37: Horse Thieves

The militia continued its slow progress through Goose Lake Valley, traveling only a few miles each day to accommodate the wagon trains. Will wished they would remain in the same camp for a few days, so he wouldn't have to load and unload his four mules each day. Though that would slow their progress toward Boise even more.

The mid-July days were hot unless they passed under an evergreen canopy. But much of the land was unforested or covered only with a mix of scrubby pines and sagebrush. So for the most part, the men and beasts sweltered under the bright sun and the radiant heat from the ground.

The evenings were cool, and the moon increased each night toward its full orb. The bright moon hid the stars from sight. Will would have enjoyed guard duty, except for the sleep he missed.

Drew sent his Klamath Indian scouts out every day to survey the land ahead and plot the route for the coming day. On the afternoon of July 17, the scouts returned to the reconnaissance force, bringing with them about twenty prospectors who'd been heading for the Malheur River. That afternoon as the expedition made camp near the head of Goose Lake, three Snake Indians also joined them.

"Wonder what they want," Joel muttered as the packers unloaded their mules. He nodded toward the Snake tribesmen. "No good'll come of having more Indians with us."

Once Drew's tent was assembled, the Snake visitors and the Klamath scouts met with the colonel. Rumors spread through the rest of the camp that the Snake tribesmen were angry to find the expedition in their territory. After his powwow with the Indians, Drew passed the word through his officers to the rest of the soldiers and packers that the Snakes had come in peace and would spend the night in camp with the militia. The prospectors would remain with them as well.

The new arrivals all put their horses to graze with the militia's herd. The guards would watch the newcomers' mounts along with the expedition's horses and mules and the animals from the wagon trains.

That evening, the packers and guest prospectors shared a campfire and a meal. Then the men turned to drink. Will had the early watch. When he returned, he sat near the fire whittling a whistle while he listened to Joel and the prospectors talk.

"Where you come from?" Joel asked a miner named Burton.

"We been workin' the Owyhee mines," Burton replied. "Now we're headin' back to the Malheur River. But we got lost, till your scouts found us. They said we could follow you as far as Surprise Valley. From there, we can find the Malheur."

Joel told the miners about his experiences in the Rogue River Valley. He'd never prospected along the Malheur, and after quizzing the prospectors about their finds, he commented, "Think I'll stay south on the Rogue and Umpqua. Country's purtier, and the yield is better."

"Maybe so," one of the Malheur miners acknowledged. "But the Malheur ain't got the winter snows you do."

The men argued good-naturedly for a while, then one miner interjected, "Did you see them Indian ponies the Snakes rode into camp? I'd like me a horse like them. Sturdy little mounts. Might just help myself to one."

"That don't sound very smart," Burton said. "I ain't got no desire to rile up the Indians in these parts."

The banter turned to how easy it would be to steal the Snakes' horses. Will listened with some alarm—Shanty's dam had been an Indian pony, and Shanty had spots on his coat like the Snake tribesmen's horses. But the men's talk died down as they got in their bedrolls.

Will turned in also, and soon was asleep.

Early the next morning, Will was awakened by a shout. "Burton's dead. Murdered."

"Burton?" Will asked Joel. "Isn't he the man we talked to last night?"

"Yep. One of them prospectors," Joel replied. "Seemed a pleasant enough fellow. Don't know why anyone would kill him."

The three Snake Indians and about half of the white prospectors were no longer in camp. One of the remaining prospectors said, "Them Indians killed Burton. Musta been them." Drew ordered a cavalry squad to ride out and investigate, and he told the rest of the expeditionary force to remain in camp.

"We ain't goin' nowhere today," Joel predicted. "Not till Drew sorts this all out."

When they gathered at the quartermaster's wagon for breakfast, Will and the other packers learned several horses had been stolen. "All the Indian ponies are gone," Sergeant Crockett reported. "Some of our horses, too. Snakes probably took 'em along with their own mounts when they left camp."

"Which of our horses were taken?" Will asked.

The quartermaster squinted at him. "Don't you ride that Indian mixed-breed horse?"

"Yes, sir," Will said, nodding.

"That's one of the horses what's missin'."

Will ran to the herd and searched for Shanty. The gelding was gone. "Where'd the thieves take the horses?" he asked one of the guards.

The soldier shrugged. "Hell if I know. Made off with 'em afore dawn."

"Weren't there guards on duty?" Will demanded.

"'Tweren't my watch. But them sneaky Indians can steal horses even with a guard."

Will swore, then went in search of Jonah. "Can I borrow your horse?" he asked, grabbing Jonah's saddle and bridle. "Shanty's gone."

"You can't go after 'em," Jonah said. "Drew's orders."

"You bet I can," Will said. He saddled Jonah's mare and galloped off.

It wasn't hard to follow the cavalry squad's fresh tracks from that morning. About two miles from camp, Will found the soldiers digging a grave for Burton. The stolen horses, including Shanty, had been rounded up and stood under guard. The missing prospectors—other than Burton—sat near their comrade's body, and the three Snake Indians sat on the other side of the grave, their own horses with them.

"What happened?" Will asked as he dismounted.

"What're you doin' here?" the corporal in charge asked Will. "Drew told everyone to stay in camp."

"They took my horse." Will pointed at Shanty.

The corporal spat. "I'll let you explain yourself to Drew when we get back. Long as you're here, start diggin'." He pointed at a shovel.

Will picked up the shovel and began digging next to another soldier. "What happened?" he asked that man.

"'Tain't entirely clear," the soldier replied. "Seems a few prospectors, including Burton—" He gestured at the body lying on the ground and the miners sitting nearby. "They decided they should steal the Indians' horses. So sometime afore dawn, they cut the Indian ponies out of the herd along with their own. Took a few extra mounts, it seems." He nodded at Shanty. "Yours musta been one of 'em."

The soldier threw a couple of shovelfuls of dirt over his shoulder, then continued, "The Snakes went after their horses, as even an Indian has a right to do. Shots was fired, Burton got hit, and he died right here. The Snakes say he was on one of their horses when they shot him. One of the horses got shot, too. Lucky your mount ain't harmed."

As they worked, another soldier said, "Senseless killing if you ask me. Hear tell Burton didn't even want to steal the horses, but his pals talked him into it. Called him an 'Indian sympathizer' or some such rot 'cause he didn't wanna go. And now he's dead."

"Where are the thieves?" Will asked.

"Some of 'em run off when they seen us," a soldier said. "Rest of 'em are over there." He gestured to the prospectors sitting beside the body. "Drew wants us to bring 'em back. Bring the Snake Indians, too."

After lowering Burton's body into the grave, the men took a break before filling in the hole. Will went to Shanty and patted his nose. He looked the gelding over—the horse seemed unscathed. "Can I take him back to camp?" he asked the corporal.

"Fine by me," the corporal said with a shrug. "We'll finish up here and bring the horses back, along with the Snake tribesmen and the prospectors what done the stealing. Report in with Sergeant Crockett when you get back. Let him know we'll return as soon as we finish burying Burton. But the quartermaster and Drew might have a few words for you."

Will rode Jonah's mare and led Shanty back to camp. When he arrived, he turned the horses into the herd and reported to Sergeant Crockett, as instructed.

The quartermaster frowned at him. "You're McDougall, right?"

Will nodded.

"Didn't you hear? Drew ordered everyone except the search squad to remain in camp."

"Yes, sir."

"Well?"

"They stole my horse, sir."

Crockett sniffed. After a moment he said, "I need to tell the colonel."

"Yes, sir."

"Go back to the packers' camp. And stay there."

The cavalry squad returned to camp late in the afternoon with the prospectors and the Snakes, as well as the stolen horses. Drew held an inquisition, and word of his findings passed quickly through the camp. The colonel determined that a few of the prospectors had acted alone and that the other prospectors had not agreed with the plan to steal the Indian horses. The Indians had their horses back, though the injured horse—one of the prospectors' mounts—had no hope of recovery and was shot. The Snakes did not blame the cavalry and left. Drew sent the surviving prospectors on their way, even the thieves.

"That's not right," Will protested to Joel when he learned the thieves would not be punished for Burton's death nor for stealing the horses.

"If the Indians don't care about hangin' the thieves, why should we?" Joel responded. "They got their horses back. They don't want white men hung when they ain't lost any property. If they insist on punishin' white men, the cavalry'll go after 'em hard in the future. Maybe start a war. 'Tain't worth it to 'em."

After the Indians and prospectors left, Drew called for Will to be brought to his tent. "You, young man," Drew said with a scowl. "What made you think you could ride off after the cavalry? Your job is to tend mules."

"The prospectors stole my horse, sir," Will said, standing straight. "I raised him from a colt."

"How'd you come to have an Indian horse?" Drew asked.

"He's half Indian pony. Out of a mare my mother purchased at Fort Laramie in forty-seven. His sire is an Andalusian stallion."

Lt. Col. Drew raised an eyebrow. "A Spanish stallion?"

"Yes, sir. He's my fa-father's stallion." Will winced at calling Mac his father.

"Who's your father?"

"Caleb McDougall. Of Oregon City."

"You sound like a well-educated lad," Drew said. "Where'd you get your schooling?"

"At the academy in Oregon City. And from my parents. My father attended Harvard, and my mother went to an Ursuline school in New Orleans as a girl."

"Harvard, hmm?" Drew frowned and rubbed his chin. "Can you write a good hand, boy?"

Will was puzzled. Why did the colonel care if he could write nicely? "I think so, sir."

"I need a scribe." Drew stood and showed Will a ledger-lined notebook. "I keep daily records of our distance and the land we pass through. I will owe my superiors a report at the end of our expedition. But I'd rather dictate my notes than write them myself."

"Yes, sir," Will said, still confused.

"Your punishment for running away is to scribe for me." Drew sat again. "Report to my tent each evening after you've tended your mules."

# Chapter 38: Business Losses

Mac spent the middle part of July dealing with Samuel Abercrombie's renewed threats against Zeke Pershing. He convinced the judge to issue a stay of any legal proceedings while the parties dug a ditch to divert some water back onto Abercrombie's property.

By July 20, Mac was ready to deal with his own investments, and he turned to the pile of correspondence that had built up in his office in town. The top letter in the stack was from Ladd in Portland.

*July 13, 1864*
*Dear Mr. McDougall:*

*I have had no communication from you in many weeks, and my banking plans are proceeding. I doubt I can save a place for you as a shareholder in this enterprise. My subscription is now filled.*

*I hope that someday in the future, we can do business together . . .*

Mac frowned. The letter had been sent a week earlier, and he hadn't noticed it while he dealt with family matters and Abercrombie's interference. It was tempting to blame his inattention on others—particularly on Abercrombie—but his investments were his responsibility. And now he had lost an opportunity.

He needed to respond to salvage the relationship he'd developed with Ladd. He picked up his quill and wrote:

*July 20, 1864*
*Dear Sir:*
*Due to matters of a personal nature, I have only just read your communication of July 8. I understand your need to seek other shareholders, and if you have already done so, I wish you the utmost success in your endeavor. If shares remain to be had, I am still interested, and I would appreciate the opportunity to work with you on your banking project and on other developments in the future.*
*Respectfully,*

There, Mac thought, as he signed his name. That was the best he could do.

A knock sounded on his office door. "Come in," he said.

Milton Elliott, Samuel Abercrombie's attorney, entered. "Got a minute, McDougall?"

Mac grimaced internally, though he rose to shake the man's hand. It couldn't be good news that Samuel's attorney had come to call. He waved Elliott to a seat across from him.

Elliott settled himself in the chair. "As you might suspect from my presence here, Mr. Abercrombie is not happy."

"I met with both Samuel and Zeke Pershing last week," Mac said. "You'd given me leave to negotiate directly with Abercrombie, and I thought we worked out an arrangement to both parties' satisfaction."

The attorney cleared his throat. "My client has had second thoughts."

Mac swore. "And why is that?"

Elliott sounded apologetic as he explained. "The creek between their properties—"

"You mean, the creek that migrated onto Zeke Pershing's land," Mac said, wanting to keep the record straight. "We diverted a portion of the water onto your client's field."

"Yes, yes, that creek." Elliott coughed. "It seems the creek is drying up."

"Creeks tend to do that in mid-summer," Mac said.

"My client doesn't think he will get enough water for his fields under the arrangement you proposed."

"The arrangement I proposed?" Mac exploded. "Your client proposed it. Your client agreed to it. You mean to tell me he now intends to renege?"

"Well—" Elliott cleared his throat again.

"Zeke Pershing has been more than fair in offering to divert water from the creek back onto Mr. Abercrombie's land. Given Mr. Abercrombie's age, Mr. Pershing and his brothers provided the labor to dig the ditch and the pond to hold the runoff. I don't know what more Zeke can do." Mac grew more incensed at Samuel's obstinance.

"He told me to pursue the case against Mr. Pershing." At least Elliott had the grace to look sheepish. "I will ask the judge to reverse his stay."

"We'll see about that." Mac stood. "I will make one more attempt to bring Samuel Abercrombie to reason, based on my longstanding acquaintance with him. If I am not successful, then Mr. Pershing will counterclaim against Mr. Abercrombie for trespass. Abercrombie has been seen many times taking water from the creek, even though it now runs through Zeke Pershing's land. That's why Zeke dug the ditch and pond. But this is the last civil recourse I shall offer before pursuing Mr. Pershing's legal rights."

Elliott nodded. "I understand."

The next morning, Mac rode out to Zeke Pershing's claim and found his friend mending harnesses in the barn. "Thought you'd be out taking more land from Abercrombie," Mac said, with a grin.

Zeke snorted. "That old coot wouldn't do as he ought on the ditch, despite our agreement. His attorney—that Mr. Elliott—was here overseeing the digging, and still old Samuel didn't follow through."

"Did Samuel say whether he would pursue the lawsuit?"

Zeke shook his head. "Elliott didn't seem to want no part of it. Told Samuel so in front of me. But Abercrombie's likely to look for another lawyer."

"Elliott's changed his spots, it seems. He came to see me yesterday. Says Abercrombie has authorized him to move ahead with the case."

"Damn." Zeke swore a long string of stronger oaths.

"I agree," Mac said. "I'll go see Samuel. Maybe I can calm him down."

"Last time I talked to him, Abercrombie said a man named Johnson was asking questions in these parts."

A cold sweat touched Mac's neck, despite the warm day. "What kind of questions?"

"About Jenny. And Will. Your family's past."

Zeke knew Jenny's full history, so Mac spoke openly. "Did Johnson tell Abercrombie I'm not Will's father?"

"I don't know." Zeke shrugged. "I didn't want to get into it with Samuel. I was mad enough at him already. No need to start blatherin' when I wasn't thinkin' straight."

Mac clapped Zeke on the back. "Good man. Don't tell Abercrombie anything. I'll go talk to him now, find out what he heard directly. But I don't want him to try to put two and two together."

Mac rode to Abercrombie's claim. Samuel was chopping kindling in the heat of the day. Mac took off his jacket and rolled up his sleeves. "Got another hatchet?" he asked.

Samuel gestured with his thumb.

Mac picked up a hatchet with a scarred wooden handle and started chopping alongside the older man. "Zeke says you weren't happy with the ditch."

"No water flowin' to my land."

"What'd your lawyer say?"

"You musta paid him off." Abercrombie glared at Mac. "You got the money to do so. But he agreed to pursue my case in court."

Mac shook his head. "I didn't pay anyone. I only got involved to help you and Zeke work things out."

"Then you left town to go after your runaway. Left us in the lurch. Made me spend money on Elliott, weasel though he be."

"Daniel and I had to look for our boys in Eugene. And once the water flows again, the ditch will provide you with your share from the creek." Mac kept chopping. He figured his labor would soothe Abercrombie eventually.

After a while, Abercrombie raised the topic Mac sought to hear about. "Man come around askin' 'bout you and Miz Jenny." The old man squinted and crossed his arms across his beefy chest. "Name of Jacob Johnson. What's that all about?"

"What did he say?" Mac asked, continuing to chop.

"Said he knew you back in Missouri. Said he was closer to Miz Jenny 'n he had a right to be." Abercrombie spat his tobacco juice across the yard. "Though he didn't say it quite so politely."

Mac stopped chopping at that and eyed Abercrombie. "You've known

Jenny for years. Have you ever known her to behave inappropriately?"

Abercrombie spat again. "I like Miz Jenny. Always have. She's a good woman. But a man wouldn't talk that way about her without some reason."

"No reason," Mac said, picking up another piece of wood. "No damn reason at all." He turned to Abercrombie. "If you see him again, I hope you tell him so. Meanwhile, let's get your woodpile stocked."

They chopped the rest of the wood in silence.

At Mac's request, Jenny followed him upstairs when he returned home. He peeled off his sweat-stained shirt and handed it to her. Then he said, "Jacob Johnson talked to Abercrombie. About us."

She sat on the bed, twisting his shirt in her hands. "Oh, no." She thought again of that evil day, as she did whenever she heard Johnson's name.

"Samuel didn't seem to know much."

"He's so unpredictable, Mac." If Samuel Abercrombie started talking to others in town, it wouldn't merely be the end of Jenny's reputation. The gossip would hurt the children as well. Particularly the girls.

And most especially Maria, who was already the subject of many raised eyebrows among women in town. Some girls in her former school had called her a squaw. The girl's mixed blood would become a bigger issue when she reached marriageable age—which she was rapidly approaching.

"You have to stop him, Mac," she said, holding her belly. Soon there would be another child to bear the brunt of the gossip.

"We're fortunate," Mac said. "Abercrombie likes you. I don't think he'll say anything."

"But you can't be sure," she whispered. "He gets so angry. Maybe we should send Maria away."

"Maria?" Mac said. "Whatever for?"

"With the new baby coming, I won't be able to teach her properly. Hannah says Abigail Duniway still needs a helper. Maybe Mrs. Duniway would be a good role model for Maria. She certainly has shown gumption in starting a girls' school in Lafayette."

Mac kissed the tip of her nose. "You have just as much gumption as Mrs. Duniway. I want Maria here. She should be helping you, not some schoolmarm."

That night, Mac lay awake as Jenny slept. He worried after hearing Jacob Johnson was in the area. No good could come of Johnson remaining near Mac's family.

The next morning, Mac went to see Sheriff Thomas. He found the lawman enjoying his first smoke of the day. His deputy, Adam Albee, sat reading the newspaper. Thomas offered Mac a cigar, which Mac took.

After Mac told the men about his conversation with Samuel Abercrombie, the sheriff frowned at him. "Are you sure there ain't more to your past with Johnson than you're lettin' on?"

Mac shook his head. "I told you I killed his father while defending my wife. That's reason enough for him to keep bothering us."

"I suppose so." Sheriff Thomas puffed on his cigar. "Now, as to Abercrombie's threats—"

"I want to stop him from slandering my wife," Mac said, pointing his cigar at the sheriff in emphasis. "What can you do?"

"Not much." Sheriff Thomas puffed again. "I can have a word with Abercrombie, but that old coot don't listen to no one." Albee snorted in agreement from behind his newspaper. "Probably best to leave Abercrombie be," the sheriff continued.

"What about Johnson?" Mac asked.

"We got our eye out, but he must have a place where he can hide out. If we find him, we can bring him in for assaulting your wife and son last spring. But I probably can't keep him locked up for long. Not unless he causes more harm." Sheriff Thomas cocked an eyebrow at Mac. "Or unless you tell me he's committed other crimes in the past."

Mac swallowed and nodded. "Let me know if you find him."

Jenny spent July 26 preparing for Lottie's birthday party. The girl would turn seven the next day.

"Do you want chocolate cake or spice?" Jenny asked her daughter.

"Chocolate." Lottie was definite. "With lots and lots of white icing."

"I think Mrs. O'Malley and I can manage that," Jenny said, smiling.

"And I want a present," Lottie said. "Something big." Her face was solemn.

"What is it?" Jenny asked, smoothing the little girl's curls away from her face. Lottie looked a lot like Jenny had as a child, though her ringlets were prettier than Jenny's straight hair.

"I have to whisper it," Lottie said.

"All right." Jenny leaned her ear down next to Lottie's face.

"I want Will home," Lottie murmured, tears clouding her blue eyes.

Jenny caught her daughter close in a hug. "So do I, precious," she whispered back. "So do I."

# Chapter 39: Becoming Drew's Scrivener

After Burton's death, the expeditionary force remained in Goose Lake Valley until Wednesday, July 20. That morning, Drew ordered the militia and wagons to move farther up the valley. They traveled eighteen miles along the east side of Goose Lake.

When they crossed the old Southern Oregon Emigrant Road, more wagons from Humboldt County and elsewhere in California joined them. These wagons were also bound for Fort Boise and wanted the security the cavalry provided.

Now, all told, Drew's militia force escorted over twenty wagons and over thirteen hundred horses, mules, and cattle. Some of the wagons were pulled by oxen, which were slower than the mules. The caravan stretched along the route, making it difficult to safeguard during the day. The soldiers rode back and forth along the wagons and packers, urging them to a faster pace.

"Cavalry don't have to push us," Joel said. "Our mules keep up with the horses, even with their packs. But them oxen creep along like snails."

"Are we gonna go this slow all the way to Boise?" Jonah asked.

"Hard to tell." Joel blew out a breath. "This ain't what I bargained for. Reconnaissance is one thing, but pokin' along ahead of a bunch of cows is another."

"But we can't leave, can we?" Will knew the answer even as he asked the question.

"Hell, no." Joel spat. "We signed a contract. And we're back on per diem now, so we get paid our daily rate, no matter where Drew takes us, no matter how slow we go. 'Tain't fun, but we ain't got a choice."

That evening after he unpacked his mules, Will grabbed a quick supper, then headed to Drew's tent. "I'm ready, sir," he announced when he arrived.

The colonel looked at him bemused, as if he'd forgotten his earlier orders. Will wondered if Drew really meant to use him as a scribe.

"Come in, boy," the colonel finally said. "McDougall, isn't it? Let's get to work." He rummaged in his camp desk and handed Will a quill, ink bottle, and paper. Then he started to dictate. Will scribbled to write as fast as Drew talked, trying to keep his penmanship as neat as Mama would have it.

"We left Goose Lake Valley at a point twenty-one miles down the east side of the lake and were joined by several heavy trains from California, including several families, all moving toward Boise." The colonel stopped. "Are you getting this all down?"

"Yes, sir," Will muttered as he continued writing.

"We diverged to the east, and soon found the old Southern Oregon Emigrant Road, which passes around the south end of Goose Lake, and thence the road heads westward into either Shasta or Rogue River Valleys. Our reconnaissance force entered the lower portion of a beautiful glade—" Drew paused and asked, "Would you call this a beautiful glade, McDougall?"

"I would, sir. It's very pretty."

Drew continued describing the flora and fauna they'd seen through the day. He also recounted the debacle leading to Burton's death. Will's arm ached by the time Drew bade him leave, but he scrawled in his own journal:

> *July 20, 1864. Camped in Goose Lake Valley after making 18 miles today. I scribed for Lt. Col. Drew this evening. The work is harder than it sounds.*

The next day was hot, and the caravan passed through both forests and parched earth in Goose Lake Valley. Will relished the time under canopies of pines and firs. Birds chirped as the wagons and mules passed, and the occasional deer watched them while grazing. By contrast, grasshoppers and ground squirrels were the only signs of life where sage and scrubby brush sprouted in open red earth. Later in the day, the forests gave way to marshes that sucked at horses' and mules' feet.

As they rode through Goose Lake Valley, Jonah seemed morose. "What's wrong?" Will asked.

"It's my birthday," Jonah muttered. "I'm seventeen. And here I am pulling mules to who the hell knows where."

Will could have retorted that it had been Jonah's idea to run away, but he just let Jonah talk.

"I wish I had one of Esther's white cakes." Jonah licked his lips. "Light as a feather. Covered with berries and whipped cream. Instead, I'm eatin' stewed beef, tough as leather."

"Might be able to catch some fish this evening," Will said. "Or a jackrabbit."

"Them rabbits ain't much better'n the quartermaster's beef," Jonah complained. "Meat's too stringy."

Joel hooted at Jonah. "Be a man," he told his younger brother. "You think I got cake on my birthday when we come to Oregon?"

"Your birthday's in December," Jonah said. "You wasn't travelin' on your birthday that year. Family was settlin' in on the claim."

"Ma was dead," Joel said, "and Esther was married. No one made me a cake."

When they stopped for their noon break, Will used a scrap of soft leather to polish the whistle he'd made and handed it to Jonah. "Happy birthday," he said.

Jonah grinned. "Thanks." He blew a piercing blast on the whistle, which startled the mules. Another packer hollered at him to stop the racket so he didn't start a stampede.

"Fandango Valley," the colonel dictated to Will that evening, "where we are camped tonight, is so named because a group of unfortunate settlers engaged in a noisy celebration when they met up with friends from California. They neglected to guard their camp and were attacked by Indians who took advantage of their inebriation." He paused and sipped his whiskey.

Will looked up from writing. "Is that true?"

Drew shrugged. "It's the story. And true enough. One can never assume the tribes are friendly. Travelers in these parts must always stay alert."

"But surely, sir—" Will rubbed his pockmarks.

Drew stared at him over another sip. "Never assume they are peaceable," he repeated. "Some Indians are, like those Snakes that came through camp recently. But question them severely before you accept their protestations of goodwill." Then he looked toward the ceiling of his tent and continued his dictation. "This valley affords excellent grazing and good water. I suggest the Army build a permanent outpost somewhere between the northern end of Goose Lake Valley and here."

By the time Will finished taking notes for Drew, his hand was so cramped he couldn't write in his own journal.

The next day the expedition traveled only six miles. They made a difficult crossing of a pass from Fandango Valley into Surprise Valley. To get their wagons up the steep route out of Fandango, the emigrants were forced to hitch double teams of oxen to their wagons.

The packers waited at the summit, watching settlers lead their oxen up the slope. "This'll take twice as many trips," Jonah complained. "Plus all the time to yoke and unyoke the oxen betwixt wagons."

Joel shook his head. "Almost as steep as California Hill," he said. "And that was just the first of our bad slopes. Laurel Hill on Mount Hood was the last, and maybe the worst." Joel nodded at Will. "Your pa almost died when a wagon got loose."

Will had heard that story—Samuel Abercrombie stopped the wagon from careening down on Mac.

"But them oxen can pull anything," old Felix Bagley said. "You can bellyache about their slowness, but mules'd have a hard time pullin' a wagon up this mountain. Good thing the quartermaster has eight mules on his wagon, and they're still strugglin'."

Joel drank from his canteen. "Oxen'll pull as long as they got breath, that's for sure. And mules can be ornery."

"All depends on whether you want speed or distance," another packer said. "But mules got more personality."

At that, Joel hooted. "Personality? That's what you want in a beast? Then give me a dog. Draft animals need to pull without complaint." And the men took to comparing each other to mules and dogs.

Will stared down the far side of the pass. Mountains ranged both to the north and south. "Are those the Sierra Nevadas?" he asked Joel, pointing south.

Joel nodded. "Yup. Wild terrain."

"Will we travel through them?" Jonah asked, sounding subdued.

"Depends where Drew takes us," Joel said.

That evening, after all the wagons straggled down from the summit into Surprise Valley, Drew called Will into his tent again. He dictated, "Today we were required to double team the wagons, which were only moderately loaded. Our travel was slow and tiresome. I recommend the trail be moved to lower ground, on the spur of mountains about a mile northward of its present location, which would render the grade comparatively easy."

As he wrote Drew's words, Will nodded in agreement.

> *July 22, 1864. A long day with only a few miles made. Camped in Surprise Valley. Most of the time, I agree with Drew. He knows this land.*

The wagons and their militia escort remained in Surprise Valley for four days so the emigrants and their animals could recuperate from the steep climb over the pass. Meanwhile, the packers and soldiers busied themselves in camp, checking their horses' and mules' harnesses and making sure the food in the packs was still edible.

Drew rode out each day with his scouts and a small cavalry guard to survey the valley. And in the evenings, he called Will into his tent to scribe for him.

Jonah seemed morose after his birthday passed. "What's wrong?" Will asked him one night when he returned to the packers' campfire after supper. Jonah lay on his bedroll, and Joel sat on a log smoking.

"I dunno." Jonah blew a tentative toot on his whistle.

"Keep that damn thing quiet," Joel said. "Or you'll have the horses runnin' off."

"Homesick, I guess," Jonah muttered. "Still wishin' I had a slice of Esther's cake. Or even her cornbread."

"The quartermaster's corn pone is all right," Will said.

Jonah blew another short toot. "It ain't just the food. I don't like all this waitin' around. This ain't the adventure I thought it would be."

"You want to go home?" Will asked.

Jonah shrugged. "I dunno. Do you?"

"Soft mattress would be nice," Will said, as he kicked away rocks and pinecones before he spread out his bedroll on the hard earth. "But I don't know what I'd do at home."

"It's different for you," Jonah muttered. "Drew keeps you hoppin.' But how many times can I check the damn harnesses? Even farmin' is more agreeable than this."

"Army life isn't what I expected either," Will said. "All the starting and stopping."

"We ain't even searchin' for a new pass," Jonah added. "Thought that was our mission."

"Colonel Drew's still thinking about the route," Will said. "He talks about how to improve it in his notes."

"As long as we're gettin' paid, I won't complain," Joel said. "It's hard work, but no harder'n prospectin.' And some other man fixes my meals."

Will chuckled at Joel's comment. But so far, he didn't relish his military experience. He thought of boys his age in the East, fighting wars against each other. Mama's younger half-brother in Missouri could be among them. All Will had to contend with were obstinate mules and a verbose colonel. He supposed he should be grateful.

# Chapter 40: A Letter Home

On the morning of Monday, July 25, while the expedition still sat in camp in Surprise Valley, Drew called Will to his tent. "Ride out with our scouting party today, McDougall. See what we do."

"Yes, sir," Will said, and rushed to saddle Shanty. He was glad for the opportunity to see something besides his fellow packers and the backsides of their horses and mules.

They explored the hills between Surprise Valley and the summit they'd recently crossed. As they rode, Drew pointed out landmarks and vegetation. "Write down what I tell you," he ordered Will. "Just a few words. We'll expand on it tonight."

Will took out a pencil and notebook and scribbled what Drew said.

When they returned to camp in late afternoon, Drew kept him for two hours, straight through supper. As Will read back his notes from the day, Drew dictated lengthy paragraphs on each topic.

The colonel spouted at length about the suitability of the area for military purposes. "Wide open expanses are visible from the tops of the cliffs," he said. "Scouts posted in these positions could see any tribesmen approaching and warn those in the valleys below. The uplands are covered with luxuriant bunch grass, and the valleys are fertile, with plenty of water, and well adapted for cultivation. Some land along Goose Lake is alkaline, but much of the shore sprouts an excellent growth of rye grass and other vegetation. The Army should build fortifications to control passage of emigrants and Indians through the valleys."

"Sir?" Will asked when Drew paused to sip his whiskey. "Wouldn't the tribes also use the hilltops to watch for white men?"

Drew's brow furrowed, and Will wondered if the colonel found his interruption impudent. "Of course," the colonel responded. "That's why the Army must take control of this region immediately. Think of passing through this valley with Indians lurking above us. Now, let's get this finished. I'm sending a courier back to Klamath tomorrow when we leave camp. He can take the notes you've written to date."

Will shivered as he thought of Indians lurking above. Maybe there were tribesmen watching them now.

When he completed the day's report, Drew dictated a brief note to the commandant at Fort Klamath. "We head to Fort Boise, escorting the Humboldt-based wagons through Indian territory. From this point on, it will be too distant to send regular reports back to Klamath. Please preserve the enclosed notes for my return."

After Drew released him, Will slunk toward the quartermaster's wagon, hoping there were still leftovers from supper.

"Just washed the last of the pots," Sergeant Beaty said when Will asked if there was anything to eat. "Stew's all gone."

Beaty kept tight charge of the militia's provisions, and Will turned to walk away. He'd have to hope for an extra biscuit in the morning.

"Got some corn pone still," the sergeant called after Will. "But you probably wouldn't be interested in that."

"Yes, I would, sir," Will said, returning with a grin.

Beaty harrumphed. "Who you callin' sir? I ain't no officer, and I hear tell you're a college-bound boy."

Will shrugged as he bit into the heavy bread.

"Don't you want some honey on that?"

Will nodded with his mouth full. He swallowed and took the plate and jar of honey the man handed him, then swirled the honey on the corn pone. He took another bite and savored the sweetness on the coarse crunchy bread. "Thank you," he murmured.

"Colonel Drew keepin' you busy?"

Will nodded around another bite of the pone.

"The colonel's always liked to hear himself talk. Likes for others to listen to him, too."

"Mmm," Will choked out.

"So, you goin' to college like Joel Pershing says?"

Will swallowed. "I'm not sure what I'll do after this expedition."

Beaty frowned. "You take every opportunity offered you, son. Not all of us git a chance like that. You git all the education you can, and use it. Scrivenin' for the colonel is a start, and based on what he tells me, you're a whip-smart lad. You best use the smarts God gave you."

Will nodded silently. But he might have wrecked any chance of Mac sending him to college by running away.

When Will returned to the packers' camp after his late supper, Jonah was already in bed. "It isn't that late," Will said. "Are you sick?"

"Nah," Jonah said. "Joel went off drinkin' in the woods with the other packers. He wouldn't let me go. You was with Drew. Nothin' to do but go to bed."

"Still homesick?" Will asked as he took off his boots.

"Some." Jonah sighed. "I hope Iris ain't forgot me. Hope she ain't found another fella."

"If she loves you, she won't forget you." Will didn't know that for sure, but that's what people wrote in the novels Mama read. And he felt sure that Mama and Maria had not forgotten him.

"She don't even know where I am," Jonah said. "No one does but you and Joel."

"Write a letter home," Will said. "Drew is sending a messenger to Fort Klamath tomorrow. He told me so tonight."

"Really?" Jonah sat up at that.

"Do you want some paper and a quill and ink?" Will asked.

"Are you gonna you write home?" Jonah asked, taking what Will offered.

Will swallowed. "Why not?" he said. Mama deserved to know where he was.

After Jonah finished a letter to Esther, Will took another piece of paper and the pen and ink and wrote:

*July 25, 1864*
*Dear Mama,*

He decided to send the letter only to Mama, because he didn't know how to address Mac.

*I am safe with the First Oregon Cavalry Militia, led by Lt. Col. Charles Drew. We are exploring the region between Fort Klamath and Fort Boise. I do not know when we will return to Fort Klamath, but I shall let you know when we arrive. Jonah and I are with his brother Joel. We have hired on as mule packers with the expedition. I also serve as Lt. Col. Drew's scribe for many of his notes and letters.*

*My love to you and the rest of the family,*

*Will*

Early on July 26, Drew called Will to his tent again to pack up the papers they'd written thus far.

"I have letters from my friend and me to our families," Will said. "May I enclose those in the packet to Fort Klamath?"

Drew nodded. "Ask around to see if any other men have correspondence. This will be their last opportunity to communicate until we reach Boise. There's little between here and there, and we do not know our route."

When Will had completed this task, he handed the mail packet to the two soldiers heading to Fort Klamath, and they rode away. Will stared after them. In part, he wished he were returning with them. In part, he wished he'd kept his whereabouts to himself. What would happen when Mama and Mac learned where he and Jonah were?

The expedition and the wagons they guarded traveled twelve miles that day, ending at Cow Head Lake, higher in the mountains toward Boise. Their route was circumscribed by what grade the wagons could climb. Drew relied on the Indian scouts who preceded them to mark the trail. The land became increasingly dry and the vegetation sparser. Some water trickled through gullies, but this late in the season, only small mountain lakes like Cow Head held enough water for all their animals.

When Jonah told Joel they had written home, Joel chortled. "Writin' home like mamas' boys." Then he sobered. "Good for you, lads. I shoulda made you write home afore we left Klamath. Esther'n Daniel will be glad to know where Jonah is. And you," he said to Will, "I know your parents care about you."

"Mac doesn't care," Will muttered. "He's glad to see me gone, I'll bet."

"That ain't true," Joel said. "Why, I never seen a pa so proud to have a son."

"What do you mean?" Will asked. How would Joel know how Mac felt?

"I was there when you was born," Joel said. "At Whitman Mission. Mac detoured the wagons to Whitman, just so Miz Jenny'd be comfortable. He stayed with her all through your birthin'—him, and Doc and Miz Tuller with him."

"He detoured the wagons?" Will knew he'd been born at Whitman Mission, but he'd never heard that Mac took the wagons to the mission so he'd be born there.

"Yes, indeed. And then when you come, he carried you out so we all could see you." Joel guffawed. "He weren't too comfortable holdin' a baby and passed you off to some woman soon enough. But he was so proud he almost popped his buttons. And don't you ever think otherwise."

What a show Mac put on about a baby who wasn't even his, Will thought, uncertain whether to believe Joel.

# Chapter 41: Guano Lake

The little valley around Cow Head Lake offered good spring water and plentiful grass for the horses, mules, and cattle. They camped on the lake for three days, while Drew and his scouts made more forays into the hills around the valley.

Jonah and the other packers lolled in camp or hunted and fished, but Will got no respite. Drew commanded his presence on the scouting trips.

"Signs of Indians all around us," Drew said one afternoon as they rode through the dry hills. "Though we haven't seen a single one."

The lead Klamath scout confirmed, "Plenty sign other tribes. Maybe Paiute. Maybe Chief Paulina's people."

Drew swore. "Why do you think it's Paulina?"

"Who's Paulina?" Will asked.

"He's the Paiute chief whose band attacked Richardson's wagons," Drew said, with an impatient glance at Will. "Or so we think."

"And he's nearby?" Will glanced over his shoulder.

"No telling." Drew said. He turned back to the scout. "Why do you say it's Paulina?" he asked again.

"Paiutes camp here every year," the scout said. "Build lodges on Warner Mountain. Trade with Snakes and Klamaths."

"Where are the signs?" Drew demanded.

The scouts pointed out tracks of unshod horses and a few broken pottery shards. "We see 'em soon," the lead scout promised.

As they rode on, Will asked the scout, "These tribesmen attacked the Richardson wagons?"

The scout nodded. "Maybe so."

"Are they peaceable now?" Will asked.

The Klamath Indian shrugged. "We find out."

That night after transcribing his notes with Drew, a weary Will crawled into his bedroll, making sure his whittling knife and rifle were within reach. Despite his fatigue, he lay awake worrying about Indians in the hills.

On July 29, Drew ordered the expedition to move up the valley. "We've exhausted the grass in this camp," he told the quartermaster. "Find another camp north of here."

"I rode that way yesterday," Sergeant Crockett told him. "Grass and water ain't as good."

"But our beasts have eaten everything around here," Drew said. "It'll do for a day or two."

So while Drew, the scouts, and Will explored again, the quartermaster moved the camp to the north end of Cow Head Lake.

That night after Will arrived in camp, Jonah complained, "You're getting off easy."

"What do you mean?" Will asked. He certainly didn't feel like he had it easier than Jonah.

"You get to ride with Drew during the days, then sit with him in the evenings. I unpacked your mules tonight," Jonah fumed, "while you sat in a shady tent."

"I've been ordered to scribe. It's work, too." Will liked the scouting and scrivening hours with Drew, though he constantly felt like he was on tenterhooks with the colonel. Drew never told him he was doing a good job, and Will thought he must be falling short in some respect. "I'd rather handle the mules."

From Cow Head Lake, the militia and their entourage moved into Warner's Valley below a mountain of the same name. As they progressed northward through the valley in early August, they camped in a different site every day or two.

The pattern continued—Drew, the scouts, and a small cavalry squad explored, while the rest of the militia guarded the slow-rolling wagons and plodding oxen.

Will tried to keep up his own journal after scrivening for Drew, but his entries were brief. After writing until his hand hurt, he had little interest in writing more. Still, he wanted to have a record of this trip, one he could keep when his travels were over.

> *August 1, 1864. Traveled 20 miles, then camped at south end of Warner Valley.*
> *August 3, 1864. Moved 9 miles up valley to springs on a small lake.*
> *August 5, 1864. Went 17 miles to Clover Camp, so named because of fine grazing.*

On August 6, the reconnaissance unit rode twelve miles away from the wagons up into the hills, then returned to camp that night—a twenty-four-mile ride, through land so arid there weren't even dry gullies, let alone any flowing creeks.

"Go to bed, son," Drew said when they rode into camp. "We'll transcribe our notes tomorrow." Even the colonel staggered as he dismounted—he must be as tired as Will.

Will nodded his thanks. After caring for Shanty, he trudged wearily to bed.

In the middle of the night, Jonah woke Will up as he left for guard duty.

"Be quiet, Jonah," Will mumbled. "I'm tired."

"You ain't had guard duty in a week," Jonah said. "And I've had the midnight shift every other day. 'Tain't fair."

"You rested in a clover patch today, while I rode twenty-four miles," Will protested. "You probably ate fresh fish, too. And I got leftover beans."

"And now I'm gonna lose sleep for the rest of the night."

"Fine," Will said. "I'll care for your mules tomorrow."

"You should take 'em for the next week to make us even," Jonah muttered.

Will pretended not to hear his friend. After Jonah left, Will whispered to himself, "I wish I'd never left home."

Drew gave the expeditionary force a day of rest on Sunday, August 7, then they set out again on Monday, traveling three days without a break. As they traveled during the hot, tedious summer days, Will and Jonah argued. They fought over whose mules were most cantankerous, who had the better horse, the height of the surrounding mountains, and how soon they'd reach Fort Boise.

On the evening of August 10, the expedition camped near a small grove of pines on Warner's Mountain, which Drew named Lone Pines. The colonel didn't ask for help that evening, so Will rested near a campfire with Joel and Jonah. Will was scheduled for guard duty later that night, and he wanted to get to bed early. But Jonah bickered with him again over whose lot in life was worse.

Finally, Joel flipped a twig at Jonah. "Act like a man," he said, which seemed to be his stock advice to the boys. "You're gettin' fed every day through little effort of your own. And paid good money to boot."

"Farmin' was easier'n this," Jonah muttered.

"Then head home soon as we get back to Fort Klamath," Joel said. "I ain't asked to listen to you bellyache."

They rested a few days at Lone Pines, then moved on again on August 13, traveling twenty-three miles through an interminable sage desert spotted with small water holes and springs. Some of the watering spots were surrounded by marshes covered in dense cane that grew as high as a man on horseback. Some of the springs were hot and others cold as snow runoff, some were good-tasting and others full of minerals.

Through the entire long day, they found no grass for their animals. Finally, Drew called the halt on a foul lake he named, for reasons obvious to Will, Guano Lake. The water teemed with ducks and geese. The men had to dig along the lake shores to find water clean enough for cooking, but no one found it palatable to drink.

"Better boil this water good afore you drink it," Joel advised.

"I can't even breathe," Jonah complained. "This place stinks."

"What do you expect from a lake named Guano?" Will chuckled. "This isn't a place I'd want Mama or Maria to know about."

Tracks of shoed horses, Indian ponies, and wagon wheels all converged on a beaten trail heading south from the lake. A small group of Indians watched from the hills above, and Will wondered if it was Paulina's band.

"Do you think they'll attack?" Will asked Joel.

Joel spat. "Depends on how many of them there are. We got a lot of soldiers with us. And a howitzer. Odds are, we're safe enough. But who knows?"

They only remained at Guano Lake one night. The poor water and need for better grass sent them on their way early the next morning. But the two Indian scouts who had been with them since Fort Klamath refused to go with them. Will overheard the conversation between Drew and the scouts.

"We leave now, Colonel," the lead scout told Drew.

"You signed on for the whole reconnaissance," Drew argued. "You can't leave."

"Wagons too slow," the scout told him. "We need go home."

"Who will lead us through the Owyhee?" Drew demanded. "We're barely into the region we planned to explore."

"Your men do fine." The scout mounted his horse. Before they left, however, he turned to Drew and said, "Chief Paulina near. You watch out."

"Damn," Drew said. "Did you see Paulina's men? Is that why you're leaving?"

The Klamath scout shrugged, and he and his fellow scout rode off, while Drew continued cursing.

When Drew's tirade ended, Will asked, "Paulina—he's the Paiute chief?"

"Yes, damn it. Those savages leave us with wagons and cattle to defend, and God knows how many warriors in the vicinity."

Now they had only one guide—a man who had joined them in Surprise Valley.

After the Indian scouts abandoned the expedition, the wagons and teams left Guano Lake. As they traveled, they saw many more tracks of horses, mules, and wagons.

During the day, one of the female travelers in Richardson's wagon train became violently ill. Dr. Greer, the militia surgeon, attended her, but Will saw him shaking his head when Drew asked for a report on her condition.

"High fever and intestinal problems," Will heard the doctor tell the colonel. "Could be from Guano Lake. Could be something else."

"What can we do for her?" Drew asked.

"Let's put her in the quartermaster's ambulance. Her constitution can't take the jostling of her family's wagon. And I'll be better able to keep my eye on her."

Drew frowned. "Will she improve?"

The doctor shrugged. "She'd be best off with a rest of a few weeks, maybe months. Even then, she's near death and might not be saved at all."

They rode on through the largest sagebrush bushes Will had seen yet. The sage slowed the expedition further, as the worst of it had to be chopped before the wagons could roll over it. They couldn't stop without water and grass, and so they pushed on. They traveled twenty-eight miles, lasting from early morning until after the sun set.

Finally, they reached a spring that burst forth from the side of a mountain about fifty miles away from the Warner Mountain peak. Water flowed into a grassy ravine wide enough for the wagons to pass, with sufficient bunch grass for the animals.

"What say we call this Isaac's Springs?" Drew proclaimed. "As a compliment to our guide."

To the relief of all, they were able to make a relatively pleasant camp near the spring.

*August 14, 1864. Camped at Isaac's Springs after trekking 28 miles. Klamath scouts left us. Drew is worried, so I am, too.*

# Chapter 42: Telegrams from Boston

Throughout August, Mac occupied his days with his business affairs. One day, he traveled to Portland to meet with William Ladd. There, Mac renewed his expression of interest in a potential bank partnership with Ladd. He described his father's and brother's banking enterprise in Boston, and Ladd was suitably impressed.

"Can we call on your family to be informal partners in our venture?" Ladd asked. "Of course, banks can only be chartered within a state, even with the new National Banking Act. But surely, enterprises with similar interests can work together across state lines."

Mac nodded. "I have not seen my family since I left the East in forty-seven. But I am on cordial—albeit distant—terms with them." He grinned. "And my father and brother have never turned down a deal that is likely to make them a profit."

"Have you explored this project with them?"

"I wrote them in the spring after you and I first discussed it," Mac said. "I recently received a response from my brother Owen that their bank is interested, but they need a prospectus. That's why I'm here today."

"And your father?"

"I believe his age has led him to turn over management of the bank to Owen. But Owen would not have responded favorably without our father's approval." Mac had been away from home so long now, he didn't really know how his father and brother worked together. But he was certain that as long as old Andrew McDougall breathed, he would not allow his empire to move in a direction he didn't support. Mac's father ruled family and business with an iron hand.

The men talked, and Ladd provided Mac with the information his brother wanted. He promised a written prospectus within a month.

Goods were slowly filling Mac's warehouses in Sacramento, and his California agent wrote to report which products were selling at the greatest profit. With gold mines in California now producing less, Mac decided to focus his attentions on supplying agricultural interests around Sacramento.

But his investment in Pengra's road in Eugene plagued him. Progress on that was pitifully slow, and the investors faced competition from another company with different proposed route through Oregon.

Mac wrote Pengra:

*August 17, 1864*
*Sir:*
    *Might I inquire as to the progress of your survey? I hear reports it is delayed. Until the road is in place and your land grants determined, I will have no return on my investment.*
        *Respectfully,*
        *Caleb McDougall*

Mac received a response from Pengra within a week:

*August 22, 1864*
*Dear Mr. McDougall:*
    *Due to the presence of warring tribes in the area, I requested a military escort for our survey. Unfortunately, all Federal and State militia units are already occupied this summer, and the survey must be postponed until next year.*
    *I trust you understand,*
        *Your servant,*
        *Byron Pengra*

Mac swore in frustration—his money was committed, and he wouldn't see any profit for more than a year to come. At least he hadn't increased his participation in the road venture when Pengra asked.

And the People's Transportation Company, the steamboat enterprise he'd had such hopes for in the spring, was thwarted at every juncture by the Oregon Steam Navigation Company. The Columbia River, both above The

Dalles and below, carried enough traffic that it ought to be able to support two steamship companies. But O.S.N. Company had started a price war, and the P.T. Company faced mounting losses. Mac made a note to visit the P.T. Company owners and discuss how they could reduce costs.

As Mac sat in his office one late August morning, a delivery boy knocked on the door. "Telegram for you, Mr. McDougall," the lad said. "Shall I wait for a response?"

Mac glanced at the telegram. It was from his brother.

*DATE: 24 AUGUST 1864*
*TO: CALEB MCDOUGALL OREGON CITY*
*FROM: OWEN MCDOUGALL BOSTON*
   *FATHER HAD STROKE NEAR DEATH MOTHER WANTS*
*YOU HOME*

Mac frowned, alarmed at the news of his father's illness. Should he make a trip to Boston after so many years? How could he? It would take weeks and months, when he had so many family and business problems in Oregon.

He paid the boy and shook his head. "No answer now."

After the lad left, Mac leaned back in his chair and stared at the ceiling. He thought of old Andrew McDougall—brusque, blustery, and always right. Mac had feared his father throughout childhood. The youngest of three boys, Mac was never good enough for his father, or so he was led to believe.

As Mac grew to adulthood, he realized he and his father simply had different approaches to life and livelihood. After seeking his father's approval for years, Mac relinquished that hope and relished making his own way in Oregon and California. Yet, he still wanted his father's respect. Many of Mac's decisions in the West had been designed to prove himself worthy of his father's regard.

Their communications in recent years dealt almost entirely with money— what investments each thought the other should make in their respective spheres. Through their correspondence, Mac came to see that Andrew McDougall did value his youngest son's experience.

It was so like both his mother and brother to demand his presence, Mac thought, without any regard to Mac's circumstances in Oregon. No mention of the difficulty of travel. No mention of his family. No mention of his need to attend to his own affairs.

When Mac showed his brother's telegram to Jenny later that day, she exclaimed, "Oh, Mac—your poor father. Will you go to him?" She knew relations were strained between Mac and his family, but his father was near death. He might feel he had to go, even if she needed him home. With William gone and a new child on the way, she wanted Mac with her. But she wouldn't keep him, she resolved.

"What do you think I should do?" he asked, sitting heavily on the sofa beside her.

She cupped his cheek in her hand. "If ever you were to return to Boston, this would be the time to go."

"But Will—"

Tears came to her eyes. It pleased her that Mac mentioned William's absence first. "I can manage." She said it as much to convince herself as to convince Mac. "I have coped for four months without William. I can cope without you also if I must. I was alone for two years when William was little."

"I wouldn't be gone that long, Jenny." Mac sighed. "But I worry about leaving you. Quite apart from Will, Jacob Johnson might still be in Oregon. The sheriff has never found his hideout."

"He must have left the area," Jenny said. Truly, she thought, if he were still around, they would have heard something. "This could be your last chance to see your father. You must go."

Mac nodded, but he seemed unconvinced.

Mac dithered all evening. His best hope of finding his father alive was to leave for Boston immediately. But he didn't want to go. Not with the situation in Oregon so unsettled. Between Will's departure, Jacob Johnson's attack, and his business problems, he thought he should remain at home.

But he hadn't seen his parents or brothers in almost eighteen years. His parents had demanded his return to Boston often through the years, and he had always put them off. He'd been angry at them when he left for Oregon for several reasons. His father had demanded that Mac join his brother's law firm. His mother had dismissed a maid who later died—preventing Mac from righting a wrong he'd done to the girl.

Families were complicated, Mac thought as he sipped his whiskey in his home study. He'd tried to be a better parent than his own parents had been. He thought he'd done a decent job of fathering. Even with Will and Maria, his adopted offspring. He did everything he could to treat them the same as his children by blood.

In part the adoptions had been recompense for the sins of his youth. The maid had been pregnant with Mac's child, though he hadn't known it until after her death. Surely raising Will and Maria as his own was sufficient atonement for his past misdeeds. Both children had come into being through unfortunate circumstances, and Mac had given them each a better life than they would otherwise have had. Will and Maria—and their entire family— were happier because Mac had taken on their care.

And he'd come to love them both dearly.

Mac's reflections on his own childhood and youth did nothing to resolve his conflict over going to Boston. As he tossed and turned in bed that night, he decided to send his brother a telegram in the morning to find out more about his father's condition.

If his father had already died, he could take his time about leaving. If his father were improving, there would similarly be no rush in returning to Boston. In any event, it would take him weeks to return East.

The next morning, he took his telegram to the office in Oregon City. As he gave it to the clerk, he remembered that early March morning when he'd taken Will and Cal to Portland—only five months ago. So much had happened since.

*DATE: 25 AUGUST 1864*
*TO: OWEN MCDOUGALL BOSTON*
*FROM: CALEB MCDOUGALL OREGON CITY*
    *REQUEST UPDATE ON FATHER REGARDS TO YOU AND*
*MOTHER*

# Chapter 43: Indian Encounters

The militia unit and the wagon trains rested at Isaac's Springs, allowing the horses, mules, and cattle to graze their fill. The first evening, Drew made sure the howitzer was ready to defend the camp. "There are likely Paiute in the area," he said. "We need to be prepared. I want the artillery manned at all times. And double the guards on our animals. Be ready to shoot."

Despite ordering extra protection for the camp, each day Drew led lightly armed reconnaissance parties to explore the surrounding valley. Then he called Will to scribe. "In addition to frequent water sources," he dictated about their surroundings, "there is an abundance of excellent bunch grass. The land rises in steppes, one above the other, forming Warner's Mountain."

When Will accompanied the scouting party one day, the cavalry soldiers pointed out signs of Paiutes. "We've left the Klamaths behind," Drew said. "We're in Winnemucca's territory now."

"Who's Winnemucca?" Will asked.

"A Paiute chief. They claim their land runs from here south to the Old Emigrant Road, east to the Humboldt River, and west to the Sierra Nevadas."

"Is Winnemucca likely to attack us for entering his territory?" Will asked.

Drew shrugged. "Don't know much about him. Paulina is the greater Paiute problem in these parts. I still think he and his men are following us. I don't know why they haven't approached us, but it makes me suspicious."

On August 17, after three days at Isaac's Springs, the expeditionary force and the wagons under their protection moved on. They traveled twenty-four miles through more desert south from Isaac's Springs on a gradual descent to Pueblo Valley.

Vertical rock walls bounded the valley on either side. A small creek ran through a deep crevice in one cliff. Grass grew rampant along the creek's banks, and there was enough space for the entire caravan to camp.

They still saw signs of Indians, as they had since they approached Warner's Mountain. But once in the valley beyond the mountain, the tracks left by the local tribes became more frequent.

"They're here," Drew murmured to Will as they worked that evening. "Indians. All around us. They go into caves in the hills in the evenings, but they're following us by day."

Will didn't know whether to believe Drew. "How can you tell?"

"I can feel them," the colonel replied.

*August 17, 1864. Col. Drew says Paulina is watching us. As we ride, I feel the Indians in the hills, just like Drew does.*

After the long trek to Pueblo Valley, they rested in camp on August 18. That evening, an Indian man was escorted to Drew's tent while Will was taking dictation.

"Humboldt Jim. Paiute tribe," the native said when asked for his name. He spoke rough English and carried a Philadelphia long rifle, which he wanted to sell. Despite the rifle, the Indian acted peaceable. The colonel questioned Jim, but relaxed when it seemed their visitor was neither belligerent nor seeking any handouts.

Then Jim said, "Chief Paulina following you."

Drew sat up straight and stared at the Paiute. "As I suspected. Where is he?"

"Paulina not bother you. He see your big gun."

"The howitzer?" Drew grinned. "So that's what's keeping him away?"

Jim nodded.

Drew chortled. "You tell Paulina I'll use my big gun on him if I see him or any other Indians approaching."

"But you let me trade?" Jim asked, sounding more concerned about his own profit than serving as a messenger to Chief Paulina.

Drew nodded, with another chuckle. "Why not? If you're alone, you're no danger. But when you leave, you find Paulina. Tell him the Army won't permit him to bother us or the wagons with us."

The Indian left, and Will continued scribing. When Drew dismissed him,

Will found Humboldt Jim in the middle of the emigrant wagons, attempting to bargain with the settlers. Jim made a deal for his rifle, then took a five-dollar gold coin out of his pocket to show one of the white men. When the emigrant offered Jim a dollar and a quarter for the gold coin, the Paiute happily accepted.

"But—" Will started to object, until the settler glared at him and shook his head.

Jim seemed delighted to receive two large coins for his single five-dollar gold coin. No wonder Indians got mad at whites, Will thought—Jim was cheated because he didn't understand how white men valued money. If he ever realized his error, the tribesman would be angry.

This next day, Will mentioned the incident to Drew, and the colonel laughed. "That's the way it goes. The natives are all assassins at heart," he said. "A horde of practical thieves, highwaymen, and murderers." He sniffed. "Though at least the Paiute don't prostitute their women as many of the tribes do."

Will frowned, thinking Humboldt Jim didn't seem anything like Drew's assessment of Indians.

Drew continued, "Though when the Paiute find a woman who's taken up with another man, they burn her alive." He guffawed, as he had when Humboldt Jim told him about Paulina's fear of the howitzer. "That tends to reduce her sinfulness."

Will swallowed hard, trying not to show the colonel his disgust.

Drew leaned toward him. "You've got to understand, McDougall. Nearly all the tribes in the West—Oregon and California both—consider murder, rape, and robbery to be virtues of the highest order. The more an Indian engages in these activities, the higher his rank in the tribe. They rape the women of their enemies when captured and enslave the women and children. The War in the East is being fought over slavery, but we fight it here in the West as well. Native slaveholders are even more cruel than white owners."

Will sat silently, not knowing how to react. Joel had told him Drew was a Copperhead, but now the colonel sounded like he abhorred the enslavement of both Blacks and Indians. Mac had taught Will that all slavery was cruel. But Drew's understanding of the tribes was far different from Mac's. Drew had fought in the Indian Wars for many years, while Mac worked in commerce and had little contact with Indians. Which man should Will believe?

"Klamaths are worse than Paiutes," Drew continued. "The Klamath kill their children and slaves with as little compunction as we would kill a venomous snake. Do not forget that in any dealings with Indians. Their ways are not like ours."

Will worried about the conversation with Drew as he lay in his bedroll that night. He'd thought Humboldt Jim was gullible, but not evil. And why had Drew hired Klamath guides, if he had such a low opinion of that tribe?

On August 19, the expedition moved on from the camp near the Paiutes and rode twenty-two miles farther into Pueblo Valley. Pueblo Mountain rose above them as they passed between it and a small alkaline lake with a hot spring at its head. The valley held little grass and was mostly a sand and sage plain, with barely enough fodder for the animals and alkaline soil that chafed the beasts' hooves. Nevertheless, they made do with a camp in the inhospitable lowlands that night.

The next morning, while the wagons and a military escort traveled five miles farther up the Pueblo Valley canyon, Drew led Will and a small squad to reconnoiter the valley. They found an abandoned Paiute village with about sixty deserted Indian lodges. Not only were there tracks from unshod Indian horses, but also from American horses, mules, and cattle. The village offered many signs the residents had profited from an attack on whites. Scraps of calico were tied on the lodge poles, and glazed pottery shards lay in trash heaps.

"Was this Chief Paulina's camp?" Will asked.

Drew shrugged. "Doubtful. Humboldt Jim said Paulina stayed in the hills. This was likely a winter camp for another band of Paiutes. It doesn't matter now—they're gone."

Drew dismounted and walked about, kicking the dirt. "There's evidence the residents here plundered an American settlement or wagon train. See the horseshoe prints? And the cattle bones are from well-fed beef." He pointed out other remnants from white settlers, then he peered up at the surrounding mountains. "The Army needs an outpost nearby."

The reconnaissance party returned to the wagons and the rest of the expeditionary force. The next morning, the entire group moved eleven miles farther through the valley to Trout Creek, which teemed with its namesake fish.

"Don't know how these fish got here," Joel commented as he fished with Will and Jonah that evening. "This creek ain't connected to any bigger river I seen."

Will didn't care how the fish got there, as long as he could catch and eat his share. They were as tasty as any of the other mountain trout the men had hooked. The three of them sat in the shade of a willow tree that grew along the stream's banks. The willows were large, but the cottonwoods were broken and bushy. Bunch grass and other wild grasses grew abundantly, and the horses and pack mules grazed contentedly. Man and beast both ate well that evening.

Will had taken notes for Lt. Col. Drew earlier in the evening, and the officer had commented on the vegetation, ending with the observation, "There is no good timber in the region until the Sierra Nevada Mountains approximately one-hundred and fifty miles distant." The colonel had not seemed impressed with Pueblo Valley as a place to encourage settlement. His only concern was its military potential.

The expedition rested at Trout Creek for several days. Drew took a small cavalry squad out each day to explore while the emigrants rested their oxen. Joel and Jonah stood guard duty or hunted and fished. But often the colonel asked Will to join the reconnaissance party as his scribe.

One day, Drew took the scouts and Will to explore the mountain that rose from the valley's floor. They rode out from Trout Creek and climbed the side of Pueblo Mountain, crisscrossing it to ease the horses' ascent.

As they approached the top of the mountain, they heard the rhythmic sound of a machine. Near the summit, they found prospectors operating a steam-powered crushing mill. "The Pueblo mines," Drew commented. "The miners grind the stones into gravel and pebbles. Then they sift through the smaller rock looking for precious metals."

"Gold?" Will asked.

"These mines are mostly copper," Drew replied. "Though the miners in these parts claim there is gold and silver as well." He asked one miner, "What are you burning to run the mill?"

"Sage." The man grinned through black teeth. "Lotta sage in these parts."

"That there is," Drew said. "What about Indians?"

"A lotta them, too," the man said. "Savages raid us every so often. So far, all they done is steal horses and a few cattle."

"Why do you stay when it's so dangerous?" Will couldn't help himself from interjecting.

"If'n we strike gold or silver," the miner said, "we'll be rich."

"You do have some means of protecting yourself, don't you?" Drew asked.

"We all got rifles," the prospector said, grinning again.

"How many of you are there in this camp?" Drew asked.

The miner shrugged. "Men come and go. Maybe thirty of us now."

Drew snorted. "And you think you can fend off a band of Paiute warriors?"

After they wandered through the mining camp for an hour, Drew motioned his men to depart. "These men are blind to everything except the possibility of gold and silver," he commented to Will as they rode away from the mine. "They're essentially gamblers."

"What will you do about them?" Will asked.

Drew sighed. "The militia is required to protect them, whether or not they're reasonable. A few rifles won't keep the tribes away." He waved an arm to encompass the mountain and valley beneath it. "We need an Army presence in the area. Part of our mission on this expedition is to find the best location for it."

Jonah was upset when Will returned. "You got to see the mine, and I didn't," he said. "I come south to mine for gold and I ain't seen nothin' about minin' yet. Only the one day pannin' with Joel in Jacksonville."

Will shrugged. "There wasn't much to see. Just a lot of sluices and rock piles."

Joel chortled. "I guess you ain't got the prospectin' bug, Will," he said. Then he turned to his younger brother. "If it's mines you want, Jonah, I'll take you to the mines around Jacksonville when we get back."

# Chapter 44: Letter from Will

Jenny rolled pie dough flat and filled pie pans as she helped Mrs. O'Malley with supper preparations. Maggie stood on a chair beside her mother and patted a bit of the dough into a little lump. "See, Mama," the toddler said. "I make pie, too."

"Yes, dear," Jenny said. "We'll get you some berries to go with your crust in a minute."

Maria rushed in. "Esther Abercrombie is here," she said. "She's brought a letter from Will."

Jenny dropped her rolling pin on the table and wiped her hands on her apron. Lifting a flour-covered Maggie onto her hip, she hurried toward the entry.

Esther stood in the front hall waving two letters, one opened and the other still sealed. "I got a letter from Jonah," she exclaimed. "And brought you a letter, too. Must be from Will. They're safe. They're with Joel, working for some militia unit." She prattled on about what Jonah had said as she handed Jenny the sealed letter.

Jenny set Maggie down, tore open the letter, and read aloud, "Dear Mama—"

"It *is* from Will," Maria murmured, clasping her hands as she peered over Jenny's shoulder.

Jenny beamed at Maria. "Yes," she said. "It's William. He's well." She led the others into the parlor. "But what are they doing with the militia?" she asked, as she continued to read.

"Joel will keep them safe," Esther said, smiling.

"But it's war time," Jenny said. "Any form of military service must bring some danger."

"We'll talk to Pa," Maria said. "He'll know."

"I do wish the boys would come home," Esther said. "What in tarnation made them leave here anyway?"

"We should send Mac and Daniel after them," Jenny said. But with the news about Mac's father, Mac would be torn—he was considering a trip to Boston.

As soon as Esther left, Jenny put on her bonnet and walked downtown to Mac's office, taking Will's letter with her. While Mac read, Jenny paced the room. "Now that we know where the boys are," she said, "we have to go after them. But you also need to see your father. Maybe Daniel can go by himself. Though they have the new baby, and the harvest will start soon." Jenny couldn't stay still as she spoke, worried about how to get William home.

"Before either Daniel or I set out, let's see if we can learn something about the boys from here," Mac said.

Jenny turned to him. "But a letter will take so long. Even to Fort Klamath, which is where he posted his letter. And that's the only place we know to write."

Mac smiled. "But now we have the telegraph."

"Oh, would you?" Jenny said. She hadn't thought about the telegraph, even though Mac now used it regularly for business and to communicate with his family back East. "Then we can decide if you should go to Boston or Klamath."

Mac headed for the telegraph office after Jenny left. He had two troubling reasons to leave Oregon City, though Jenny's pregnancy was reason to stay home.

One reason to leave was his father. He'd had no update from his brother about his father's condition, so he assumed the older McDougall still lived. It would take weeks to get to Boston. If he had any intention of seeing his father before the old man died, he needed to leave immediately, and it might already be too late. His relationship with his father had been stormy at best, but now he wondered whether to rush back to Boston hoping to make amends.

The other reason to leave was to find Will. Still, despite Jenny's worry, Will should be safe enough with the militia. Mac had feared the boys had run away to serve in the War in the East. By comparison, the Indian skirmishes in Oregon and California were tame. A man could get hurt, even killed, but these battles weren't wholesale slaughter like the Eastern campaigns.

But Jenny wanted her oldest son home. Mac did, too, truth be told. Will's departure left a hole in their household. Despite the boy's moodiness over the last year, he was part of their family.

Jacob Johnson's interference had only accelerated a rift between Will and his parents that would have happened anyway. Much like Mac's rift with his own parents, though Mac liked to think he'd been a better father to his children than his father had been to him.

Now Mac wrestled with whether to focus on his father's generation or his son's. He was trapped between them. Which relationship was it more important to repair?

And then there was Jenny.

Mac's first telegram went to Fort Boise, because Will's letter indicated the expedition was headed there.

*DATE: 31 AUGUST 1864*
*TO: COMMANDER FORT BOISE*
*FROM: CALEB MCDOUGALL OREGON CITY*
*MY SON WITH DREWS EXPEDITION WHEN DREW*
*EXPECTED BOISE*

He asked the telegraph operator to have any responses delivered to his office. An hour later, a boy knocked on the door. Mac paid the lad a penny and took the telegram.

*DATE: 31 AUGUST 1864*
*TO: CALEB MCDOUGALL OREGON CITY*
*FROM: MAJOR LUGENBEEL COMMANDER FORT BOISE*

*DREWS ARRIVAL UNKNOWN KLAMATH REPORTS THEM
EN ROUTE*

Mac swore. Will's letter had informed them of that much. So he returned to the telegraph office to send a telegram to Fort Klamath.

*DATE: 31 AUGUST 1864
TO: COMMANDER FORT KLAMATH
FROM: CALEB MCDOUGALL OREGON CITY
    WHEN DREW EXPECTED AT KLAMATH MY SON WITH
HIS EXPEDITION*

Again, he waited for a response. It was late in the day before he received the following:

*DATE: 31 AUGUST 1864
TO: CALEB MCDOUGALL OREGON CITY
FROM: COMMANDER FORT KLAMATH
    DREWS WHEREABOUTS AND ARRIVAL UNKNOWN NO
WORD SINCE 26 JULY*

July 26 was the date of Will's letter. The expedition was wandering in the mountains of southern Oregon. Mac remembered passing through the Snake River basin in the weeks before Will was born. The entire region was barren desert, covered with little other than sage, sand, and lava rocks.

There was no help for it—retrieving Will was impossible at the moment. He and Jenny would have to wait for Drew's expedition to reach one of the forts. At least the commandants knew Will had parents waiting for him at home.

His competing options were returning to Boston or staying home. And there was no guarantee he could reach his father in time.

Mac told Jenny he'd learned nothing from the fort commanders. "I think I should stay here," he told her. "Wait to hear from Will."

"Oh, Mac," she said. She cradled her belly with an arm, the way she always did when she was upset during pregnancy. "What about your poor father?"

Mac shrugged. "My father has lived without me for almost two decades. He hasn't demanded my return since I told him I planned to make my home with you in Oregon. It's only now that Father might be dying that my brother wants my presence."

"But you should make peace with your family," Jenny said. "If you can."

"Do you want me to go to Boston?"

Jenny bit her lip and shook her head. "No."

"Do you want me to go to Fort Klamath?"

"You just said we didn't know when William would return there."

Mac nodded. "That's right. We have no idea." He took her in his arms. "I can help most by staying here and taking care of you." It was the right decision, he believed, but he still felt a pang of guilt over not trying to see his father.

# Chapter 45: Camp Alvord and Beyond

After resting the animals at Trout Creek for several days, Drew led the expedition and emigrants on toward Camp Alvord in Stein's Valley. They made a long trek of twenty-eight miles on August 25 to Horse Creek, then continued another ten miles the next day to reach Camp Alvord.

As they rode toward the camp, Will asked Joel, "What's Camp Alvord? Another Army fort?"

Joel shrugged. "Beats me."

So Will asked the colonel, who replied, "No, not a fort. A simple camp. Company E of the First Oregon Cavalry Militia is there, led by Captain George Curry."

"Are we meeting them?" Will asked.

"I hope so," Drew said. "I want to find out what Curry knows about Indian troubles north of here. He's been on campaign all summer. Our quartermaster is low on supplies, and we need to proceed post-haste to Fort Boise to reprovision. I want all the intelligence I can gather before we head there."

"I thought we was exploring the Owyhee Basin," one soldier said.

"We've lost so much time moving at the slow pace of the wagon trains that fulfilling that part of our mission is doubtful," Drew said. "Though I hope we can engage in more reconnaissance on our return to Klamath. We won't have the emigrants with us then."

When they arrived at Alvord, they found Captain George Curry's troops settled into camp. Many of Curry's soldiers were ill with dysentery, and Curry planned to remain in camp for an extended period. The militia had built a few defensive earthworks around the Army's tents, but nothing

244

permanent.

Drew's party and their accompanying emigrants camped on a small mountain stream about two miles away from Curry's earthen outpost, where there was abundant grass for the animals. Wild grasses waved in the breeze and mixed with clover and small brush.

The men fixed their own supper their first evening in Camp Alvord. "Sergeant Crockett ain't well," one corporal told the packers. "Fend for yourselves tonight. Drew ain't named a replacement yet."

They remained at Camp Alvord for several days. Lt. Col. Drew named Sergeant Beaty as the temporary mess sergeant responsible for food preparation and rationing the militia's provisions. Sergeant Crockett suffered some stomach ailment and kept to his tent.

"And I'm naming Sergeant Geisy to have full charge of the packers until Sergeant Crockett can return to his duties," Drew announced.

Jonah and other packers grumbled at that. Geisy was stricter than Crockett in keeping the packers to Army regulations.

"At least we know what's what," Joel said. "I'd rather deal with Crockett, but Geisy is predictable—more so than the colonel, truth be told."

Will was silent, not wanting to malign Drew. He liked Crockett better than Geisy, but he'd rather follow the colonel than Geisy.

Crockett wasn't the only one sick. The woman emigrant who had sickened at Guano Lake remained critically ill. And others reported a variety of ailments. Surgeon Greer moved from one patient to the next.

Rather than sit in camp, Will and Jonah rode out into Stein's Valley when they weren't on guard duty. The valley was another basin covered with dry alkaline soil, but there were several grassy spots where creeks or springs provided water. Some streams appeared to run year-round, and other watersheds were now dry in the late-August heat.

"I'd rather sit in camp," Jonah complained. "It's too hot to ride."

"I thought you wanted to see the country," Will said.

"I'd most rather fish," Jonah said. "Or move on so's we can get home sooner."

One evening, Drew ordered Will to accompany him to talk with Captain Curry. "Take notes of what Curry says," Drew said.

"Chief Paulina has been following you," Curry told Drew.

Drew puffed on his cigar, then said, "I heard that from a Paiute who visited our camp, but I wasn't sure I believed him." Will raised an eyebrow at that, knowing how cautious Drew had been after Humboldt Jim's description of Paulina's actions.

"Our unit pestered Paulina's band through June and July, which sent him south," Curry said. "That's when he began pursuing you."

"The Paiute said our howitzer scared him off."

"Could be." Curry grinned and pointed his cigar at Drew. "Or could be he merely wanted to rest his men with food and water on Warner Mountain. Get them ready for raids later in the year."

"What are the tribes doing to the north between here and Fort Boise?" Drew asked Curry.

"Some marauding bands of Snakes, but you can handle them," Curry replied. "They're looking for easy targets, like prospectors who don't watch their backs. Or emigrant wagons."

"I don't know what to do with the wagons we're escorting," Drew said. "I'd thought to take them to Boise, but I'm not sure they can make it through the desert between here and there. And one of their women is gravely ill. We all need rest, but my cavalry unit must get to Boise for provisions."

"You could split up," Curry commented after a long puff. "Leave your sick and the wagons here."

"Might do that," Drew said. Then he and Curry turned to a map of the region, plotting out a route for a portion of the reconnaissance unit to reach Fort Boise quickly.

The next morning, Drew mustered his cavalry and the civilian teamsters and packers. "I'm dividing our forces," he said. "The next camp is thirty-three miles through rough terrain. On Crooked Creek. Some of the emigrant wagons can get there, but others need to rest. The weaker wagons will stay here, as will most of the militia. I'll take the packers, a cavalry squad, and the abler wagons in the emigrant companies on to Fort Boise."

Late in the afternoon of August 30, Drew sent the stronger wagons toward Crooked Creek. "I will lead the reprovisioning party. We'll travel until full dark," he instructed. "Then rest until first light. We'll do our best to make it to Crooked Creek before the heat of the day tomorrow." He ordered nineteen of the cavalry's enlisted men and the best horses to accompany the wagons.

"The rest of you," he instructed the other soldiers, "will remain in Camp Alvord with the weaker wagons and Captain Curry's unit. Sergeant Moore will be in command here at Camp Alvord while I am gone. And Surgeon Greer will stay to assist our invalids. The mule packers will come with me to haul supplies back from Boise. Sergeant Crockett reports he is well enough to come with us to Boise, but Sergeant Geisy will have direct supervision of the packers."

Will turned to get his mules ready to depart. "You, McDougall—where do you think you're going?" the colonel bellowed after him.

"Yes, sir?" Will asked.

"Stay with me. Tell the Pershing men to handle your mules. Without full packs, they should be able to handle your four beasts plus their own."

Will swallowed. Jonah would be mighty peeved.

*August 30, 1864: The packers will accompany Drew to Fort Boise. I am glad Sgt. Crockett will be with us, though Geisy is coming as well.*

Per his orders, Drew led the healthier portion of the expeditionary force, the packers, and the stronger emigrant wagons on a long night march toward Crooked Creek. They paused well after midnight for a few hours' rest, then continued at dawn, arriving at the creek around noon. Sergeant Crockett stayed in the quartermaster's wagon, and Geisy kept the packers in a tight group for the entire march.

Crooked Creek was a welcome respite after the long ride, an oasis of green in the middle of dry, parched land. As they'd passed through the desert, Will wondered whether he'd ever find a drop to fill his canteen.

The next morning, while they packed up their camp, a huge hailstorm beat down on them briefly. Will tried to shelter Shanty's head, but the gelding bucked when the icy pellets struck his haunches. "Whoa, boy," he murmured. "Bet you wish you were back at Camp Alvord with the sick folks."

The storm was over as quickly as it began, though the skies remained threatening. The men and beasts in the reprovisioning force continued their journey.

It was now September, Will realized in surprise, as they traveled along Crooked Creek. He would have been on his way to Harvard with Mac, or already there, if he'd followed Mac's plan for him.

Instead, he was a military man, intent on making it to Boise then back to Klamath. He wondered how long he would continue with Drew's outfit after the expedition. He wanted to leave the militia as soon as he could, though he would fulfill his contract, as he had committed.

That evening, after leaving his mules and Shanty in the herd, Will again sat in Drew's tent taking dictation. "Crooked Creek meanders through this volcanic valley as a thin trickle," Drew said. "Occasionally, it widens enough to permit a little grass to grow, but it passes mostly through country covered with lava, sand, and sage."

"How do you know that, sir?" Will asked. He often wondered at Drew's characterizations of the mountains and valleys they traversed.

"Know what, boy?"

"Know about volcanoes and lava and such?"

Drew puffed on his cigar and sipped his whiskey. Then he said, "I've been studying this land for over a decade. And I have an imagination."

"Did you go to college, Colonel?"

Drew frowned at Will. "Are you college bound?"

Will shrugged. "I was. Now I don't know. My fa-father—" Again, he saw no need to enlighten Drew on his family's tortured past. "My father went to Harvard before he came West."

"Ah, yes." Drew puffed on his cigar again and studied Will. "You'd do all right in college. But you'd get a faster start in life with a commission in the Army. I'd put in a good word for you. You're a bright boy. You can follow orders, and you have some sense." He pointed his cigar at Will. "Apart from that incident when you went after your horse."

"Thank you, sir." Will didn't want to join the Army after this expedition. He'd seen enough to know that by now. But he didn't want to cross Drew while he was still under the colonel's command.

*September 1, 1864. Drew wants me to join the Army. This expedition will be enough for me.*

After he was in his bedroll, Will thought more about his conversation with Drew. He didn't want to wake Jonah and Joel, but he wanted to talk to someone who knew him, who knew Mac. Drew commanded this expedition. But did he have the right approach to handling the tribesmen? Will remembered the emigrants and soldiers laughing at Humboldt Jim. Drew didn't seem to take the Indians seriously, except for when they were killing. Then he talked as if they were savages.

On the other hand, Drew treated the Indians fairly in the incident when Burton was killed. Drew recognized that those prospectors brought the violence on themselves.

Maybe the matter wasn't black and white on either side. Maybe Mac had the better side of the argument. But the world needed soldiers like Drew who could keep the peace. And Drew was better than many of them.

Will turned over and stared at the dying campfire. For the time being, he had no choice. He had to follow Drew's orders.

# Chapter 46: Special Express

Drew led the packers and the emigrants accompanying them from Crooked Creek into the Jordan Creek Valley. The mountains above the valley were covered with fir and pine, with cottonwoods lower on the slopes. The first day away from Crooked Creek, they traveled seventeen miles, and the second day took them another twenty-two miles.

Late on September 3, their second day into Jordan Creek Valley, as they were looking for a place to camp, two soldiers rode up. "Colonel Drew?" one shouted. "Is this Colonel Drew's party?" Their horses blew heavily as the newcomers slowed to a halt.

Drew turned his mount around. "Yes? I'm Drew."

"Sir." The soldier saluted, then took a paper out of his pocket. "I have an urgent message from Fort Klamath. We found part of your force at Camp Alvord, and we've followed you from there."

Drew held out a hand for the message, broke the seal, then read it with a frown. "We'll camp here," he said to Sergeant Geisy. Then he turned to the newcomers. "You men can stay the night. I'll have a reply for the Fort Klamath Commandant in the morning."

"Yes, sir." Both soldiers saluted and followed the cavalry in Drew's unit.

After they'd set up camp and eaten supper, Drew called Will into his tent. "Take this down," he said, then dictated, "To Commandant, Fort Klamath. From Lt. Col. Charles S. Drew. I am in receipt of your orders to return immediately to Fort Klamath for treaty negotiations with the tribes. However, my unit is in dire need of provisions. I must proceed to Fort Boise, obtain what we need, and rejoin my full force at Camp Alvord. Only then can we return to Klamath."

He turned to Will. "Read that back." Will did so, then Drew signed the document. "Take it to the messengers. Tell them to leave for Fort Klamath at first light."

"Yes, sir," Will said.

After Will completed Drew's order, he made his way to the packers' tents. Jonah lolled on his bedroll, and Joel sat smoking by the fire. "What's the news?" Joel asked.

"Drew's been ordered back to Klamath," Will said. "To negotiate a treaty with the tribes. But we're going to Boise first."

Joel snorted. "He don't follow orders well."

"We need provisions," Will protested. "We have to go on."

Joel blew a puff of smoke, then said, "Drew does what he likes. Not much of a soldier, if you ask me."

From beneath his blanket, Jonah murmured, "Suits me. I like seeing the country."

"Hah," Joel said. "Say that again when our mules are fully loaded after we hit Boise."

The messengers were gone when Will awoke on the morning of September 4. Drew's unit continued through Jordan Creek Valley. They reached the creek that evening, then camped on Jordan Creek for three nights, letting the wagons and their teams rest while Drew and a few of his men explored the region.

Once again, Joel waxed on about how Drew wasn't following orders. "We's supposed to be headed to Klamath, and he's restin' on the way to Boise? This is just like when he didn't bother arrivin' in Klamath until late July. The man is a law unto himself."

"But the wagons can't travel—" Will said.

"He could let the wagons fend for themselves," Joel argued. "They ain't a part of his mission. His first orders were for a reconnaissance expedition, and now his orders are to return to Klamath. He ain't done either with any speed."

Jordan Creek itself was a series of pools with dry stretches in between. The larger pools were deep and full of fish, with willows growing along the banks.

While the others lay near their campfires, Drew asked Will to scribe for him. "You thought any more about what I said?" Drew asked.

"Sir?" Will didn't know what Drew meant.

"About the Army." Drew was already drinking, though it was only midafternoon. "You're the type of young man the Army needs."

"I'm not sure I want to fight Indians, sir," Will said.

Drew squinted at him. "That's our responsibility, boy. We must protect the Christian whites who want to profit from this land."

Will couldn't help glancing outside the tent at the barren land.

Drew barked a laugh. "Well, this valley's a little dry for settlers, except for right along the creek," he acknowledged. "But much of Oregon is prime land, wouldn't you say?"

"I know lots of farmers making a good living," Will agreed. "Jonah Pershing's family, for example."

"And they couldn't farm if they faced savages rampaging through their claims, could they?"

"No, sir," Will said. "But my father told me the Indians were generally responding to wrongs done to them by white men."

Drew snorted. "You got some growing up to do, son. Understand the white man's place in the world." He waved his cigar at Will. "You do that, you'll be a credit to the Army."

"What about the treaty negotiations?" Will ventured to ask.

"What about them?" Drew said.

"Your orders—"

"My orders are mine to deal with. I know enough about the tribes in these parts to have some concern about how the negotiations might proceed." But that was all Drew offered on the subject.

Will didn't want to press him any further. He couldn't tell if the colonel supported treaty negotiations or thought them pointless. He left his session with Drew more confused than ever.

On the expedition's first evening on Jordan Creek, settlers living in the area joined them in camp. "We sleep here near the creek every night," one man told the militia members. "We mine during the day, or farm our fields, but we come together for protection at night."

"What about your mining supplies and farm implements?" Drew asked.

"We just hope they're there in the morning. But them murderin' varmints done killed enough of us already. Better our goods is stolen than we die."

"Do you mean the local tribes have killed whites in the area?" Drew asked the man.

"Yes, sir. They done killed Jordan back in the spring, along with several other men."

"Who was Jordan?" Drew asked.

"He found this valley, started the placer mine." The man gestured at the rest of the group. "We all followed him. It's good prospectin' land, but we can't live in peace with the tribes on the rampage."

"Jordan," Drew mused, as if he were trying to remember. "Ah, yes. I remember hearing of the incident. Colonel Maury from Fort Boise forayed here when he learned of Jordan's death."

"Yes, sir, he did," the prospector said. "But he and his men was too late. We'd gone after the murderin' bastards, but they got away."

"So now you're waiting for them to attack again?" Drew asked.

"That's why we band together." The man nodded. "We aim to keep our scalps, even if they steal our tools."

"What would you need for better protection from the Army?" Drew asked.

The prospectors went into a lengthy description of the need for a military presence in the valley. "Them Indians rendezvous about forty miles south of here. We need cavalry right there, where the soldiers can guard the Humboldt route and the mines in this valley."

Drew told Will to write down what they heard. "I'll add the prospectors' perspective into my report."

The next morning, while the emigrants and packers rested their animals, Drew took his soldiers and Will to visit the mines. They followed the prospectors who had stayed with them the night before.

The placer mines were concentrated in a small area near Little Jordan Creek. As they stopped at one miner's digs, Drew asked the prospector, "How much gold do you pull out of the ground in a day?"

"'Bout fifty dollars at most," was the reply. "Usually less'n that. A lot of silver mixed in the ore. More silver than gold. We make a livin', though we ain't got rich yet."

"Yet you keep mining," Drew mused aloud.

The cavalry squad rode through the district and found a few quartz mines beginning to replace the placer mines. Drew swept an arm to encompass the land they saw. "Quartz mining will take over the entire district within a year," he told Will. "They can be worked more cheaply. These men already have mills that will be ready to work within weeks. But the region won't prosper until they can get machinery in here to purify the metal before it's shipped."

That evening, when they were back in camp, Drew dictated, "I agree with the prospectors that this valley and its citizens deserve the Army's protection. With the numbers of tribesmen passing through and rendezvousing at the head of the valley, a military outpost could well be justified."

*September 5, 1864: The miners in this region are determined to stay despite the danger. Drew wants to protect them, but how much can one military fort do to protect such a vast area?*

# Chapter 47: Reaching Boise

On the evening of September 6, while Will scribed for Drew, Drew called Richardson, the emigrant wagon leader, to his tent. "Do you want to press forward with us to Fort Boise?" Drew asked, showing his rough map of the region. "Or head out on your own?"

"We planned all along to end up near Ruby City," Richardson said. "Some of us want to mine there, and the rest of us plan to supply the miners with food and game." He pointed to a dot on the map. "Ruby City is due north of here. No need for us to go farther east to Boise, then backtrack."

"You think you're safe enough without my cavalry?" Drew asked.

"Route to Ruby seems doable. We should be all right."

"If you run into trouble, send a man back here," Drew said. "I'm taking the packers with me to Boise, but I'm leaving most of the cavalry squad here. We'll be back in a few days with our provisions, then we need to return to Alvord and thence to Klamath. But the soldiers I leave here can come to your aid until I'm back from Boise."

On those terms, the wagons left the expeditionary force. On September 7 Drew took the packers and their mules forward toward Fort Boise. He took only a few soldiers under a unit led by Corporal Biddle. The quartermaster, Sergeant Crockett, accompanied the Boise contingent to supervise the reprovisioning. And Sergeant Geisy came with them to manage the packers.

"We'll move fast now," Drew told the men. "Get to Boise in a few days, then head back here." Despite Drew's promise of speed, they only made twelve miles that day before camping on another creek. But on September 8, they pushed hard and reached the Snake River after a twenty-five-mile trek.

A man named Enoch Fruit operated a ferry across the Snake. The ferry was constructed of logs lashed together with ropes. Oarsmen rowed wagons across the river for four dollars and a man on horseback for one dollar.

The expeditionary force had no wagons, only mules, and Drew decided the men and their beasts could swim the river.

Will thought of Mac's and Jenny's descriptions of crossing the Snake River on their trek to Oregon in forty-seven. He would have the opportunity to experience the same thing, though he had only cantankerous mules and no wagon to lead.

He also remembered how he and Jonah had used the Molalla ferry on their way to Jacksonville. If he were making the trek now, he'd swim Shanty across. He'd come to realize he and his horse were tough enough to handle it.

They camped on the west side of the Snake River that night, then made the crossing at dawn. Once across the Snake, they rode thirty miles, and arrived at Fort Boise on September 9 as the sun set behind them.

Will was exhausted, and he was glad Drew didn't ask him to work that night. He barely got any impression of the fort after tending to his mules. As soon as he could, he fell into his bedroll and slept.

The next morning after breakfast, Drew sent a soldier to bring Will to the commandant's headquarters at Fort Boise. Will was currying Shanty and checking his horse's hooves. He needed to see to his mules, then he wanted to wander around the fort. But he followed the soldier, assuming Drew needed a scrivener.

"Yes, sir?" he asked the colonel when he arrived.

"Major," Drew said to a man seated behind a large table covered with papers and ledgers. One pile of paper was weighted down with a pistol. "This is young William McDougall. McDougall, this is Major Pinkney Lugenbeel, commander of Fort Boise."

"Sir." Will gave a small bow to the fort commandant.

"I had a telegram a few weeks back from a Caleb McDougall," Major Lugenbeel said. "You know him?"

Will was confused for a moment, thinking the major referred to his brother Cal, then he realized. "Mac," he said. "Caleb McDougall is my fa-father. Everyone calls him Mac."

"Yes, he said you were his son." The major ruffled through the papers on his desk. "Here it is." He picked up a page and read, "'My son with Drew's expedition. When Drew expected Boise?'"

Will stood mute. So the Army had discovered his and Jonah's flight from home. What would Drew do to him now?

"Your father didn't know you were on this expedition?" Drew demanded.

"No, sir," Will said. "Not until I sent my mother a letter in the last dispatch to Fort Klamath."

"I see," Drew said.

Major Lugenbeel looked down at his desk, a hand over his mouth, like he was hiding a grin.

"How old are you, boy?" Drew asked. "You and young Jonah Pershing."

"Jonah's seventeen," Will said. "I'll be seventeen next week."

The fort commander chortled behind his hand. "A birthday you'll be having, is it?"

"Yes, sir."

"Well, Colonel Drew," the major said, after another guffaw. "What will you give him for his birthday?"

"Dock his wages for the telegram I'll send his father," Drew said. "This isn't the first time the lad's made trouble."

"I've done everything you asked of me, Colonel," Will protested.

Drew shook his head. "You're a decent scribe, all right. But remember how you got the job? Running away to find your horse in the middle of an Indian attack? Seems you have a propensity for running."

"Those Indians weren't attacking," Will muttered.

"We didn't know that at the time," Drew countered. "You disobeyed my order then, and it seems you also hired on as a packer under false pretenses. What shall I tell your parents? That you and young Jonah will return home as soon as we get to Fort Klamath?"

"Yes, sir," Will said. What else could he say?

Will stood silently while Drew dictated the telegram to Mac and Major Lugenbeel arranged for it to be sent. Then Drew gestured for Will to follow him back to his quarters.

Once Drew was seated at his desk, he frowned at Will. "You'll be treated as a regular packer from now on. No more scrivening. No more special treatment. You're a young runaway, not the aspiring officer I had hoped to make of you."

"Yes, sir," Will said.

"Your father must be worried sick over your absence, not to mention your mother. How could you do that to them?"

Will remained silent. He wanted to shout that Mac wasn't his father, would never be his father. He wanted to tell Drew and everyone else in camp that he was no better than the man who had fathered him—whoever that was. A criminal. A violent rapist. He wanted to crawl under a rock and hide.

"Report to Sergeant Geisy," Drew ordered. "You're to follow his orders until we reach Camp Alvord. Along with the other packers."

"Yes, sir." Will could see his future now—he'd be sent home in disgrace. Mama and Mac would never let him leave Oregon City. He wouldn't be able to make anything of himself. He'd be stuck doing whatever Mac let him do, never part of the family, and never able to escape it either.

"What happened?" Jonah asked as soon as Will returned to the mules. "Why'd Drew want to talk to you?"

"They know we ran away."

"What?" Jonah said. "How?"

"Mac wrote the fort commander here. Now Drew knows we didn't have our parents' permission to join the militia."

"Your pa? How'd he know we was here?"

Will shrugged. "It doesn't matter. Major Lugenbeel responded to Mac's telegram weeks ago. So Esther and Daniel must know, too."

"So?" Jonah asked. "We're both seventeen now. Or near enough. Old enough to join up."

"We were only sixteen when we left," Will said. "Drew knows we lied."

"Damn," Jonah said. "Is he mad?"

Will nodded. "He won't let me scribe for him anymore."

"Well, that's good," Jonah said. "You can load and unload your own damn mules now."

"I've done most of the loading and unloading," Will argued. "You only had to tend them when I worked for Drew."

"Some work. Writing in a cozy tent." Jonah spat, looking just like his older brother.

Will jumped on Jonah's back. Jonah staggered, but threw Will off, and the two fell to the ground, fists flying.

"What's going on?" Joel bellowed, appearing behind them. He grabbed Will by the collar and pulled him off Jonah.

"He hit me first," Jonah yelled, lunging for Will again.

Joel got between the boys. "What's going on?" he repeated, as he shook Will.

"Sorry," Will muttered. "I'm in trouble, and I took it out on Jonah."

"Trouble?"

"Drew found out we ran away." And Will repeated the story for Joel's benefit.

Joel laughed, just like Major Lugenbeel had. "Well, you deserve your punishment. So take it like a man."

They finished their work with the mules, then the three of them wandered around Fort Boise. It sat on a small creek, a large parade ground with two or three buildings on each side. The new quartermaster's facility was a large sandstone building. Throughout their exploration of the fort, Will kept an eye out for Drew, hoping to avoid the colonel for as long as possible.

That night, before Will crawled into his blankets, he wrote:

*September 10, 1864. Drew learned Jonah and I ran away, and he won't let me scribe. Will he ever forgive me? And what will Mac do to me when I get home? Will he come after me?*

The next morning, Will, Joel and Jonah were all called to Drew's quarters. "Did McDougall tell you about his father's telegram?" Drew asked Joel.

"Yes, sir," Joel responded. "I still vouch for the boys. They done good work."

"My unit doesn't take runaways and liars," Drew said. "If he'd known they needed their parents' approval to join up, Captain Kelly would never have hired them on as packers."

"I'm sorry, sir," Joel said. "I'll take responsibility for them until we return to Klamath."

"It's Captain Kelly you should apologize to," Drew said, as he stood. "And I will hold you accountable for their behavior and their safety. But whether you take responsibility does not matter. I am in charge of this expedition, and I am responsible for everything. If the lads are harmed, I will be the man the Army holds liable. And most likely, the man their fathers will hold liable as well." He waved them away. "Go tend to your mules. And stay out of trouble."

The packers and cavalry soldiers rested at the fort until September 13. A small town had sprung up around the fort, and the men were allowed to wander the town. "If I hear of any shenanigans," Sergeant Geisy said, "I'll keep you all on the fort grounds."

Will and Jonah hunted and fished during the day. Jonah accompanied Joel and the other packers to a saloon in the evenings, but Will was too upset to go with them.

On September 13, Sergeant Crockett instructed the packers to bring their mules to the quartermaster's building. They loaded provisions into the panniers as directed by Sergeant Crockett. By now, Will could heft and balance the loads with ease.

"Let the mules rest tonight," the quartermaster instructed. "Bring 'em here at dawn. We'll leave as soon as they're loaded."

*September 13, 1864. We begin our return tomorrow. When this expedition is over, I must face the music.*

# Chapter 48: William's Birthday Coming

When Jenny awoke on September 16, she immediately thought of William—it was his seventeenth birthday.

She remembered his birth. She'd been so frightened, bouncing in the wagon as they approached the Whitman Mission. At the time, Jenny was in too much pain to realize Mac detoured the wagon train to the mission to provide her with some measure of comfort as she labored. Later, Zeke Pershing described for her the arguments between Mac and others in the company over the detour.

After Mac returned from California a few years later, she asked him why he'd taken them to Whitman Mission. "I had a responsibility to you as well as to the others," he said. "I cared about you."

She grew braver in her questions. "Do you think we should have married then? That fall?"

He sighed and looked at her. "I asked you. Remember? You weren't ready."

"Yes." She stared into the distance. "But I would have come around."

"Maybe," he said. "We'll never know. In the meantime—" He rose and came to her chair, leaning over to kiss her forehead. "We've come to a happy place, haven't we?"

She'd smiled. "Yes, we're happy now."

But now, over a decade later, she was unhappy. Her oldest boy, that child born at the Whitman Mission, was gone.

The baby in her belly turned over, and her womb hardened in response. Soon, there'd be another child. She had a month to go before this one would be here.

As Mac ate breakfast that morning, he realized Jenny was melancholy. He followed her into the pantry after the meal and asked her what was wrong. "It's William's birthday," she said, a catch in her voice. "I miss him."

"We know he's with the militia," Mac said, trying to soothe her. "Colonel Drew said he was fine. The boy will be home soon."

"But I worry," Jenny whispered. "The papers report Indian attacks south of here."

"Drew's expedition is surveying mountain passes, not fighting Indians," Mac said. He'd sent a note to Bryan Pengra asking how Drew's mission fit with the new military road. Pengra replied that Drew's primary purpose was to find a shorter route between Boise and Klamath and to determine if a military post in the area was needed.

Pengra's letter also revealed that Drew's militia unit guarded wagon trains attacked by tribesmen. So Jenny was right—there was some danger to Will. But Mac wouldn't tell Jenny any more than he had to.

After breakfast, and only slightly reassured by her conversation with Mac, Jenny gathered the mending from Cal's and Nate's room. She glanced across the hallway at William's room, the bed neatly made and unoccupied for so many months. She wondered how her oldest child coped with soldiers all around him. He relished the privacy of his little room under the eaves.

Nate had gone to school that morning, but Caleb begged off, claiming a toothache. Now he sat on his bed reading.

"Is your tooth better?" Jenny asked. Cal winced and gingerly touched his cheek. She suspected the wince was mostly for her benefit, and his tooth didn't hurt as badly as he said. "Shall I get you more camphor oil?"

"No, thank you, Mama," he said. "I'll be all right."

She picked up clothes off the floor, sighing. These boys would never learn to care for their garments. Will was a neat child, but Cal and Nate were careless with their belongings.

"Where do you think Will is on his birthday?" Cal murmured.

Dropping the clothes on Nate's bed, Jenny sat beside Cal and brushed his hair off his forehead. He didn't feel feverish. Maybe she should have made him go to school. "Are you worried about your brother?"

Cal nodded. "He left because of me. I wanted him gone, but not for this long."

Stilling her hand on his head, Jenny asked, "I thought we talked about this earlier. It's not your fault William left."

"He teased me so." Cal whimpered. "I hated him sometimes. I told him so the day before he left. After he hit me for breaking Maria's horse."

"Oh, Caleb," she said, patting his shoulder. "You shouldn't ever say you hate someone. Particularly not your brother or sister. We all have spats sometimes. Brothers often have them." Jenny'd been an only child and didn't know how brothers felt, but surely siblings were no different from other friends. "William didn't leave because of you. And he'll come home safely. You'll see."

Mac spent much of the day in his office in town. He drafted letters to Ladd in Portland, to Pengra in Eugene, and to his contacts in the P.T. Company. He wanted updates on these Oregon investments.

In midafternoon, a delivery boy brought Mac a telegram. After paying the boy, Mac read:

*DATE: 16 SEPTEMBER 1864*
*TO: CALEB MCDOUGALL OREGON CITY*
*FROM: OWEN MCDOUGALL BOSTON*
*    FATHER WORSE DOUBT YOU CAN REACH BOSTON IN*
*TIME*

What did that mean? Mac wondered. He rushed out and went to the telegraph office.

*DATE: 16 SEPTEMBER 1864*
*TO: OWEN MCDOUGALL BOSTON*
*FROM: CALEB MCDOUGALL OREGON CITY*
*    CANNOT LEAVE OREGON HOW BAD IS FATHER*

As he paid for the telegram, Mac regretted he hadn't attempted to get to Boston immediately upon hearing of his father's illness. Now, if his brother was right, it was too late. Too late to make peace with his father. Too late to mend the breach that had lasted for decades.

But too late to leave Jenny also—she was distraught over Will and would soon bear Mac's next child. Mac couldn't abandon her now.

His family in Boston had done without him for eighteen years. He might well miss seeing his father again in this world, but at some point he should make amends with his mother and brothers.

Still, Mac agonized over his father. He should have visited sometime in the past eighteen years, if only to clear the air between them. When he'd left home, Mac had been little more than a college boy. In the years since, he'd made a success of himself. He'd made money in several enterprises and could talk his father's language—the language of money. Perhaps they could have built a relationship as men of commerce, if not as father and son.

Late in the day, Mac received another telegram from his brother, this one with a black border.

DATE: 16 SEPTEMBER 1864
TO: CALEB MCDOUGALL OREGON CITY
FROM: OWEN MCDOUGALL BOSTON
    FATHER DECEASED MOTHER HYSTERICAL ADVISE YOUR
ACTIONS

Mac rubbed his forehead, his head spinning with regret. He'd been right that morning—it was too late to forge a relationship with his father. Should he return to support his family? He'd seen his mother hysterical before, and he didn't care to deal with her in that frame of mind again. Owen was closer to her—let him handle the situation. Mac couldn't do anything from Oregon, no matter how much remorse he felt.

He would plan a trip to Boston some other time. After Jenny delivered their child. After Will returned home. Perhaps after they'd found Jacob Johnson and dealt with him. If he convinced Will to go to Harvard next year, Mac could accompany him to Boston then.

He sent another telegram, specifying it should be delivered with a black border:

*DATE: 16 SEPTEMBER 1864*
*TO: OWEN MCDOUGALL BOSTON*
*FROM: CALEB MCDOUGALL OREGON CITY*
*TELL MOTHER I GRIEVE WITH HER LETTER TO FOLLOW*

As soon as she saw Mac's face that evening, Jenny knew he was in turmoil. "What's wrong?" she asked.

He told her about his father's passing. "Oh, Mac," she said, embracing him and resting her head on his solid chest. "I'm so sorry. I wish you'd gone to Boston as soon as you heard he was ill."

"What's done is done," he said, sighing. "I wouldn't have made it in time to see Father." He laid his cheek on her hair. "I'm not leaving you now. Not until the baby comes. Not until we get Will home."

"When will that be?" she murmured, her heart pounding as it did every time she thought of her boy with the militia.

She felt Mac shrug. "Who knows? Probably not more than another couple of months. They'll return to Fort Klamath before winter, I would think."

Winter. Now Jenny had a new fear—William could freeze in the Cascades. Those mountains ran right into the Sierra Nevadas, where the Donner party had starved to death so many years ago. She sighed.

"Don't worry, Jenny," Mac said, rubbing her back. "If Will isn't home by the time the baby arrives, I'll go after him. Once I know you're well."

"Caleb is troubled also," she said. "He told me he and Will had a disagreement before Will left. He said he told Will he hated him. You should talk to Caleb."

"All right," Mac said. "Though there's nothing we can do about it now. They'll have to make up once Will is home."

Jenny's womb tightened again. She'd felt it frequently in recent days, but it was too early for the baby to come. It was only false labor, she was sure.

# Chapter 49: A Present for William

Jenny went to bed right after supper, then lay in bed praying. The pains were stronger, more regular. It was too soon—the baby wasn't due for another month. But the pains continued through the evening until she couldn't contain her moans.

Mac heard her and asked, "What's wrong?"

"It's the baby," she whispered. "It's coming. Now."

"I'll get the midwife," Mac said, already donning his coat. "And call Maria to stay with you while I'm gone."

Jenny lay groaning and praying. Maria sat by her side. Mac seemed to be gone forever, but then he was back with the midwife.

"Go to bed, Maria," Mac said. "The midwife and I will be with her."

"But Mama—" Maria said.

"Go to bed," Mac said again.

After that, Jenny gave into the pain. Wave after wave of pain. She'd been through this so many times now, how could she forget? But each time it seemed new again.

Pain. More pain. Then more waves, faster and faster.

Now, as with all her births, Mac was beside her, soothing her. "Go away," she yelled at him in the worst of it, wanting only to be alone. But he stayed.

And throughout the ordeal she moaned, "It's too soon." She remembered poor Hattie Tanner and the little girl she'd borne too soon, a baby who never took a breath. Was this baby destined to return to heaven just as quickly? "It's too soon. Please, God, it's too soon."

"Push, Mrs. McDougall," the midwife ordered. "It's time."

She bore down. "It's too soon."

Mac stayed with Jenny through her labor. Shortly before midnight, as Jenny continued to moan, the midwife said, "This baby comin' now. Nothin' I can do to stop it."

Jenny wailed, she pushed him away, he tried to calm her, but she cried, "It's too soon." Her tears mixed with perspiration, and he wiped her face.

Mac wished there were some way to remove the pain. He always wished it, each time he'd seen Jenny in labor. He cursed God's plan, letting women suffer to propagate the species. Will's birth was Mac's first experience seeing a woman in labor. Will might not be Mac's son, but he'd suffered as much through Will's delivery as through any of Jenny's later labors. Each one caused Jenny pain, and each time Mac vowed it would be the last child.

But he loved his wife, and so more children came. Maybe this one would be the last.

At least Jenny was strong and healthy now, unlike at Will's birth, when Doc Tuller said she was too young. Yet now Mac feared for the child coming into the world too soon as much as for Jenny.

If the child died, he feared for Jenny's sanity. She'd been bereaved for months after her earlier miscarriage. And also when little Abram died. Mac grieved after Abram's death as well, but it seemed harder for a mother to cope with a child's death than for a father.

This year, Jenny had lost Will—would she lose another child tonight?

William would never meet this little one, Jenny mourned as she bore down in pain. This baby would die before Will returned. If Will returned. She screamed and pushed and cried and prayed.

A baby's thin cry came. Once.

"A wee boy," the midwife announced, holding the infant up for Jenny to see. "Let me clean him up." And she whisked the newborn away to a table across the room.

Jenny sobbed, and Mac cradled her in his arms.

Hearing nothing from the baby, Jenny moaned, "Why isn't he crying?" She clutched Mac's arm as she remembered Hattie's little daughter again. Clarence Tanner had tried and tried, but the baby wouldn't breathe.

Then a small whimper. And a choking sound. A cough.

"He's gonna make it," the midwife said. "At least through the night."

Mac ushered the midwife out of the house, then returned to their bedroom and sat beside Jenny, who held his newest son. Maria crept back into the room and sat at the foot of the bed. The other children slept through the night's excitement.

"What shall we call him?" Mac asked, touching his finger to the baby's hand. The baby's arm wasn't much thicker than his finger.

"Andrew?" Jenny suggested. "We named William after my father. Let's name this one after yours. Or would that distress you?"

"Andrew." Mac tried the name out, thinking of his tumultuous relationship with his father, his failure to reconcile before the older man died. Perhaps naming this new son after the crusty old banker made sense. He smiled at Jenny. "You should have a part of him as well. Let's call him Andrew Calhoun McDougall."

Maria laughed. "That's a big name for such a little mite. Do you think he'll grow into it?"

Mac laughed, too. It felt good to laugh. There hadn't been many reasons for joy recently, what with Will's departure, his father's death. And the fear this baby wouldn't make it.

"He ain't out of the woods yet," the midwife had said after telling them to keep the newborn warm and comfortable. "He's little. You gotta guard against chills."

But for now, they could be happy.

"If only William were here," Jenny whispered. "This little one came before midnight—still on Will's birthday."

Mac left Jenny to sleep and stole downstairs to his study. He'd placed Andrew beside his wife in a little cradle and sent Maria back to bed. Now, he poured himself a glass of whiskey and lit a cigar, feeling drained after the night's ordeal.

Retrieving the cradle from the attic had brought back memories. He made that cradle for Will not long after they arrived in Oregon City. His first task in Oregon was to build the cabin and barn. But during the long cold evenings that winter, he needed something to do with his hands. He wasn't skilled at carpentry, and the cabin and barn were largely the work of Clarence Tanner, Zeke Pershing, and other friends. But Mac made the cradle out of love for Jenny. He did most of the work himself, relying on Tanner only for guidance.

He didn't realize he loved Jenny then. He didn't figure it out until he left her, not until he learned Zeke wanted to marry her. Then Mac raced back to Oregon to claim Jenny himself.

Mac thanked the Lord every day she hadn't married Zeke and had waited for him.

Now he thanked God again for Jenny and for delivering her of their new child. And he prayed his son Andrew would live.

He was relieved now he hadn't gone to Boston. He should have made the trip years ago, perhaps. But at this moment, he was heartened to have been with Jenny during Andrew's early birth. And comforted to know she wouldn't wait alone for Will to return.

It was strange, Mac thought—he felt no more strongly about Andrew's birth than he had about Will's. Andrew was his, while Will was another man's child. Except Will wasn't another man's child. Mac had lived through the trials of raising Will, save only the two years Mac spent in California. Will's personality was due more to Mac's toils and training than to any blood from the man who fathered the boy.

Mac felt every inch Will's father. Somehow, he would have to prove it to the boy. He hoped Will would return so he could.

He picked up his pen and started a letter:

*September 17, 1864*
*Dear Mother,*

*I received Owen's telegram yesterday. It is now the wee hours of the morning, and my wife has just been delivered of a son we named Andrew, after Father.*

*I regret he has passed from this life without my seeing him again. I am sorry for your loss and for remaining away from you for so many years. Perhaps I can rectify my absence within the year, but until certain family matters are resolved here, I cannot leave Oregon,*

*Please be assured of my continued prayers for you and for*

*my brothers and their families,*
          *Your loving son,*
          *Caleb*

Jenny slept late the next morning and awoke to find baby Andrew nestled beside her. He rooted at her chest, trying to nurse, and she tapped his cheek to help him. His suckling felt weaker than her other babies' early efforts, but he worked at it until he tired. She would try him again shortly.

She thought again about William. Would Will meet his newest brother? She still feared this baby wouldn't live long. She'd felt that dread with each child since Abram. Abram had been stronger than Andrew at birth but succumbed to a fever not many weeks later.

"Oh, William," she whispered, "please come home."

# Chapter 50: Leaving Boise

At dawn on September 14, the packers and their heavily laden mules followed Drew and his cavalry squad out of Fort Boise. They began retracing their path to Camp Alvord, where the bulk of the expeditionary force awaited their return. The first night out, after the long trek of thirty miles, they stopped at the Snake River. They forded the Snake the next morning and traveled twenty-five miles to Runnel's Creek. Two hard days with cantankerous mules that protested every step after their rest at Boise.

September 16 was Will's birthday. He spent it riding from Runnel's Creek to Little Jordan Creek, a trip of only twelve miles, but twelve of the driest, most desolate terrain they'd encountered.

While he rode Shanty and pulled his four recalcitrant mules behind him, Will pondered his circumstances. He was seventeen now. A year ago, he could not have dreamed he would spend his next birthday in the Owyhee Basin as a packer for a militia unit. He thought of the birthday party Mama planned for him last year—a frothy white cake from Mrs. O'Malley, his first dance in their parlor. He'd danced with Maria and other girls, practicing the steps Mama taught him.

What did he have to show for this last year? He'd abandoned school, discovered his family was a lie, run away from home, and destroyed his mother's and Maria's faith in him.

And now he'd alienated Lt. Col. Drew—the one man Will knew who could help him forge a career out of the shambles he'd made his life. Since their confrontation at Fort Boise, Drew hadn't said a word to him. Of course, Will tried to avoid the colonel, not wanting to receive another scolding.

Will wished he could have remained at Camp Alvord, instead of

271

accompanying the reprovisioning group to Boise. Then he would still be in blissful ignorance of Mac's telegram to the fort commander. But as a packer, he had to pull his mules.

That evening, Drew announced the group would rest for a day at Little Jordan's Creek before heading through the Jordan River Valley. The next morning, the quartermaster commandeered Will to peel potatoes for the noon meal. "Hear tell you lied to the colonel," Sergeant Crockett said.

"I suppose so," Will said. Though he thought he was more guilty of an error of omission, rather than an affirmative lie—he and Jonah simply hadn't told Captain Kelly they'd run away from home. Still, he'd fibbed about his age, and it embarrassed him that Sergeant Crockett—someone he liked—knew of his offense.

"Colonel Drew is a fair-minded man," the quartermaster said. "But he expects the truth from those around him. Especially from his subordinates." The sergeant picked up another potato. "And we're all his subordinates." He pointed his paring knife at Will. "Particularly young lads like you."

"Yes, sir."

Will and Sergeant Crockett peeled potatoes in silence until they amassed enough for the group. When they'd finished the task, Will slunk away to find Jonah, and the two of them fished in the creek.

"Trout'll go well with them spuds you peeled," Jonah said. "'Bout time you took your share of orders from the quartermaster."

The next day, the reprovisioning party continued back through Jordan Creek Valley toward Camp Alvord, camping at the same spots where they'd stopped each night on their way to Boise. The weather turned decidedly autumnal, with brisk nights that made Will shiver until his body heat warmed his bedroll.

The men traveled every day, but Drew did not push the force along, despite his orders to return to Fort Klamath as soon as he could. "Wonder why he's lollygagging," Joel commented one evening.

"We're moving at the same pace we did from Alvord to Boise," Will replied as he whittled a small figure of a mule. "I wouldn't say we're moving slowly."

"But we had wagons with us part way to Boise," Joel said.

"And now we have fully laden mules," Jonah said. "Do you want us to kill 'em?"

Joel snorted. "Take more'n a fast pace to kill these mules. No, it's somethin' Drew don't want to do back in Klamath, I suspect." He turned to Will. "You have any idea what Drew's hidin' from?"

Hiding? Will had never thought Drew might be hiding from anything. "He's supposed to help negotiate a treaty with the Indians," Will said. "I don't know why he wouldn't want to be there. But he doesn't tell me anything these days."

On September 22, Drew and the packers made their final push of thirty-three miles to Camp Alvord, arriving after sunset. The militia men who'd been left at the camp let out a cheer.

"Why are they so happy?" Jonah said, staggering as he slid off his mare's back.

Will was as tired as Jonah. He merely shook his head as he, too, dismounted wearily.

"They want the grub we brung," Joel said. "But they'll have to wait till tomorrow. I ain't unpacking the panniers tonight."

"We have to unload the mules," Will said.

"Sure," Joel said as he hefted the first pannier off his lead mule. "But we don't got to unpack the panniers. We can leave 'em beside the quartermaster's wagon."

But Sergeant Crockett insisted the packers unpack the provisions and stack them neatly near his wagon. And he made the packers do all the work, fending off the soldiers who wanted to root around in the packs. "You men ain't stealin' what we worked hard to bring you," Crockett yelled. "Wait till tomorrow. You can eat your fill then."

# Chapter 51: Fires

After Drew and the packers reached Camp Alvord with provisions, the remaining emigrant wagon trains and their cattle left the militia's escort and headed north toward Fort Boise. Their rest at the camp for several weeks had enabled the beasts and their human drivers to regain their strength. Even the woman who'd been so ill could now travel. Will hoped they would reach their destination safely, though based on what he had seen of the territory, their biggest risk was lack of water and grass, not Indian attacks.

As soon as the wagons departed on September 24, Drew's reunited expeditionary force also left Alvord and headed back toward Fort Klamath. But rather than retrace their route through the Pueblo Valley, they headed into the Pueblo Mountains.

"We have sufficient supplies from our reprovisioning at Boise to explore the region as we return to Klamath," was the only announcement Drew made to the reconnaissance party. "We will search for a new pass through the Sierra Nevadas, which was our original mission."

"Drew still ain't rushin' back to Klamath," Joel muttered. "Don't seem to matter what his orders say."

"Maybe he's trying to find a shorter route," Will said, defending Drew. The colonel might have a harsh opinion of Indians, but Will considered him a reasonable man. "You always said you'd go where you were told, as long as you got paid," he argued.

"That I did," Joel responded. "But winter'll hit these mountains soon enough. I'd rather be holed up in a warm cabin in Jacksonville than shiverin' with a string of mules through the Sierras."

As Drew led them south toward the Pueblo Mountains, Will heard him tell the quartermaster, "I'm hoping to find a pass that shortens the route to Klamath. But the pass must be suitable for wagons."

"All we can do is forge ahead," Crockett replied. "If our wagons can get through, surely future emigrant trains can, too."

"That's my thinking as well," Drew said. "And it would save a couple hundred miles on the trip from Boise to Klamath. Well worth it, even if we need to clear a path."

*September 24, 1864. In the Pueblo Mountains. Drew hopes to find a new pass. I don't know what I'll do when we return to Klamath.*

On their third day out from Camp Alvord, Will smelled strong wood smoke as they rode through the forested hills. He wondered if there was a farm or Indian village nearby, but the odor seemed too pungent for a single house or small encampment.

"Forest fires," Sergeant Geisy said, when Will asked him about the smell. Will watched for flames, but all he noticed was the haze and acrid stench. The horses grew nervous. By midafternoon, the odor intensified, and they rode beneath smoky skies.

The militia force stopped early that evening. The next morning they could not continue because smoke obscured the trail.

Drew sent out a small party to discover whether the smoke cleared farther along the route, but those soldiers returned in a few hours. "Can't get through," Will heard them tell Drew. "Smoke's too dense. Can't see more'n a few feet ahead of us. Can't see the mountain peaks above us. Ain't no way to find the pass. Plus, there's signs of Indians. 'Tain't smart to go on when we can't see 'em comin'."

Drew cursed at the new delay. "First, we were forced to guard emigrants and their putrid sicknesses. Then I was ordered back to Klamath. Now wildfires. It's as if the Almighty doesn't want me to find the pass." He frowned at the scouts and asked, "Did Indians set the fires or was it lightning?"

"Can't tell, Colonel," the lead soldier said. "Can't tell nothin' through the smoke."

*September 25, 1864. Fires stalled our progress. They're worse than anything I've seen before. Everything smells of smoke.*

As they sat in camp waiting for the skies to clear, Will wished the expedition were over. He feared what would happen when he returned home and didn't want to face it, but he also worried about Mama—her baby would come soon.

"Wish we'd never have come on this trek," he complained to Joel as they sat near their bedrolls. Will whittled a small figurine from a pine branch. He'd started another little horse for Maria to replace the one Cal broke.

"I never told you to run away," Joel said. "I woulda been fine without you boys. Probably better off. Now I got Colonel Drew mad at me—he thinks I bamboozled Cap'n Kelly into hirin' you."

Will pared off a scrap of wood with his Bowie knife. "When do you think we'll get back to Klamath?"

"Could be another month or more," Joel said. "Depending on our route, whether we find a good pass or not. Whether Drew dilly-dallies any longer."

"Maybe we'll be home by the harvest dance," Will said.

"Who you gonna dance with?" Jonah asked, poking Will in the side with a stick.

"Don't matter," Will said, though he thought of Maria. He'd have to dance with other girls as well, but he'd make sure to dance with Maria.

"Maybe I should go north with you," Joel said. "I been thinkin' I should see my family more, too."

"Am I the only one glad we left?" Jonah asked. "I like bein' out here. Though I do declare I'd like a dance with Iris. I suppose when I get back, I'll ask her to marry me. My wages from the Army should make a dent in what I need to save afore we can wed."

"You might like roughin' it now," Joel said. "But come winter you won't be so happy. Some nights are already too cold for my old bones." Joel leaned back, his saddle behind him, seeming wistful. "Wish I'd gone home to see my pa more often afore he died. But I didn't."

"That was years ago," Jonah scoffed. "He died in fifty-one."

"Our pa was a good man," Joel told his brother. "You didn't know him when he was in the Army. A fine sergeant, he was. As good as any of the cavalrymen with us now."

"I barely remember him," Jonah said. "All's I recall is an old man who let our stepmother push him around. And she was mean to our brothers'n sisters, too. They've all told me so. I was lucky to be livin' with Daniel and Esther."

Joel shook his finger at his younger brother. "You remember that, Jonah. You remember what a good thing Esther did, takin' you to raise like she did. Or you coulda been stuck with Mother Amanda like the other young'uns was. Daniel was a capital fellow to let Esther have you. Not many young men want a baby that ain't theirs, not so soon after marryin'."

Jonah brushed the dirt around his bedroll with a twig, not saying a word. Will thought about what Joel said. Mac had taken on both Jenny and Will, and then Maria, though he didn't have to. He wondered again why Mac did so.

Late on September 28, after the troops and packers had all gone to bed, a shout went up from the guards. "Stampede—herd is bolting!" The men all pulled on their boots and raced to the pasture where the animals grazed.

A count revealed that about twenty-five horses and mules had escaped. "We caught the rest of 'em," one guard said. "Afore they followed the others." Will was thankful that this time Shanty was still with the herd.

"Musta been the smell of fire," another guard said. "Them horses sure were skittish."

Sergeant Crockett led a search party to find the missing horses and mules. "McDougall, you're with me," Crockett ordered, as he named the men to accompany him. Though the searchers couldn't see the surrounding mountains, they could track the stampeding animals easily enough. Broken twigs and hoof marks in the forest floor left a clear path.

They found the runaway horses and all but three mules with a band of Indians camped nearby. Then a dispute broke out between the search party and the tribesmen over whether the Indians had stolen the beasts. "We found 'em. They're ours," the chief said, and refused to return the horses and mules.

Crockett argued the cavalry had been in full pursuit of the beasts and the tribe had no right to keep them. He threatened to unleash the might of the U.S. Army if the animals were not returned. But it was only when he agreed to leave two Army horses behind that the tribesmen permitted the search party to cull the rest of the expedition's horses and mules from the Indians' herd.

When they returned to camp, Will heard Crockett tell Drew, "We lost two horses and three mules. They musta run off separate." The sergeant didn't tell the colonel they'd left two horses with the Indians. "Didn't see hide nor hair of 'em," Crockett said. "The tribesmen done us a favor catchin' the rest of 'em. Saved us gallivantin' all over the mountain."

"Chasing horses isn't a pleasant way to spend our time, that's for sure," Drew responded. "Do we have a chance to find the other beasts?"

"I doubt it, sir," Crockett said.

After Drew dismissed him, the quartermaster told the packers, "You'll have to load the remaining mules more heavily. Make up for the three what's gone." Will looked sidelong at Sergeant Crockett, wondering at the lie he'd told Drew. The quartermaster was no better than Will and Jonah, despite what he'd told Will about Drew not countenancing untruths from his troops.

Later that morning, Drew announced, "I'm sending an advance party up Mount Warner. We can't remain in this camp any longer. Not enough grass and water for us to wait for the smoke to lift." He ordered the scouting detachment to build signal fires as soon as they found water and grass.

*September 29, 1864. Horses and mules stampeded. We found most of them. Now our scouts seek a route through the smoke. My eyes water constantly.*

Will debated mentioning Sergeant Crockett's negotiations with the Indians, but decided not to snitch on the sergeant, even in his journal.

Those in camp watched all day for the signal, but it never came. On the morning of September 30, a faint glimmer of light flickered through the heavy haze. Drew ordered the company to pack and leave immediately, and they met the advance party several hours later.

The full reconnaissance unit marched more than twenty-seven miles that day over parched land covered in huge sage bushes. But by evening, they reached some springs where grass and water were plentiful.

The next day—now October, Will realized—the expedition traveled another nineteen miles to another spring. The horses and mules picked their way slowly through a field of sharp lava, while Will wondered how much longer it would take to reach Fort Klamath.

By the end of the day, however, they reached their outgoing route from Klamath. "By my calculations," Drew crowed, "we saved sixty-seven miles. From Camp Alvord we've traveled about seventy-three miles. On the way to Alvord, we rode one-hundred forty miles from this point. At least this journey has netted us some advantage."

# Chapter 52: A Present for Jenny

Jenny awoke on October 4 feeling unsettled. Her birthday—she was thirty-two. She'd spent more than half her life in Oregon, she realized, arriving in the territory mere days after her fifteenth birthday.

From the cradle next to her, a demanding cry sounded. She got out of bed and picked up little Andrew. He was still so tiny, but his voice grew stronger every day. She carried him to the rocking chair across the room, untied her nightgown, and began to nurse him. As she felt him latch on and her milk flow, she calmed and smiled. He was a greedy little mite—he'd grow to match his voice.

And what about her eldest? Where was William?

Later that morning, Esther Abercrombie and Hannah Pershing visited to wish Jenny happiness on her birthday. She sat in the parlor with them, while Maria helped Mrs. O'Malley assemble coffee and a plate of pastries.

Esther brought Martha with her, now almost four months old and already trying to roll over. Next to Andrew, she looked huge.

Esther and Hannah exclaimed over Andrew—how small he was, how lustily he cried, how much he looked like Mac. "He's the spittin' image of his pa," Esther said.

"Then it's a good thing we gave him a name from Mac's family," Jenny said. "Though it was an easy choice because Mac's father just died. We wanted to honor him."

"Perhaps someday you'll take his namesake back to Boston to meet the rest of Mac's family," Hannah said.

"Perhaps," Jenny said, but privately she doubted it. Mac didn't seem in a hurry to return East. If his father's death hadn't prompted a visit, what would?

As usual this year, the conversation between Esther and Jenny turned to their missing boys. Jenny told her friends the only birthday gift she wanted was for William to return home.

"I have prayed for Jonah to come home every day since they left," Esther said. "Particularly on his birthday. But it didn't happen."

"I do the same," Jenny said. "Then Andrew came on William's birthday. Perhaps that is a sign our boys are well."

"At least you know they're with Joel and in a militia unit that is surveying, not fighting," Hannah said. "Think of those poor mothers in the East—both Union and Secessionist women. They must worry about their sons being killed every day."

After that, the women spoke somberly about the War reports they read in the newspapers. Jenny and Hannah firmly supported the Union. Esther's sympathies tended in that direction, though she said little. "Old Samuel Abercrombie is a Confederate through and through," she said. "Because he hails from Tennessee. I try to stay away from talk of the War when he's around."

"The battles in Tennessee have been fierce," Hannah said. "Has he lost any loved ones in the War?"

"If he has," Esther said, "no one's written to tell him."

"I wish Mac would go find William," Jenny said.

Esther nodded. "I've talked to Daniel, too. He says he can't leave until after harvest—the end of this month. By then, I hope Jonah is home."

As she left, Hannah asked Jenny, "Have you thought any more about sending Maria to work with Abigail Duniway?"

Jenny shook her head. "Not since Andrew was born. I need her with me now. And Mac didn't like the idea of her leaving home."

"It might be good for her to get more schooling," Hannah said. "And to see how others live. You keep her so sheltered."

Jenny sighed. "I suppose. Maybe I'll talk to Mac again." But she didn't intend to do so any time soon.

Mac walked to his town office early on the morning of Jenny's birthday. He'd left her to sleep as late as she could—Andrew didn't give them much rest. Mac would be glad when the baby slept through the night. As it was, the infant fed every two hours, day or night. That made for very long nights for his parents—or short nights, depending on one's perspective, Mac thought wryly.

He'd heard nothing about Will since the one telegram Drew sent from Fort Boise. That had been almost a month ago. He wondered whether the expedition was near Fort Klamath yet. Surely if they had arrived, Drew would have telegraphed Mac again.

Mac thought he and Daniel should travel to Klamath to meet the returning militia. He wanted a word with the colonel to complain about the Army hiring young boys for a military expedition without their parents' consent. But Daniel said he needed to finish the harvest.

Mac grew bored with his paperwork and returned home to saddle Valiente. When he found Esther and Hannah about to leave after visiting Jenny, he offered to escort the ladies back to their farms. "I want to talk to Daniel, so I'm headed in your direction."

"We have shopping to do in town," Esther told him. "You go on ahead. You should find Daniel with Zeke cutting corn today."

Mac rode to the country and found Daniel and his father Samuel reaping Daniel's fields with the help of Zeke and his brothers. "I've a mind to start for Fort Klamath soon to find the boys," he said. "By my reckoning, they should arrive there by the end of this month."

"What makes you think so?" Daniel said, leaning on his scythe.

"If they left Boise shortly after September 10 when I heard from Colonel Drew, they could easily make Klamath by the end of October. They might be there already if they pushed it."

"Wasn't they lookin' for a new pass through the Sierras?" Zeke asked.

"Yes," Mac said, "but they'll want to beat the snows in the mountains. Remember the Donners were caught in mid-October in the Sierras."

Samuel Abercrombie spit a long stream of tobacco juice. "That were a lot farther south, weren't it?"

"Not that much farther," Mac said. "And the whole of the Sierra range can be treacherous."

Daniel gestured at his crops. "I can't leave yet."

"Your fields is almost done," Zeke said. "I'll help Samuel finish your land and his. Me'n my brothers have enough brawn amongst us to get it done afore the first freeze."

Daniel looked at his father. "That all right by you, Pa?"

Samuel eyed Zeke. "What's to guarantee Pershing'll keep his word?" he asked. "What's to say he won't welch the way he done on the ditch?"

"I ain't—" Zeke began.

"Zeke did exactly what he was supposed to on the ditch, Abercrombie." Mac was tired of Samuel turning every conversation into an argument. "Your lawyer agreed and refuses to represent you any longer."

Zeke picked up his scythe again and moved to the next row of corn. "If you don't want Daniel to leave, Abercrombie, I'll go in his place. Jonah is my brother as much as Esther's."

"I raised the boy, Zeke," Daniel objected. "It's my place to go."

Mac turned to Abercrombie. "See what you started? One of them is going. You decide who it should be. Will you let Zeke help you so your son can do the right thing, or will you stand in his way? I'll take either man as a companion."

After hemming and hawing, Samuel agreed Daniel should go and Zeke could help finish the Abercrombie harvest.

When Mac returned from the country, he settled Valiente in his stall, then went inside. "Happy birthday, sweetheart," he said to Jenny, kissing the top of her head as she nursed the baby. "Daniel and I plan to leave Thursday for Fort Klamath. We'll bring our boys home." He reached out to touch Andrew's fuzzy hair.

"Oh, Mac," Jenny said, taking his hand and laying it against her cheek. "Thank you. Next to having William home already, that's the best present you could give me."

At supper that evening, Mac told the other children of his plans to go after Will. "We know he'll return to Fort Klamath soon," Mac said. "I hope to be there before he arrives."

"I want to go, Pa," Cal announced.

"Oh, Caleb—" Jenny murmured.

"No, Cal," Mac said, seeing Jenny's crestfallen face. "You must stay with your mother. You'll be the man of the house while I'm away."

After supper, Cal came to see Mac in his study. "I need to go with you, Pa," Cal said. "Will won't come home unless I do."

"Whatever do you mean, Cal?" Mac asked, putting down his cigar.

"Before he left, he told me he didn't want to be here as long as I was."

Mac frowned. "Why would he say such a thing?" Brothers argued, as he well knew. But they didn't usually tell each other they wouldn't live in the same household.

"After I broke Maria's horse," Cal said, stifling a sob. The boy was trying to act grown up, but he was still a child, Mac realized. Only twelve, his voice as yet unchanged, his cheeks still round and soft. "He said he hated me. I said I hated him, too. And then he said he had no place here, that I'd taken his place, that I broke the best whittling he'd ever done, and he didn't want to live around me anymore. Then he ran away."

"I'm sure he didn't mean it," Mac said.

"But he did," Cal insisted.

"Regardless, you cannot go with Daniel and me to Klamath."

"I have to, Pa. To tell him I'm sorry."

Mac thought a moment. He didn't want this son to run away like Will had done. Jenny would come undone. "I'll tell you what, Cal. If you write Will a letter, I will make sure he gets it before we head home. And I will assure him you want him to return. Will that do? You must stay here to care for the rest of the family."

Cal sniffled. "All right, Pa. I'll write him tonight."

# Chapter 53: The New Pass

After crossing Warner's Valley via the same route they'd taken in August, the expedition took a new path that ascended the western rim of the valley. "Hope we're saving some miles," Joel said, as their horses trudged slowly up the steep mountain grade toward the summit. "This ain't as easy as the route we took before."

Will felt his lead mule lag behind Shanty and gave the beast's rope a tug. "Without the emigrant wagons, we can make it."

"Maybe," Joel said. He looked back over his shoulder and nodded toward the quartermaster's wagon. "But the sergeant's wagon is purty heavy. Hope his mules can pull it."

"As long as he don't offload any goods from the wagon onto our mules," Jonah muttered. "I'm draggin' these beasts up the mountain already."

They continued through the day, through pine forests and open scrub. The lava fields were behind them now, and the earth beneath the animals' hooves was smooth. By evening, they reached the eastern foothills of the Sierras and camped at the head of Honey Creek.

*October 5, 1864. The country sure is pretty. Tall mountains and fresh water. Drew still won't talk to me.*

The next morning, the expedition climbed higher into the Sierras. The route ascended through forest glades, a steep but pleasant passage for the mules and even for the quartermaster's team. The path was wide, grass-covered, and surrounded by timber, with abundant water along the way. That night, their camp was still on the eastern slopes of the Sierras, but they appeared to be near the summit.

After the long climb, they rested in that camp on October 7. Drew sent out an advance party to scout the summit and find a route down the west side of the pass. "Next valley is Goose Lake Valley," the report came back. "We saw the lake from the heights. Once we reach Goose Lake, the way to Klamath is clear."

On October 8, the reconnaissance force resumed its journey, following the scouts' lead, until they crossed the summit and reached the western slopes of the Sierras. The pass they traversed was at least a half-mile wide, burgeoning with timber, grass, and water.

"Well, I suppose that is a shorter route," Joel commented as they started their descent into Goose Valley. "And easier because it's wide, even if it's steeper."

As the men made camp, Drew confirmed Joel's impressions. "Only forty miles from Warner's Valley to Goose Lake Valley," he told his men. "Convenient camps along the way, with good grass and water. Finding this route is another accomplishment of our expedition."

Cheers arose from the soldiers and packers, and the cheers increased when Drew announced, "A ration of whiskey from the quartermaster for each man."

Drew's enthusiasm was contagious, and the mood of the entire expedition lightened. Will was glad the reconnaissance endeavor had succeeded. Even Jonah quit his grousing.

Soon we'll be back in Klamath, Will thought. Then what will I do?

That evening, Drew called Will to his tent. "I have a fair amount to write this evening," the colonel said, then paused to light a cigar. "Will you take my notes?"

"Yes, sir," Will said, trying not to show surprise. He sat at the table, picked up a quill, and dipped it into the inkwell. Would Drew berate him again about joining the expedition without his parents' consent? It seemed not, as Drew immediately launched into a summary of their journey, as if nothing had happened.

"We have accomplished our mission through the country between Fort

Klamath and the Owyhee region," Drew dictated. "Our contributions to the nation are the following: First, we have explored this part of the country, of which little was previously known. Second—Are you keeping up with me?"

"Yes, sir," Will said, writing furiously.

"Second, we have maintained peaceful relations between the Indians and the white citizens of the land. The hostile chief Paulina was unsuccessful in his plans to attack us." Drew paused with a frown, then continued, "Third, we have discovered many hiding places of the Snake and Paiute tribes, which will enable us to thwart their advances in the future. Fourth, although not part of our original mission, we provided for the safe conduct of several wagon trains that had been attacked by Indians." He pointed his cigar at Will. "You still with me?"

"Yes, sir." He thought Drew had overstated their accomplishments in discovering Indian locations, but he didn't want to get crosswise with the colonel again.

"Fifth, we have found a new route from Northern California and from Southern and Middle Oregon to the Owhyee and Boise regions. This route shaves fully two hundred miles off the Humboldt trail and affords better grass and water with more regular camps than any path previously used. Sixth, this route opens a line for direct communications between Fort Klamath and Fort Boise and shortens the old Southern Oregon Emigrant Road by several hundred miles."

Drew had Will read back the transcription. The colonel made a few corrections, then sent Will away without any mention of his transgressions.

The next day, the militia unit continued its descent into Goose Lake Valley. As they traveled, Will thought again about his return home. First, of course, he and Jonah would have to get themselves from Fort Klamath to Oregon City. If Jonah even wanted to go home.

"Jonah," he asked his friend, "are you staying with Joel when we get back to Klamath, or are you ready to go home?"

"I ain't done any prospectin' yet," Jonah said. "I'd like to stay."

"What's Joel say?" Will asked. He didn't relish the idea of traveling north on the Applegate Trail by himself. After these months with the Army, he knew he could do it, but two weeks alone didn't sound appealing. If he'd learned anything on this expedition, it was that men needed each other for support in the wilderness.

Joel had overheard Jonah's answer, and he responded to Will's question. "You're goin' home, boy," Joel said to Jonah. "Maybe I'll even go with you. I might have a hankerin' for Esther's cookin'."

# Chapter 54: Traveling to Klamath

Jenny helped Mac search the attic for blankets, camp utensils, and other necessities he hadn't used since camping with William and Caleb a few years earlier. He hadn't traveled in the wilderness in a long time.

On the morning of October 6, when Daniel arrived at their door ready to depart, she kissed her husband goodbye. "You'll reach Eugene tonight, won't you? And stay in a hotel?" She snugged Mac's coat around his neck as if he were no older than Nate.

"Yes, the real trek doesn't begin until tomorrow." He held her close and kissed her.

She breathed in his scent, wishing she could keep him with her, even though she'd urged him to go. After a last hug, she turned Mac toward Daniel, who waited patiently on his mare with a pack mule in tow behind him. "Can Daniel's mule carry enough food for you both?" Jenny asked, already worrying about Mac as much as William.

Mac leaned over and kissed her again. "I'll bring Will home safely," he said, then mounted Valiente to ride to the steamboat dock.

After the men left, Jenny and Maria sat silently in the parlor sewing. Andrew lay in a basket at Jenny's feet, and Rufus snored and woofed on the floor by Maria. "Penny for your thoughts," Jenny said to her daughter after a while.

"Just worrying about Pa and Will," Maria said.

"I am, too." Jenny sighed. Then she looked at Maria. "Have you ever thought about going back to school? After William returns, of course."

Maria shook her head. "I didn't like the girls in town. And they didn't like me."

"What if we looked for a school in another town?" Jenny picked up another pair of pants to patch.

"Leave home?" Maria's voice rose an octave. "Oh, Mama."

"I don't want you to go either," Jenny said. "But we must consider what's best for your future."

Andrew let out a muffled cry. "Shh," Jenny crooned, "you'll meet your oldest brother soon. Your papa will bring him home. Until then, Maria and I will take care of you." Then she told Maria, "We won't decide until Mac and William are back, but I want you to think about it."

Mac and Daniel rode to the steamboat dock in Oregon City and bought their tickets. They repeated the journey they took earlier in the year after hearing the boys were sighted in Eugene.

The boat trip up the Willamette River was lovely this time of year—the maples and cottonwoods turning bright colors, the autumn air crisp and cool. Mac was glad of his woolen coat and scarf against the chill from the water, but it was a beautiful day to be on the boat.

"How long you reckon it'll take us to ride to Klamath?" Daniel asked.

Mac shrugged. "A week or ten days. It's roughly two-hundred and fifty miles from Eugene to Klamath, and we're both seasoned riders with little baggage."

Daniel grinned. "Maybe I'm seasoned, but you're a city man now. Gettin' soft, I suppose."

"We'll see." Mac clapped Daniel on the back. "I can still ride horseback all day if I have to."

"And your horse is gettin' old," Daniel ribbed Mac further. "Valiente's over twenty now, ain't he?"

"I think he's twenty-three this year." Mac squinted at his mount. "His muzzle's turning gray, but his spirit's strong."

"How many colts has he sired? The two I bought from you are the best horses I ever had."

"I haven't kept count." Mac chuckled. "It's hard enough to keep track of the children I've fathered."

Their banter continued as the steamboat headed south.

The boat arrived in Eugene late that afternoon, and after a night in the hotel, Mac and Daniel mounted their horses to head south. They stopped first to talk to the storekeeper who'd spotted Will months earlier. The man had not seen the boys, nor heard anything about them.

"Not surprising," Mac said, as they remounted after leaving the store. "We know they're out in the field with Colonel Drew."

They rode south out of town. Pushing hard that first day, the two men made twenty-five miles before stopping to camp in a glade along the trail. The next day, they rode hard again and reached Roseburg.

"What say I spring for a room in a hotel tonight?" Mac asked.

Daniel chortled. "I said you was goin' soft. That why you need a bed?"

"You're almost as old as I am," Mac said. "Bet you'd appreciate a comfortable bed."

"Sounds all right," Daniel said. "Particularly if it comes with a glass of whiskey."

"I can make sure it does," Mac said.

As they ate in the restaurant on the hotel's ground level that evening, Mac asked the waiter how far it was to Fort Klamath.

"It's a ways," he said. "But if you move fast, you can make Grant's Pass in two days. Fort Klamath is another three days or so from there."

They followed the waiter's advice, and rode from dawn until dusk for two days, arriving at Grant's Pass late on their fourth day out from Eugene.

It was another long ride from Grant's Pass to Jacksonville, but they reached the mining town shortly after sunset on October 12. They went to a saloon in Jacksonville for supper.

"Anyone know anything about Colonel Drew's expedition?" Mac asked as they were served their meal and whiskey.

The barkeeper shook his head. "They telegraphed from Boise in mid-September, but ain't been heard from since. Should be close to Fort Klamath by now, I expect."

"We're headed to Klamath. How far is it?" Daniel asked.

"'Bout seventy-five miles," the barkeeper replied. "Maybe a tad more."

"That's at least three days," Mac said.

"Most men take four," the man said. "But a good horse can do it in three."

"We don't mind hard days," Mac said. "We'll rest when we get to

Klamath."

Daniel nodded grimly.

Despite their best intentions, Mac and Daniel were slow to leave Jacksonville the next day. The pack mule cast a shoe. "Might as well have a good breakfast while the blacksmith does his work," Daniel said.

So they returned to the saloon for pancakes and ham while they waited for the mule to be re-shod.

That night they camped on a creek that crossed the trail.

"What're we going to do with the boys when we find 'em?" Daniel asked drowsily as he lay on his bedroll after their supper of jerky and fried potatoes.

"I don't know," Mac confessed, then grimaced. "I told Jenny I'd bring Will back in one piece, but I'm tempted to whale his hide when I see him. How could the lads be so callous toward Jenny and Esther?"

"Not to mention you and me," Daniel said. "Remember my plan to deed Jonah a corner of my land? That's on hold now, until I see how he behaves back home."

"And I don't know whether to send Will to Harvard or put him to work in Oregon City." Mac sighed. "We'll have to see what they have to say for themselves."

Mac and Daniel continued toward Fort Klamath the next day. They camped on a small lake nestled in the shadow of Mount McLaughlin. The mountain air was the coldest they'd felt thus far on their journey.

"Pretty place," Mac said, gazing around the forested shoreline as waves lapped at his feet.

"But there's snow on the peak already." Daniel gestured at the mountain. "We'd best find those boys and head home quick. Country we've come through, it could see snow any day now."

Mac remembered their trek around Mount Hood back in forty-seven. They'd encountered freezing rains and snow in October that year. Mount Hood was higher than Mount McLaughlin, but Daniel was right—winter could arrive at any time. Drew's party only had to get to Fort Klamath to avoid the snows, but then he and Daniel still had to get the boys home.

October 15 was another long day in the saddle. Mac and Daniel left the idyllic little lake at dawn and rode until sunset. They saw Fort Klamath in the distance as dusk approached. "We can make it," Mac said. "There's a full moon tonight."

Despite the full moon and myriad stars, it was too dark to see more than silhouettes of buildings by the time they reached the fort. Once the Army guards admitted them, they sought food and a place to camp. Talking to the fort commander could wait until morning.

# Chapter 55: Jenny Waits

After Mac left, Jenny's worries doubled. Mac could take care of himself in the wilderness, and she trusted Daniel as his traveling companion. Still, anything could happen in the untamed land they would travel.

These days, Caleb disturbed Jenny as much as Mac and Will. Something happened between Mac and Cal shortly before Mac left, but she didn't know what.

"What's wrong, Caleb?" she asked her son the afternoon after Mac left. The two of them were alone in the kitchen, the boy sitting at the kitchen table while she made him a sandwich after school.

"Nothing."

"Something is bothering you," she said. "Tell Mama what it is."

Cal threw her a look of scorn. She sighed—he didn't like her treating him like she did toddler Maggie. She would have to try again.

"I know you're old enough to have secrets from me," she said. "But maybe I can help."

"I told Pa."

"What did you tell him?"

"What I told you earlier. Will ran away because I didn't want him here."

"Oh, Caleb." Jenny knelt by her son's side. "It took more than a brotherly squabble to make William leave. I don't know why he left, but I'm sure it wasn't your fault." That was probably a fib—Will had almost certainly left because of what he'd learned about Jacob Johnson, but she wouldn't tell Cal that.

Cal brushed away a tear. "If you don't know why he left, how do you know I'm not the cause?"

"Because I know you and I know William." She brushed Caleb's hair out of his face. "You're both good boys, and you love each other. Brothers fight, but they make up afterward." She hoped with all her heart that her two sons would patch up the bitterness between them.

October 16 was another McDougall child's birthday—Eliza turned nine. Despite Mac's absence, Jenny tried to make the day special for her daughter. With every month, the little girl looked more and more as Jenny had as a child—same light brown hair, same stubborn mouth.

Jenny hoped to give Eliza—and all her children—a happier childhood than her own. She wasn't much older than Eliza when her parents uprooted their home in New Orleans and moved to the farm outside Arrow Rock, Missouri. All her troubles started after that move. Her papa died, then her mama married a wicked man.

To celebrate Eliza's birthday, Jenny invited Esther Abercrombie and her brood, as well as Zeke and Hannah Pershing and their two children, for cake and a party after Sunday services. When they gathered outside the Methodist Church in Oregon City, Zeke said, "I'll feel mighty out of place without Mac and Daniel there for support. What if I take the lads down to the river for a spell? If'n you save us some cake, I think me'n the boys would call it square."

Hannah laughed and patted her husband's arm. "You wouldn't enjoy our hen talk?"

He smiled at her. "My druthers'd be to escape it."

Zeke took all the boys old enough to carry a fishing pole to the banks of the Willamette. The women and younger children went home with Jenny. They set aside a large hunk of cake for Zeke and the boys, then ate their fill. Afterward, Maria and Cordelia led the younger children upstairs to play, leaving the three women to talk.

"I surely hope Mac and Daniel find those boys and return home soon," Esther said. Little Martha squirmed on her lap, so Esther set her on the floor and gave her a rag to chew. Jenny held Andrew safely on her lap to avoid Martha's probing fingers.

"Yes," Jenny said, with a sigh. "Now I'm anxious about both our husbands and the boys."

"I can't wait to tan Jonah's hide," Esther said. "He may think he's too big, but he ain't."

"I just want William safe," Jenny murmured.

"I spoke with Abigail Duniway last week," Hannah said. "She's still looking for a young woman to help with her school. She cannot pay, but she would provide room and board and an education to whomever she hires. It might be an opportunity for Maria or for Cordelia."

"My Cordelia?" Esther exclaimed. "She has no interest in book learnin.' She says she's done with school. And I need her help at home."

Jenny thought again about Maria. Her daughter helped with the younger children and housework, but Jenny could hire a maid to take Maria's place. She'd rejected sending Maria away when Hannah brought it up earlier, and she hadn't yet raised the subject with Mac again. Maria didn't want to leave, but she needed to experience life outside the shelter of their family home. Abigail Duniway could show Maria possibilities for her future beyond keeping house. Plus, having William and Maria at home together might prove to be a tinderbox. A little distance wouldn't hurt the two of them.

"What if I talk to Maria?" she said. "And we'll have to wait until Mac returns to decide. But we'll think about it."

The next day, a Monday, Jenny and Maria washed the baby's laundry. Jenny sent out many of Mac's and the older boys' clothes to an Indian laundress in town, but she did the delicate baby clothes and lacy items herself. Having a laundress was an indulgence she appreciated, remembering the years when she did all the heavy work herself.

"What would you think about going to boarding school?" Jenny asked Maria. She scrubbed one of Andrew's little shirts and handed it to Maria to rinse.

Maria looked at her with a stricken gaze. "You want me to leave home?"

"I'm thinking of your education," Jenny said. Her hands were wet and soapy, but she wanted to hug the girl. "It's not because I want to send you away."

"I was so unhappy at the school in town."

"This is a school in Lafayette," Jenny told her. "Run by Mrs. Abigail Duniway—you've met her. She's a very resourceful woman. Her husband was injured, and she now supports her family by running a boarding school for girls."

"Does she want me?" Maria asked.

"She wants a girl to assist her," Jenny said, wringing the soap out of another shirt. "You could help Mrs. Duniway and get experience teaching younger children. Plus, you would receive some schooling from her yourself."

"Do you want me to go?"

"Even girls should have an education, Maria. I've tried to provide you with lessons here at home. But with all the younger children, I can't teach you properly. And you need to become comfortable with people outside our family and friends." Jenny wished Mac were there to help her with this conversation.

"Does she know I'm part Indian?"

Jenny dropped the laundry in the tub and dried her hands. Then she placed her hands on Maria's shoulders and turned the girl toward her. "Whether you are part Indian has nothing to do with your education. And whether she knows about your heritage has nothing to do with it either, though she knows you're adopted."

"Does she know about my mother?"

"Maria." Jenny tried to hide her exasperation. "Your mother did the best she could under the circumstances. She made choices I would not have made, choices I hope you will never even have to consider. But you must fight to become the woman you want to be, not let the situation of your birth decide your fate." She squeezed Maria's shoulders gently. "Now, do you want more schooling or not?"

Maria nodded. "Yes. I just don't want to be embarrassed."

"You are my daughter and Mac's daughter. You can hold your head up proudly anywhere in Oregon."

# Chapter 56: Another Trek to Klamath

After reaching Goose Lake Valley via the new pass, Drew's expedition retraced the route they'd taken away from Fort Klamath in the summer. They reached Drew's Valley on October 11 and continued to the Goose Lake Mountains on October 12, camping that night in a glade near the summit.

Nighttime temperatures turned bitterly cold, and Will was reluctant to leave his bedroll the following morning. Joel toed both boys with his boot, first Jonah, then Will. "Get up, lazybones," he said. "We're almost back to Klamath. Don't slow us down now."

Once out of bed, the boys hastened to break camp and load their mules. Then they and the other packers followed the cavalry down the mountain.

Due to the steep terrain, Will leaned back in his saddle, almost standing on the stirrups, while underneath him Shanty grunted at every step. His mules plodded along on their sure feet.

Will worried about how Mama might chastise him for running away. And how would Mac treat him? He would surely be punished—and he would deserve it all.

Will regretted letting Jonah talk him into leaving. He'd learned something in the almost six months he'd been gone, particularly in his time with the expedition. He'd learned to pull his own weight with the rest of the packers. He'd learned to follow orders. And he'd learned there were consequences for failing to do as he was told.

The men around him had each taught him something. Drew showed him the value of an education—scribing for the colonel was far more interesting than loading and unloading his mules each day. Sergeant Geisy's tirades taught him about the importance of order and attention to the care of his mules. Sergeant Crockett stressed the importance of truthfulness, despite his own lie to the colonel.

His encounters with Humboldt Jim and his conversations with Drew led Will to conclude Mac was right about the Indians, more so than Drew or Samuel Abercrombie. Though caution was necessary around the natives, white men were as deceitful and violent as the tribesmen, and white men's violence led to many Indian reprisals.

Perhaps most surprising to Will, he'd learned more about Mac and Mama. He'd listened to Joel's description of how Mac had taken care of Mama before Will was born, even detouring the wagon train to the Whitman Mission. Mama wasn't the only one who'd tended to Will all his life—Mac had as well, despite not being Will's father.

But what lay ahead for him? Will still had no idea what to do with his life.

And how did he feel about Maria? Did he love her? Jonah waxed on about Iris whenever he had the chance, though Will wondered whether Iris felt as strongly about Jonah as Jonah did about her. How did Maria feel about Will? She hadn't resisted his kiss, but maybe he had startled her into passivity.

She was young, and he had nothing to offer a wife. He wasn't ready for marriage, but when would he know? How would he know whether Maria was the woman for him?

The questions reverberated through his head with every step and sway of Shanty's hips, with every gaseous expulsion as the horse descended the mountain.

On October 13, the expedition reached the Sprague River, one of their first landmarks after leaving Klamath months before. Seeing the familiar burbling stream seemed almost like arriving home. They traveled along the Sprague River for two more days, then rested on its banks on October 15 before making their final push forward.

"We'll take a Sabbath rest tomorrow," Drew announced to the men on the evening of October 15. "Start sprucing up your gear. We'll want to make a good appearance as we ride into Klamath in a few days."

But his orders to the cavalry to spend their rest day cleaning gear didn't seem to apply to Will. On Sunday morning, Drew called Will to scribe for him. "I have some summary thoughts I want to capture," the colonel said.

Once again, Drew ignored his earlier rebukes of Will.

When Will was settled with quill and ink, Drew began, "The land from the Owyhee to the new pass was mostly volcanic. The lava beds ran north to south, so we crossed them at the perpendicular as we headed west, making travel fatiguing. But we took care to find the best passes over the mountains, despite the rugged terrain. We crossed through two large watersheds, one heading north to the Columbia, and the other south toward the Sacramento."

Drew spoke on for several minutes, while Will tried to keep up. After describing the land in more detail, Drew made his recommendations to his superiors. "I suggest a permanent post at the northern end of Goose Lake Valley, which would benefit the frontier settlements throughout Northern California and Southern Oregon. A post established in Goose Lake Valley would permit the rapid movement of troops in any direction to protect our citizens."

Then Drew paused. "This next section is confidential," he told Will. "I expect you to keep it to yourself."

"Yes, sir," Will said. He didn't plan to get crosswise with Drew so near the end of their journey. He'd been in the colonel's bad graces twice, and that was plenty.

Drew continued, "I am indebted to the men under my command for the success of this reconnaissance. Sergeant James Moore ably commanded the detachment left in Camp Alvord, and he is worthy of higher rank. Sergeant Garrett Crockett was my staff officer and quartermaster. Sergeants A.M. Beaty and Geisy were diligent in performing their duties on our reprovisioning foray to Boise." Drew went on about the other sergeants and corporals in the group, then said, "The uniform cheerfulness and alacrity with which the enlisted men performed their duties added to my pleasure and interest in this expedition."

Will noted that Drew did not mention any of the packers. But then, this report was for military commanders who would appreciate commendations for their soldiers, rather than for the hired packers. Still, Will wished he knew what the colonel thought of him.

Sunday evening, Will and Jonah lay on their blankets. Joel sat beside the nearby campfire, smoking a cigarette he'd rolled.

"Joel?" Jonah murmured drowsily.

"Hmm," his brother responded.

"I aim to stay with you in Jacksonville this winter."

Joel puffed the cigarette and released a cloud of smoke. "I told you, I ain't sure I'll stay in Jacksonville."

"Ain't you going to prospect?" Jonah asked, rising on one elbow to stare at Jonah.

"Maybe not," Joel said. "I ain't decided yet."

"What would you do instead?" Will asked, curious, though not involved.

"Maybe take you boys back to Oregon City. Stay there the winter," Joel said. "We got to let Esther know where you are."

"But if'n you stay in Jacksonville, can I stay with you?" Jonah asked. "I ain't tried my hand at prospectin' yet."

"Minin' ain't easy," Joel said. "Can't find gold just sittin' on the ground, like back in forty-eight and forty-nine. Easy pickin's are all gone."

"But men still make fortunes, don't they?" Jonah asked.

"A few do," Joel said. "But I ain't never made mine."

Will remembered Mac telling him Joel had made and spent several fortunes, while Mac saved and invested his earnings. "Mac says the real money is in serving the miners," Will told Jonah.

Joel pointed his cigarette at Will. "You remember that, McDougall." Then he turned to his brother. "And you, too, Jonah. If I was as smart as Will's pa, I'd be sittin' in the lap of luxury in San Francisco right now. If you make money, keep it. Don't do like I done and spend it all."

"What'd you spend it on, Joel?" Jonah asked.

Joel grinned wickedly. "You boys ain't old enough for me to tell you."

# Chapter 57: Reunion

The expedition moved into Klamath Valley on October 17 and camped at Gabb's Springs. "We're only a few miles from Fort Klamath," Sergeant Moore said to Drew. "Shouldn't we ride on tonight?"

Drew gestured at the night sky. "It's already dusk. We'll camp here and ride in tomorrow morning. Tell the troops I want everything spic and span by dawn."

"He still ain't in a hurry to get to Klamath," Joel muttered. "Moon's bright enough to light our way. I still wonder what he's hidin' from."

Will shook his head. Drew never mentioned his orders to attend the treaty negotiations.

Despite the frosty evening, every soldier and packer unpacked and repacked his gear, stowing everything as neatly as possible. Will was glad the mules' packs were considerably lighter after the monthlong journey from Boise. The men had eaten most of the provisions.

The next morning, October 18, the expedition rode the last four miles to the fort. Drew ordered the bugler to announce their arrival, which he did with gusty blows.

After entering the fort, the packers took their mules to the supply building to unload. They stored their remaining provisions and equipment where Sergeant Crockett ordered.

"Take the mules to the stables," the quartermaster then said. "The stable master will want to make sure they're healthy and fit."

As Will and the others led their horses and mules toward the stables, he heard a shout. "William McDougall, get over here."

He turned around—Mac. And Daniel Abercrombie stood beside him.

Mac spotted Will as the boy led Shanty and four mules across the fort's open yard. Jonah and Joel Pershing were with him. Mac ran toward Will, calling his name. Still holding the leads for the five animals, Will turned to look at Mac and moved toward him.

A sergeant stepped between Will and Mac. "Not so fast, McDougall," the man told Will. "You're mine till you've dealt with your mules."

"Yes, sir," Will said.

The sergeant said to Mac, "This your son?"

"Yes." Mac nodded.

"He's a fine lad, but he has a job to do. He needs to finish it."

Will shrugged, then followed the sergeant.

Mac turned to Daniel. "What do you make of that?"

Daniel grinned. "I'd say we have two soldiers instead of boys."

Will was embarrassed by Mac's shout across the stable yard. Though he was startled to see Mac, he realized he'd half-expected to be met at Fort Klamath. He'd known Mama would want Mac to find him. In fact, he'd wondered from time to time if Mac would appear over the hilltop along the trail between Boise and Klamath.

It took Will and Jonah most of the morning to get their mules inspected. Then they led the beasts to pasture. Will slapped his mules on their rumps to send them out with the rest of the herd. Shanty wanted to follow them, but Will pulled the gelding along to find Mac—they would face the music together. Jonah followed with his mare. Joel remained behind.

"Scared of Daniel, ain't you?" Jonah taunted his brother.

"You see what's what," Joel said. "I'll check on you in a bit. If Daniel'n Mac ain't too mad, you wave, and I'll join you."

Will and Jonah found Mac and Daniel camped on the outskirts of the fort. The men had a noon meal cooking, and its savory scent made Will's mouth water. They'd eaten all right on Army food, but this smelled almost as good as Mrs. O'Malley's cooking.

Will stood apart from the campfire until Mac looked up. "You have a bowl, son?" Mac asked.

Will grimaced, but with Daniel and Jonah there, he simply replied, "Yes, sir." He got the bowl and spoon out of his pack and let Mac ladle stew into it. Jonah did the same.

"Sit down, boys," Daniel said. Then the four started eating.

"Why did you run away?" Mac asked after Will had taken a couple of mouthfuls.

Will rubbed his cheek as he glanced at Jonah.

"I wanted to prospect," Jonah said. "I knew Joel was minin' near Jacksonville. We went to find him, only to learn he'd signed on with the militia to pack mules."

"And you?" Mac asked Will again.

Will shrugged. "Jonah asked me to go. Nothing better to do."

Mac's lips tightened and he looked angry. But he remained silent.

"Why didn't you tell me you wanted to prospect?" Daniel asked Jonah. "We coulda written Joel first. Asked him, or at least let him know you was comin.' We wouldn't have worried so."

"Esther would never let me go," Jonah protested. "And you kept me farmin' dawn till night. I wanted to make my own fortune, not work for you. I still got years afore I can file a land claim."

"I meant to give you your own land for your birthday," Daniel said. "But seeing's how you don't want—"

"My own land?" Jonah said, his eyebrows shooting up. "Really?"

"Forty acres," Daniel said. "It ain't much, but it's enough for a cabin and some crops."

"I could get hitched with forty acres," Jonah said.

"Get hitched?" Daniel looked surprised. "You want to marry?"

"Iris Hayes," Jonah said. "I want to wed her soon as I can build her a home."

Daniel swore. "You're only seventeen."

Jonah sat up straight. "You was only nineteen when you married, and Esther just fifteen."

Will listened to Jonah and Daniel argue. At least they talked—he and Mac seemed to have nothing to say.

After the four of them finished their meal, Daniel and Jonah ambled off to find Joel. Mac and Will cleaned up the stew pot in silence, then Mac said,

"Walk with me, son." Mac noticed Will's jaw clench, but the boy nodded.

They walked along a path outside the fort along a little bubbling stream. "Does this creek have a name?" Mac asked.

Will shrugged. "It's just called Fort Creek."

Mac wasn't sure how to get the boy talking. A few minutes later, he said, "You have a new brother. His name is Andrew. Born on your birthday. We named him after my father."

Will glanced at him, eyebrows raised.

"He came early," Mac added.

Will stopped abruptly. "Is Mama all right?"

Mac was glad Will cared about Jenny. "She's fine. So is the baby." Then he tried again. "My father died in September."

Will resumed walking. "I'm sorry for your loss," he said in a stilted tone.

Mac sighed. "We'd been estranged for many years. Ever since I left home in forty-seven. My father was a hard man to please. I never wanted to be that kind of father."

"You haven't been." Will's response lifted Mac's heart.

"I don't feel I've done well by you, son." Will winced as Mac called him "son." So the boy still hadn't come to terms with his paternity. Mac tried again to reach him. "Your mother has missed you. So have I."

Will nodded.

Mac patted his pocket. "I have a letter for you from Cal." He handed it to Will.

Will read it aloud, "'Dear Will, I'm sorry I said I hated you. I don't. I didn't mean to make you leave. Please come home with Pa. Your brother, Cal.'" He gave a short laugh. "I didn't leave because of Cal."

"I know," Mac said. "You had a lot more on your mind than a brothers' squabble." He sighed, wishing Will's stiffness with him could be settled as easily as the dispute between the two boys. "You will come home with me, won't you?"

Will shrugged. "Well, I don't want to stay with the militia."

# Chapter 58: Authorities Clash

Mac had more to do before taking Will home to Jenny. He and Daniel spent the afternoon purchasing food and supplies at the fort. They had their horses and mule examined by the stable master and made sure the boys' horses were also inspected.

That evening, Mac found Joel drinking with other mule packers and called him aside. "What were you thinking, taking those boys on the expedition?" Mac demanded.

Joel eyed him. "I already discussed this with Daniel."

"Well, you're discussing it again with me."

"I signed on as a packer afore the boys arrived. I couldn't back out, not and keep my good name in these parts. The militia needed more packers, and Jonah and Will were eager to go along."

"Why didn't you send the boys home? Or send me a telegram—there's a direct line through Oregon now? Or at least have Will and Jonah write home before they left?"

Joel shrugged. "They's old enough to make their own decisions. As old as I was when we set out for Oregon. I did a man's job then. I figured they could do the same."

"What's your plan now? Are you coming north with us?"

Joel stared at the darkening sky. "Told Daniel I'm staying put here."

"Will said you'd told him you were returning to Oregon City."

"Changed my mind."

"Why?" Mac asked.

"Bein' with family makes me feel trapped. Like I can't get any air. I need open space. I need to be able to move on."

"This expedition kept you trapped, doing what the Army required."

"I've had enough of that, too. Think I'll go prospectin'."

"What do we tell your family—Esther, Zeke, and the others?"

"I'll visit 'em sometime. Maybe next spring."

Before he left Klamath, Mac also wanted a word with Lt. Col. Drew. The morning after the expedition returned, he sought the officer out in his quarters. "Might I have a moment, Colonel?"

Drew looked up from paperwork, then stood and held out his hand. "You're Caleb McDougall, William's father?"

"I am." Mac shook his hand, then sat when Drew gestured to a chair across from him. "I'm here to inquire why you took two underage boys with you on a military expedition."

"They told Captain Kelly they were eighteen."

Mac raised his eyebrows. "And you took them at their word? Did Joel Pershing confirm his younger brother's age?"

"I always take my men at their word until they give me reason not to." Drew took two cigars out of a drawer and offered one to Mac.

Waving his hand, Mac declined the cigar. "Will says you learned he was underage."

"Not until we reached Fort Boise and I learned of your telegram. That was far too late to send him home, Mr. McDougall. It was safer to keep the boys with us." Drew lit his cigar and leaned back in his chair. "Your boy has fine potential. Did he tell you he acted as my scribe for much of the journey?"

"Yes."

"He's intelligent, quick on his feet, and willing to follow orders," Drew said. "Well, most of the time."

"What do you mean?"

"Will first came to my attention when he ran after his horse."

"Shanty?"

Drew chuckled. "Is that the horse's name? His mount and others were stolen by a gang of prospectors who thought they were stealing Indian ponies. I gather the horse has some Indian blood."

Mac nodded. "His dam was an Indian pony."

"Young Will acquitted himself well and came to no harm. When I learned he had some education, I asked him to take my dictation. It relieved my sergeants of that duty and my hand to hold my glass of whiskey. I called it Will's punishment for disobeying orders, but I suspect he enjoyed the task." Drew paused to puff the cigar. "Because I thought he liked the scrivening, I stopped it when I needed to punish him further."

"And why did he need punishment?" Mac had mixed opinions about Drew's leadership skills, and it still upset him that no one had questioned the boys closely before taking them into the wilderness.

"Because I learned he was only sixteen." Drew took another puff. "Though I understand he had a birthday a few weeks ago."

"I see," Mac said. "So as punishment for being too young, you ended the oversight you provided him while he scribed for you."

Drew shrugged. "This is a military operation, not a boys' school. I need to show discipline to my troops. And Will lied to Captain Kelly." He leaned forward toward Mac. "Despite his occasional lapse in judgment, your son would make a fine Army officer, if you care to support him in that direction."

"I'll have to talk to his mother." Jenny's father had been an Army officer, but Mac didn't think she wanted Will to pursue a military career. And certainly not while the War in the East continued. It would ultimately be Will's choice, of course, but Mac wasn't about to push the lad toward an undertaking Jenny didn't condone. "I've been encouraging him to study at Harvard, as I did."

"Harvard?" Drew grinned. "Will mentioned you'd gone there. How'd a Harvard man get to Oregon?"

"There are plenty of us in the West," Mac said. "Even Harvard men relish the challenge of creating a civilized society out of wilderness. As it is, you kept Will on the trail too late for him to start in Boston this fall. When can the boys leave your command?"

Drew shrugged. "I have no more need of them. They can check out with the quartermaster and draw their pay. You can leave tomorrow." He rose behind his desk. "And now I must present myself to my superiors to explain my delay in reaching the Indian treaty negotiations." He sighed. "Unfortunately, I do not have high hopes that the government will make good on its promises to the tribes."

Mac could tell when he was being dismissed. He stood, gave a curt nod to the colonel, and left.

That afternoon, Will listened to Mac berate him for leaving home. Mac no longer used the softer approach he'd taken the day before. Will supposed he deserved the admonishments. He hadn't wanted to hurt Mama, but he'd known she would worry. At the least, he should have left a note.

But the note wouldn't have said anything about the Owyhee Expedition, because Will had known nothing about the militia when he and Jonah left Oregon City. All he would have told Mama was that they were on their way to see Joel.

And if he'd told Mama they were searching for Joel, Mac would have been on their tails within hours. He and Jonah wouldn't have made it to Jacksonville, they wouldn't have found Joel, and they wouldn't have gone on Drew's expedition.

Will listened to Mac lecture him with half an ear. Mostly, he reflected on the past few months. Was he glad he'd gone on the expedition? It hadn't been enjoyable, but he'd learned some things about himself. He'd learned he had the physical stamina to keep up with grown men like Joel and the quartermaster. He could do his superiors' bidding and keep them satisfied with his performance. He had the courage to make decisions on his own when necessary—he'd rescued Shanty. He could think as well as a career military officer—he'd kept up with Drew and debated with him on occasion.

He heard Mac ask him again for the thousandth time, "Why'd you do it, son?"

"I'm not your son," he answered. "I did it to find out who I am."

Will's response silenced Mac—the boy still didn't see him as his father. That part of his answer was startling enough. But the other part of his answer surprised Mac even more—that Will sought to discover who he was.

At some point, every man had to look within and decide what kind of person he wanted to be. For Mac, the answers had come later than for Will, assuming Will had learned something over the last several months. Mac left Boston in forty-seven ashamed of himself, remorseful over lives he'd destroyed. Finding Jenny and rescuing her from the Johnsons and her stepfather felt like redemption. But after he took Jenny away from her home,

Mac hadn't known how to extricate himself from his responsibility for her. It took him years to discover his attachment to Jenny was no encumbrance. He came to welcome his care of Jenny and their children as his best path to salvation. And his salvation they had become.

Now, Mac asked Will, "What did you find out about who you are?"

Will shrugged. "I can do more than I thought I could. I can think for myself. Do for myself. Match wits with men around me."

Mac nodded. "Those are excellent lessons for a man to learn." He paused, then continued, "I asked you yesterday if you'd come home with me. Are you ready to do for yourself back home?"

Will sighed. "I'm still not sure where my home is," he said, then added, "But I don't have anywhere better to be. And I want to see Mama."

# Chapter 59: Returning Home

The next morning, Will and Jonah got in line to draw their pay. Will would have preferred to remain at the fort a while longer before leaving for Oregon City, but he was sure Mac wouldn't agree to any delays.

"We'll depart as soon as you've settled up," Mac told Will. "I don't want to be away from our family any longer than we must."

Still, as he stood in line with other packers, the men shouting profane goodbyes as they headed in various directions, Will wished he had a goal in mind, something to look forward to, a plan. He wished he didn't have to hightail it home with Mac like a small child.

The boys returned to Mac and Daniel, coins and bank drafts in hand. "They only paid us part in coin," Jonah complained. "The rest we need to get from these drafts."

"I'll honor them," Mac said. "When we reach Oregon City, I'll exchange your drafts for coin. Face value, no discount."

"Thank you, Mr. McDougall," Jonah said.

Their saddlebags were crammed full, and Daniel's mule carried provisions for the journey home. "Do we have enough food for the four of us?" Daniel asked.

"We might need to hunt or fish along the way," Mac said. "But with four able-bodied men, we should survive until we reach the steamboat in Eugene."

And the four of them rode out of Fort Klamath toward Jacksonville.

They followed the same route they'd taken to get to Klamath—west to Jacksonville, then north on the Applegate Trail to Eugene. They left Klamath on Thursday, October 20, and reached Eugene on Friday, October 28. They traveled hard, riding until dusk most days. Once they stopped early to fish, and another day Daniel left them briefly to shoot grouse for their supper. Otherwise, they ate food purchased in Klamath—hard tack and bacon or jerky.

Mac rode alongside Will when the trail was wide enough, though Will seemed disinclined to talk.

"It's too late for Harvard this fall," Mac commented one morning. "But maybe next year."

"Maybe." Will pushed Shanty ahead as the trail narrowed.

Mac kneed Valiente to catch up to Shanty when the path widened a bit. "Have you given your education any thought while you've been away?"

"Not a lot."

"What do you plan to do next?" Mac asked.

"I don't know."

Mac wondered what it would take to get more than a three-word answer out of Will. After a moment he said, "You mentioned you'd discovered some things about yourself. Care to expand on that?"

"Not really."

"What more do you hope to learn?" Mac asked.

Will shrugged without a word.

He was getting nowhere with the boy, Mac decided. And so they rode in silence for the rest of the morning.

They saw early snows in the Cascade peaks to their east. Mac had packed warm clothing for himself, but he wished he'd brought another coat or blanket for Will. The boys left home in late April when the weather was warming. Now, each night seemed more frigid than the last. He offered Will one of his blankets, but the lad shook his head. "I'm all right."

On their last morning before reaching Eugene, they awoke to a campsite covered with snow. More snow fell as they ate their morning meal and packed their belongings. Mac was glad he and Daniel found the boys when they did—much later would have risked serious weather.

Will knew Mac wanted him to converse as they rode, but Will had no desire to talk. The last six months might have taught Will something about himself, but he still didn't know how to handle the fact that Mac was not his father. Nor how to live in a family that was not his.

Mama was his mother, and the other children therefore his half-siblings. Except for Maria, of course. But the rest of the family seemed like a unit—Mac was their father, and the youngsters all clamored to be with him.

Will had been like that once, wanting Mac's approval for everything he did. No longer. He would make his own choices now, though he didn't know how he would spend the coming winter, nor the rest of his life. Could he work with Jonah and Daniel, maybe live in that cabin Jonah wanted to build until Jonah and Iris married? Or would he have to work with Mac in an office? He had liked scrivening for Drew, though he didn't see any appeal to spending all day with Mac, not with their relationship so ill defined.

He glanced over at Jonah, who rode as quietly as Will did. Daniel, too, attempted conversation from time to time. Jonah responded as sullenly as Will supposed he did himself.

Nothing had changed, Will thought. Nothing. He'd done a man's job on the expedition, yet he knew no more about his future—or his past—than he had in April.

They rode the steamboat downstream from Eugene to Oregon City. Jonah perked up once they were on the boat—he'd never ridden the steamboat before. Will chose not to roam the vessel with Jonah. He sat on a barrel and stared at the shore. The cottonwoods had lost most of their leaves, though other trees still wore their fall colors.

Sooner than Will expected, they arrived at the Oregon City dock.

The kitchen door opened, and Jenny rushed to see who it was. She startled at every sound these days, hoping Mac and Will had returned.

"William," she exclaimed when she saw her son, rushing past Mac to hug her firstborn. Then she turned to Mac and embraced him. "You brought him home." She returned to Will and squeezed him again. "William, you're home."

They were both dirty, and the scent of horse and wood smoke wafted around them. "We need baths," Mac said.

"Let me feed you first," she said. "Are you hungry?"

"We can wait for supper," Mac said. "I'm going upstairs to change."

"Oh, William," Jenny said, hugging him again. "Let me look at you." She stepped back, still clasping his arms. He must be three inches taller than when he left in April. And broader. He looked like a man, instead of her little boy. Her eyes teared. "You've grown so."

"I'm sorry I ran away, Mama." Will enveloped her in a bear hug. He even smelled like a man.

The younger children raced into the kitchen. "Will!" They all clamored and clustered around him. Maria hung back, holding a swaddled infant. Will stepped over to Maria and took the baby from her arms. "So this is Andrew." The infant yawned, unimpressed at meeting his oldest brother.

Jenny watched the children, her tears falling freely. Her family was together. Life would be perfect now.

# Chapter 60: Late Autumn Blues

Will tried to fit in with the family, but truth be told, he was bored. Harvest was over, and his Pershing and Abercrombie friends didn't need his help on their farms. He rode Shanty out to Daniel's and Zeke's houses to ask how he could assist them. Daniel and Jonah made work for him, but they were also at loose ends.

Will finished whittling the little horse he'd started on the expedition and gave it to Maria. She seemed glad to spend time with him, though something worried her—she wouldn't tell him what.

Mama hovered over Will until his teeth crawled. He knew she was glad he was home. He regretted hurting Mama by running away, but he wished she didn't watch him every minute with wounded eyes.

Will spent as much time in the carriage house as he could, caring for the horses. "I don't know how long I can stay," he whispered to Shanty. "No one needs me here. At least in the militia, Colonel Drew needed me. Or so he said." Sometimes Will wondered whether Drew really required help with his notes, or if the officer merely wanted to keep him out of trouble.

One day Cal came into the carriage house while Will was there. "Oh," the younger boy said, "I didn't know you were here. I brought carrots for the horses." Cal handed one to Will to give to Shanty then busied himself with the carriage horses.

After a bit, Cal asked, "Did you get my letter?"

Will nodded, impressed that his younger brother would bring it up. "I didn't leave because of you. I'm sorry I said I hate you."

"Why did you leave?"

Will shrugged. "I needed to get away. And Jonah asked me to go with

**315**

him."

"It wasn't because we fought?"

Will shook his head. He thought his little brother deserved more. He turned to Cal and said, "If you ever decide to leave home, tell your parents first. Don't do what I did—I was wrong not to tell Mama."

But though he knew he'd been wrong to leave, Will still felt stifled by Mama's attention.

A few days after the conversation with Cal, Maria found Will in the carriage house. "Mama wants you inside," she told him.

"Why?" Will said. "So she can pat my head again? Kiss my cheek? I don't need her hanging over me."

"She missed you, Will." Maria sat on an upturned bucket and smoothed her skirts down.

Will wished he could stay in the carriage house with Maria forever. He sighed. "I know Mama loves me, but I'm not a little boy anymore."

"Maybe that's what she's afraid of," Maria said. "That you'll leave again. Are you going to leave?" Her voice trembled.

Will turned to her, ignoring Shanty nosing at his pocket. "Would you miss me, Maria?" He would miss her—Maria's calm and gentleness drew him more than Mama's brooding.

"Of course, I would," she said. But she sounded perfunctory. Will couldn't tell if Maria yearned for his companionship the way he yearned for hers.

When William and Maria returned to the house, Jenny gave them a swift glance. She'd wondered aloud where Will was, and Maria offered to find him. But Jenny fretted when the two of them spent time alone together. Maria had been so distressed after William kissed her in April. Mac and Jenny had discussed it, but neither of them knew where Will's infatuation might lead.

"She's his sister," Mac insisted.

Jenny shook her head. "But she isn't. And they both know it."

"They were raised as siblings."

"Perhaps so," Jenny said. "But it wouldn't be wrong for them to find love with each other."

Mac harrumphed, clearly not convinced. "They're too young."

Jenny agreed with him on that point. She wondered whether they should send Maria to live with Abigail Duniway to nip any developing relationship between the two teenagers.

Jenny sent Maria off to braid the little girls' hair and asked William to help her peel apples for a pie. They sat in the kitchen paring the fruit over a bucket between them. "Are you happy here?" she asked him.

William glanced up with a wild look in his eyes. He shrugged.

"Tell me the truth," she said. "I want to help you."

"I don't know, Mama," he said, his voice sounding strained. "I want to be here, but I don't."

"What's the reason you don't want to be here?"

"There's nothing for me to do." He waved the paring knife in one hand and a half-peeled apple in the other. "I don't need the academy anymore. You don't need me at home. Mac doesn't have much for me in town."

Jenny swallowed hard when William used Mac's name. He hadn't called Mac "Pa" since he'd found out about Johnson and the others. She pressed her lips together so as not to comment.

William continued, "I didn't like the militia, but at least it had a purpose."

"What purpose do you want?" she asked her son.

"I don't know." And he turned back to peeling the apple.

The next day, Will rode Shanty to Daniel's farm to see Jonah. After living together for months, they had spent little time together since their return.

Jonah was cleaning the barn with Daniel and some of Daniel's children. It was a messy job and not very interesting, but Will pitched in. Afterward, they went into the house for cider and cornbread. Esther served them but seemed angry with Will.

"The rapscallion returns," she said as she plunked his plate in front of him and gestured at the honey. "Help yourself."

"Thank you, Mrs. Abercrombie," he muttered.

She sat next to him and leaned her elbows on the table. "Just what did you think, taking Jonah off to Jacksonville?"

"Esther," Jonah said, "I told you. 'Tweren't Will's fault."

Esther continued to glare at Will, who shrugged and ate, washing the bread down with a gulp of cider.

When they finished, Jonah gestured to Will, and they returned to the barn. "I don't know what bee Esther has in her bonnet," Jonah said. "She's convinced you made me go south. I told her otherwise."

"It doesn't matter, I suppose." Will sighed. "How are you doing, now we're home?"

Jonah chewed on a piece of straw. "Fine, I guess. Daniel says he'll deed that land to me next spring. If I prove myself this winter while we clear a field to build on. We'll build a cabin, so I can marry Iris next summer, once I'm eighteen."

"And is Iris willing?" Will said with a grin.

"I ain't asked her proper," Jonah said. "I want the land deed first. But I'll bet she'll say yes. She kisses me like she will."

Will grinned to himself. So now Jonah had kissed Iris. With a pang, he thought of Maria. He hadn't tried to kiss her again. Maybe he never would. But he wanted to every time he saw her.

As Will rode home, he thought about how settled Jonah seemed. He'd given up on his dream of prospecting and returned to the life Daniel and Esther offered him. A small bit of land to farm until he could file his own homestead claim. A wife soon, and babies after that, most likely. Meanwhile, Will drifted aimlessly.

Mac spent every hour he could in his office, catching up after his weeks-long absence retrieving Will. His business endeavors all needed his attention. The banking proposal seemed dead in the water, because Mac's brother Owen wouldn't respond to his missives about a partnership with Ladd's bank. The steamship company was embroiled in a fare war. The road survey would not resume until next summer. His Oregon investments were not reaping any profits—it was a good thing the California properties were thriving. Construction of the transcontinental railroad east from San Francisco kept workers in California prospering.

On November 8, Mac took a break from his paperwork and voted in the federal election. He cast his ballot for Abraham Lincoln, of course. He hoped the President would be reelected and the War would end soon. Union forces were making headway through the South—the papers were full of

Sherman's march through Georgia toward the Atlantic.

Will stopped by his office that afternoon. "Did you vote?" he asked Mac.

"Certainly."

"Any word on the local results?"

"Not yet," Mac leaned back in his chair and gestured for the boy to have a seat. "Polls aren't even closed yet. It'll be at least tomorrow before we know how Oregon voted. Getting the national count will take time."

"I hope Lincoln wins," Will said as he sat.

"I do, too, son."

Will's face went blank, as it often did when Mac called him "son." But Mac wasn't about to stop the appellation. He'd called Will "son" ever since the lad was a toddler. He'd tried to become the boy's father, and he thought he'd succeeded. He wished Will felt the same.

Will could tell Mac didn't have time for him. Nevertheless, after they discussed the election, he asked, "Is there anything I can do for you?"

Mac shook his head. "I need to catch up on my correspondence."

"Could I draft your responses for you? Or take your dictation? Colonel Drew thought I was pretty good at it." Will tried not to sound too eager.

Mac shook his head. "I've tried using a secretary, but I find it's faster to handle my letters myself. I think better as I write." Mac leaned forward. "Shall I seek your admittance to Harvard next fall?"

Will shrugged. "We don't need to decide yet, do we?"

"No. Next spring will be soon enough. But you seem at loose ends, and I thought maybe if you knew what was coming next—"

"I am at loose ends," Will admitted. Maybe Mac had some idea of how he could occupy his time. "I need something to do besides help Mama peel apples."

Mac laughed. "I can see that's not a fit occupation for a young man of your talents. What about a job in town? Shall I ask around?"

"Why not?" Will thought Mac's work would likely be more interesting than a job elsewhere in Oregon City. But any job would be better than sitting around the house.

That night, when Jenny and Mac were alone, she asked, "Do you think we should send Maria away to school? Abigail Duniway needs a helper, and Maria is so good with the younger children."

"I thought we decided against that," Mac said as he washed his face.

"I worry about having William and Maria together at home, neither of them with any meaningful ways to spend their time."

"I'm going to try to find Will a position in town," Mac told her. "Perhaps at the newspaper. Or the telegraph. He's a bright lad, and any establishment would be lucky to have him."

"Can't you make a place for him in one of the companies you've invested in?" she asked. "Keep him where you can watch him?" She wanted William to stay nearby. If not at home, then at least where Mac could oversee her son's activities.

Mac grimaced. "The last thing Will needs is for me to be breathing down his neck. It would be better if he did something independent of us. He knows that, deep down. He's been on his own for months, and he'll chafe if we monitor everything he does."

"But what if he leaves again," Jenny said. That was her greatest fear.

Mac embraced her, and she rested her head on his chest as he rubbed her neck. "He's going to leave sometime, Jenny," Mac murmured against her hair.

"I suppose," she whispered. "But I missed him so. And worried so."

"But now you want to send Maria away?" he asked.

She sighed. "No. I want to keep them all close. But I can't, can I?"

# Chapter 61: Some Things Never Change

Will's days continued to pass monotonously. Saturday, November 12, was a mild day, and in the afternoon, he took Cal and Nate down to the Willamette to fish. The fish were active in the cooler waters of late autumn.

They found a spot away from the steamship docks where the water was relatively still. The younger boys cast their hooks in the river, but Will decided to read instead. "I'll help you if you land a big one," he said to Nate, ruffling the little boy's hair. Then he settled himself on the riverbank and opened *Great Expectations*. Will had read a few serialized chapters of the story, but never the whole book. Mama and Mac had purchased the three-volume novel while he was away.

"Will?" Cal asked after they'd been fishing about half an hour.

"Hmm?" he said, not even taking his eyes off the page.

"Did you kill any Indians while you were in the Army?"

At that, Will looked up. "Kill Indians? No."

"But you saw them," Cal said, turning to Will.

"I saw some," Will said, thinking of Humboldt Jim and the Snakes whose horses were stolen with Shanty. "Watch your pole."

Cal faced the water, then said, "Did you carry a gun?"

"Yes," Will said. "We were all issued rifles."

"Did you shoot it?" Nate asked.

"Yes. We hunted." Will closed his book. "But mostly the rifle was for protection."

"Protection from Indians?" Cal asked.

"Yes," Will said. "Or from bears and the like."

"Did you like the Army?" Cal asked.

**321**

Will shrugged. "It was hard work. I loaded and unloaded mules over and over again. Can't say I liked that. But I enjoyed scribing for Colonel Drew. And I liked seeing the country, barren though it was."

"I want to join the Army," Cal said. "And fight Indians."

"Why do you want to fight them?" Will asked. "Have you talked to your father about fighting Indians?"

"Pa? What does Pa know about Indians?"

"Ask him," Will said. "He told me about being in the militia after the Whitman Massacre. And about being on posses through the years. He didn't like fighting."

"If Pa didn't like the militia, why'd you join up?" Cal wanted to know.

"I didn't have much choice," Will said. "Joel Pershing had signed on, and Jonah and I didn't have anywhere else to go."

"If I can't shoot Indians, I can shoot Johnny Reb." Cal held his fishing pole like a rifle and made shooting sounds.

Will decided he'd better try to dissuade Cal's interest in the Army, or Mama would cry again. "The Army's no place for boys, Cal. You wait until you're of age before you decide whether to enlist. There's no call to shoot a man unless he needs shooting. Most Indians don't do us any harm. And the War will be over long before you're old enough to join."

"There'll be another war," Cal said, casting his line back into the water.

When they returned, Will helped the younger boys clean their fish in the yard. They threw the innards to Rufus, then Cal and Nate took their fish inside to show off to Mama and Mrs. O'Malley.

Maria came outside as Will washed his hands at the pump. "Cal and Nate are so proud of their catch," she said, smiling. "Thank you for helping them."

Will shrugged. "It was better than moping about here."

"Are you still sad, Will?" she asked, handing him a towel.

"Just lost, I guess," he said. "Nowhere to go. Nothing to do." He frowned at her. "Would you like to take a ride on Shanty tomorrow? We could visit the Abercrombies."

She blushed. "We'd better not."

Will saw her pink cheeks. "I'm sorry I kissed you, Maria."

The blush deepened. "Are you?"

Will handed her the towel back. "I don't know. I liked kissing you."

"I liked the kiss."

"Do you care for me?" he asked. He wanted to know how she felt, but he wasn't sure what he was asking. Or what he wanted the answer to be.

"Of course, I do, Will. I've cared for you for as long as I can remember."

"How do you care for me?"

She turned away and stared toward the setting sun, waving a hand aimlessly. "I don't know. It's so confusing. I love you. I want you here. I like to spend time with you. But I don't know what that means."

Will sighed. "I don't know what it means either. But I feel the same way."

Talking with Maria only brought Will more turmoil. He knew Mama and Mac didn't want him to kiss Maria again, but he thought another kiss might clarify his feelings. If he knew what Maria wanted, he'd do it. But she hadn't said.

And Mac hadn't yet come up with any work for Will, not in his own office nor with any of his business acquaintances in town.

It was up to Will to find something to do. He walked into town the following Monday and talked to storekeepers and other businessmen. On a whim, he walked into Sheriff Thomas's office. Deputy Albee sat at one table reading the newspaper, while the sheriff smoked a cigar.

"Do you need anyone to help out here, Sheriff?" Will asked. "Another deputy?"

The sheriff frowned and pointed to a chair. "Sit down, boy."

Will sat and waited while the sheriff eyed him.

"What kind of work are you looking for?" the sheriff said. "Do you really want to be a deputy?"

"I don't know, sir. I figure I can do about anything."

"What'd you think of your time with the militia?" the lawman asked, taking a deep draw on his cigar as he squinted at Will.

Did everyone know his business? Will swallowed, then said, "Well, sir, we found a new pass that'll save emigrants several hundred miles on their trek. The expedition did all right."

Sheriff Thomas nodded. "The reconnaissance was successful, I hear. But how did you like being in the Army?"

"It wasn't the real Army, just a militia unit," Will said. "But I guess I did all right."

"I guess you did, too, according to your pa," the sheriff said. "But did you like it?"

Did the sheriff truly want to know? "I didn't much cotton to the regulation. It was hard work. I did the work, but I don't want to do heavy labor for the rest of my life. I don't plan to join the Army for good, sir, if that's what you're asking."

"Yes, that's what I'm asking." The sheriff squinted at him again. "So why do you want to work with me? Any lawman has to follow regulation—ask Albee here." He gestured at his deputy, who grunted. "We have heavy work, unpredictable work. It ain't much different from the Army, except we sleep in our own beds most nights."

Will was quiet a moment, then said, "I need to find something productive to do, sir. I can't sit at home all day, simply because my mama wants me there."

Sheriff Thomas chuckled. "Well, boy, I can sympathize with you there. No man wants to sit home with his mama. Let me talk to your pa, and we'll see what I can do for you."

"Why do you have to talk to Mac?"

"Because you're still underage, son. I won't hire you without McDougall's agreement."

Jenny had watched William and Maria talking by the pump on Saturday. She saw Maria blush at whatever William said to her, and she worried about that blush all night. But she said nothing to Mac—he would probably get mad at Will again. While they were sewing Monday afternoon, she asked her daughter, "Was William bothering you the other day? Out by the pump?"

"No, Mama." Maria shook her head, then sighed. "I just don't know what to think."

"About what?"

"About Will." Maria hesitated, then said, "I love him. Like a brother. He's always been good to me."

Jenny paused before she asked, not sure if she wanted to know the answer, "Do you think you might feel more for him?"

"I don't know," Maria whispered. "But maybe."

Jenny closed her eyes in a silent prayer for her two children. "Give it time, Maria. You're only fourteen. You have years before you have to decide."

"What if Will grows up and goes away?" Maria asked.

Jenny swallowed hard. That was her fear also. "He's likely to, Maria. He's already grown, and he's likely to leave again at some point." She took a deep breath. "We will have to hope he comes back. If he's meant to return, he will."

They sewed in silence after that. Jenny worried about her family. Everything had fallen apart after Jacob Johnson's attack last spring—her own anguished memories rekindled and William's life shattered. She didn't know how to put their family back together. And she felt it was her fault they were broken.

# Chapter 62: Another Sighting

On Tuesday, November 15, Mac received a letter from William Ladd in Portland. The banker wanted to discuss Mac's individual participation in the bank and other investment opportunities, even if the McDougalls in Boston weren't interested. Ladd wanted Mac to meet him in Portland the next day. Mac dashed off a telegram to accept and gave it to a messenger boy to take to the telegraph clerk to send.

Just as Mac settled back into his office to deal with other correspondence, Sheriff Thomas arrived. A cool breeze through the open door alerted Mac to the sheriff's entrance. He rose and shook the lawman's hand.

"Your boy came to see me yesterday," Sheriff Thomas said as he slumped in a chair across from Mac.

"Oh?" Mac was surprised.

"He wants a job."

"A job? With you?" Mac cleared his throat. "I don't think that's wise. He's only seventeen."

"That's why I'm here." The sheriff leaned back in his chair as if he planned to stay awhile. "I wouldn't hire him without your approval. But I think we should discuss his future."

"Why should you worry about his future?"

The sheriff shrugged. "Will has the makings of a fine young man, but he don't have a way to use his smarts and gumption. If you can't give him a job, maybe I should. Otherwise, he might turn his talents to less savory activities."

"What would you have him do for you?" Mac asked. He didn't like the idea of Will working with the sheriff, but he hadn't found anything else for the boy to do.

"Mostly checking out reports of petty crimes." The sheriff tapped his steepled fingers against his lips. "Maybe make him a junior deputy. I ain't given it a lot of thought yet."

"After his militia experience, I thought of sending him to work with the road surveyors out of Eugene," Mac said. "But they won't start again until next spring. Plus, his mother probably won't countenance his leaving home."

Sheriff Thomas chuckled. "Mothers can be that way."

Mac sighed. "I suppose I could assign him something with the P.T. Company."

"The steamship operation?" The sheriff raised his eyebrows. "Are you a part of that?"

Mac nodded. "I provided some of their financing. Enough that their boat would hire Will on as a dockhand if I asked."

"That's rough work," the lawman commented. "Maybe rougher than looking for thieves in town."

"Maybe," Mac agreed. "Give me some time to think about it. And to talk to Jenny and Will."

"All right." Sheriff Thomas stood. "There's another thing I need to tell you. That man Johnson is in the area again. The one who invaded your house last spring. I heard tell he was in Myers Mercantile recently asking about your family."

Mac stood at that. "What did he say about us?"

The sheriff shrugged. "I didn't get any details." He frowned at Mac. "I asked you before—does he have a reason to go after your family?"

"As I said, I killed his father. But that was in self-defense. And it was eighteen years ago."

"It appears Johnson hasn't forgotten." Sheriff Thomas turned to go. "Let me know if you or your family have any trouble with him."

"I'm going to Portland tomorrow. Will you or Albee ride by our house while I'm away?"

The sheriff nodded.

Mac rode out to the country that afternoon. He had business with both Zeke and Daniel. He went to Zeke's house first and found the farmer mending leather harnesses in the barn with the help of his younger brothers.

After they concluded their business discussion, Mac took Zeke apart from the other Pershings and asked, "That man I told you about last spring—Jacob Johnson?"

"Yes?" Zeke said.

"The sheriff says he's back. Have you heard anyone asking questions about me or Jenny or Will?"

Zeke shook his head. "Not a word. What's he look like again?"

Mac described what Jenny and Will had told him last spring. "Most notable thing about his appearance seems to be a damaged left arm. He doesn't use that arm much."

"I'll keep a lookout." Then Zeke grinned. "Didn't you tell me the arm was Jenny's doing?"

Mac nodded grimly. "She shot him back in Missouri. Maybe that's why he's hanging around."

"Or it could be young Will." Zeke's face turned serious. "Johnson might not let up until he's had it out with the boy. Who might be his son."

"I hope to hell that's not it," Mac said.

He mounted Valiente and rode to Daniel's claim, where he had a similar conversation with Daniel.

That evening, Jenny listened to Mac describe his conversation with the sheriff about Jacob Johnson. "Johnson might come by here again," Mac said. "So be careful. I'll tell Will to stay here also."

Jenny's heart raced and her stomach clenched. "Oh, Mac," she said. "William won't like that—he feels so confined anyway." She was afraid of Johnson, but she also worried about Will's reaction. He was like a caged beast most days, standing at the windows gazing outside and pacing when he thought no one noticed.

"I can't risk Johnson hurting you or the children, Jenny," Mac said. "Will's grown since the spring, and he's had the militia experience. He's the best protection I can provide for you, other than myself."

"Where will you be?" she asked. She felt safer when Mac was home.

"I'll stay here as much as I can. But I told William Ladd I'd meet him in Portland tomorrow. I'll leave in the morning. I'll only be gone two days, and I've asked the sheriff to keep an eye on the house. But up here on the cliff, it'll be hard for him to get here much."

"Can't you delay your trip?"

Mac shook his head. "I would if I could. But I failed Ladd before, and I don't want to do so again."

That night, Jenny lay awake for a long time. What would happen if Johnson returned? She'd keep a loaded pistol in her pocket, though she hated to with little children around. If anyone was going to shoot Johnson, she wanted it to be her, not William or Maria, and certainly not one of the younger children. The dreadful memory of Maria holding the rifle on Johnson last spring was etched in Jenny's memory.

As was her long-ago memory of the first time she'd shot the brute.

Will lounged in his room, trying to read, when Mac knocked on the door. "Come in," Will said, and sat up.

Mac entered and closed the door, then turned the desk chair toward the bed and sat facing Will. "We need to talk," he said.

That sounded ominous. Will waited for Mac to continue.

"The sheriff says Jacob Johnson is back in town," Mac said.

"Do you think he'll try to attack Mama again?" Will asked, an icy fear settling in his gut.

"I don't know. He might. He might also come after you."

"Me?"

"You attacked him last time. So did Maria." Mac sighed. "And he knows you might be his son."

Everything in Will recoiled at Mac's blunt statement. He was no part of Johnson. He was nothing like the man. He refused to be. And Maria—if Johnson went after Maria, Will would kill him. Or Mama—the same went for Johnson attacking Mama again. Will would go after the brute, no matter how afraid he was.

"I need you to stay close to home," Mac said. "I have to go to Portland tomorrow. I need to rely on you."

Will nodded. He hated being confined to the house, but there was no help for it. "I'll be here. I won't let Johnson hurt anyone."

"You left last spring after I told you to stay."

Will's face went hot, embarrassed to remember his earlier action. "I was wrong then. I won't do it again."

"Good man." Mac nodded in approval. "Sheriff Thomas says you came to him wanting a job."

Will shrugged. "I need to do something. The storekeepers turned me down."

Mac sighed. "Did you know Johnson's father Isaac was a sheriff? Did I tell you that? And Jacob was his deputy."

Will's stomach lurched. Had he inherited the Johnson men's predilections without intending to? He shook his head.

"I'd rather you not work for the sheriff," Mac said. "When I get back, we'll see about finding you a job with someone here in Oregon City. So your mother won't be uneasy."

The next morning, Mac took the steamboat to Portland. He almost didn't make the trip. Before he left the house, he leaned over to kiss Jenny, still sleeping with the baby beside her. "Good-bye," he whispered when she stirred at his touch.

At his voice, she bolted upright. "You're leaving now?"

He nodded.

She got out of bed and began dressing. He saw her slip his pistol into her pocket.

"Maybe you should give that to Will," he said. "Let him guard the house."

"I will take care of our children, Mac." Her mouth was set in the stubborn line he'd loved for so many years.

"I'll make sure Will has my other pistol," Mac said. He roused Will, gave him the gun, and left, a prayer on his lips.

His business with Ladd went well. They agreed on how Mac might invest in the bank. "I plan to expand early next year," Ladd said. "You're still in time to be on the ground floor of this enterprise. With or without your brother in Boston."

Mac sat in the hotel restaurant that evening nursing a whiskey after he ate. He would give anything to be home with his family.

The next morning, he stood at the bow of the sidewheeler as it churned upriver toward Oregon City. As soon as it docked, he raced home.

All day long, Will stared out the front window. Except when Mama and

Maria sat in the parlor sewing. Then he went to watch out the kitchen window, trying to act nonchalant as Mrs. O'Malley bustled about.

He didn't know what to expect. If Johnson showed up, would Will be at the right place to stop him? He wished he had Jonah or someone else to help him guard the house.

Mama looked tired and worried all day. Will wanted to tell her to rest, that he would handle everything. But truth be told, he needed her assistance. He couldn't watch both sides of the house at the same time. At one point, he murmured, "Should we tell Maria?"

"No." Mama's voice was sharp. "I don't want any of the other children to dwell on this. It's bad enough that you do."

Shortly before supper, Maria asked Will why he kept peering out the window. "Just watching it snow," he said. A soft sleet fell and melted on impact.

"What's wrong, Will?" She touched his arm, and he startled. "You're scared of something."

He shrugged.

She sat in the chair beside him, saying nothing.

He turned to her. "You should go upstairs."

"Why?" She picked up her needlework bag and pulled out a sock she was knitting.

"Move away from the window." He tried to sound as stern as Mac.

She frowned. "Tell me why."

Will sighed and gave up. No matter what Mama wanted, he needed to talk to someone. "Jacob Johnson. He's in the area again."

Maria gasped. "Is he coming here?"

"We don't know. But Mama and I are watching."

"I was the one who got rid of him last time," Maria said, sounding irritated. "Someone should have told me he's back."

"I just did." Will turned back to the window, gazing out through the snow.

"I'll help guard," Maria said. "My bed is right by the upstairs front window. I'll watch tonight while you get some sleep. I'll wake you toward dawn."

Will turned to her. "Make it sooner. Mama will be up as well, and I don't want her alone. One of us should be awake, too."

Maria nodded grimly.

Will remained in the parlor with Mama after the other children went to bed. "Go on up, William," Mama said. "I'll stay here."

"Maria is watching also," Will said, kissing Mama's cheek. "I told her."

Mama frowned at him. "I told you not to."

"She guessed something was troubling us." Will went to the door and turned back. "I'll be back downstairs later. Then you can sleep."

Maria shook Will's shoulder sometime in the middle of the night. "It's your turn," she whispered.

Will hugged her briefly. "You go to sleep now. I'll be fine."

He waited and watched for the rest of the night and all the following morning. Will was glad when Mac returned in midafternoon.

"Did you see anyone?" Mac asked Will.

Will shook his head. "No one."

# Chapter 63: A Posse Sets Out

The day after he returned from Portland, Mac stayed close to home. He'd left Jenny and Will to manage long enough. He worked from his home study, then went to town briefly to pick up his mail after the noon meal. When he returned, he took his correspondence into the parlor to read, sitting where he could look out the window every few minutes.

All remained quiet until midafternoon when a knock sounded on the door. Mac opened it to find Sheriff Thomas. He shook the sheriff's hand and ushered him inside.

"I can't stay but a moment," the lawman said, standing in the foyer. "I came to tell you Albee found what we think is Johnson's hidey-hole. He's got a shack on an abandoned claim northeast of town. In the hills, isolated in a little hollow."

"Have you arrested him?"

The sheriff shook his head. "I'm taking a posse out tomorrow to bring him in. Do you want to be part of it?"

Will gasped from behind Mac.

"Of course," Mac told Sheriff Thomas.

"Meet at my office at first light," the lawman said.

"Who else is going?" Mac asked.

"I'll round some men up," Thomas said. "You're the first."

"Why don't I ask Zeke Pershing and Daniel Abercrombie?" Mac suggested. Zeke and Daniel knew the full story of Johnson's association with the McDougall family, and Mac wanted them with him. So far, he'd kept the saga from the sheriff.

Sheriff Thomas nodded. "They're good men. Make sure they're in town by dawn. I'll have Albee with me. That's five men—should be plenty to capture Johnson. He ain't got any henchmen we know about."

"We'll be there," Mac promised.

The sheriff tipped his hat and left.

"I'm going, too," Will said, as Mac shut the door.

Mac turned to him. "You are not."

Mac saddled Valiente and rode to Zeke's farm first. "Sheriff Thomas found Johnson's hideout. Will you help us ferret the bastard out tomorrow?" he asked Zeke.

Zeke eyed him. "What's this about?"

Mac went through his conversation with the sheriff, ending with, "I'm asking you to go as a favor to Jenny and me." He knew Zeke still had a soft spot for Jenny. And Mac wasn't above using Zeke's friendship in this situation. "I want Johnson, dead or alive. He can't continue to threaten my family—I won't have it."

Zeke nodded. "Does Sheriff Thomas know Johnson raped Jenny?"

"He knows I killed Johnson's father and Jenny shot Johnson. He knows Johnson attacked both Jenny and Will this spring. But that's all he knows."

"I'll be there," Zeke said.

Then Mac went to Daniel's claim. After Mac's request, Daniel didn't ask for any details. He merely said, "I'll go. But I need to tell Pa, so's he can look after Esther and our brood while I'm gone. My brother was killed on a posse hunt, and Pa will worry. I don't want him caught unawares."

"Make sure Jonah stays home," Mac said. "Will is aching to go along, and I told him he couldn't."

Daniel nodded. "Johnson sounds like a mean son of a bitch. I don't want the boys hurt."

The next morning, Mac awoke when it was still dark. He dressed and donned his gun belt, shoving the pistol Jenny had kept into its holster. As he left their room, Jenny sat up in bed and whispered, "Be careful."

Mac clenched his teeth and gave a grim nod. He came to the bed and kissed her, then patted Andrew sleeping in the cradle beside her.

He started downstairs for the carriage house, half-expecting Will to follow him. But only Maria peeked out of her bedroom. "I love you, Pa," she called softly.

Mac went back and kissed his daughter's cheek. "Take care of Mama and the children," he said, as he hugged her.

The house remained dark as he crept outside. No one joined him in the carriage house, and Shanty was still in his stall. Mac saddled Valiente, put his rifle in its scabbard, and checked to be sure he had plenty of ammunition for both pistol and rifle. Then he mounted and rode to the sheriff's office. Flakes of snow fell softly as he rode. It would be snowing more heavily in the hills.

When Mac arrived, the sheriff and Albee were there, along with Zeke Pershing and Daniel and Samuel Abercrombie. Mac was surprised to see the elder Abercrombie. "Morning," he said, nodding at the group.

"Let's go, men," Sheriff Thomas said. "Johnson's holed up northeast of here. We go north out of town, then east into the hills."

As they pulled into line along the road, Daniel trotted next to Mac. "I couldn't get Pa to stay home," he murmured. "He wouldn't let me go alone."

Mac shrugged. "I suppose the more men, the better."

"Pa's still a good shot," Daniel said.

"I thought your brother's death had made him wary," Mac said.

Daniel sighed. "He says he wants to avenge Douglass's death. Thinks riding with this posse'll do it, though Douglass's murderer was hung long ago."

Will waited until he was sure Mac had left. He planned to hang back until after the posse left the sheriff's office, then follow them. He could catch up when they'd gone too far to send him home.

But he had to leave the house before Mama got up, or she would stop him surely. He waited until first light, then trod quietly down the stairs.

He startled and almost yelled when Maria whispered from the parlor, "Will, what are you doing?"

"Why are you sitting in the dark?" Will hissed. "You half-scared me to death."

"I got up when Pa left." Maria sighed. "I'm too frightened to sleep."

"I'm going after him," Will said. "Don't tell Mama."

Maria rushed over and grabbed his sleeve. "You can't, Will. Mama and Pa told you not to. It's too dangerous."

"I'm going anyway. It's me Johnson wants. I know it is. And I want to have it out with him." Will touched the pistol he'd kept nearby since watching for Johnson a few days earlier. It now hung through his belt, and he'd filled his jacket pockets with ammunition. He'd looked for Mac's other pistol, but Mac must have taken it.

"Will, don't go," Maria pleaded, trying to hold him back. "Please don't go."

"I have to, Maria." This was man's work, and Will didn't expect her to understand. But he couldn't stay away from Johnson. He had to be a part of confronting the man.

"Oh, Will," Maria whispered and flung her arms around him.

Will couldn't help himself. He might not see her again. He leaned over and touched his lips to hers. This kiss was as sweet as the first one. "Wait for me. I'll be back. You'll see." He hoped his words would convince them both.

Jenny came down the stairs in time to see William kiss Maria. She gasped, and both children turned to her.

"Mama," Maria exclaimed.

Jenny ignored her daughter and focused on William bundled in his heavy coat and holding his hat in his hand. "Where are you going?" she asked.

Will straightened to his full height, towering over her. "I'm joining the posse, Mama. I have to." He turned and rushed out the back door toward the carriage house.

Jenny ran after him and found him saddling Shanty. "You can't go, Will. Your father and I forbid you."

"Mac isn't my father," Will said, glaring at her. "And Johnson might be. Are you telling me I don't have a part in this?"

"Whatever your part is," Jenny said, tugging on Will's arm, "it isn't going with the posse. I can't lose you again."

Will pulled away from her. "I have to, Mama."

She retreated when he pulled Shanty out of the stall. "Please, William," she whispered, her heart pounding and her voice catching. "No." She watched him mount and ride away, tears streaming down her cheeks.

Will worried he might be too late to see which direction the posse took out of town, but they were just leaving the sheriff's office as he approached. He hung back far enough that he hoped Shanty wouldn't call to Valiente. He'd have to be careful, or the gelding might give him away. Once they left town, there weren't many forks in the roads, and Will should be able to follow the horses' hoof tracks in the light coating of snow.

There were six men in the posse—he'd only expected five. He'd heard the discussion naming the sheriff and his deputy, Mac, Zeke, and Daniel. It didn't matter to Will, but he wondered who the sixth man was. Then he heard a deep voice boom—Samuel Abercrombie. Will hoped the old blowhard didn't bollix their search for Johnson. Will wanted to confront Johnson face to face.

He waited until he could barely see the men in the faint light of dawn. As they disappeared into the morning flurries, he followed.

# Chapter 64: On the Hunt

The posse rode north through the streets of Oregon City. At the far end of town, near where the Clackamas River joined the Willamette, the sheriff gestured to the right. "We head east along Abernethy Road," he said. "After a few miles we turn north between two creek beds. That's where Albee found Johnson's lair." Sheriff Thomas gestured at his deputy.

"How'd you find it?" Mac asked.

"Got word from a farmer in those parts," Albee replied. "Said he seen a man in the woods near a farm what's been abandoned. The description of the man matched what we know about Johnson. Bad left arm. Confederate garb. I checked it out yesterday. Saw signs of a man living in an old shack. I didn't approach 'cause I was alone. But I marked where to head north from the road. I can find it again easy enough."

They followed the road through forested hills and dales. The snow ceased, but dank clouds hung overhead, keeping the day gloomy and gray. About an hour's ride from town, Albee stopped them. "There's my mark." He pointed to a small pile of rocks beside a twisted pine. "We turn off the road here."

Mac gazed up a creek bed descending the hill above them. Another creek trickled down about a hundred yards farther along the road. Patches of snow lay where no sun could reach the ground. "What's the best way to approach so we don't chase him off?"

The sheriff peered upward, just as Mac had done. "Better split up," he said. He and the deputy conferred about the terrain and about how to pinch Johnson's camp between two groups of men.

"All right," Sheriff Thomas said after he and Albee reached a decision. "Here's what we'll do. I'll head up this creek bed, takin' two of you with me." He gestured at the deputy. "Albee will take the other two, go up the other creek bed. My group will stop below the shack, and Adam's group'll head up above it and drive him down to me. If Johnson stays put, we'll attack him from both above and below."

"I want to be in on the kill," Samuel Abercrombie said. "I'll go with you, Sheriff. Daniel, you're with me."

The sheriff caught Mac's eye and raised an eyebrow.

"I'm fine with that." Mac grinned. "If you all make too much noise, we might be the ones making the arrest." He raised an eyebrow at Zeke, who shrugged his assent.

"Give us a chance to get started," Deputy Albee said. "We have a longer climb."

Mac and Zeke followed Albee to the other creek bed, and they turned up the hill. "Have you been this way?" Mac asked the deputy.

"Yep. I went up this path yesterday," Albee said. "And come down the other creek bed, trying to find the best route. The two paths are about even in terms of difficulty. This route's longer, but the other has more fallen trees to get over or around."

"Serves old Samuel right," Zeke murmured to Mac. "He'll have fun jumping his fat gelding over the logs."

Will stayed far enough behind the posse that he could barely hear the horses' hooves clopping along the road. He almost caught up to them several miles out of town along Abernethy Road. Shanty's ears perked up and he tossed his head. "Whoa, boy," Will whispered, and stopped the gelding to stay behind a curve from Mac and the others.

Will dismounted and tied Shanty to a tree, then he crept into the forest and inched toward the posse, which was stopped at a gully that crossed the road. He heard the men discuss splitting up, then watched as Mac, Zeke, and the deputy rode a bit farther along the road until they turned up a second creek bed. About ten minutes later, the sheriff and the two Abercrombies started up the first gully.

Will raced back, untied Shanty, and headed toward where the posse had halted. Which group should he follow? He didn't relish letting Mac shout at him, but he had no interest in spending the day with Samuel Abercrombie.

"God damn it," he heard Abercrombie bellow from up the hill. "This path

**339**

ain't nothin' but downed logs."

That clinched it. He wouldn't follow Abercrombie. Will urged Shanty along the road and up the path Mac's party had taken.

Will followed the hoof prints of the horses ahead of him, trying to stay back far enough to avoid being seen. Soon, however, he heard them not far ahead. "Can we jump the log, do you think?" he heard Zeke say.

"Valiente can take it," Mac said. "Your horse is bigger and younger."

"I did it comin' downhill the other day," Adam said. "But uphill is harder."

Valiente whinnied, and Shanty whinnied back.

"Who's there?" Mac called.

Will urged Shanty forward. "It's me." He looked uphill to see three men with rifles turned on him. "It's just me."

"God damn it, Will," Mac said. "What in the hell are you doing here?"

Mac rarely cursed around him. "I-I wanted to be part of the posse," Will said.

"You were supposed to stay with your mother," Mac said, sheathing his rifle. "We almost shot you." Mac gestured for Albee to put his rifle away. Zeke had already put his back in its scabbard. Mac waved from Will to the deputy. "Do you remember my obstreperous son William?"

The deputy nodded. "Is he goin' with us?"

"You left your mother alone with the children?" Mac asked Will.

"Yes, sir," Will said. "But if Johnson's up here—"

"We don't know that for a fact," Mac said. "And I ordered you—"

"I'm here now," Will said. "And I'm staying."

Mac sighed and pointed his finger at Will. "You will do exactly as you're told. Whatever I say or Albee says or Zeke says. Do you understand?"

"Yes, sir."

"If you don't, you could be killed."

"Yes, sir."

Mac glared at Will, then turned to the deputy. "He's staying."

Albee's portion of the posse continued up the hill, the deputy leading, Mac following, then Will, and Zeke bringing up the rear. Will's heart pounded. He didn't know what they would face. He'd been on scouting forays with Colonel Drew looking for Indians, but now the posse pursued a known villain. On the reconnaissance expedition, they'd hoped not to encounter hostile Indians, but now they hoped to find and capture Johnson.

He and Jonah had been fortunate with the militia, Will realized now. They hadn't been at war like their counterparts back East. Seventeen-year-olds joined both the Union and Secessionist forces and shot one another. Like those boys, Will and Jonah had lied about their ages to join Drew's expedition, but they hadn't faced wartime battles.

Joel had repeatedly admonished Jonah and him to act like men. This was Will's time. Time to be a man.

The uphill route zigzagged across the creek bed. They detoured around fallen logs and huge boulders. Occasionally, they had to jump a log. Soon they neared the top of the hill, and gray sky peeked through the forest in a patchwork pattern. Snow began to fall again.

The deputy held up his hand to halt them, and they gathered close to talk softly. "We'd best go wide to the east," Albee said. "We want to be sure we come down on the cabin from the top, drive Johnson toward the sheriff's group."

After Will joined them, Mac sat rigidly on Valiente's back, his spine almost too stiff to sway with the horse's gait. His jaw clenched, and his head felt like it was in a vise. How could Will have been so stupid? If they were closer to town, he would have insisted his son return home. As it was, they were near enough to Johnson that Mac wanted to keep an eye on the boy—he might be safer with the posse than alone on the road.

Why had Will disobeyed him? Perhaps Will no longer considered him his father, but still, Mac was an adult and a reasonable man. As long as the boy lived in Mac's household, he expected Will to follow simple instructions—such as to stay home and take care of his mother.

Surely both Mac and Will had Jenny's interests in common. Surely Will could understand Mac's desire to protect Jenny. And Maria. And the rest of the children. After all, Will was their half-brother.

Whatever Will thought, Mac considered the boy to be his son. He'd worked hard for many years to treat Will like Mac wished his own father had treated him. He'd listened to the boy prattle about childhood nonsense, and he'd taken it seriously. He'd taught the lad how to fish, how to shoot, how to saddle a horse. And recently, how to shave.

What more did Mac have to do to prove himself to Will?

Surely Will didn't think of Jacob Johnson or the other rapists as his father.

"Mac," Zeke called softly from behind Will. "Tell Albee to stop."

Mac gave a low whistle, and the deputy turned around. Mac gestured at Zeke, and the men gathered close.

"I seen somethin'," Zeke said. "A clearing of some type. Maybe a shack there as well."

Albee peered through the trees. Mac followed. Off to the left, slightly below them on the hill was a small house, not much more than a shack. A woodpile and a chopping block sat in an open area in front of the dwelling.

Albee nodded. "That's it."

Will swallowed hard when the deputy nodded. His stomach churned and he wanted to retch. But the other men didn't seem scared.

"See the door and window on the front," Albee said. "Another door on the back."

"What's the plan?" Mac asked.

"We spread out on this uphill side," Albee said. "At my shout, we ride toward the shack. Johnson either returns our fire, or he runs out the back toward the sheriff's group. They should be close enough he'll run right into 'em. Watch out, in case there's another man with him. I ain't seen no one yesterday, but he could have a partner."

"What if he holes up and shoots at us?" Zeke asked.

"There's four of us, only one of him. Maybe two," Albee said. "And we'll be coming at him from four directions, plus the sheriff's men below."

Zeke nodded.

"Will, stay behind me," Mac said. "If you ever had reason to obey me, this is it."

"All right," Will whispered. He took the uphill flank, with Mac nearby, the deputy facing the front door of the shack, and Zeke on the deputy's far side.

Albee shouted, Zeke whooped in response, and the four of them charged the cabin.

# Chapter 65: Finding Johnson

Mac kicked Valiente into a gallop down the hill. They crashed through the underbrush as fast as Valiente could take the descent. Will on Shanty rode behind him, and Mac prayed for the boy's safety. He couldn't let Will get hurt, or Jenny would never forgive him.

Mac kept himself between Will and the cabin as they attacked. He saw Albee ahead of him on his right, and he heard but couldn't see Zeke beyond the deputy.

"Stay back, Will," Mac shouted as they approached the cabin.

Will was petrified, his fingers clutching Shanty's reins too tightly.

But he couldn't hang back, even though Mac ordered him to. He was part of this posse, and each man had to protect the others. He'd learned that much in the Army. He had to act like a man. He might be scared, but he feared letting Mac or the others down more than injury to himself.

Mama would never forgive him if Mac were wounded or killed. Will knew how much Mama loved Mac—he'd known it all his life. Mac was the most important person in the world to Mama. And Will wasn't about to let Mac come to harm now.

He urged Shanty down the hill behind Mac.

A shot rang out from the cabin. Mac dismounted, unsheathed his rifle, and dodged behind a tree. "Will," he called. "Stay here with the horses."

Mac crouched low and crawled forward. Valiente and Shanty squealed behind him, and he hoped Will did as he'd ordered. He couldn't take time to look.

More shots from the cabin, then Zeke and Albee returned fire. Mac raised his head above a downed tree log and saw Johnson peeking out the window. He hadn't seen the man in almost eighteen years, but he recognized him. Mac aimed his rifle and fired.

Johnson ducked, then returned Mac's fire. More bullets from Zeke and Albee.

Albee rushed down the hill and took cover behind a tree just outside the clearing. "Come out, Johnson. We're here to arrest you for the attack on Jenny McDougall and her family."

Johnson fired at the deputy. Zeke, Mac, and Albee shot back. Johnson let off another round.

Mac heard a moan from his right. Was it Albee or Zeke? He fired, then scuttled toward the moan. More shots from either Albee or Zeke.

After a pause, more shots from Johnson.

A crash on his left, slightly behind him.

"Will?" Mac turned to look.

"I'm fine. I think Albee's shot." Will raised a bit and fired at Johnson. "I'll cover you."

Mac shook his head. How'd Will learn about covering a man in a gun battle? "Stay here," he told his son.

The moaning stopped, but Mac worked his way in that direction until he halted next to Albee. The deputy gasped, then his eyes glazed over, staring sightlessly until Mac closed them.

Just then Zeke approached Mac from the other direction. "Johnson ain't shooting so fast now," Zeke said. "I bet he's almost out of bullets or maybe wounded. I'm going in. Cover me. When I signal, stop shooting."

From right behind Mac, Will said, "Got it." Damn it, the lad hadn't obeyed—he'd followed Mac.

Mac and Will shot volleys at Johnson, and Johnson took single shots in return.

Zeke ran to the corner of the cabin. He waved. Mac and Will stopped shooting, and Zeke plunged through the doorway. A cry sounded, then Zeke pulled Johnson out of the shack with an arm around the villain's neck.

As Will was reloading, he wondered whether he was firing on his own father. But he couldn't do anything else. He was part of the posse, and his job was to cover Zeke.

He'd seen Deputy Albee go down. That's when he'd rushed toward Mac. He couldn't let either Mac or Zeke get hurt. They were part of his life—Johnson was not. Even if Johnson was his father by blood, the man was evil.

Will once told Joel Pershing he didn't have to be like his drunken father. Zeke and Joel had the same father, and Zeke wasn't a drunkard. Will didn't have to be evil like Johnson or the other men who'd raped Mama.

As Will watched Mac close Albee's eyes, he swallowed a huge lump in his throat. Mac was the man he wanted to be like. He wished Mac were his father in truth, but Mac had raised him, and that's all that mattered.

Weapon now ready, Will fired at the cabin until Zeke's signal to stop. When Zeke dragged Johnson into the clearing, Will followed Mac toward them.

Mac tramped down the hill toward Zeke and Johnson with his rifle trained on Johnson. Will followed behind him.

"Go inside the cabin and look for something to tie him up with," Mac told Will. He kept his gun on Johnson.

"You're McDougall, ain't you?" Johnson said, spitting. "Ain't seen you since you was in Missouri. You gonna kill me like you killed my pa?"

Will came out of the cabin, a ragged rope in hand.

"Tie him up, Will," Mac said.

"Well, young Will," Johnson sneered. "You think you're gonna tie up your own pa?"

Will said nothing but shot a look at Mac.

"Go on, Will," Mac said. "Tie him up."

Will bound Johnson's hands. Then, after Zeke threw the scoundrel to the ground and held his legs, Will bound Johnson's feet.

Zeke checked the knots, then nodded at Mac. "He ain't goin' nowhere."

"Where's the sheriff?" Mac asked, lowering his rifle but keeping an eye on Johnson.

"Who knows?" Zeke said. "Maybe got held up by Abercrombie. Or a rotten log."

"What's next?" Johnson taunted. "You gonna shoot me?"

Mac looked at Will. "What do you think, Will? Should we kill him now? He murdered Albee, and you know what he did to your mother."

# Chapter 66: Will's Decision

"Kill him?" Will startled at Mac's question. Why had Mac asked him what to do?

He thought about all the trouble Johnson had caused. First, raping Mama all those years ago, and heaven knew what other crimes he'd committed in Missouri. This year, the man attacked Mama and Will in their own home and threatened the entire family. He was a Secessionist deserter. He'd hidden out for months in Oregon, probably stealing from farmers for his sustenance. And now he'd killed Deputy Albee.

But if the posse shot Johnson now, while he was trussed on the ground, it would be cold-blooded vigilantism. Akin to murder of their own. Will wanted Johnson gone from their lives forever—and he dearly wished he'd never known about the man's existence. But did his evil deeds justify the three of them killing him now?

Mac wanted Johnson dead. The bastard had caused enough misery in their lives. Johnson's malevolence began even before Mac knew Jenny, and his vile deeds still influenced their family. Without Johnson and his two fellow rapists, Jenny might have married Mac in forty-seven, and they could have lived happily.

But she wouldn't have married him because Mac wouldn't have taken her with him to Oregon. And they wouldn't have Will. Nor Maria—for it was doubtful Mac would have gone to California and met Consuela. And if he hadn't married Jenny, none of the other children would exist either.

Everything that was good in Mac's life had come from meeting Jenny, bringing her to Oregon, marrying her, and raising their family. Sometimes, evil acts brought good consequences—if the victims could overcome the depravity through righteous behavior.

Mac hoped he and Jenny and their children had been righteous.

At the moment, Mac wanted Will to feel he had a role in the decision what to do with Johnson. Will, more than any of them, had a stake in the outcome. No matter how expedient it might be for Mac to simply pull the trigger and kill the man, Will would still have to face the truth that he had been fathered by a rapist.

Mac and Zeke kept their rifles trained on Johnson and waited for Will to speak.

Mac had killed Johnson's father, Will remembered. As Mac told the story, it had been in self-defense—the older Johnson had fired at Mac first. How would Mac deal with killing two of the three men who might have been Will's father? Was it right to put that burden on Mac?

Was Will willing to pull the trigger himself? If he wasn't, he couldn't ask another man to do the job for him. He couldn't ask Mac.

It was one thing to let the courts try the criminal and rule as they saw fit, after finding the man guilty. Even if Johnson were sentenced to hang. It was something else to pull the trigger here in the wilderness, with only Will, Mac, and Zeke standing in judgment.

Will shook his head. "We'll take him back to town, Pa."

As Will spoke, three horsemen trotted into the yard.

"Whoa," Sheriff Thomas said, as he pulled his mount to a stop, the two Abercrombies behind him. "What happened? Where's Albee?" He turned to Will. "And what the devil are you doing here?"

Mac and Zeke told the sheriff and the Abercrombies about the gunfight. Then the men lashed Johnson to a saddle on an old, scarred mare found behind the cabin—probably a horse Johnson had stolen from the Army when he deserted. "Tie his hands to the reins," the sheriff said. "And we'll hope the horse throws him. Pershing," he said to Zeke, "since you captured him, you lead him into town."

The lawman helped Mac and Will wrap Albee's body in a dirty blanket from the shack and place it across the back of the deputy's horse. "I'll lead his horse," the sheriff said. "Adam was a good man." He looked at Johnson. "I hope you hang for this."

The somber posse rode back to Oregon City. Any time Johnson started to talk, Zeke kicked him. Will saw a glance pass between Mac and Zeke, and he realized Zeke didn't want Johnson saying anything about Will being his son. Will nodded gratefully at Zeke, who grinned back at him.

As they returned to town, Will reflected on his realization that Mac's raising him made Mac his father. It didn't matter whose blood ran in Will's veins. Mac had contributed far more than blood to Will's character.

No one knew who sired Maria either, but Mac was her father, too. And Mac treated both Will and Maria the same as he treated their siblings he'd fathered in blood. Will wondered what all this meant for his attraction to Maria, but those considerations would have to wait for another day.

When they reached the sheriff's office, Sheriff Thomas supervised the jailing of Johnson, then dismissed the posse. "You men go home to your families," he said. "I'll take Adam's body to the undertaker, then visit his wife. She'll be devastated. They have a little baby."

Will hadn't known Deputy Albee was married. He thought again of Mama, alone in Oregon with a baby after Mac left. Now the deputy's wife was in a worse predicament—her husband would never return.

Will and Mac said good-bye to Zeke and the Abercrombies. "Let's go home, son," Mac said, clapping Will on the back.

"All right, Pa."

Jenny cried when Mac and William entered the kitchen through the back door. "We're filthy," Mac said as she ran to him. But he put his arms around her and held her close. He smelled of woods and horse and sweat and blood.

She turned to William. "Are you all right?" she asked, hugging him in turn.

Will leaned over awkwardly to return her hug. "We're both fine," he said.

"Deputy Albee was killed," Mac said. "But no one else was hurt."

"And Johnson?" Jenny was almost afraid to ask.

"He's in jail," Mac said. "Sheriff will turn him over for trial as soon as he can."

"Then it's over with him?" Jenny asked.

Mac shook his head. "Can't say for sure. He'll be found guilty of Adam's murder, that's for certain. And with that murder, it's unlikely any other charges will be necessary. Maybe Sheriff Thomas can keep our family's name out of it. But I can't tell you Johnson won't start rumors."

"If he does, he does," William said. "We can withstand rumors." He put his arm around Jenny's shoulders, and she leaned into him a bit, taking strength from his assurance. "He can't hurt us, even with the truth."

Jenny nodded. The secret she'd feared William learning would not harm him in the long run. He was more resilient than she'd thought.

Mac went upstairs to wash, and Jenny followed him.

"You should be proud of Will," Mac told her. "He acted like a man today."

"But we told him not to go on the posse." Jenny pulled a clean shirt from the wardrobe for Mac and handed it to him.

"Yes," Mac said. "But he did a man's job while he was with us." He told her about Will covering for him and then for Zeke.

She closed her eyes and shuddered at the picture of her son risking his life, even for Mac and Zeke. "Land's sake," she whispered.

"And I asked him what we should do with Johnson. I wanted him to think through the options—vigilante justice or bringing the man back to town for trial."

She sat on the bed facing Mac as he washed. "So Will decided to let Jacob live, even after everything the felon has done?"

"He did." Mac wiped his face with a towel. "It was the right decision, and I'm proud of him."

That evening, after he'd gone to bed, Will heard a soft tap on his door. "Come in," he said.

It was Mama. She sat on the edge of his bed and brushed his hair back from his face, like she had when he was little. "I'm proud of you, William."

"What for?" he asked.

"Mac told me you decided to let Jacob Johnson stand trial." She smiled at him. "When did you grow up to be so wise?"

He shrugged, embarrassed by her praise. "It's just the way I was raised."

She rose and turned to leave. "Mama?" he said.

"Yes?"

"I'm sorry. I'm sorry I treated you so badly when I found out about him. I shouldn't have said those things about you." He'd called her a whore, he remembered. Maybe some other things, too.

She sighed. "It's all right, William. As I said, I never wanted you to find out who fathered you."

"Mac's my father in everything but blood," Will said. "I know that now."

She walked to his bed, leaned over, and kissed his forehead. "Yes, he is. And I'm glad you have come to see it."

# Chapter 67: At Church on Sunday

Will accompanied his family to church on Sunday, the day after the posse. He felt eyes on his back as they filed into their usual pew, filling it from side to side.

The minister droned on, and Will didn't hear most of what he said. The sermon was something about "there but for the grace of God go I."

That was true, Will thought, as he let his thoughts roam. Only God's grace had brought Will into this world, though the Almighty had had a pretty brutal way of bringing him into existence. Only God's grace had brought Mac into Mama's world, and therefore into Will's. Only grace had kept Jonah and him safe when they ran away, only grace had kept Mac and him alive on the posse and saved them from the fate that befell Deputy Albee. How long would it be before Albee's family could find grace after his tragic death?

When the congregation stood to sing, Will heard Mama's lovely soprano loud and strong. He looked over the heads of the other children to see her singing:

> *Through many dangers, toils, and snares,*
> *I have already come;*
> *'Tis grace hath brought me safe thus far,*
> *And grace will lead me home.*

"Safe thus far," Will thought. He'd been brought safe thus far. He'd come through dangers, toils, and snares this year—the worst year of his life. And he had survived. Not only survived, but grown from the adversity.

He still didn't know what the next phase of his life would bring, but he knew he had a family's love to support him. Maybe that was enough for now. Maybe it would always be enough to keep him safe.

After the service, Mac led his family out of church, letting them all precede him down the aisle. Last out of the pew was Jenny carrying their infant Andrew. She smiled at Mac as he ushered her ahead of him.

Once in the churchyard, Mac raised his face to the sky. The pale late November sun shone through high wispy clouds, but a breeze chilled him to the bone. Winter would soon set in.

His older children separated quickly once they were outside, looking for their friends. Only Maggie and Andrew remained with Mac and Jenny. He scooped up Maggie and carried her across the yard to where Zeke and Hannah Pershing stood.

"Good morning," Mac said in greeting.

Hannah smiled and reached out her arms to take Maggie, who went willingly. They stepped apart from the men and greeted Jenny, who had followed Mac.

Zeke asked Mac, "Heard anything more about Johnson?"

Mac shook his head. "I stayed home all day yesterday. Figured the family needed my attention. Jenny was shaken up over Albee's death."

"I went to see the sheriff," Zeke said. "Apparently, Johnson is spouting off about being Will's father. Thought you should know."

Mac swallowed. He'd hoped Johnson would be silent—after all, if the McDougalls told their story, the villain could be prosecuted for rape as well as murder. "What does Sheriff Thomas say?"

Zeke shrugged. "Says it's none of his business. All he cares about is getting Johnson hung for killing Albee."

Mac sighed. "I'll go talk to the sheriff tomorrow morning. See what we can do to get us all through Johnson's trial as quickly as possible."

Samuel Abercrombie joined them. Both Zeke and Mac fell silent.

"Guess we showed that Johnson bastard what we Oregonians can do," the old man boasted. He seemed to have forgotten that Jacob Johnson was a Southern sympathizer like he was.

"Why'd it take you so long to reach Johnson's cabin?" Zeke asked. "You were supposed to be waiting for us when we came down from the top of the hill."

"Them damn logs," Samuel said. "Sheriff's old nag couldn't make the jumps. He led us around."

Mac thought the sheriff had probably saved Samuel's neck—the old man could have fallen off his gelding if they jumped. But it wasn't worth commenting on.

"I been hearin' some odd rumors 'bout Johnson and Miz Jenny," Abercrombie said. "Just want you to know I don't countenance what that bastard says at all."

"Good to know, Abercrombie," Mac said.

# Chapter 68: Caleb's Birthday

On Saturday morning, November 26, Mac sat in his home study, reading a letter from the People's Transportation Company. That steamship outfit had succumbed to a lawsuit from the Oregon Steam Navigation Company in Portland—the P.T. Company would no longer run a boat on the upper Columbia River. He sighed. It had been a good prospect, but now at least, he could focus his energies and finances on the bank proposal from Ladd. Or that would be his focus until Byron Pengra renewed his survey on the Central Oregon Military Road next summer.

From outside his study door, he heard children laughing and shouting and Rufus barking. The house was full of commotion—it was Caleb's thirteenth birthday, and Jenny was preparing for another party that afternoon. "Boys," he heard her cry. "Put the dog outside."

He sighed. He would have to offer himself up to obey Jenny's orders about the party soon.

The posse had captured Jacob Johnson over a week ago. The man would be tried for murder in a few weeks. Mac had little doubt about the outcome—killing Deputy Albee would bring Johnson a swift hanging. He hadn't talked to Will about the likely resolution, but he should.

He should also talk to Will again about Harvard. There would be talk in town for a while after Johnson was brought to justice—there was no way to escape it. Will would do better if he left Oregon City until the rumors died down. After some time away, Will could make his way here in Oregon, if he chose. He'd done well on the expedition and he'd impressed the sheriff during the posse—even though he had been an uninvited member of that group.

But Mac still believed Will's true talents lay in using his mind, rather than his muscle and guns. Neither the Army nor law enforcement were the best use of Will's intelligence.

It was odd, Mac thought, that Will's talents mirrored his own in many respects. Will was more cautious, perhaps, than Mac had been as a youth. Mac had craved action. Will could handle action, though he waited until he was forced to. But more than Cal or Nate, Will used his head—he would do well in law, probably better than Mac ever had. However, to become a lawyer, a college education would be useful, followed by an apprenticeship with an attorney back East.

After the cake was cut and most of the guests had wished Cal a happy birthday, Will approached his younger brother and cuffed him gently on the side of the head. Then he put an arm around Cal's shoulders.

"Much happiness, little brother," Will said.

Cal grinned up at him. "I'll be as tall as you soon," he said. "Taller maybe."

"That'll be the day, short stuff." Then, in all seriousness, Will put his hand in his pocket and brought out a whittled horse. "I made another for Maria, but this one's for you."

Cal turned sober. "Gee, Will, this is splendid. It's like the one I broke last spring. I'm sorry for that."

"It took me a couple of tries to get the one for Maria right. This was one of my attempts. It's not quite like Shanty. The wood wouldn't let me get the markings right."

"I like it fine," Cal said, rubbing his thumb over the wood.

"Enjoy your party," Will said, and sauntered off to find guests his own age. Maria was across the room talking with Jonah, Cordelia, and Sammy.

"What's next for you, Will?" Jonah asked him. "You gonna work with Sheriff Thomas?"

Will shrugged. "Maybe. If Mac can't find anything for me to do."

"I don't know how you could be so brave," Cordelia said. She didn't quite bat her eyes at Will, but she came close. He caught Maria's eye as she tried to stifle a smile.

"I just did what anyone would." Will wondered how much of the tale Daniel had told his family. And, of course, Daniel hadn't been there for the most important part.

"Well," Cordelia said, putting her hand on Will's arm and leaning into him. "I was never so scared as when Pa told us the story. And I worried so about Grandfather Samuel—Pa said he fell off his horse on a jump."

Will raised an eyebrow. So that's why the sheriff's group had been delayed—Samuel Abercrombie had taken a spill. He was glad the old man hadn't broken any bones, but he shouldn't have been there in the first place. He'd caused the posse's plans to go awry, which might have contributed to the deputy's death.

Later, as the party wound down, Will thought again about Jonah's question. What did come next for him? He still needed an occupation.

When the guests had departed and the women were cleaning up, Mac called Will into his study. He might as well talk to the boy now.

"Have a seat," Mac invited.

Once Will was seated, Mac poured his son a single finger of whiskey and handed him the glass. Will took it with a look of surprise. Then Mac poured two fingers for himself. He held up his glass, "To Cal—may he have many more birthdays."

"Many more," Will said, and sipped. Mac suppressed a grin when Will stifled a cough.

"I want you to consider going to Harvard next fall," Mac said. "I think it would do you a world of good."

"What do you mean?" Will said.

"You're a bright young man, and you would do well to further your education. You're bored here in Oregon, and you need a vocation that will occupy your mind."

Will hesitated, then said, "Why would you send me East?"

Mac hadn't expected that question. "You're my son. I want the best for you."

Will heaved a sigh and stared at his glass.

Mac leaned across his desk toward Will. "The world has seen you as my son since the day you were born. I have treated you as such since I returned from California when you were just a lad. I love your mother, and you are her child—and I love you as my own."

Will nodded, but his face remained skeptical.

Mac sat back in exasperation. "Have I ever treated you any differently than Cal or Nate?"

"No."

"Have I ever treated Maria any differently than Eliza or Louisa or Maggie?"

"No."

Mac waved his hand, careful not to spill his whiskey. "Jenny mothers all of you equally, including Maria, and I seek every day of my life to live up to her example. I fail many times in many ways to win her approval, but I pray to God I do not fail in treating you as my son."

Will's face relaxed. "You don't, Pa. But why send me away?"

Mac breathed a sigh of relief when Will called him "Pa." Maybe Will was simply concerned about leaving home. "Don't you want to go East?"

Will hesitated, then said, "I'd like the education. But I'd miss Mama and the youngsters. I still don't know where I fit in here."

Mac leaned forward. "Jenny's father was a scholar as well as an Army officer, Will. She says you take after him. But it doesn't matter where you got your intelligence. As your father, it is my responsibility to help you make the most of what you can be. And that's why I want you to go to Harvard. The college helped me find my path away from my parents, and I believe it will help you as well."

"Then you're not just trying to send me away?" Will asked. "To get me away from the family. And from Maria."

Mac set his glass down with a thump. "Is that what you think? That I want you out of the house?" He chuckled. "Believe me, there are cheaper ways to get rid of you than sending you East to college." Then he turned serious. He should talk to Will about Maria. "There's no legal reason you and Maria can't marry someday, if that's what you both want. But marriage is a complicated relationship. So take it slowly, Will. If you want to marry her, then earn her trust and her love. Be the best man you can be before you ask her."

Will nodded slowly and sipped his whiskey. "I understand, Pa."

Mac felt his throat grow thick, and he gulped his whiskey to conceal his emotion. Then, until they both emptied their glasses, he and Will spoke of mundane things.

That night, Will sat in his room thinking. Pa was right—an education at Harvard would open many doors—including doors to opportunities Will couldn't even fathom now.

He didn't like leaving home. It felt like he had just come home, just found his family again. He'd lost his family when Johnson attacked them in the spring. He'd felt so far away from Mac—Pa—and from Cal and the younger children. Only Mama and Maria had seemed to care for him.

But Pa came to get him at Fort Klamath—and he'd searched for Will before that. Mama told him she'd pushed Pa to go after Will, but they hadn't known where to look. She'd said Pa stayed in Oregon to be there when Will returned, rather than go to Boston after his father's death.

And after Will's return from the reconnaissance expedition, he and Pa had vanquished Johnson. In that battle, they'd begun to forge a new path together as father and son. Pa was trying to build that path, and Will would try, too.

Yes, he'd go to Harvard. To make Pa happy. But even more importantly, because it would be another reconnaissance—this time into what Will could become as a man.

He took out his well-worn journal and wrote,

*November 26, 1864. Pa gave me whiskey tonight and we talked. I will go to Harvard next fall. The prospect excites me.*

# Chapter 69: Heading East

Will stood on the deck of the steamship in Portland, Pa beside him. They were leaving for Boston. It was July 1865. The War was won, and President Lincoln was dead. As was Jacob Johnson—hung after a quick trial just weeks after the posse caught him.

Will waved to Mama below them on the dock. The whole family had traveled from Oregon City to Portland two days earlier to see Will and Pa off. The younger children had never been as far as Portland. It amused Will to watch Cal lord it over their younger siblings, pointing out various landmarks that Cal had only seen once before—when they'd made the trip with Pa to see the telegraph office.

Mama blew Will a kiss. He couldn't blow a kiss back to his mother—no grown son would do that. But he felt his eyes glisten as he waved his arm wildly. He would miss her. She cried when she helped him pack his trunk.

Maria waved at him also. She had spent several months at Abigail Duniway's school, but she grew homesick, and Mrs. Duniway had not had much need of her assistance. Maria came home for good in May, and she and Will spent many hours together during the weeks after her return, usually under the close watch of Mama or Pa.

But one evening the week before Will was to leave, he found Maria alone in the garden. Mama peered out the kitchen window, but she left the two of them to talk by themselves.

"Do you care for me?" Will asked Maria, as he had when he returned from the militia expedition last autumn.

"Of course, I do, Will."

"Do you love me?" he asked. "As a woman loves a man?"

"Oh, William," she said, with a wistful sigh. "I don't know. I don't know any life without you, so I don't know how you will fit in my life ahead."

"Do you think you might love me?" he asked.

She turned to him and touched his cheek. "I might."

"Will you write to me while I'm away?" Will took her hand and pressed it to his lips.

She smiled then. "That I will certainly do."

He'd extracted one promise from her. That was all he needed at this point. But he hoped for more promises someday.

The steamship chugged away from the dock and down the Columbia toward Astoria and beyond.

"Come, Will," Pa said. "Let's stand in the bow and watch where we're heading." He slung his arm around Will's shoulders.

Will grinned at his father, and they walked forward together.

# THE END

*Find more books from Theresa Hupp at*
*https://www.amazon.com/Theresa-Hupp/e/B009H8QIT8*

# Author's Note

This novel relied more on specific history for its plot than my earlier books. Lieutenant Colonel Charles S. Drew commanded Company C of the First Oregon Cavalry Militia in 1864, and he led a military reconnaissance expedition through the Owyhee Basin. I have relied on Drew's report to describe the events of that expedition. See *Official Report of the Owyhee Reconnoissance* [sic], *made by Lieut. Colonel C. S. Drew, 1st Oregon Cavalry, in the summer of 1864*, available at https://ia800906.us.archive.org/9/items/officialreportof00unitrich/officialre portof00unitrich.pdf.

For more about the expedition, see also *The Deadliest Indian War in the West: The Snake Conflict, 1864-1868*, Chapter 6, by Gregory Michno (2007), available at https://www.google.com/books/edition/The_Deadliest_Indian_War_in_the _West/5ZExU-tGSz8C, and Bancroft, *History of Oregon*, available at https://www.google.com/books/edition/History_of_Oregon/l-gNAAAAIAAJ.

There is no evidence that Drew used a scribe, but I liked this as a plot device. I summarized and paraphrased Drew's report in his dictation to Will, but I tried to be true to the attitudes Drew expressed in his report.

There is no clear explanation why Drew delayed in setting out on the expedition, though Michno indicates he wanted to keep his men safe, as well as the wagon trains once they joined him. I also did not find any clear rationale for why Drew did not rush back for the treaty negotiations (which he actually reached on October 15, 1864, on the Sprague River, the day the negotiations concluded). Bancroft states Drew did not believe the government would keep its treaty promises.

I made some changes to the actual events of the Owyhee Expedition. For example, the theft of Indian horses that led to Burton's death took place away from the cavalry's herd, but I wanted Will's horse stolen as well. Also, Humboldt Jim was a real visitor to the expedition's camp, but he did not tell Drew that Chief Paulina was following the cavalry. Paulina's Paiutes really did follow the expedition and Paulina decided not to attack because of the howitzer, but Drew did not learn this until after he returned to Fort Klamath.

In addition to Lt. Col. Charles S. Drew, other historical characters in his reconnaissance force who found their way into this novel include Captain Kelly and Sergeants Crockett, Geisy, and Moore. However, I do not know the specific roles these men played in the reconnaissance force, nor do I know anything about their characters. When Drew reported that men left the unit or stayed behind at certain points, I tried to be true to those events.

Captain George Curry (or Currey) commanded another company of the First Oregon Cavalry Militia in 1864, and Drew's company met Curry's at Camp Alvord.

Even though no battles were fought in Oregon between North and South, the Civil War had an impact on the state. Both Northern and Southern sympathizers argued their positions vociferously. All the regular Army units in Oregon were called to the East to fight. As a result, Oregon raised its own local militia, of which Drew's cavalry unit was a part. But the Oregon militia was understaffed, and in the summer of 1864, all units were on field assignments managing the Native American population, which did in fact cause Byron Pengra's road survey to be delayed until 1865.

Many deserters from both the North and South did drift west during and after the Civil War.

With respect to the age of enlistment, boys under the age of eighteen could not enlist in the Army without a parent's consent. Younger boys could enlist with consent. Of course, a lot of lying went on by boys eager to participate in the War.

The businessmen Mac encountered—William S. Ladd, Byron Pengra, and the steamship company owners—were real Oregon pioneers engaged in the enterprises I described.

Abigail Scott Duniway was an early suffragette in the West. When I discovered her, I decided to include her in these pages, and I hope to feature her in a future novel as well. Duniway was a pioneer on the Oregon Trail, a farmer's wife, a teacher, a businesswoman, a newspaper publisher, and an author of fiction and nonfiction, as well as an advocate of voting rights for women in several Western states. Her autobiography can be found in *Path Breaking: An Autobiographical History of the Equal Suffrage Movement in Pacific Coast States*, by Abigail Scott Duniway (1914), available at https://www.google.com/books/edition/Path_Breaking/LYtJAAAAIAAJ. But although she did run a girl's boarding school in Lafayette in Yamhill County, Oregon, in 1864, there is no indication that she hired anyone to help her with the school.

Some of the weather described came from a diary by James Virtue, a prospector who made a trip to Boise in the summer of 1864. His diary depicts a miner's life in the 1860s, and can be found at "'May Live and Die a Miner': The 1864 Clarksville Diary of James W. Virtue, by Gary Dielman, *Oregon Historical Quarterly*, Vol. 105, No. 1 (Spring 2004).

As always, any errors or deviations from history in this novel are my own, and I take full responsibility.

# Discussion Guide

These questions are to help book clubs and other reading groups discuss *Safe Thus Far*. They might also make good essay topics for students reading this novel for the classroom.

1. What did you know about the involvement of West Coast states in the Civil War before reading *Safe Thus Far*?

2. How did the arrival of the telegraph in Oregon make life easier for residents in the West? Did it make life harder in any respects?

3. Was it realistic that in 1864 at age sixteen, Will and Jonah could join a militia unit? Why or why not?

4. What did you think of the depiction of militia life in this novel? How does it mesh with other Civil War novels you have read?

5. What attitudes did different characters in *Safe Thus Far* have toward Native Americans? Which attitudes do you think were realistic for the times?

6. How would Native Americans tell the story of Drew's expedition? Would their stories be different in 1864 and today?

7. How did Will and Jonah resemble sixteen-year-olds today? How did they seem different?

8. What did you think of Will's reaction to learning that Mac was not his father?

9. When did Will run away from something or someone, and when did he run to something or someone?

10. If you were Mac, would you have gone East to Boston to see your family or stayed in Oregon? Why did you choose the way you did?

11. What would you have done to Johnson—kill him or let him live? Why did you choose as you did?

12. Which character was your favorite in *Safe Thus Far*? How did this person change and develop through the story?

13. If you have read earlier books in this series (particularly *Lead Me Home* and *Now I'm Found*), did Mac and Jenny and their friends mature as you thought they would?

14. Where do you see Will, Jonah, and Maria in five or ten years?

*If you enjoyed* **Safe Thus Far**, *you might also enjoy my other novels,* **Lead Me Home**, **Now I'm Found**, **Forever Mine**, *and* **My Hope Secured**.

*All books are available on Amazon and Barnes & Noble, or find them here:*

https://www.amazon.com/Theresa-Hupp/e/B009H8QIT8

# Acknowledgments

The Sedulous Writers Group (my writing critique group) was an immense help in the development and shaping of this novel. I also appreciate the marketing advice and support of Write Brain Trust. The knowledge and expertise of the authors in these groups have made me a better writer and publisher.

My thanks as well to early readers and editors of this book, specifically Lisa, Mike, S.J., Sally, and Sylvia.

No author should write a novel without a community of support, and I am greatly indebted to my friends and colleagues for their help.

# About the Author

Theresa Hupp grew up in Eastern Washington State and the Willamette Valley in Oregon. Her ancestors include 19th century emigrants to Oregon and California, and her great-grandfather was a sheriff in Polk County, Oregon. She now lives in Kansas City, Missouri.

Theresa is the award-winning author of novels, short stories, essays, and poetry, and has worked as an attorney, mediator, and human resources executive.

Winner of the Missouri Indie Author Project adult fiction prize, *Lead Me Home* (2015) tells the story of Mac McDougall and Jenny Calhoun on their wagon journey along the Oregon Trail. *Now I'm Found* (2016) follows Mac and Jenny through the early California Gold Rush days. *Forever Mine* (2018) explores the Oregon Trail trek from the points of view of other members of the same wagon train and provides additional perspectives on the journey. *My Hope Secured* (2019) gives Zeke Pershing from the wagon company his own love story.

Theresa has also published two corporate thrillers under a pseudonym, as well as an anthology titled, *Family Recipe: Sweet and saucy stories, essays, and poems about family life*. In addition, Theresa has written short works for *Chicken Soup for the Soul*, *Mozark Press*, and *Kansas City Voices*. She is a member of the Historical Novel Society, the Kansas City Writers Group, Missouri Writers Guild, Oklahoma Writers Federation, Inc., and Write Brain Trust.

You can follow Theresa on her website and blog, http://TheresaHuppAuthor.com, on her Facebook Author page, http://facebook.com/TheresaHuppAuthor, and her Amazon page at http://www.amazon.com/Theresa-Hupp/e/B009H8QIT8. You can also subscribe to Theresa's monthly newsletter through her website.

# Readers' Praise for Earlier Books

*Lead Me Home:*

> . . . on the challenging Oregon Trail of 1847 . . . the going is slow and scary and dusty behind a team of oxen. . . . [Hupp] takes us on this journey and shows how her characters cope and grow under these difficult circumstances.

> . . . an incredible story, amazingly and beautifully written.

*Now I'm Found:*

> Hupp has done extensive research on . . . traveling the Oregon Trail and prospecting for gold in the California mountains. The descriptions of those closely related periods of history are exciting backgrounds for a tender love story.

> . . . Hupp does history and fiction well!

*Forever Mine:*

> Hupp researches her books with care, plots them well, describes the land beautifully, and makes the people of these books come alive with vivid characterizations.

> For any true lover of the western and the hardships of the pioneers who were willing to put their life in danger. . . .

*My Hope Secured:*

> Historical fiction done right! The author does an amazing job of researching the time period. . . . If you are interested in pioneer history this is something you should not miss.

> . . . A wonderful story of finding love and family in the frontier of Oregon.

Theresa Hupp's books are available online at Amazon or Barnes & Noble, in paperback or ebook formats. Your local library might also have the ebooks through Overdrive.

Made in United States
Troutdale, OR
06/20/2023

10709578R00206